WILLOW WEEP

A standalone sequel to
Under the Willow

WILLOW WEEP

TRINITY RAPTURE PUBLISHING

MADGE HURLEY JONES

WILLOW WEEP

Hardcover ISBN: 978-1-7365630-3-8
Paperback ISBN: 978-1-7365630-4-5
Ebook ISBN: 978-1-7365630-5-2

Library of Congress Control Number: 2023918234

Book and cover design by The Brand Huntress
TheBrandHuntress.com

First printing 2023

Willow Weep is dedicated to the memory of Hunter Draminski, the young man who, as a small boy, stole the hearts of his neighbors.

Hunter, as I wrote this book, I never imagined that Jesus would call you home so soon. You will always be dearly loved.

Hunter J. Draminski
March 23, 2000—February 14, 2022
Geneseo, Illinois

"Those who touch our lives stay in our hearts forever."

1

THE RUNAWAY

Danielle did not care that she was cold, wet, and trembling as she ran through the thunderstorm to the willow. She was hurt, angry, and could no longer deal with the unjust accusations and lies which kept her life in constant turmoil. She needed peace in her life—true peace—and not just stolen moments of it.

Danielle breathed deeply, trying to calm herself by listening to the sounds around her. The splashing of the brook, the gradual ceasing of the rain drops, and the leaves rustling with every puff of wind brought clarity. The time had come. . . and she was prepared.

Heavenly Father, I've always tried to find ways to please my family and withstand their rejection, but I can no longer live this way. Please give me peace in my life as I follow through with my decision. I believe it is best for all concerned. I ask for Your strength and guidance as—

"I knew I'd find you here!" The grating voice tore its way into her moment of resolve. "So you've managed to cause trouble again." Her half-brother smirked as he tossed back the blonde curls from his broad forehead.

He then heaved his heavy-thighed leg forward, landing his

hard-toed boot in the bottom of Danielle's foot. He laughed as she cringed in pain.

"Only a fool like you would be sitting out here soaking wet." Glaring hatefully at the branches dripping around him, he snarled, "I've always hated this tree. It's time I cut it down. This will be the last time I'll be sent *here* to find you."

His eyes narrowed on his stepsister. "Don't think I won't be settling up with you after father has seen what you've done." His stare turned vicious. Delbert thrived on finding ways to make Danielle look like a constant troublemaker—and their mother, Esther, goaded him on.

Danielle vaguely remembered walking to the house and entering the kitchen door. She would have to endure one more of her mother's demeaning rants.

"There you are. . . and soaking wet!" She spared no time in using her usual snappish tone toward Danielle.

Esther Simpson rushed to the mirror to make certain not one auburn hair was out of place. "Because of *you*, I've barely had time to get ready for my meeting with Mr. Grant. I'm ashamed to have you for a daughter! Delbert saved for *months* to buy that briefcase for his Father. Harold didn't even have it a week. Then you do *this*.

"Your stepfather has been good to you, so I'll make no excuses. You're on your own. Since the help is off today, make certain the housework is completed." Esther gave Danielle a bitter look and stomped out of the room.

No matter how fierce the abuse had been, Danielle had always cowered—but *today* was different. She was going to put an end to it all.

Esther and Delbert had made their accusations after Harold's new briefcase had been found badly splattered by a knocked over bottle of ink. Danielle had not been near the desk where the case was sitting, but she suspected Delbert had, since he was always rummaging through his father's desk for one reason or another.

Danielle and the staff had given the house a thorough cleaning and laundered the clothing the day before, so she gave no thought to her mother's demands. Even if the work had not been done, she was through being a chore maid for her family. The ironing would go undone, and there would not be a dinner waiting for the Simpsons this evening.

After gathering a few of her things from the laundry, Danielle hurried up to the attic. Even though no one was home, she was so afraid of being caught that she had jumped when the door latch clicked behind her.

Danielle moved the old, maple dresser from the wall and pulled out the two carpet bags hidden there. They were both in good shape, a nice size, and would work perfectly for her needs. She spared a second to lovingly stroke the flowers embroidered on her grandmother's elegant bags. They were the only connection she had with her own father's family.

Danielle took the bags and placed them in the safety of her room, locked the door behind her, and hurried off to bathe. Removing her damp clothes and stepping into a warm bath would go a long way in soothing her anxiety.

Catching a glimpse in the mirror revealed her messy blonde hair and mud-streaked face. It was humiliating to know her mother and Delbert would have the satisfaction of remembering her being so unkempt and distressed—but it was of little consequence now.

Relieved to find her savings still inside the black carpet bag, Danielle removed the money to make certain it was all there. But this time, placed between the bills was an envelope with a note on the outside. The script read *For Danielle.* Inside the envelope were three twenty-dollar bills.

At first Danielle panicked. Since it was such a large amount, she wondered if someone was trying to trap her, but there was no time to dwell on it. This was her chance. If the person meant to cause problems, she would deal with it when the time came.

The black bag was used to pack Danielle's limited, but stylish, clothing. Fortunately, there was enough room inside for everything, including toiletries, a favorite book, and a Bible. Harold Simpson was a wealthy man and did not seem to mind supplying his stepdaughter's needs—although it was resented by the rest of her family. To avoid facing more of their hostility, Danielle had learned to fend for herself—even to the point of designing and sewing her own clothing.

The navy bag was already filled with items she had purchased in preparation for the day she would leave. Necessities for cooking, sleeping, and ironing were among the things one could not do without. When the packing was finished, Danielle tested the weight of her luggage and felt it would be manageable while traveling.

She pulled her new day dress from the closet and slipped it on. After pinning up her hair and putting on the blue hat with the roses and feather, Danielle was ready to leave the only home she could remember.

She whispered her love as she passed little Sherry's room. Sherry had not yet been tainted by their mother's contempt toward Danielle—but she feared it would have been only a matter of time.

Moving quietly along the hallway, she gave little thought to

Margaret, her other half-sister, who was Delbert's twin. Margaret was beautiful and quite taken with herself. She usually ignored Danielle unless she needed something—but even then was rude and condescending.

Danielle hurried down the spiral staircase and through the marble foyer, her heart beating faster with each step. Reaching the tall, ornate front door, she turned the knob and claimed the first moments of her journey toward freedom.

2

SAYING GOODBYE

Even though her mother and Margaret would be home within the hour, Danielle knew she must drop by Jean and Everett's home to say goodbye.

Leaving the carpet bags behind the rock at the willow, she took the muddy footpath to avoid being seen. By the time she reached the Johnsons' home, Danielle had to take a second to rest. She scanned the patches of flowers and foliage scattered throughout her friends' shaded lawn. *Jean will surely keep heaven's gardens someday.* Saving the scene in her memory, Danielle hurried across the porch to the back door.

Just as she was about to knock, Jean pushed open the screen door, ready to pitch a bucket of dirty water into the yard. Although startled, the woman managed not to spill its sloshing contents.

"Dani! I wasn't expecting anyone to be out here." Setting down the bucket, Jean placed a hand on her chest, and her usual comforting smile appeared.

"Look at you in that new dress. It's perfect with your blue eyes. You've become an excellent seamstress. And you finished it in no time. It's a good thing I have something in mind for your next project." The dear woman always had a plan to bring a little cheer into Danielle's life.

When there was no reply, Jean looked more closely into the girl's eyes. Seeing something was terribly wrong, she led Danielle to the wicker porch swing. "Those eyes are telling me something I don't want to believe."

Neither made a direct reference to the situation, but it was understood that Danielle was leaving. Jean knew the visit would need to be brief, and she must make the most of it.

"Dani, we were outside in the garden this morning. The willow isn't far off and. . . well. . . voices carry. You needn't worry about the willow. I don't know if I've mentioned it, but the tree is actually on *our* property. We'll be waiting for Delbert."

"Thank you for telling me." Danielle's burdens felt somewhat lighter in hearing her willow would be spared.

"Sweetheart, your family has treated you despicably. But, because you've trusted the Lord through it all, you've acquired a spiritual depth seldom found in a young person. Please never let bitterness settle in your heart. Still. . . you must have had some good times at home." Jean was never one to leave things on a critical note.

"There were some. When we were small and before mother. . ." Danielle decided not to speak of it. She had enough to cope with for the time being.

"Promise me you'll never stray from the Lord. . . and remember we'll always be praying for you and your family. Everett and I love you so."

"I will not stray, nor will I ever forget your love." Danielle looked up into Jean's face with saddened eyes. They both knew their time together must come to an end.

Jean went through the motions of straightening Danielle's

collar. "You were just a little bitty thing when you started going to church with us. You've been like our own daughter." Then Jean forced herself to quench her sentiments.

"You and Everett have supported and guided me well, and I thank you for that. I don't know what I would've done if the Lord hadn't brought you into my life. I love you both."

Danielle hugged Jean one last time with instructions to share it with Everett when he returned. Unable to say more, she placed her hand on Jean's cheek and then ran down the path toward the willow.

Jean immediately felt the sting of loneliness creep into her heart and wondered if they would ever see their Dani again.

3

ON THE WAY TO NOWHERE

"Destination?" the serious-looking man behind the counter called out.

Danielle had no idea what her destination was. She had never traveled far, nor had she ever been inside a train station. She tried to be subtle while searching the board for any town that did not sound nearby.

"Bristol!" she called out, louder than she had intended. Then she glanced around to see if anyone had noticed.

"Cutting it close, aren't you? Train's due any minute. That's a fair distance for a young woman to travel. . . unescorted."

"It can't be helped." Danielle had intentionally spoken the words sharply. *The nerve of the man—as if it was any of his business!* Snatching the ticket from his hand, she gave a curt bow of her head.

Trying to keep out of sight, Danielle went to stand behind a group of people who appeared to be traveling together. Even though it was only a few minutes before the train would arrive, Danielle's heart was racing in fear of being caught. She was so close to putting the Simpson family and the town of Grandville behind her.

"Train now boarding for Fortville, Bristol, and Remington!"

Danielle did not think she had ever heard sweeter words.

Holding her breath, she started the risky walk toward the train. It was only a few more steps and then a few more minutes until the train would pull away from the station. Danielle was almost free.

Harold Simpson stepped out of his shipping company office to light up a pipe and take a stroll to relieve the stress of the day. He often walked to the nearby train station to watch people sharing a loving hello or a tearful goodbye. It was one of the few pleasures in his life.

But *this* stroll would be different. As he approached the board-walk, a young lady who was about to board the train caught his eye. *Surely not! That can't be Danielle.* Harold, determined to find out, walked faster. Still a distance away, he saw the girl climb the steps and take a seat by a window. Just as the train lunged forward, a group of adolescent boys crossed in front of him, blocking the way. By the time his path was clear, the train was moving.

He hurried to the side of the car and could distinctly see Danielle through the window. Wanting to catch her attention, Harold pounded on the glass as he walked beside the train. He would always remember the fear on her face once she had recognized him.

Harold nodded with a reassuring smile, blew her a kiss, and patted his heart. Unable to keep pace with the moving train, he stopped and waved. In return, Danielle gave her stepfather a grateful smile.

Run, little girl! Run just as fast and far as you can! It was the only thought in Harold's mind as he watched the train fade in the distance. Then sadness and guilt overtook him. She would not have needed to leave if he had been the man he should have been—the man who should have stood up to her mother—his wife, Esther Simpson.

He began to recall the whole ugly story of how Danielle had come to live in his home.

The first time Harold had noticed Esther Snodd was at a summer dance. He had thought she was the most beautiful creature that ever walked the earth. Not only was Esther attractive, but she was sweet, elegant, and charming. Harold had fallen in love with her almost immediately and had given into her every whim. Right away there was talk of marriage between them.

Then the unexpected happened. Harold's father was found dead after a heart attack. The devastating loss turned Harold's life upside down. Not only was he grieving, but now the entire shipping company and estate were in jeopardy without a strong leader at the helm. Since his mother had no understanding of business and his brothers were much younger, Harold had to fulfill his obligations and take charge.

To make the situation more difficult, Esther began insisting they marry. Yet, Harold, knowing he needed time to settle the estate and move into his role as head of the company, realized their marriage must be delayed. Instead of being empathetic, his fiancée became angry and broke their engagement.

A few days later, Esther left town to stay with a relative, leaving Harold with a broken heart. Soon after, he received a letter from her stating she had married a farmer by the name of Daniel Harrison.

Totally devastated, Harold drowned his sorrows by delving into the operation of the successful shipping company. He was a natural at growing the business and increasing the family's wealth.

Just when life was starting to seem a little brighter for him, Harold had received a letter from Esther stating she now had an infant daughter but, unfortunately, had chosen badly in marrying

Daniel Harrison. She claimed that, among his many other improprieties, the man was an abusive drunkard who had threatened to harm the child if Esther tried to leave. She pleaded for Harold to rescue her, insisting she was fearful of what her own father might do if he was informed of the circumstances.

Immediately Harold's feelings for Esther returned. Risking his own good reputation, he had done the unthinkable. He had boarded a train, met Esther in a secluded location near her home, and returned to Grandville with the married woman and her child.

Esther and her father, concerned for what little social standing the family had attained, fabricated a lie to conceal the disgraceful divorce. The invented story declared Esther's husband—supposedly on a business trip—was one of the passengers killed in the well-known Wilmington train accident. Esther's father, an unscrupulous attorney, had dealt with the divorce swiftly and quietly, clearing the way for a hasty marriage between Harold and Esther.

Once the two were married, everything changed. Esther—no longer sweet and charming—became cutting, critical, and, above all, obsessed with social climbing. Harold, confused by the abrupt transition in his wife's demeanor, tried unsuccessfully to do everything he could to appease her.

One morning, not long after their marriage, Harold had returned home to pick up some important papers he had left in the study. Upon entering the house, he had heard a heated argument between Esther and a gentleman caller. He started to enter the room but decided to take a moment to listen. He recalled the conversation as if it were yesterday:

"Esther, it is *distinctly* spelled out in the divorce agreement—as long as I keep my identity quiet in Grandville, we have joint custody of Danielle. We both agreed on the visitation schedule. You know I *refused* to sign the decree until a schedule was established. Not to mention, I've even waited for you to get settled in your new home before coming to get her. But now, I'm here to take Danielle home with me for my allotted time."

Realizing the man must be Daniel Harrison, Harold feared for Esther's safety. But it was *then* that he had heard Esther laugh at her ex-husband in a most spiteful manner.

"Surely you don't believe I have any intention of honoring your *schedule*. I only agreed to it so you would sign the divorce papers.

"I told you before I left that I only married you to make Harold jealous. I had planned to leave you soon after we married and would have if it hadn't been for *the child*. Rest assured. I have no intention of letting people find out that I was married to *a farmer*. You will not be coming around to spoil my credibility in Grandville."

"It's always society and money with you, Esther. So, do you even care for Simpson? Obviously, you don't love him. Are you using him too?"

"I do care for him somewhat. I care for his money and social position. What I don't care for is *the child*."

Harold recalled becoming nauseous in overhearing the deplorable confessions made by his wife.

"How can you say such a thing about your own little girl? Surely you don't mean it."

"*I do*—and I'll tell you another thing—if you set one foot in this town again or do anything to ruin my chances, I'll have you brought up on charges of wife beating and child neglect and any other accusations I can create. My father has the connections, and I now have the money to put you behind bars if need be. Just keep in mind that anything that affects my reputation will always be transferred to your daughter. She would be an outcast for life.

"Although, I must admit I would have left Danielle with you if word of my pregnancy hadn't already reached Grandville. Having her underfoot will make things difficult now that Harold and I are expecting *our* first child."

Harold had been shocked to hear that Esther was expecting. He already had regretted not listening to his parents when they had pleaded with him not to marry or have anything to do with Esther Snodd. But after hearing he was going to be a father, Harold had known he was trapped in the marriage.

"But I was a *good* husband to you, and I never laid a hand on you or neglected Dani—nor would I ever. Why are you making such a threat?"

"Because I want you to completely disappear—no contact with us whatsoever." Esther had spoken the words precisely, leaving no doubt that she was dead serious.

Trying to comprehend what he had just heard and knowing he had been a complete fool, Harold walked away, determined to help Daniel Harrison. So, in the months to follow, Harold had scheduled several secret meetings between Daniel and Danielle. The two men soon became close friends and had planned a course of action for the biological father to gain custody of his daughter.

Unfortunately, Daniel Harrison had contracted pneumonia and passed away while Danielle was a toddler. Harold was sorry for the loss of his comrade and sorry that Danielle Harrison would never know the love of her own father.

Throughout the years, Esther monitored Harold's contact with Danielle. If he made the mistake of showing her too much attention, Esther's jealousy and resentment were undeservedly turned toward Danielle. She did nothing to harm her first born physically but totally detached from her—even going so far as to delegate

Danielle's complete care to the staff. The child was denied nearly every joyful moment shared by the family and was seldom allowed in public. However, Esther did permit Danielle to attend church and a local school, where she was loved by all who truly knew her.

What was to have been Harold and Esther's first baby turned out to be their extremely spoiled twins—Margaret and Delbert. As time passed, the two learned to follow their mother's example. They seldom interacted with their older sister and treated her callously.

Harold now realized that he, as head of the family, had allowed the harassment to go on. He was just as guilty as Esther.

But things were about to change in the Simpson household.

4

DO NOT PROVOKE ME

Danielle watched Harold Simpson from the train window until he seemed to fade into her past. The fear which shot through her at seeing her stepfather had caused an emotional upheaval, but Danielle still managed to savor the feeling of freedom.

Having never envisioned herself traveling by train, she was well pleased with the comfort the passenger car offered. Even though she welcomed the serene atmosphere created by the gentle swaying of the coach, the bewildering encounter with Harold Simpson soon resurfaced in Danielle's thoughts. If she interpreted Harold's gestures correctly, he must love her and approve of her going away. At least she hoped that was true.

Harold was a lonely, quiet man who worked most of the time, and his absence had allowed Esther to do as she pleased. Danielle did recall times when her stepfather had tried to show her some affection, but it was eventually limited to a smile, a wink, or a simple word of encouragement at crucial times when Esther was on a warpath. Her mother had made it clear that she did not want Danielle and Harold to bond.

There was no doubt in Danielle's mind—Harold must have

expected her to leave someday. It was evidently he who had put the money in the carpet bag, and she would always think of him fondly because of it.

❧

"Where have you been?" Esther had no problem using her most demanding voice with her husband.

"Not that I need to account for my whereabouts, but I had a late appointment with the lawyer and one of his associates." Harold's very stern response shocked his overbearing wife so much that it rendered her speechless—for a moment.

"Well, you might like to know that Danielle hasn't lifted a finger to fix dinner and has left the ironing undone." By this time, Esther's face was pinched into one of its nastiest forms.

"And why *should* she? Danielle is not one of the hired help. As you recall, we have an excellent staff that is paid well to care for this home and those who live in it." Harold suddenly realized he was enjoying his newly found voice. "And I expect such treatment of Danielle never to happen again!" He suppressed a chuckle, knowing only he understood the truth in his statement.

"How dare you use that tone with me! Who do you think you are?" Esther expected Harold to back down as he always had.

By this time, Delbert and Margaret had entered the room to see what was going on.

"I'll tell you who I am. As a matter of fact, I will tell all three of you *exactly* who I am." Harold took a deep breath.

"I am the husband. . . the father. . . the head of this family. . . the *sole owner* of this house, two major shipping companies, and everything that goes with them.

"Not to mention—other than a small portion of money which I have set aside for each of you—nothing I own is in your names—nor is *anything* willed to you. Rest assured it will remain so until I deem it otherwise. And there had better be genuine changes in each of your lives *or* you will never see another dime."

Harold was just warming up. He had kept this speech inside far too long.

"As for the ink spilled on the briefcase, Danielle was *not* responsible. Delbert was searching through my desk when *he* knocked it over. You should be more aware, boy. I was sitting in the winged chair when it happened. So don't try accusing her.

"Which brings me to my next point. . ." Harold stopped momentarily, observing his son sitting on the sofa with a smug expression.

"Delbert, a couple days ago, I was taking a break near the hedge outside my office. On the other side of that hedge were three young men discussing *you. . . and* the briefcase. Evidently you attained it by swindling the apprentice at the leather shop. The poor lad is now forced to pay the shop owner the entire price of the case.

"You, sir, will work at the docks in the shipping yard to pay back every cent. Tomorrow you will apologize and commit to the payments for the case. You will also continue to work at the docks until I feel you're responsible enough to use that education I paid for.

"Son, you're a lazy bully. You will grow up and learn to respect others, or you will leave this home."

"Father, surely you don't believe those scoundrels. They were deceiving you. You were set up." Delbert was confident he could dissuade his father.

"Hush, boy. I've heard enough of your lies."

Delbert's face turned red. Not only was he angry, but he was beginning to believe his father might follow through with the threats.

"Margaret, you, too, are lazy. . . vain. . . and disrespectful. At this time, there is no longer a dowry for you to buy yourself a husband. We shall see how many proposals you receive on just your looks. In the meantime, I am arranging for another school—away from your mother. You will learn how to appreciate and treat others, *or* you will be dismissed from this house—just as I promised Delbert."

"But Daddy, I have prospects. You wouldn't send me away—"

"Quiet, Margaret." Harold gave her a determined look.

Esther folded her arms.

"Unfortunately, I'm even more to blame than your mother for what this family has become. I've been foolish to let Esther rule over me all these years. I've allowed you to be spoiled and have watched idly as she has instilled her reprehensible ways in both of you. But none of it compares to the way Danielle has been treated by her *own mother*. Esther, you should be horse-whipped—just as I should be."

Harold was about to continue when Esther spoke up. She had had enough of his arrogance.

"Harold, none of these threats will be carried out. I have no idea what has come over you, but it will stop this instant. You've always been a weak man. Pay no heed to him, children. I will bring him to heel."

"Mrs. Simpson, I am through with you and your ways. The only reason I have allowed you to stay in my home is because I love our children and have an obligation to care for them.

"I was outside the door two decades ago when you were black-mailing Daniel Harrison. I heard every word, including the way you used him to get to me and my money. You and your parents—who are next to paupers—are still using our marriage to further your status. In addition, I have the signed documents of Daniel Harrison's testimony of your efforts to blackmail him and con me into a sham marriage."

Esther sat down in shocked silence as she absorbed the information. "Nothing you have against me would stand up in court!"

Her husband looked at her long and hard.

Harold then turned to Delbert and Margaret. "You are not children. You are adults and have been for quite some time. I advise you to take me seriously."

Then he turned back to Esther. "And you, woman, have no idea what I *do have* that *will* stand up in court. You are skating on very thin ice. Please don't provoke me."

With that, Harold left the room, went to their quarters, and locked the door behind him. Esther had to find other accommodations.

5

A FRIGHTENING PLACE

Considering there were no longer any certainties in her life, Danielle had slept well during the night. Only God knew what would take place once she stepped off the train in Bristol.

Looking around at the other passengers, Danielle wondered if any of them had been forced to flee into the unknown. If so, maybe they felt as she did. Her inner struggle wasn't about trusting God—because she *was* trusting Him to guide her future. It was about *not knowing*.

"Would you mind if I take this seat beside you?" The question came from an older lady who looked the epitome of neatness. She appeared to be fragile due to her petite frame, but her voice had an air of sweetness and confident strength. Her elderly beauty was emphasized by a creamy complexion and silvery-white hair.

"Please. I would love to have company."

"I've been watching you. You seem to be a little apprehensive in your traveling. Is this your first train trip?"

"It *is* my first train trip. Is it so obvious?"

"Maybe a bit. I travel by train to visit my son quite often. When I'm not reading, I have developed a bad habit of studying people.

You caught my attention when the gentlemen knocked on your window. Because of it, you became somewhat of a mystery to me."

"No mystery. I'm not that interesting. I've left home to begin a new life on my own. The man was my stepfather wishing me well." Danielle did not feel it was necessary to explain her life's story, nor did she feel the lady was intending to be nosey.

"My name is Danielle Harrison."

"A lovely name. Mine is Mrs. Belinda Gray. It's nice to meet you. I'm on my way home to Bristol—"

"Bristol is where my trip ends. Is it a large town? I know nothing of it." Danielle had not meant to interrupt Mrs. Gray, but she needed any type of information the lady could share.

"It's a good-sized place—just teetering over into being a city—with every type of shop or business you would ever need. The residents love to stroll the downtown area since it has a garden-like charm. Bristol is nice but on the expensive side if you're thinking of settling there."

"I never considered one town might be more expensive to live in than another. Thank you for mentioning it. I'll need to find a job as soon as possible. Although I'm not destitute, I do have limited funds. Hopefully, I can secure a position as a seamstress. Do you have any idea if it might be possible?"

"From what I've gathered, finding a position as a seamstress is difficult. Very few seamstresses leave the trade once they secure a spot. As a matter of fact, it's hard to find any employment in Bristol. People are moving there from all over the country, so any available jobs are normally filled right away."

"I hadn't considered that finding employment might be difficult either. It may be best for me to find lodging first. Would you happen to know of any suitable rooming houses?"

"You may need to find a hotel for at least a day or two. The boarding houses are supposed to be a rare find. I'm sorry. I'm not meaning to discourage you."

"Of course not. I appreciate your honesty. Then can you recommend a hotel?"

Mrs. Gray seemed reluctant to answer the question. "There are hotel rooms available, but finding one appropriate for a lady will be difficult.

"I do have a suggestion, but I'm afraid it might not be ideal. I have a dear friend who owns an inn not far from the Bristol train station. It's in a small town called Willow Weep. Rosa, the owner, recently lost a trusted and longtime employee. She wanted to take time to reevaluate the position before rehiring. That's the only reason the job is still open. But she did ask me to inform her if I came across any prospects.

"You might consider starting your search there. It's a waitressing position, but it's in a very respectable and nice establishment. Rosa is so kind. Would you happen to have any experience in the field?"

"Only that I've been waiting on people all my life."

Mrs. Gray pulled a paper from her handbag and began to write on it. "Ask for Rosa Smith at this address. I'm writing a note of introduction just in case you decide to see about the job.

"Well, I must gather my things. We'll be pulling into Bristol soon. It was so nice to have met you, Miss Harrison."

Danielle's mind was preoccupied as she joined the other passengers exiting the train. Stepping onto the platform, she was now concerned the newly found freedom she relished might prove to have more obstacles than anticipated. Pushing the thought aside, she went into the station to hire a ride into the city.

Downtown Bristol was as lovely as Mrs. Gray had described it. There was a variety of shops, restaurants, and hotels all set along a wide, stone walkway. Each business had its own frontal flower garden designed to set it apart from the others. Even though it was still morning, people were already busy shopping in the area. It all looked so inviting, but Danielle had to deal with the tasks before her.

After several tries to find employment in dressmaking shops, she again found Mrs. Gray to be correct—there were no known jobs for seamstresses. Not long after, she came to the same conclusion about finding housing. There were no decent, available rooms at hotels or boarding houses in the area.

It was well past noon, and she was beginning to feel desperate. Bristol had just become a frightening place. Danielle did not know what to do next.

Feeling overwhelmed, she took time to pray and remembered the note given to her by Mrs. Gray. As much as she disliked the idea, the waitressing position was her only hope. Danielle decided to return to the train station to hire a ride to Willow Weep.

"Excuse me, sir. Are you available to take me to Willow Weep? I need to get there as soon as possible."

The plump man with a scruffy beard looked up at her as if she should recognize who he was. "No, I'm not one of 'em. I only do intown runs."

"Then, can you please point me to someone who might take me there?"

The man looked around the lot. "Doesn't seem to be any of 'em here. No tellin' when one'll get back. Could be five minutes or a couple hours. Depends on where they took their customers."

"Is there any other way to get to Willow Weep?"

"Hoofin' is the only way I know of—unless you can hitch a ride." The man was starting to seem irritated.

"Then, would you please give me directions to Willow Weep?" Danielle hated to bother him again, but she was beginning to panic.

This time he let out a long, disgusted sigh and pointed to the road. "See that road right there. Take it about three to four miles until you come to the sign pointing to Willow Weep. Take that road about a mile and a half." He then turned and went back to picking the horse's hoof.

Time was passing quickly as Danielle hurried down the road toward Willow Weep. It would be difficult with both carpet bags, but at least it was a nice day.

6

THE BREWSTER BOYS

The walk was becoming strenuous, so Danielle stopped to give her tired arms a rest. Just as she was setting the bags down, a horse—galloping at full speed—rounded the corner. The buckboard behind it slid to one side and fishtailed. Danielle had to jump out of the way for fear of being run over. While she was trying to make sense of what had just happened, the man driving brought the horse to an abrupt stop.

Immediately, he and two other young men jumped from the wagon and approached Danielle. "Well, what do we have here?" The driver, with bright red hair and a face covered with freckles, was intentionally being forward. His attitude encouraged the other men to follow his lead.

The redhead put his face directly in front of Danelle's. "I wouldn't be a gentleman if I didn't offer this sweet thing a ride. Where are you going? We'd be more than happy to take you there."

He and the others broke out into laughter.

Delbert had tried to torment Danielle many times by getting in her face. In return, she would stare straight ahead, not giving him the satisfaction of thinking he had intimidated her. Out of habit, the same defensive, blank stare was given to *this* hateful bully. Danielle was not sure if she was doing the right thing, but it was too late.

Once the men realized Danielle was not reacting to their intimidation, their laughter stopped.

Baffled by the response, the redhead began walking back and forth in front of Danielle with his hands clasped behind his back. "Well, boys, this one doesn't seem to think she can talk. But I think she can. What should we do?"

The skinny one started laughing so hard he could barely get the words out. "She. . . she's pretty enough. Let. . . let's take 'er for one of your *gentlemanly* rides."

The three of them broke into another round of laughter. The one with stringy, blonde hair—who obviously had been drinking—fell onto the ground and had to be helped up.

As they dusted him off with their hats, Danielle breathed a prayer. She knew God would never leave nor forsake her, so she looked around for a way to escape. There was none. She was trapped.

The driver grabbed her by the arm and started pulling her toward the buckboard. The blonde picked up her bags and was about to throw them in the back when he yelled to the other two that someone was coming.

Before Danielle could turn to see what was happening, the three offenders were in the buckboard and moving out at a faster speed than when they had arrived.

Heavenly Father, you are my protector. . . my deliverer. . . I thank you for—

"Are you hurt? They didn't harm you, did they?" The man yelling the questions pulled his farm wagon up beside her.

"I'm fine. . . just frightened." Danielle was too embarrassed to face him. "They hadn't been here long. Thank you for scaring them off and stopping to ask."

She walked over to pick up her belongings but became dizzy and lost her balance.

The man jumped from the wagon just in time to catch Danielle as her legs gave out. She recovered quickly, but not before looking up into his strong, handsome face and noticing his thick, dark hair. As he steadied her, it was obvious to Danielle that his muscular strength had come from hard work.

"What are you doing out here all alone? And carrying baggage? Don't you know a woman alone is an easy target—especially so close to Bristol? What were you thinking?"

In a split-second Danielle was offended. "Excuse me, sir. While I appreciate your kindness, I don't appreciate the scolding.

"I happen to be on the way to Willow Weep by foot because I couldn't find transportation or anything else in Bristol. Now, please excuse me. I need to gather my things and be on my way." Danielle straightened her shoulders, leveled the hat atop her light blonde hair, and reached for her bags.

"Look, under most circumstances, I'd leave you to it and be on my way. However, I must ask you to come with me to Willow Weep. . . for your own protection. Bristol is a growing town with all sorts of people coming and going. It's not as safe in this area as it once was."

"If that's the case, how do I to know *you're* to be trusted?" Danielle was intentionally being argumentative.

"Look, you're extremely fortunate I came along. I know those men. They're not to be trusted, and I wouldn't put anything past them. At the very least, they could've robbed you. What if they return?"

Since most of her money was hidden on her person, his comment did cause Danielle to realize the seriousness of the situation.

"Ma'am, I have no way of convincing you that my intentions are honorable, but keep in mind there are *three* of them." He grabbed her bags and deposited them in the wagon. Then he climbed up and offered her his hand.

Danielle hesitated, but she did feel this know-it-all man was reliable. Besides, she had no other choice. Danielle took his hand to allow him to assist her into the wagon. After taking a seat, she scooted as far from him as possible, perching on the very edge of the bench.

Although still fuming over her ingratitude, he felt an introduction was necessary. "I suppose I should introduce myself. I'm Hunter Jackson. May I ask your name?" Then, after having taken the initiative, he wondered if the girl with the pleasing looks and spunky attitude was going to respond.

Danielle, still hesitant to give her name or other personal information, began to choose her words carefully. "I'm Danielle Harrison. I guess I should reaffirm that I appreciate your kindness in assisting me in a most trying circumstance. Ordinarily, I wouldn't have taken a deserted road in an unfamiliar area, but in this case, it was warranted." Danielle tried to keep her explanation as cool as possible.

"So why are you so desperate to get to Willow Weep?" Hunter, at least, was attempting to have a civil conversation.

"I'm on my way to see about a waitressing position. But whether I'm hired or not, I will need to find lodging by the end of the day."

"Any particular reason why you chose Willow Weep?"

"As I mentioned earlier, I couldn't find a job or even a place to stay in Bristol. At this point, I am a beggar, not a chooser."

"Then what brought you to Bristol?"

"Mr. Jackson, I don't see why you're interested in my affairs. But if you must know, I decided to start a new life for myself."

"I see." Hunter's reply and his face could easily be read.

"No, Mr. Jackson, I'm *not* running from a husband. I have no attachments—romantic or otherwise." Danielle chastised herself for including the word *romantic*.

As Hunter turned onto the road leading to Willow Weep, the wagon wheel hit a rut, bouncing Danielle into the air. He grabbed her arm to prevent her from falling. As she stubbornly slid farther back onto the seat, Hunter couldn't help but notice that Danielle crinkled up her nose each time the wagon hit a rut. He probably would have thought it adorable if he had not been so frustrated with the girl.

Not long after, they pulled into Willow Weep. "Where would you like me to take you?"

"I'm to see Rosa Smith at the Willow Inn. If you wouldn't mind taking me there, it would be most appreciated."

"Rosa's place? I know her well. She's a wonderful lady. It's a well-respected establishment. I have dinner there on the days I pick up lumber." Hunter did not realize it, but the news had put a smile on his face.

When they arrived at the Willow Inn, he helped Danielle from the wagon. Once on the ground, she held out a fair amount of money for him to take. "I want to pay you for your trouble."

"Miss Harrison, I'm not for hire. My offer of a ride was out of courtesy." With that, he climbed back into the wagon and drove away.

As Danielle watched Hunter Jackson leave, she regretted her actions and wondered why she had been so impertinent toward the man who was kind enough to offer her protection.

7

IS SHE HIDING SOMETHING

Danielle stood outside the Willow Inn trying to gather enough courage to go inside. She had never applied for a job and did not know what it entailed. Before entering, she thought to check her appearance. After all, she *had* traipsed the downtown area of Bristol, walked a third of the way to Willow Weep, been dragged by a hooligan, and bounced around in a dusty wagon. She could only imagine how she must look.

Taking a mirror from her reticule, Danielle tucked in a few strands of hair and then looked down at her dress which seemed to have fared well. Having no more time to waste, Danielle stepped inside the restaurant.

Just as she entered, a smartly dressed, middle-aged lady with chestnut hair and a cheerful smile greeted her. "Good afternoon. May I find you a table?"

"If you please, I'm Miss Danielle Harrison, and I've come to inquire about the waitressing position. I was told to see Mrs. Smith at the request of Mrs. Belinda Gray." Danielle's voice was shaking by the time the words were spoken, but at least she had managed to sound pleasant.

"From Mrs. Gray? Indeed, my friend is true to her word in trying to help me find a suitable replacement. I'm Rosa Smith. It's nice to meet you, Miss Harrison. Although, I'm afraid you have come at a bad time. We're quite busy. Would you mind waiting in my office until I can find my way free to speak with you? It might be awhile."

Danielle was relieved. "I'd be happy to wait."

With that, Mrs. Smith ushered Danielle to a small, well-organized office just inside the swinging doors of the kitchen.

"I must return to the front but feel free to look at the magazines beside you." Then Mrs. Smith rushed off, not even giving Danielle a moment to say thank you.

Having been granted the opportunity for the interview, she was glad Mrs. Smith had offered a quiet place where she could calm her thoughts and have time to consider what she might do if she didn't receive the position. Danielle knew she couldn't allow herself to be daunted by the events of the day.

⚜

"Miss Harrison, I am so sorry you were kept waiting. However, I believe we shouldn't be disturbed for a while. So, you mentioned being sent here by Mrs. Gray. May I ask how you're acquainted with her?" Mrs. Smith's speech was hurried, making it seem as if the woman never had a spare moment.

"Mrs. Gray and I only met briefly on the train this morning. While we were talking, I mentioned I needed employment. I have a note of introduction from her." Danielle handed the proprietor the badly wrinkled piece of paper on which the note had been scribbled.

Mrs. Smith put on her glasses and scrutinized the note. "Without a doubt, it's Belinda's handwriting, but I find it strange she recommended you after such a brief encounter. I must say, it does give me cause for concern, but I've never had reason to doubt Belinda's judgment.

"I'm sorry to be so frank, but I must ask why you've come to Willow Weep."

"I had originally planned to settle in Bristol, but Mrs. Gray discouraged me. She suggested that applying for the waitressing position might be a better choice. After exploring Bristol, I could see Mrs. Gray's opinion was well grounded. That's why I'm here."

"But what was your purpose for coming to Bristol *or* Willow Weep?" Mrs. Smith was starting to sound suspicious.

"I'm relocating to start life on my own."

"And your family approved of you striking out alone?"

"I'm old enough to make my own decisions. But my stepfather did see me off at the train station—as Mrs. Gray can attest." Danielle's conscience was pricked since she knew she had just stretched the truth.

"I see. What else can you tell me about yourself?"

"I'm unmarried, in my early twenties, a school graduate, a seamstress. I've worked at odd jobs, but I've never held a position outside of my home. However, I had many responsibilities there. I'm also a hard worker." Danielle was grasping to recall anything which might make it sound as if she had experience.

"But no experience in restaurant work?" At this point, Mrs. Smith sounded even more skeptical.

"I've waited on people within my home. Other than that. . . no." Danielle was becoming disheartened again.

"You're telling me you've left the comfort of your home to start a new life without plans for your future?"

"Yes, I did. It wasn't an ideal plan, I must confess."

"So where *is* your home?"

Danielle wanted to change the subject. It would not do for Esther to ever receive word of her whereabouts, and she wondered if it had been wise to use her true identity. "Mrs. Smith, I can assure you I'm of the highest moral character and have no ulterior motive. I'm only seeking an independent life."

"Please excuse me a moment, Miss Harrison." With that said, Mrs. Smith scurried out of the room, leaving Danielle to wonder what her departure must mean.

Rosa walked into the dining room to see if Hunter Jackson was still in the restaurant. She thought he might be able to answer some questions about this perplexing, young woman. Fortunately, he was paying his bill and had not left.

"Hunter, may I have a word before you leave?" Rosa motioned him aside where they could have some privacy.

"I have a girl in my office seeking the waitressing position. I believe I saw you assist her from your wagon earlier. Am I correct? A Miss Danielle Harrison?"

"You did. How may I be of help?"

"I must admit she puzzles me. Belinda Gray recommended the child see me after only having met her on the train this morning. The girl seems the decent sort, but I feel as if she's hiding something. Her answers to my questions are on the peculiar side. Can you tell me what you know about her?"

"I happened across her on the way to Willow Weep—and none too soon. The Brewster boys were about to force her into their wagon. They took off when they saw me coming. She was unharmed but badly shaken.

"I insisted she ride to Willow Weep with me. We didn't get off to a very good start as far as introductions go. I spoke sternly to her after seeing she was walking alone with baggage." Hunter was reluctant to mention this to Rosa since she often lectured him about his bluntness.

"Hunter, when you're agitated, you *must* learn to think before you speak. You're such a wonderful, young man. It gives people the wrong impression of you.

"Regardless, what else can you tell me about this girl? And what is your opinion of her? Do you think she is trustworthy?"

"I do believe she's hiding something, but I didn't get the impression she's done anything wrong. Although, I do think Miss Harrison would walk away from the job rather than reveal what she's keeping inside.

"I believe she's trustworthy, but beyond that, I can't say. I should also mention that Miss Harrison told me she didn't have a place to stay tonight.

"Well, if that's all, I need to get this load delivered."

Feeling encouraged by Hunter's and Mrs. Gray's opinions, Mrs. Smith decided to hire Danielle. Yet, after talking to Hunter, she could not help but be concerned for the girl's welfare.

Mrs. Smith breezed back into the room as quickly as she had breezed out. "Well, Miss Harrison, I *am* willing to take you on. However, since you have no experience in this field, I cannot start you off at full salary. You'll receive full wages when you prove yourself.

"I also reserve the right to let you go for any just cause during training. Is that agreeable?" Mrs. Smith's face went from professional seriousness to a welcoming expression.

Danielle could not believe what she was hearing. She had been concerned she might need to get back on the train just to have a place to spend the night. But Mrs. Smith had just given her hope.

8

THE NAGGING QUESTION

"Miss Harrison, I'm afraid I have only the one uniform on hand. It'll be big on you. It belonged to Bets. All my employees are expected to dress the same. It's a pretty dress style, don't you think? The waitresses, however, do wear full white aprons over them."

"I must agree. The uniforms are very becoming."

"Well, I believe this is everything. Show up Monday at ten so we can get you started. Do you have any questions?"

"I do, but they don't pertain to the job. I need to find a bank and a place to stay." Danielle was hoping her employer would have some recommendations. It was late in the afternoon, and she had no idea where to begin.

"I see. Undoubtedly our rooms here at the inn are much too expensive for someone on a budget. . . but I *do* have a friend who's hoping to rent out a little one room cottage. She had been using it for storage, but since her husband has passed away, she needs to use it to bring in extra income. It's a very lovely, little place. I believe it would be within your budget, and you might be allowed to move right in if you agree to clean it out. Hattie hasn't been feeling well lately, or it would've been cleaned and rented by now."

Once Mrs. Smith had written down the directions for the rental and the bank, Danielle went on her way to see what else God had in store.

The first order of business was to get her funds safely tucked away. Danielle put the money Harold had given her in a savings account for emergencies. The rest of the money—minus what would be needed for getting settled—was put in a regular account. If frugal, she hoped she could live off the wages from the restaurant. With the banking completed, Danielle hurried off to see Mrs. Hattie Pence.

Hattie was a thin, stooped-back, elderly lady who shuffled along the best she could. The woman's face lit up as soon as Danielle introduced herself. The two liked each other at once and decided to be on a first name basis. Danielle agreed to the rent and terms without looking at the cottage. She was in no position to be choosey, and if the condition of Hattie's home was any indication, then the cottage would be a sanctuary.

Danielle followed the path through the trees and across a bridge spanning a trickling stream, and then on toward the stone cottage laden with morning glories and surrounded by weeping willows. Her new home was picturesque, quaint, and in excellent repair. Danielle even had her own stone walk, a manicured yard, and a wooden bench.

However, the inside of the cottage definitely needed to be cleared out. It was not dirty, but it did have discarded treasures which needed to be hauled away or burned. Danielle had noticed a fire pit in Hattie's backyard, so burning would not be a problem. Fortunately, there was furniture she could use—not to mention an indoor working pump, a small sink, and a tiny, wood-burning stove. The floor was varnished and in good shape.

Danielle thought she could easily remove the unneeded items, clean the cottage, and set up the furniture by dark. She planned to work into the night to complete everything and have free time for shopping the next day.

Excited at the prospects, Danielle hurried off to get the cleaning supplies Hattie had promised to set out. To her surprise, placed beside them was a plate filled with ham, bread, cheese, fruit, and cookies. Along with the tempting meal was a cold glass of lemonade. Mrs. Pence was going to be a wonderful landlord.

❦

Once she had finished eating, Danielle started pulling the unwanted and broken items from the cottage. She fed a burn pile with the things that were not salvageable and set the rest together for the junk dealer. The last item, found hidden in a corner under a pile of feed sacks, was a sewing machine. Danielle's heart leaped with excitement. She hoped Hattie might allow her to keep it in the cottage for sewing projects. When the sorting was done, it was time for Danielle to set up housekeeping.

It was still daylight, so Danielle gave everything a good scrubbing—including the walls, floor, and the kitchen sink. By the time night fell, she was ready to move the chosen furniture in place to make her little cottage a cozy home.

Using the tools left in the building, Danielle managed to put together the iron bed and placed it in the middle of the back wall. Being blessed with the luxury of a nice mattress and having brought her own bedding, she would sleep in comfort.

An ornate, cherry table was put by the bed as a nightstand. Her Bible and an etched glass lantern were set on top for reading at night.

Danielle pulled the little, round kitchen table and two mismatched chairs near the corner by the sink. A smaller lantern brought from home was centered on the table for more lighting. The cherry chest of drawers went beside the window to the right of the foot of the bed. A small, intricately decorated church pew was placed against the wall opposite the chest, and a tapestry-covered trunk fit well at the end of the bed for storage.

From the junk pile, Danielle rescued the wooden corner shelf and put it back in its place. She now realized the wooden rod on it was for holding hangers, and the extra shelf would definitely come in handy. The Turkish rug placed on the floor matched well with the trunk, and the various colors in the rug gave Danielle a color scheme and inspiration for further decorating.

The last task for the night was to make a list of the things she needed to finish setting up her cottage.

⚜

The next morning Danielle awoke well rested and hoping to make the needed purchases. After her devotions, she hurried to dress and set out to shop in her new hometown.

Other than being on a smaller scale, the downtown area was just as lovely as Bristol. There were several shops, and each had its own specialness.

Danielle liked the warm feeling of Willow Weep and felt it was probably best she was beginning her new life in a small town. The city of Bristol might have been a major challenge, considering her limited knowledge of life and people.

Then, there it was—the most magnificent weeping willow to ever catch Danielle's attention. The trunk was huge, the branches were perfectly formed, and the limbs were full of leaves swaying in the wind. Danielle could not have imagined a more perfect welcome to Willow Weep.

The tree was located within a well-cared-for garden in the middle of town. The town's people had every reason to take pride in their majestic willow. There were flowers and benches to draw one to the area. Danielle wanted to linger beneath the tree but knew her plans for the day could not wait.

⁂

The mismatched chairs and kitchen table looked inviting once given a new coat of paint. After asking Hattie for permission to use the sewing machine, Danielle made a simple bedspread by sewing two sheets together and using an old blanket for the inside padding. The curtains, pillows, and tablecloth were a quick project made from the newly purchased, blue and burgundy fabric.

Danielle tacked a new covering on an old ironing board and stored her few dishes and cookware in a drawer beneath the sink. For a homey touch, a vase of wildflowers was placed on the dresser.

When finished unpacking and hanging up the rest of her clothing, Danielle took the cutting from her own willow and placed it in a frame above the bed. The rest of the day was free for relaxing and doing simple things like reading a book, exploring the area, and hopefully, visiting with Hattie.

Her new life seemed filled with hope. Yet, she could not overcome the nagging question: Would she succeed as a waitress?

9

IDIOTS

"Delbert! I told you to be up and dressed by six-thirty to start work on the docks. Get out of bed and get moving!" Harold was already furious with his lazy son and could only imagine what a day at work with Delbert would be like.

"Seriously, Father, you don't actually expect me to work on the docks. Don't you have some bookwork or something I can do? I had a late night, and I'm not up to it. Besides, it's already warm out." Delbert was using his most pitiful, whiny voice—a ploy which always worked with his mother.

"Get those work clothes on and be ready to leave in five minutes! The men at the docks will already be working by the time we get there. The foreman will have to take time out of his day to show you the ropes."

It was a full fifteen minutes before Delbert came lumbering to the carriage. Harold felt bad for pushing the product of his failed parenting onto the dedicated men employed by him, but he could not think of an alternative. It might be the only possible way to reach his son.

Harold's face displayed no pride when he presented Delbert

to the workers. The men had been loading shipments for almost an hour and were already dripping with sweat.

"I apologize for our late arrival. My son didn't seem to think I was serious when I told him he would start working on the docks this morning. I'll see that it doesn't happen again.

"This is Delbert. I expect him to put in the same hours, carry the same workload, and receive the same salary as any other new employee.

"Bill, as foreman, you will need to train the boy. It's an extra burden, especially this late in the morning. I'll see that you're properly compensated. It will come out of Delbert's salary.

"Delbert, Bill is your boss. You're to do anything and everything he tells you to do. You are expected to put in a full day of hard work—just like the rest of the men. Do I make myself clear?"

Delbert folded his arms, leaned back against a wagon, and crossed one leg over the other. Then he gave a cocky smile with twitching lips as if he was about to laugh. "Sure."

Harold Simpson was embarrassed for his son. It was obvious Delbert was not smart enough to be embarrassed for himself.

Moving closer, Harold looked him squarely in the eye. "I'm not fooling, boy. Don't test me. Do your job."

During the morning, Harold would stop work to watch his son's progress. Each time he checked, Delbert was working hard, and each time his father would breathe a sigh of relief.

✦

At noon, Harold pulled his son off the job and walked him down to the leather shop. He explained to the owner and the apprentice that Delbert would be paying the full value of the briefcase. Harold then asked his son to apologize to the shop owner and to the young man.

Delbert gave an insolent laugh. Then putting his hands together, he got down on one knee and pretended to beg for forgiveness.

The owner looked at Harold, shook his head in disgust, then glared at Delbert. "He can keep his apology. I want nothing from the likes of him." He then walked back to his shop.

The young apprentice leered at Delbert in amazement. The look he gave Harold was even more belittling than the one the shop owner had given. It was a look of pity. "I don't want his money either. *I'll* pay the debt."

Harold was shamed and ashamed. He would have preferred a beating over what he saw in the eyes of the apprentice and shop owner.

"Idiots!" Delbert was pleased with himself, and it was apparent he thought he had brought his father down a peg or two.

Wearing his usual arrogant expression, Delbert climbed into the buggy and stretched his arm across the back of the seat. The only reason Harold did not turn his son out into the street immediately was that he had observed Delbert laboring responsibly on the docks that morning. He felt the job might be the avenue to reach his son.

Margaret was waiting at the door for Harold when he arrived home and wasted no time in issuing her attack. "Father, I know you were testy yesterday, but I need to speak to you about sending me off to another school. You do not have the right to make such a decision on my part. I am of age and I refuse to—"

"My dear Margaret, you are exactly right. You do have the right to refuse to go to another school—just as I have the right to tell you to pack your bags and leave the premises. As I stated before, you will go to the school of my choice *or* you will leave this house." With that, he walked into his study and closed the door.

On the desk, Harold found several bills from high-priced dressmakers. He was ready to put an end to Esther's spending. However, when he went to speak with his wife, he was informed by one of the staff that Mrs. Simpson again was visiting with Mr. Grant.

Harold had no actual qualms with Esther spending time with Mr. Grant. In general, anytime the woman was out of the house was bliss for Harold, but he did have reason to be interested in the particulars of their relationship. As it was, he would have his lawyer inform the dressmakers that Mrs. Simpson's accounts were to be canceled.

"Mother! Father! Hurry! I've found a note from Danielle. She left home on purpose." Sherry stood in the foyer, waving the paper clutched in her hand. Harold arrived in time to watch her wipe the tears from her cheeks. Pulling Sherry up and into his arms, he could not remember the last time he had held his little girl. But that would no longer be the case. Harold would show as much affection for Sherry as he so chose.

"Sherry! Was that you shouting? It will not be tolerated! You are a lady!" Esther yelled.

"Now, what's all this about Danielle running away? Put that child down, Harold. I don't want people seeing our children crawling all over you. Leave the children to me."

"Hush, woman. You no longer tell me what I will or will not do with our children or anything else. I'll hold my little girl as often as I choose." Harold had not raised his voice but had spoken with a commanding presence.

"Harold, what has gotten into you of late? I want the way in which you have been speaking to me to cease." Esther—being uncertain if she wanted to provoke Harold further—had lowered her voice.

"My dear—just to remind you—you're currently penniless. So be careful."

This time she was starting to wonder what her husband's insinuations truly meant. Choosing to ignore what Harold had said, she changed the subject to Danielle. "Let me have that note. The girl has been nothing but trouble since the day she was born."

Esther took the note, but Harold snatched it from her hand, read it, folded it, and put it in his inner pocket. "Danielle has left home with no plans of returning. She'll be praying for us. There were no further details."

"How dare Danielle bring disgrace on me! Let me see that note. I have a right to read it. After all, she's my daughter. She's nothing to you."

"Didn't you mean to say that she's nothing to *you*? I distinctly remember hearing you say similar words to her time after time. Most likely that's the reason she addressed the note to *me*. You care nothing for Danielle, and she's no longer in your life. It should make you incredibly happy."

"The disgrace! We must hire someone to find her." Esther's face was blotchy red with anger.

"Esther, you didn't even care enough for Danielle to check to see if she came home last night. Don't you lift one finger to try to locate the girl, or I'll tell our friends why she's a runaway." With that said, Harold left the room with Sherry in his arms.

10

A STUBBORN AND GRUDGE HOLDING WOMAN

Danielle walked in the back door of the Willow Inn exactly on time. Mrs. Smith was already in the kitchen giving the cook instructions for the lunch menu. A smile came to her face as she walked over to greet Danielle. "I hope you had a good weekend. Did you rent the cottage?"

"I did. It's such a perfect little place—just what I'd hoped for. Hattie and I are getting along wonderfully. We even had devotions together on Sunday. Since she wasn't feeling up to going to church and I haven't had time to find one, we spent the entire morning together."

"I'm so glad to hear it. I almost drove by Hattie's to see how she was doing and whether or not you had taken the cottage. Is there anything you need?" Rosa seemed as excited about the rental as Danielle.

"Actually, I'm all set up. There was enough furniture to make it comfortable, and I went shopping on Saturday for the other things I needed."

"That's wonderful news. God even takes care of the details.

"Well, I guess we'd better get you to work—although, I do want to mention how nice the uniform looks on you. Most waitresses don't bother to alter them. Now, let me explain what your duties will be."

❧

Danielle froze when she was asked to wait on her first table. Everything suddenly went out of her head. One of the other waitresses stopped to ask Danielle if there was a problem. "I'm scared. I don't think I can do this." The waitress was kind enough to repeat the routine serving procedure and tried to encourage her.

Unfortunately, the lady's kind intentions did not help Danielle. She kept forgetting to take the water pitcher to fill glasses, and even when she remembered the pitcher, she missed filling some glasses, overfilled several, and knocked one glass over—which meant the tablecloth had to be changed. When delivering orders, she could not remember who ordered what. Twice she over-poured coffee, causing it to flow into the saucers. But the worst was when Danielle dropped an entire plate of food.

That evening, Mrs. Smith sat down with Danielle to have a talk. "Dear, you didn't do well today. To be honest, I've never seen a worse start. Why was it so difficult for you?" Mrs. Smith was as kind and understanding as one could be under the circumstances.

"I was unnerved and unable to organize my thoughts. It was as if my brain had frozen. Evidently, I'm uncomfortable working so closely with people. It would probably be best if I leave before you invest more time in me. I don't feel it's something time will change."

"Waitressing looks easy, but it does require a clear head and an excellent memory. What is easy for some isn't always easy for others. I've seen what you described in other workers I've hired. Through no fault of their own, some people's brains just shut down when they get nervous. Remember, we're not all meant to be farmers or opera singers. God made us all different. Some of us are equipped to work around people, while others are meant to work alone. But we all have at least one niche in life. On the other hand, I may have started you off too quickly."

Danielle was relieved when Mrs. Smith had not scolded or fired her.

"Why don't you return in the morning and try the breakfast and lunch shift. Afterward, if you still feel waitressing isn't for you, I have another plan."

Danielle left work, humiliated and concerned for her future. Thanks to Harold, there was enough money to get by while she looked for another job, but it might mean leaving Willow Weep. Danielle could not keep from wondering if Esther and Delbert were right. Maybe she *was* stupid and worthless. She needed to pray.

⁂

The next day was somewhat better. Breakfast was not so demanding, but Danielle still made more than her share of mistakes. The cobwebs in her head did not go away. It was plain to see, she could not thrive in this situation.

At the end of the shift, Mrs. Smith called her into the office. "You had another difficult day, but I'm willing to work with you if you're still interested in being a server. However, if you no longer want to be a waitress, then I would like to offer you another position."

Danielle hung her head. "Evidently I'm not a waitress. But I am interested in hearing about the other job you have in mind."

Mrs. Smith's expression was laced with empathy. "Well, while you were knocking over glasses and over-pouring coffee cups yesterday, I had another employee resign. My head housekeeper has recently married and is expecting her first child. Therefore, I'd like you to consider the position. It pays well, but you *will* have employees under you. Also, I'd like it if you'd fill in as a waitress from time to time. It might help you with your challenges."

Danielle was astonished—especially knowing her performance as a waitress could have affected Mrs. Smith's business reputation. "Your offer is so kind. Of course, I'd love to take the position. And I won't disappoint you this time."

Having received the details for the new assignment, Danielle arrived at the cottage with a lifted spirit. When living at home, she had helped with all household chores and knew what was expected of the head housekeeper. Once again, God had taken a bad situation in her life and turned it around.

Since Hattie had not been feeling well, she had gone to stay with her son's family for a while. Danielle was lonely and bored. So, with the afternoon free, she decided to change clothes and take a walk to see the town. Willow Weep was much prettier than she had imagined. The town was full of trees, rocky streams, and flowers. For her, the place was a dream come true. The afternoon walk eventually led Danielle to a public library which looked relatively new. It had been a long while since she had been allowed to spend time looking through rows of books. Having established residency, she now had a library card. Going there would be something to do in her spare time. For that reason, she only checked out one book, a classic novel.

From the distance, she noticed the willow tree in the town

garden and decided it would be a good place to read. Since the book was so interesting, she hadn't noticed the sky was darkening with storm clouds. It was not until she heard giggling that she looked up to see a pretty, young lady and a gentleman approaching. When they walked out of the shadows, she could see the man was Hunter Jackson. Unfortunately for her, he noticed Danielle at the same time.

"Miss Harrison, I see you are enjoying the Willow Garden."

"I am, Mr. Jackson. I discovered the willow while shopping. I have a great fondness for them. Since I'd just visited the library, I couldn't resist sitting down for a while to read."

"I sometimes sit here myself when I'm in town. Oh, you must excuse me. May I introduce Miss Sally Mee. . . Meeker. Miss Meeker, this is Miss Danielle Harrison."

Sally did not even acknowledge Danielle or give her time to speak. "You silly thing, you act as if you don't know my name." Then Sally giggled, slipped her hand under Hunter's arm, and snuggled close to him.

Being a Christian, Danielle would not allow herself to think how much she did not care for Sally Meeker. "It's nice to meet you, Miss Mee. . . Meeker."

Hunter could not keep his lips from showing a faint smile at Danielle's subtle humor. And Danielle could not keep from noticing the jealous look on Sally's face—nor did she miss seeing the death grip Sally had on Mr. Jackson's arm.

"I came into town to pick up some papers from an attorney for my uncle and decided to eat at the Willow Inn. I assumed you would be working. You did get the position?"

"I did, but it seems I'm not the waitressing type. Instead, I was offered the position of head housekeeper." Danielle was embarrassed to tell him but knew it was likely he would hear it from Mrs. Smith or someone who had witnessed her inadequacies.

"She's a *housekeeper*?" Sally distastefully emphasized.

"I'm glad to hear it, Miss Harrison. Not to change the subject—but there's a storm headed our way. May I take you home while I drop Miss Meeker off at her house? I wouldn't like for either of you to get caught in the storm."

"Thank you kindly, Mr. Jackson, but I'll be fine. I like to walk in the rain. Besides, I wouldn't want to intrude."

"No intrusion. But I must insist. The clouds are rolling in quickly." Hunter then recalled suffering repercussions the last time he had spoken to Danielle Harrison with similar words.

"Mr. Jackson, I believe we've been down this road before. As I said, I'll be fine."

"Miss Harrison—"

"Hunter, the girl said she'd be fine. Now, let's go." Sally gave Danielle a menacing look, while pulling on Hunter's arm.

"Well, if you insist on walking, Miss Harrison. . . then, good evening."

Hunter was upset with himself. He did not understand why he cared so much for Danielle's welfare—especially when she infuriated him so. And he was even more upset with Sally, who managed to track him down every time he was in town.

As soon as Hunter and Sally drove away in the buggy, Danielle started the walk back to the cottage. Hunter was right. It was not long before huge drops of rain began to fall. To protect the library book, she wrapped it in a giant hosta leaf she found along the way. A short time later, lightning began to flash, thunder began to roll, and the rain began to pour. Danielle was immediately drenched.

Suddenly, Hunter's buggy appeared beside her. The rain and thunder were so intense she could barely hear what he was yelling.

"Get in the buggy! I'll take you home! It's dangerous out here!"

"No—"

He then jumped down in front of her. "You are the most stubborn, grudge-holding woman I've ever met! Now, please, get in the buggy!"

"No, I—"

"I don't believe this!" With that, Hunter picked Danielle up, put her in the buggy, and climbed in beside her.

"It's too dangerous to be out walking!" He then slapped the reins and took off down the street, "*Now*, will you tell me where you live, so I can get you home safely?"

"Yes! I live back there in Hattie Pence's cottage where you picked me up!"

Without a word, Hunter turned the horse around, returned to Hattie's driveway, assisted Danielle from the buggy, and disappeared into the raging storm.

11

THE DAMAGE WAS DONE

What was I thinking?

Hunter always thought things through before acting—but since meeting Danielle, he seemed to be losing his ability to be levelheaded.

Why do I feel as if I'm Danielle Harrison's caretaker? I barely know the girl. I've made a needless trip to Willow Weep just to see if she is faring well. Instead of riding my horse, I drove this rig to town just in case she might need a ride. The next thing I know, I'm chasing her down in a rainstorm and throwing her into my buggy. I've made a complete fool of myself. Well, it won't happen again.

The storm was still raging, but being so discomposed, he had foolishly left town rather than seeking shelter. The dirt road was now washed out more than normal, so he slowed the horse to carefully navigate each rain-filled hole. Fortunately, he had taken his uncle's oldest buggy.

Hunter was the middle child of a wealthy family. According to his parents, he was the rebellious one—not because he was unruly, but because he would not conform to society's standards. His parents were wonderful people, but they did take pride in their social status. As a boy, Hunter was forced to attend certain balls and parties to meet other young people who were considered his equals. His parents believed it was one of the steps necessary to prepare him to take his proper place among the wealthy. Hunter had great respect for his family and did what was expected of him socially—until after graduating from college.

Upon Hunter's graduation, his parents insisted it was time for their middle son to take a wife. They even hinted at a marriage of convenience. On the other hand, Hunter felt it was time to live his life as *he* saw fit.

Hunter was not attracted to most young ladies of money and found many of them to be snobbish, shallow, and pushy. There had been only one who had intrigued him, but the romance had not ended well. Their relationship had convinced him that he was not ready to take on the responsibilities of a family or sit behind a desk giving orders. Someday he would likely inherit a portion of his family's fortune. But, in the meantime, Hunter's aspirations were to build his own life and make his own money through his own hard work—whether he ended up a man of means or not.

Most of Hunter's views mirrored those of his father's brother, Melvin Jackson. His Uncle Mel was a reasonably wealthy man who would only make principled investments and was a devout Christian who did not hold to social demands. Mel did not believe people deserved respect because of their earthly possessions but felt people *earned* respect by the good way in which they lived their lives. He followed the biblical principal of treating all others the way he would want to be treated. Mel was just as likely to be found working in the fields with his hired hands, as sitting behind his expensive desk.

Hunter's parents were not accepting of their son's beliefs. To avoid causing further discord within the family, Hunter had sought employment as the overseer of his uncle's farmland, forests, and gardens. For the time being, he was very content.

⚜

Danielle was extremely upset and confused by Hunter Jackson's actions. *What was he thinking? The nerve! To pick me up! I told him I would be fine.*

But when she was honest with herself, she realized it was a very thoughtful gesture. He had tried to warn her about the storm, and the storm did end up being as violent as he had predicted.

Then she became upset all over again. *He was probably just passing by and happened to notice me. Hunter Jackson probably thinks I'm not smart enough to come in out of the rain! In all probability, he wasn't being a gentleman at all.*

Danielle wrestled with her thoughts for the rest of the night.

⚜

The next morning when Danielle entered the back door of the Willow Inn, she was greeted by applause. To her surprise, Mrs. Smith had asked the staff to meet in the kitchen to encourage her in the new job and confirm that no one had a bad opinion of her.

Danielle was touched by the gesture and thanked everyone profusely. When a few of her fellow workers began teasing about her blunders, she and everyone else laughed. That is, everyone laughed except Mildred Haines.

Danielle readily took to the job. She knew many tricks of spotless cleaning and the way to do them efficiently. Those working under her appreciated the changes she enacted to ease their work load.

Mrs. Smith was extremely impressed with Danielle's work, and one day called her into the office. "Miss Harrison, I've always been pleased with the performance of my previous heads of housekeeping and could take pride in the cleanliness of my inn. But since you have come, everything has an extra sparkle. What is your secret?"

Danielle was surprised by the comment—but knew the answer. "Over the years, my family has had many excellent housekeepers. I was required to work with all of them. They each had their own ways of doing things, so I learned all of their methods. As your employee, I'm applying the best of those methods."

"Sweetheart, you've learned well. Please accept my compliments.

"Now, let's get down to the reason I called you here. I've come to think very highly of you and hope you consider me a friend. So, outside of the workplace, I'd like for you to call me *Rosa*. I also hope I may call you *Danielle*."

Danielle was honored that her boss would take time from her busy day to ask if they could be on a first name basis. Having had few friends in her life, she considered this the highest of compliments.

A couple evenings later, Danielle decided to explore the property that was behind her cottage. A short distance into the woods, there was a creek where she could see several people fishing. Danielle assumed it was public domain and began to wander along the bank. It was a pleasant walk, and it seemed everywhere she looked there were willow trees and wildflowers. Occasionally, she would pick a flower and drop the blossom in the water just to watch it float away. Everything seemed so peaceful along the creek bank and in her life as well.

During the stroll, Danielle came to a spot where she needed to cross to the other side of the creek. Fortunately, there were several rocks in the water to use as stepping stones. Without giving it a second thought, she began to cross. But as she stepped onto the fourth rock, a fishing line and fly swished directly in front of Danielle's face, causing her to lose balance and almost plop into the creek on her bottom. Just in time, a strong arm reached out to prevent her from falling. There was a moment's pause, but then a familiar voice drifted to her ear.

"Well, Miss Harrison, it seems I can't escape you."

Danielle looked up into the face of Hunter Jackson once again. "I agree. I don't seem to be able to manage to avoid you either. To be perfectly honest, I would rather have fallen into the creek."

Hunter shot back with just as much frustration toward her as she had just shared with him. "I will keep that in mind. . . should another occasion arise when you need my assistance."

"Of course, it wouldn't have happened had I not been startled by your fishing tackle."

"Then may I remind you again to take note of your surroundings, Miss Harrison."

"May I remind you that I've never asked for your assistance?"

This time Hunter could not hide the hurt in his voice. "That's true. Like I said. . . I will keep it in mind."

At once Danielle realized how her sharp words had affected him. The damage was done, and Danielle did not know what to do about it.

Hunter began reeling in his line. To his disgust, hooked on the fly was one of her flowers. Danielle would never forget the wounded look on his face as he jerked the blossom off the hook, pitched it away, and headed down the creek.

"I'm sorry," Danielle said softly as she watched him walk away.

12

OBNOXIOUS AND MEAN AND PLAIN LAZY

Harold was exhausted after spending a week in Perrysville clearing up problems in his company there. He had hoped to spend the first day back in Grandville doing paperwork but found Bill waiting in his office when he arrived.

"Bill, good to see you. We usually don't cross paths this early in the day. Is there something I can do for you?"

"Well, that remains to be seen, Mr. Simpson. I've come to discuss some serious business." Bill was somber, and his jaw was set.

Since Bill was always jovial and cordial, Harold was jolted by his friend's tone. "Certainly, what is it?"

"Another company has made an offer to me and several members of my crew. We have decided it is to our advantage to accept."

Stunned by the information, Harold could not speak for several seconds while he processed the man's words. "Bill. . . I don't understand. I've always thought we had a good working relationship. Is it a matter of money? If so, I'd be more than willing to consider your terms—although I've always felt I paid my workers generously."

"It's not the money, sir. It's the working conditions."

"The working conditions? But you've never mentioned

there was a problem. Bill, you've been here for years. Tell me what's wrong."

"Harold, it isn't the money or the job. It's *Delbert*. He's obnoxious, mean, and just plain lazy. He has spent his time here doing absolutely nothing and has been threatening us with our jobs if we report his behavior. The men are intimidated by him. They have families and can't afford to go without work. He also harasses and curses the workers. Since you've been away, it has become unbearable. Frankly, the entire crew would rather leave than work another day with him."

Again, Harold took time to absorb what he had just been told. "You're telling me Delbert *isn't* working? But I kept an eye on him to be certain he was doing his part before I left on the trip. He was always hard at work."

"When you're at the window, he can see you. He *waits* for you to appear. Delbert was only acting like he was doing his job. It's a game to him. He sees you and everyone around him as stooges to be manipulated. I'm sorry to be so blunt. . . but Delbert is a vicious bully, and I refuse to work another day with the man. So you have my resignation effective immediately."

"Wait, Bill, *please*. I should have known. Allow me to make this right with you and the crew. Delbert will be fired, regardless. . . but as a friend, I'd like a chance to explain what's going on."

⚜

Delbert had been unaware of his father's return the night before and had shown up at work on his own. To confirm the foreman's story, Harold watched his son through an open door at the dock. He saw he had definitely been duped by Delbert.

A few minutes later, Harold tied the boy's horse to the back of the buggy and entered the shipping yard to remove his son from the premises. Delbert was obstinate and refused to leave. But after some friendly persuasion from a couple of the dock workers, Delbert decided it would be in his best interest to abide by his father's wishes.

⚜

When they entered the house, Harold spoke with one of the staff and then directed Delbert into the study. Delbert started to take a seat, but Harold interfered. "Don't sit down. You won't be staying long." He then scribbled out a check.

"Here's an allowance for you to start out on. It's sufficient for lodging, food, and general necessities. You will receive the same amount each month for one year—and not a penny more. I suggest you get a job. In anticipation of your departure, I've had a banking account set up in your name." Harold tapped a piece of paper and told his son to sign it.

Wearing the expected smirk, Delbert leaned over and signed the paper.

"You were warned what would happen if you refused to change your vile ways. I've asked one of the staff to pack some of your clothing. The bags will be at the door on your way out. The rest of your belongings will be delivered once I receive a letter stating where you've settled.

"You're to leave the house immediately, and you're not to return unless I say so. My attorney has already been notified of my decision concerning your departure, and he will act accordingly. I've hired security for this property, so don't try lurking around here for any reason."

Delbert crossed his arms in defiance. "Mother will never allow this. Besides, you aren't man enough to see this through. I had the entire dock crew under my dictation while you stood at the window and watched. I outsmarted you then. . . and I can outsmart you now. So, if I were you, I'd stop this little charade while you can."

"Delbert, it's difficult for me to make these decisions. I know I'm to blame for the person you've become. But until the day arrives when you want to change, I'll tolerate your behavior no longer.

"Learn, boy, or you will end up paying a high price for your choices. I suggest you start with seeking God's forgiveness. I had every intention of raising you children in the ways of the Lord, but I let Esther interfere. And—as for your mother—she has nothing to say in the matter. I fear she will soon have her own issues to battle."

"Come on, Father. If you expect me to leave, who's going to make me? You? Just try it!" Delbert uncrossed his arms as if he were ready to fight—daring his father.

After hearing Delbert defy and threaten him, Harold drew back his hand and slapped his son across the face, causing Delbert to reel and land in the chair beside him.

"Now, you need to leave."

Delbert, with his face red from the slap and tears in his eyes, scrambled to his feet and headed for the door—cursing his father and issuing more disgraceful threats.

What hurt Harold the most was realizing he was relieved to see his own son walking out the door.

✦

Having arrived home late that night, Esther had been unaware that Delbert had been sent away. By the time Harold arrived home the next afternoon, his wife was pacing with anger and issued her verbal attack as soon as he entered the door.

"You imbecile! I can't believe you threw my son out without consulting me. I won't have it! You will find him and bring him home at once."

"Hush, Esther." He directed her into his study. "Do you not know the staff gossips about what goes on in this house?"

"I do. It was one of the staff who informed me that Delbert left after you struck him. Go find him, or I'll have you brought up on charges. My father has connections and—"

"I slapped Delbert since he left me no alternative. He was defying and threatening me. We can only hope that someone will rescue our cowardly son if he ever gets into a fist fight with a girl.

"As for your father's connections. . . due to his crooked ways, he seldom sees a client. He's been blacklisted by his colleagues. It appears your father is lacking in funds and will soon be unable to keep his office afloat. I assume cutting off your ability to pilfer my money to him is now adding to his financial problems."

Esther gasped and did not speak another word.

"What little money your father once had was spent trying to rub elbows with the affluent. So, you see, Esther, I can have *you* brought up on charges as well. I believe the terms are. . . forgery and embezzlement. Tread lightly, Mrs. Simpson."

Harold turned and left the room.

After Harold had gone to work the next morning, Esther combed all the lodging in Grandville and found Delbert in the most expensive hotel in town.

"Mother, this pittance father has given me won't do. You need to provide me with more money."

"Where do you think I'll get it? Your father has found us out and has taken charge of the finances. Currently I'm in the same position as you."

Delbert went into a fit of rage, throwing pillows and vases. His face was flushed with anger as he stomped like a small child across the floor and plopped into a chair.

"Calm down, dear. I'll find you a less expensive hotel or boarding house."

"Mother, I can't live in squalor!"

"What choice do we have at the moment? This will only be temporary. I have other plans in the making. Have I ever failed to come out on top? Just trust me."

After much searching, Esther managed to find her son a room in a boarding house. Delbert was incensed, but, as might be expected, it was only a few days before he was evicted because of his rudeness.

The next option was to move in with his grandparents. It seemed like the perfect arrangement since they were in desperate need of money. Unfortunately, he was acting aggressively toward them and spending his allowance on liquor and cards, instead of paying for his keep. Because of his behavior, Esther was forced to make daily trips to check on her parents' safety.

⚜

In the meantime, Harold received word that there was an opening with a missionary family who was willing to take on Margaret's special situation. The minister and family had built a mission church and school among the impoverished found deep in the Appalachian

Mountains. The mission was well established, and although the work there was difficult, it was also rewarding.

Pastor Allen and his wife had been touched by the plea received from Harold Simpson—a desperate father hoping to reach the daughter he had allowed to be overindulged. The couple had felt the Appalachian people could be an inspiration to someone such as Margaret.

The attorney informed Harold that Pastor Allen and his family had impeccable recommendations and had proven to be reliable. Harold was pleased with the lawyer's research and instructed him to proceed with the arrangements.

"Father! You can't mean it! You definitely told me I was to go to another finishing school. I refuse to go to an Appalachian mission! Those people wear dirty clothes."

"I had planned to send you to another finishing school, but none met your needs. . . and you're older than most of the young ladies. No, Margaret. I want better for you. I want you to learn to appreciate your lifestyle and respect people for who they are. This is my offer."

"Harold, you've lost your mind! Don't think for a minute I'll allow you to send Margaret away to such a horrid place."

"Esther, you have nothing to say in the matter. You've had your way with our children and look what you've done to them. Please leave this room now. . . or shall I call the attorney?"

To Harold's astonishment, Esther said nothing and left the room.

A few days later, Harold escorted Margaret to the station. Still irate, she would not acknowledge or wave to her father as the train left the depot. He had given Margaret only enough money for food. The rest of her allowance had been mailed to Pastor Allen to manage.

Harold Simpson hoped sending his daughter away was not as cruel as it felt to him at that moment, but he wanted his children to be responsible and caring individuals. In spite of the way they had been raised, they deserved a chance to have a truly fulfilling life. Harold prayed that Margaret would be wiser than her brother.

13

THE DIAMOND NECKLACE

Hattie returned home feeling spry and ready to work in the garden. The change in the older lady was easily detected by the sparkle in her eyes. On the way to the inn, Danielle stopped by to welcome her home. The little cottage would not seem so lonely now that Hattie was close by.

Rosa was going over the menus with the chef but managed to give Danielle a wave of acknowledgment. The inn was fully booked with guests who were in Willow Weep to attend a wedding. For that reason, every member of the staff was scheduled for the weekend to accommodate the party.

That morning, several of the lady guests had gone out to explore the shops, while the men went fly fishing in Willow Creek. The housekeeping staff hustled to get the rooms back in perfect order and set up the banquet hall for the evening dinner.

By the time the banquet room was completed, the ladies and gentlemen had returned to dress for another outing, making it necessary to tidy the guests' rooms again.

Later in the afternoon, the hotel supplied each room with light refreshments so their patrons could relax before dressing for the evening. One of the kitchen girls asked Danielle to assist by taking the final tea tray to room seven. With the trays all delivered, Danielle breathed a sigh of relief. The night shift would take over once the diners were seated in the banquet hall.

Since everything seemed to be in order, Danielle went to Rosa's office to finalize the paperwork from the long shift. But just as she was preparing to leave, Rosa bolted into the room. "*Danielle*, one of the guests has lost a diamond pendant with a gold chain. The lady and I searched the entire room repeatedly and didn't find it. Now she's accusing one of the housekeepers of theft. Please gather the day staff before they leave. This *must* be remedied at once."

Fortunately, Danielle caught the housekeepers at the door and escorted them to the office.

Rosa briefly explained about the missing necklace and began questioning the girls. She asked each one to recall their workday and what they could remember about room seven.

It appeared the room had been in the care of a trusted employee who had worked at the inn for many years. The only other person known to have been in room seven was Danielle while delivering the tray. After reviewing all the information, the final conclusion was that Danielle had been the last person to enter that particular room. Rosa felt she had no choice but to ask Danielle not to return to work.

"*Rosa*, I didn't do it. . . I didn't *see* the necklace, nor did I *take* it. I would never do such a thing." She squared her shoulders and left the building.

As soon as Danielle was through the back door of the Willow Inn, she began to weep uncontrollably. Blinded by the tears, she ran into the parking lot and straight into Hunter Jackson. He immediately closed his arms around her. Hunter knew he should not—but he could not stop himself. Danielle Harrison was hurting.

Hunter comforted her for a few seconds before he made the mistake of speaking. "What is it, Miss Harrison? What has caused you to be so upset?"

As he had expected, Danielle did not look at him. She just shook her head and ran away.

Hunter did not walk to the front entrance but barged in the back door and asked the kitchen staff where he could find Rosa. One of the workers indicated to check the office. Not finding her there, Hunter went through the swinging doors and into the dining area. He stood in the middle of the floor and surveyed the room.

Finally, catching a glimpse of Rosa in the banquet hall, Hunter went straight over and nearly demanded to speak with her. Seeing the seriousness in his eyes, she led him to an unoccupied hallway.

"Rosa, I was coming through the back parking lot and found Miss Harrison in tears. What's happened?"

"Oh, Hunter, I don't know if I should dare tell you. It's most horrible for the girl, but I didn't know what else to do under the circumstances. I was so preoccupied with the inn being full of guests that I made a snap decision. The poor dear! I'm certain Danielle mistook my meaning. She must think I'm awful—a fair-weather friend."

"Rosa, please, what happened?"

"Well, most of housekeeping knows, but they've been warned—so you must speak of this to no one.

"There is a necklace missing from a guest's room, and since we couldn't find it, the woman insists it's been stolen by one of the staff. There were only two people known to be in the room—Phyllis, who is a longtime, trusted employee. . . and Danielle. To appease the guest, I had to ask Danielle to leave. I didn't want to involve Officer Brown prematurely, but if I don't report it, the woman expects *me* to replace an expensive piece of jewelry."

"You know Miss Harrison didn't take it, don't you?"

"Of course, I do. I just didn't know how to handle the situation at the time. I've never had to deal with anything like this. Although I do suspect the necklace was stolen—but by whom, I don't know."

It was clear to Hunter that Rosa was at her wit's end and was just as distraught over the situation as he and Danielle were. "You must get to the bottom of this. She can't be expected to take the blame. Would you like me to take her a message?"

"Oh my, yes, if you'd be so kind. Please follow me to the office, and I'll write it directly."

Danielle cut through the woods and ran along Willow Creek to reach the cottage. Fortunately, there were only a few older men fishing, and she managed to get by them without being noticed. The door slammed behind her as she ran to the bed to pour out her heart in prayer. "*Father, I don't understand. I don't want to leave Willow*

Weep, but what choice do I have?"

The hurt inside was all too familiar. Her mother and Delbert had falsely accused Danielle all of her life. She had hoped such hurt was behind her.

Hunter had mounted his horse and promptly coaxed him into a full gallop. Petra was a sure-footed and quick-responding horse that anticipated Hunter's every cue. The animal swiftly maneuvered the back alleys, and within seconds they were on the street headed for Hattie's place.

Hattie answered the back door and was delighted to see Hunter. They had become friends at Faith Chapel Church soon after his arrival in the Willow Weep and Remington area. Hunter, being a well-rounded Christian, was always willing to get involved whenever a need arose and had come to Hattie's aid several times since her husband's passing.

This evening, Hattie was unusually talkative, so it was several minutes before he was able to tactfully interrupt their conversation to request permission to deliver the note. Hattie was impressed by his consideration and gladly gave consent.

Hunter, being eager to deliver the message, found himself beating, instead of knocking, on the cottage door.

"Who is it?"

He could tell by Danielle's reluctant response that his pounding had caught her off guard. "I'm sorry to disturb you, Miss Harrison. It's Hunter Jackson, and I'm here to deliver a message from Mrs. Smith."

Danielle cracked the door and peeked out. Seeing her mussed hair and swollen, teary eyes, Hunter could hardly resist the desire to hold and comfort her again.

"Miss Harrison, I know what you think of me, so rest assured, this is not a social call. I've only come to deliver a note from Mrs. Smith since she is unable to come in person. She asked for you to please read it at once. I found her very distressed. Will you please accept and read it?" Danielle appeared dazed and confused.

"Miss Harrison, are you all right? Do you need assistance? I can get Hattie."

Danielle shook her head slightly to indicate not to bother her landlord. "I'll accept the note."

As Hunter handed her the message, the tips of their fingers touched ever so slightly. He could no longer deny the connection he felt to Danielle Harrison. "May I wait on the bench for a reply?"

Danielle looked at the note, nodded her head, and closed the door.

It was at least a full fifteen minutes before she opened the door and stepped outside. Her face looked refreshed and she seemed relieved.

"Thank you for waiting and for taking the trouble to deliver the note. I would appreciate it if you'd take this message to Mrs. Smith."

"Will you be all right? You had me a bit concerned."

"I appreciate it, Mr. Jackson, but there's no need to be. I'm accustomed to such treatment." Danielle realized she had said too much. "Again, Mr. Jackson, I thank you for your kindness, but I'll be fine."

She then gave a polite nod to excuse herself and went back into the cottage.

Rosa was waiting in the dining room for Hunter's return. As soon as he walked through the door, she asked Madison to make him a plate.

Hunter went directly to Rosa with the note. She read it and closed her eyes momentarily. "Danielle understands the situation and has accepted my apology. Honestly, Hunter, I didn't mean to give the girl the impression she was fired. I only meant she shouldn't return until the situation was straightened out. But Danielle was out the door and gone before I realized the damage I'd done."

"So that's why Miss Harrison is so distressed. Rosa, I believe she has been treated badly by someone in the past. When I expressed my concern for her, she told me I shouldn't worry because she was accustomed to such treatment. After making the statement, she retreated into the cottage."

"I agree. Danielle is hiding something. . . or from some-one. . . or both."

"Rosa, if you don't get to the bottom of this missing necklace by tonight, it may be too late. Can you think of anyone who had reason to hurt Miss Harrison?"

"I don't know of anyone. It would almost have to be one of the staff, and such things are usually kept between the workers." Just then Rosa was called away to attend to a matter in the banquet hall.

Madison was on her way to the table with Hunter's food when she was stopped briefly by Mildred Haines. Hunter noticed that the slight conversation between the two seemed to affect Madison's demeanor.

"Madison, is something wrong? I noticed Mildred seemed to have said something to upset you."

Looking too disturbed to answer, she shrugged her shoulders.

"Will that be all, Mr. Jackson? If not, I can ask one of the other waitresses to check on you. It's past the end of my shift."

Hunter was about to reply when Rosa returned. He gave Madison a polite wave of thanks as she quickly turned and walked away.

"I don't know what I would've done without Mildred this evening. Seeing how busy I was, she just took charge of the housekeepers and the servers in the banquet hall. Normally, I find Mildred's domineering streak irritating. It's the reason I passed her over for the housekeeping position."

"Sounds like Mildred's trying to impress you. But did I understand you correctly? Mildred had applied for the head of housekeeping position?"

"She did. And, of course, she wasn't pleased with me when I told her I had hired Danielle. I was sorry, but Mildred simply isn't kind to the other workers. I just couldn't—" Rosa's eyes widened as she realized why Hunter had asked the question. "Hunter, you may have hit on something. But how would we prove it?"

"I don't know. It's just a hunch, but she certainly put the fear into Madison just now. Excuse me, Rosa. I'm going to move Petra off the street to the back lot. I have a feeling we're going to be here awhile."

Hunter had finished tying his horse by the water trough when he heard whispering. He stopped to listen.

"Mr. Jackson. . . Mr. Jackson!"

He moved toward the storage shed. It was darker there, but he could see it was Madison. "Madison, what is it? And why are you still here? You're trembling."

"Please, be quiet, Mr. Jackson. I'm afraid of being caught—but I need you to tell Mrs. Smith something for me. Mildred has warned me not to say anything. I'm afraid she might try to harm me, and I can't afford to miss work. Since mom died, we need my wages to help support our family. But I lied to Mrs. Smith today."

"What do you mean? Does it have something to do with Mildred?"

"Tell Mrs. Smith that Miss Harrison wasn't the only other person in room seven. I came around the corner a little while before the tea trays were delivered and saw Mildred coming from the room. She was putting something in her apron pocket. I didn't think anything about it until we were called into the office. The looks Mildred gave me at the meeting still make my bones chill, and she has warned me a couple times since. Please let Mrs. Smith know what I saw and tell her I'm sorry." Madison then turned and hurried down the alley.

Hunter knew he had the information needed to clear Danielle's name—and he knew just how to go about it.

14

HAND IT OVER

Rosa was still in the dining room when Hunter returned and motioned her into the hallway. He shared Madison's confession along with his idea to settle the matter of the stolen necklace. Since Mildred's shift was about to end, they needed to act quickly. Officer Brown was immediately summoned and filled in on the theft, along with the plan.

The officer, Rosa, and Hunter had just arrived in the kitchen as Mildred was rushing through on her way to the back door. Rosa was the first to approach her.

"Wait a minute, Mildred. I noticed the apron you're wearing is on the dingy side, so I've brought you a new one. I'll take the one you're wearing to the laundry for a good soaking."

"No bother, Mrs. Smith. I'll give it a soaking tonight, and it'll look as good as new tomorrow. You'll see."

"I'm sorry, dear, but I must insist. I can't take a chance with a home washing this time. You know dingy aprons give our customers the impression our facility isn't as clean as it should be."

While Mildred was trying to think of a response, Officer Brown closed in behind her.

Rosa then took charge. "Hand over the apron, Mildred."

Mildred looked around for a way to escape and broke into tears when she saw the officer. She slowly untied the apron and handed it to Rosa, who then handed it to Officer Brown. He checked the apron pockets and pulled out the diamond necklace.

Tears filled Mildred's eyes. "Mrs. Smith, you have to believe me! I wasn't stealing the necklace. I was going to sneak it into the lady's baggage before she left tomorrow. I just wanted the head housekeeper's job so badly. I deserve it. I thought if I got Miss Harrison out of the way, you would see I was the best person for the job."

"Mildred, do you realize how much harm you've done? Not only have you ruined *your* reputation, but you were willing to risk Miss Harrison's. You've also damaged my name and the good name of the Willow Inn."

"Mrs. Smith, please don't let Officer Brown arrest me. I don't think I can bear it!"

"Ma'am, you're mistaken if you think Mrs. Smith can keep you from going to jail. It's out of Rosa's hands. You didn't steal the necklace from Mrs. Smith or the Willow Inn. You stole the necklace from a guest."

Mildred—not having fully considered the consequences involved if caught with the necklace—began to wail with fear. Out of desperation, she rattled off all the details of the theft— even admitting to her plan to have Danielle deliver the tea tray to room seven.

Continuing to plead for forgiveness, Mildred finally begged to speak to the owner of the necklace. Although Brown knew it was against protocol, the small town officer relented and asked Mrs. Perry to join the others in the kitchen.

Since the necklace had been returned, Mrs. Perry volunteered to keep the theft quiet. However, she refused to drop the charges against Mildred for at least a week, feeling Mildred needed time to consider the seriousness of her actions.

Mildred was then cuffed and taken to jail.

Although it was near bedtime when the details of the theft were finalized, Hunter knew Miss Harrison would be agonizing over the accusation. He insisted she be notified of the arrest immediately and—as a courtesy—volunteered to escort Rosa to the cottage.

Concerned that entering the driveway might wake Hattie, Hunter drove the buggy through the little wooded area in front of the cottage and up to the door. They were both relieved to see a light shining through a window. Hunter assisted Rosa to the door and then stepped aside while she knocked.

"Dear, don't be frightened. It's Rosa. I need to speak with you."

Danielle opened the door and held out a lantern so Rosa could see to enter.

Hunter, being content that Miss Harrison had been cleared of any wrongs, went to sit on the bench.

Rosa's heart wrenched when she saw the pain in Danielle's face and felt the full effect of her careless words. She hugged her as an apology. "Sweetheart, I've come with good news. You've been completely absolved of any wrongdoing."

Danielle smiled in relief. "But how. . . and so quickly?"

"One of the housekeepers saw Mildred coming out of the room earlier in the afternoon. Mildred has admitted to everything—even to having you deliver the tea tray so you would be accused. She was angry because you were given the head of housekeeping position. She's been taken to jail."

"But I've *never* been unkind to Mildred. I try to treat all the housekeepers fairly."

"I wouldn't take it personally, dear. But, what about us? Are we still friends after the way I mishandled the situation?"

Danielle leaned over and gave Rosa a kiss on the cheek. "Of course, we're still friends."

Rosa smiled in appreciation. "Well, it's getting late. We both have a busy day tomorrow. And Hunter is waiting outside for me. He still has quite a ride ahead of him."

"Mr. Jackson is outside?" The inadvertent touch of their fingers was still fresh in her mind.

"Oh my, yes. He purposely stayed in town to help. As a matter of fact, he's responsible for putting the information together and coming up with the plan to get Mildred to confess. If it hadn't been for Hunter, you might still appear to be a suspect. He also insisted I visit you tonight to put your mind at ease—even volunteered to drive me here. He's a most thoughtful and caring young man—always willing to pitch in when someone is in destress."

Although Danielle's heart had leaped at learning Hunter had been her hero, she was disheartened when hearing Rosa's last sentence. She felt silly for having had the foolish notion that his concern for her was more than friendship.

⚜

The next morning, Madison was waiting for Danielle at the back door of the inn. "Miss Harrison, I'm sorry I didn't tell Mrs. Smith right off that I saw Mildred coming out of room seven. She threatened to get even if I told." Madison's eyes still reflected the fear of being found out.

"Thank you for your apology, Madison, but it wasn't your fault. It was Mildred's fault for plotting the theft. I don't understand her thinking, but I pray she has learned her lesson. It was brave of you to do the right thing, and I'm so glad you did."

The two girls walked into work together—feeling the bond of a new friendship.

15

AN EXCUSE

Now that warm weather had set in and the crops were planted, it was time to concentrate on the grounds of the estate. Hunter's Aunt Helen and Lonnie, her head housekeeper, were out weeding the vegetable garden, excited about the bounty they would share. The two were determined to care for the plot by themselves—although Hunter doubted their busy schedules would allow them to keep up.

Most of Helen's time was spent sewing dresses to support an orphanage in the West. As for Lonnie, her new husband had left the job as the Jacksons' groundskeeper to buy a nearby farm. When she was not working at the Jacksons', Lonnie was at home caring for the children. Hunter assumed he soon would be picking up the slack of their neglected garden.

Heading for the lumber mill that day, he gave the ladies a more animated wave than usual. His uncle had asked him and the crew to start construction on a new barn, and he would now have a legitimate reason to make frequent trips to Willow Weep.

The sawmill needed a little time to finish the first load of lumber, so Hunter decided to have an early lunch at the inn. He talked with Rosa for a while and was disappointed when she mentioned it was Miss Harrison's day off. After paying his bill, he walked to the Willow Garden to relax and had just taken a seat when Danielle appeared.

"Mr. Jackson. I'm sorry. Am I disturbing you? There's usually no one here this time of day."

"No, not at all." Hunter quickly stood to his feet. "Just killing some time while the mill finishes my order. So, Miss Harrison, what brings you to the willow?"

"I usually visit the library whenever I have time—which seems only to be on my days off." Danielle stopped talking long enough to shift around the books in her arms. "My original plan was to take one book home at a time, but as you see—"

Hunter lunged forward just in time to catch a book on its way to the ground. "Here, Miss Harrison, let me help you with those." He took the stack of books from her arms and sat them on the bench.

"It seems, Mr. Jackson, I'm at your mercy once again." She managed a smile but could not bring herself to make complete eye contact. "From what I've been told, I owe you much gratitude for helping solve the mystery of the missing necklace."

Hunter did not respond, fearing he might be interrupting what sounded like words of appreciation coming from Miss Harrison.

Danielle took a breath and finally forced herself to look into his blue eyes. "And I don't know how to express to you how grateful I am. But I do want to thank you for coming to my rescue.

"To be honest, I want to thank you for *all* the times you've rescued me—even the time it wasn't necessary." Apologizing to Hunter after the way she had treated him was difficult, but Danielle wanted to make peace between them.

Hunter laughed slightly at her last comment about the humiliating rainstorm incident. "Well, thank you, Miss Harrison. I'm glad I could be of assistance. I can't take all the credit. I believe God was at work."

Hearing Hunter give credit to God melted Danielle's heart. "I agree. . . sometimes we forget who truly should be praised. But God also needs someone with a willing heart to carry out His plans. I've been told you possess such a heart." Once the words were out, she was embarrassed for being so forward.

Hunter was equally embarrassed. He put his thumbs in his back pockets, looked at the ground, and shuffled one foot.

"Mr. Jackson, I have treated you badly since our first meeting. I was overly defensive due to my circumstances at that time and mistook your concern. But now I understand you are a person who speaks and acts from a caring heart."

"No, I had no business lecturing you. I was definitely too outspoken a couple of those times."

"Only a couple?" Danielle came back forcefully.

Hunter's eyes opened wide. He had done it again. Then Danielle laughed, and he realized she was joking.

"And I think we are well enough acquainted to drop some of the formalities. I would appreciate it if you would call me *Danielle*. . . but only if you will allow *me* to call you *Hunter*"

"I think that can be arranged."

"So, here you are. I'm ready." Hunter felt Sally Meeker's hand slip under his arm.

He gave Sally a disgusted look. "What do you mean?"

"For you to take me home. . . as always."

Hunter took a few calming breaths while trying to think how to handle the pestering Miss Meeker. . . and finally decided to ignore her.

He then turned to continue his conversation with Danielle. But Danielle and the books were disappearing down the street.

16

THE OPPORTUNIST

It had been difficult for Esther and her parents to manage Delbert's rebellion—until she had pointed out that such actions could put his social standing in jeopardy. His popularity always stroked his ego, so he became selective in his misbehavior. Although Delbert did have one major shortcoming when it came to socializing—overindulging in liquor.

Beyond that, Delbert needed to hide the fact that he had been banished from his father's home with little money. The story concocted was that Delbert was concerned for his grandparents and felt it was necessary to move in with them. He hid the lack of money by only accepting invitations to parties. For more costly gatherings, Delbert used the excuse of having prior engagements. He—like his mother—was a seasoned manipulator.

⚜

Benjamin Dice sat behind his desk wearing a solemn expression. "Harold, as your attorney and friend, I must inform you that my assistant, Mr. Long, has come across some unsettling information.

It is never pleasant to deliver bad news—especially when it's to a friend—but you've hired me to do a job."

"Get on with it, Ben. We've always been straight forward with one another. You know all there is to know about me and my family. No need to start tiptoeing around now."

"All right then. . . Esther has been seen by Mr. Long and other witnesses in a compromising situation with her friend, Mr. Grant. And that's not all— "

⚜

After leaving Attorney Dice, Harold went straight home to speak with Sherry. His little girl's life was about to change even more drastically than it already had. Since Delbert and Margaret basically ignored her, she had handled their departure with little fuss. On the other hand, Danielle's leaving had hurt her deeply. Even at that, what Harold was about to share with his youngest daughter was an altogether different matter.

Harold found Sherry in her room serving her dolls tea and cookies. It was such a sweet picture. He wished he did not need to interrupt.

"Hello, Daddy. I wasn't expecting to see you today. This is the day you work late." Sherry jumped in his lap as soon as he took a seat in the tufted chair.

"I know, sweetie, but I've taken the afternoon off because I have something extremely important to discuss with you. I'm afraid it's not good news, and you're going to need to be very brave."

"No one ever seems to want to discuss anything important with me. I'll be most happy to listen to anything you have to say." Sherry was still innocent and had escaped her mother's influence thus far. Harold wanted to preserve that innocence.

When Sherry was born, neither parent had wanted more children. Harold thought it was best for the obvious reasons, and his wife did not want another child interfering with her life. Even though Esther did seem to love and tolerate their youngest daughter, she showed little interest in her. Esther's parental attention was always channeled toward the twins. As it turned out, much of Sherry's care was left to the staff and later to Danielle. At first Harold had tried nurturing Sherry, but his wife gradually began criticizing his efforts, causing him to back off. Sherry was bright, perceptive, and wise beyond her years. But most of all, she possessed a loving spirit. With Delbert and Margaret out of the house, Harold was afraid Esther would soon turn her attention to Sherry. He was not about to let his wife ruin this little one too.

"Sweetheart, I'm certain you're aware that mommy and daddy disagree from time to time." Harold was trying to ease into what he was about to share.

Sherry's eyes widened. "Oh, I am! Sometimes your disagreements become most fierce. When they are, I plug my ears and hide under the covers." The statement was delivered with intense animation.

Hearing what Sherry's reaction was to the strife between him and Esther crushed Harold. He had not realized the effect the disagreements had on the darling child—and probably the entire household. "I'm sorry to hear that. Had I known, I would have made certain we were more discreet."

"It's okay. It only bothered me and Danielle. Delbert and Margaret thought it was funny when mother backed you in a corner. I heard them say so."

"I suppose they did." It wounded Harold deeply to know his

own children had laughed at his weakness.

"Because we couldn't work out those fierce disagreements, mother and I will be going our separate ways. I know you are only eight, but do you understand what I'm saying?"

"I do. It means one of you won't be coming home at night."

Harold almost laughed at her wittiness. "We will talk about where you heard such an expression later. . . but apparently you understand the meaning.

"Sherry, it's my desire for you to live with me instead of your mother. I know it's a lot to ask of a child, but I think it's in your best interest." Harold felt almost cruel being so honest with his young daughter, but he had to prepare her for what was to come.

Sherry twirled a lock of her hair around her index finger while she gave her father's statement much needed thought. "I think. . . I'd like that very well. I do love mother, but I don't care for her very much. She is grouchy and bossy and seldom pays attention to me. Although, I wouldn't mind seeing her on occasion."

His sweet little girl's answer warmed his heart. He hadn't wanted to tell Sherry that she had no choice in the matter. "I'm overjoyed to hear you'd like to stay with me. However, I must explain that the changes will be taking place this evening. I'm sorry I wasn't able to tell you before today. I hope you'll find it in your heart to forgive me."

"Think nothing of it, Father. One must do what one must do."

Harold gave a slight chuckle—amazed again by Sherry's mature perception and happy to see what a little trooper she could be.

When his wife arrived home, Harold opened his office door and asked her to join him. Esther was infuriated by the request and intentionally made putting away her wrap and umbrella an especially long process. When finished, she walked into the office and slammed the door behind her.

"Now, what do you want?" Esther was flabbergasted when she realized it was Attorney Dice on whom she had unloaded her wrath. The attorney just raised his eyebrows in reply.

"I'm over here, *dear,*" Harold informed her curtly.

She looked over to see her husband sitting at his desk. "You should have mentioned we had company." By this time, she had sweetened her tone.

"Sit down, Esther. Benjamin is here on official business."

She was vexed by his sharp reply but sat down. "What official business?"

Harold shifted some papers in front of him to sort out the ones he needed first. "Well, since you're so anxious to hear, we'll get right to it. As it is, Benjamin has three signed statements by witnesses who are willing to testify they saw you embracing and kissing your *friend,* Mr. Grant. I believe that is referred to as being unfaithful."

"What? They're lying! There's no possible way anyone could have seen us behind that wall." Esther cringed inside at hearing her own words.

"Well, that didn't take long. I thought at the very least we'd have to pry it out of you." Harold was astonished at his wife's stupidity. The truth was out and Esther had sealed her fate.

"So, what of it? It was just a harmless kiss." Her attempt to explain it away fell on deaf ears.

"Benjamin has prepared some papers. I should mention that, among the papers you *will* be signing, there are documents to give me full custody of Sherry. Once we have your signatures—except for a quick visit with Sherry—you're to leave this home immediately and not return.

"If you recall, I spoke of what would happen if you continued in your ways. Therefore, your bags are packed and on their way to a property which I've recently had renovated. You may live there for as long as you so choose—provided you bring no further disgrace on my family's name. I'm certain you don't fancy another shameful divorce.

"It's a nice home and should be sufficient enough for the type of society you'll be entertaining. Other than providing you with a place to live, I've set aside a monthly allotment, rated according to the lifestyle to which you were accustomed before you conned me into marriage."

Esther left her seat to stand before Harold in an intimidating move. "I won't sign anything! I'll fight this in court."

"Esther, you will sign these papers, or I will expose you as the person you truly are—a deceiver who roped Daniel Harrison into a marriage you had no intention of honoring—an unloving mother who used her eldest daughter as a house drudge—a liar who fabricated the death of her husband to cover up a disgraceful divorce—a fraud who beguiled me into a loveless marriage only for my money and social standing—a forger and embezzler who stole my money so her crooked parents could secure a place in society—an opportunist who chases after men in the hope of snaring a wealthier and more influential husband. Shall I continue?" He stopped and stared at his wife long and hard.

"You can't make me leave. I won't stand for it. Consider how society will view you for doing such a thing to me." Esther was seething, and her face so distorted with anger that neither man could see a hint of beauty.

"As you are aware, Esther, I have no aspirations for social standing."

At that moment Attorney Dice laid the legal papers beside Esther as he attempted to hand her a readied ink pen.

"You are mistaken, Benjamin. I have no intention of signing anything. I refuse to be blackmailed."

"That will be fine, my *dear*. You may take your claims to court, but we're only trying to protect your good name. You must understand we also have signed testimonies from two women who are also willing to appear in court—a Mrs. Andrews and a Mrs. Sissle.

"So let's consider Mrs. Andrews's statement. It appears you pursued her husband until he asked her for a divorce. Yet, you abandoned the relationship once informed the fortune you sought belonged to *Mrs.* Andrews."

Esther did not realize her mouth was agape. It was apparent her confidence in winning a court case against Harold was beginning to wane. "I can ex—"

"No, no," Harold said, as he picked up another paper. "Shall I paraphrase the details of the next person's statement?

"According to Mrs. Sissle, you had mistaken her husband for a blueblood and for being much wealthier than he was—before you faded into the sunset. Now, Esther, do you still want to take this to court?"

The color had drained from Esther's face. The woman was literally shaking as she was handed each paper Attorney Dice placed in front of her. Once the signing was completed, Esther left without visiting Sherry.

17

A NITWIT

As soon as his wife had left the premises, Harold went straight to Sherry's room. Esther had not even taken the opportunity to speak with her daughter. As a matter of fact, she had signed over custody without opposition or even inquiring about visitation. He feared Sherry would be heartbroken and might feel her mother did not love her.

As Harold Simpson tapped lightly on Sherry's door, he heard the clinking of dishes and listened as his baby girl excused herself from another tea party for her dolls. The knob turned and the door opened slowly. Then two bright, blue eyes greeted him, followed by a happy grin. "Hello, Daddy. Do come in. The ladies and I were just sitting down for tea. May I pour you a cup? It's still steaming hot, and the cookies are scrumptious. Please have a seat."

Harold could not resist picking Sherry up, swinging her into the air and onto his hip. "I believe I will have to forgo the ladies' tea today, but can you schedule me in for Saturday at two? I believe I'm free this weekend."

"I'm not sure. I will need to get back to you on the date and time. My calendar is nearly full." Sherry gave a teasing giggle, wrapped her arms around her father's neck, and kissed him on the cheek.

"Please sit down with me, my sunshine. I need to speak with you." Harold hoped to keep the conversation light.

"You came to say that mother left without coming to see me. I watched the carriage drive away. It was quite rude. But that's the way she is. At least she won't be able to take her anger out on Danielle this time." Sherry wiped a tear from her cheek with the back of her hand.

"I'm sorry. I guess your mother wasn't thinking straight after meeting with me and the attorney."

"It doesn't matter, Daddy. I'm just happy it was mother who left and not you. You and I can be a happy family together."

"My little princess, how did you become so wise and strong?" Harold hugged her, as he thanked God for the opportunity to raise Sherry.

⚜

Esther halted for a short time and took in every detail of the newly renovated home. The place did have a stately appearance, and it did give the impression of prominence and wealth. Still, it was not the grand home she had just left, and she was not pleased.

She proceeded up the steps and burst through the front door, pushing the housekeeper aside. After taking time to assess the impressive foyer, she then turned and demanded, "Who are you, and what is your purpose here?"

"I'm Wilma, the housekeeper Mr. Simpson hired to care for this home." She and the other three staff members had been fore-warned not to allow Mrs. Simpson to gain control over them. Esther was to be considered only as a guest in the home, and she had no control whatsoever. The employees had been handpicked by Harold because they were intelligent, trustworthy, and reasonable—not to mention each of them had the correct personality needed to deal with his wife.

Esther went from room to room to see what she had been allotted in a home. Finding the house was on a smaller scale, but elegantly decorated, annoyed her, since she would have no reason to complain.

Upon her return to the foyer, she found the staff waiting. "Why are you all standing around? Don't you have work to do? We aren't paying for your idleness."

"As the staff hired to care for this home, we have gathered for a proper introduction—which, of course, is customary." Wilma made the statement in an authoritative manner.

"Then, where's the rest of the staff? If you insist on an introduction, everyone should be present. Am I correct?"

"You are correct, Mrs. Simpson, and, as you see, we *are* all present."

"The entire staff? This is totally unacceptable. Mr. Simpson and I will need to remedy this at once. And I will be choosing my own people, so you should expect to be replaced."

Before dismissing everyone, Esther demanded that a carriage be readied. She was going out.

Neither Wilma, nor the rest of the staff, went out of their way to hurry.

⌖

When Esther arrived at Mr. Grant's mansion, she hurried up the steps and briskly knocked on the front door. The maid, knowing who it was, answered reluctantly.

Upon asking to see Mr. Grant, Esther was told he was not receiving guests. The reply did not suit Esther, so she pushed her way inside and headed to the study where Horace Grant spent most of his time. Seeing her enter the room and approaching his desk, Mr. Grant quickly stood.

"Why am I being interrupted? Was it not made clear that I am not receiving guests?"

"Dearest, I have come with the most wonderful news. Harold has acknowledged our loveless marriage and is willing to sign for a divorce. Horace, we can be married as soon as the papers are signed." She approached the man with her arms outstretched and engulfed him in an affectionate embrace.

Unfortunately, the romantic relationship between Esther and Mr. Grant had not developed as she had hoped it would, so Mrs. Simpson knew she had to be shrewd in the way she approached the matter at hand. Acting as if it was Horace's idea they marry seemed like the best option. After all, he was elderly and should be overjoyed to have a much younger, attractive woman as his wife.

Grant grabbed Esther by both arms and shoved her away from him. "What's the meaning of this? Mrs. Simpson, I've put up with your constant hounding far too long. I've reached my limit with you. Furthermore, you've refused to acknowledge my obvious hints for you to leave me be. I'm still outraged that you cornered me at the park and intentionally forced a kiss on me against my will. I now realize I've been a buffoon for not being blunt with you from the start."

"Darling, you don't mean a word of it. You must be overtired. We have been seeing each other romantically for some months. My sweetness, you are only uncomfortable because I initiated the kiss.

Regardless, we've both wanted that kiss for quite some time." Esther was certain her logic would convince the older man he was confused.

"Mrs. Simpson, you mistake me. Since the day we met, I've never had any interest in you. . . even as a friend. Are you such a nitwit as to believe you're the only woman who has tried to entrap me into marriage for my money and my social rank?" He eyed Esther with total disgust.

Esther drew her lips tight. Grant had sized her up.

"Mrs. Simpson, you're a married woman with children. Your name has come up at the clubs as being the woman who has caused problems in more than one marriage in this town. How dare you compromise my good name! Now—just in case I have not made myself clear—please leave my home and do not return." Grant extended his hand toward the door.

Esther was seething and humiliated beyond expression. She had been expelled by two men of social standing in less than two hours. It had also been brought to her attention that her antics were being discussed within the gentlemen's clubs. Mrs. Simpson had to find a way to clear her name, or her reputation would soon be damaged beyond repair.

Since Grant was concerned with his name being compromised, he would keep her indelicacies quiet. Her current husband was a different matter altogether. Esther needed to find a way to make Harold Simpson appear to be totally responsible for her present circumstance.

But when it came down to it, Esther knew the true source of all her misery had been the birth of her eldest daughter—the product of a hasty marriage. Someday, she would destroy Danielle's happiness the way Danielle had destroyed hers.

18

THAT DID NOT GO WELL

All was going sufficiently well in Danielle's life since her last encounter with Hunter. She was happy to have made peace with him and even happier they were on a first name basis. However, it seemed evident he and Sally Meeker were courting. Danielle decided it was best to avoid Hunter Jackson since it was clear Miss Meeker did not want them conversing.

With summer edging closer, the inn was full for the weekdays as well as the weekends. The village ambience lured people to Willow Weep for leisurely visits. Not to mention, the town and surrounding area had their share of weddings and reunions which brought in many guests. Willow Weep felt safe and exciting to Danielle. It was as if God had miraculously carried her to an earthly paradise. Still, amid all the pleasures she now cherished, there was a heaviness deep within her, and she did not know the cause.

"Danielle, I have been trying to track you down all day. I was afraid I'd missed you." Before proceeding, Rosa smoothed her hair at the temples where a bit of gray was sneaking in. "I have a favor to ask of you."

"I'm in no hurry to leave. What may I do for you?"

"Well, I have asked some of my dearest friends from church to have dinner at the inn tomorrow evening—"

"You aren't going to ask me to serve, are you?"

Rosa gave a little laugh at the panicked look on the girl's face. "No, hon, nothing of the kind. But I *am* inviting you to join us. I want to show you off to my friends. They are anxious to meet you. Please say you'll come."

Danielle was moved by Rosa's request. Even with the many dinner parties Esther had hosted, Danielle was never allowed to take part in one, "I'd love to attend, but Madison and I have made plans to have a picnic by the creek. She works so hard to help her father provide for their family. I can't disappoint her. I know how it feels to have few pleasures in life." Again Danielle had not meant to mention her past.

"Why don't you invite Madison? I promise you will both enjoy the evening."

"If you're certain you don't mind. I think Madison would love to come as much as I would."

"I'm so pleased to hear it, and thank you for changing your plans. I'll expect you both at seven." Rosa then rushed off as she always did.

✦

Danielle went directly to inform Madison of the dinner invitation, and the girl was thrilled to be included. Never had she dreamed of dining at the Willow Inn as a guest. However, there was a kink in their plans. While Danielle had just finished sewing a new dress for such an occasion, Madison did not have anything acceptable to wear and felt she had no choice but to decline. Danielle would not hear of it and promised to find Madison a dress—although she did not have a clue where to get one.

Before allowing Madison to return to work, Danielle took her friend's measurements, and they prayed for a dress. Madison, trusting God would provide, went back to work.

Danielle left the hotel pantry, wondering if she had made the right decision in making the promise to Madison. There was not enough time to design and sew a dress for her friend. But at that exact moment, a guest paged her from down the hall, carrying two dresses in her arms. Remarkably, the nice lady asked if Danielle knew of anyone who might have need of them. The woman had made several purchases while in Willow Weep and did not have room to pack the disfavored garments. Danielle gratefully accepted the dresses while thanking God for His timely provision.

There was not time to design and sew a dress, but there was time to alter one. Even though it required working into the early morning hours, Danielle successfully turned one of the donated frocks into a proper dress for Madison.

✦

The young waitress gave a periodic giggle while trying to keep her eyes squished shut until the transformation was complete. When finished, Danielle led her to a full-length mirror. Madison squealed with delight upon seeing her reflection. The floral fabric and dress design slimmed and flattered her short, slightly plump figure. Danielle had also painstakingly formed soft curls and gathered them into a hairstyle to emphasize Madison's sweet face. Both girls were pleased with the outcome.

While Danielle nervously readied herself for the dinner, she wondered if it was possible for her to fit in among Rosa's friends.

⚜

"There you are! I have been watching for the two of you." Rosa took Danielle by the hand and led her toward a group of friends. Madison had been detained at the door by a lady who was admiring the altered party dress.

"Here she is—my Danielle, whom I've spoken so much of lately. Danielle, please meet Mr. Melvin Jackson and his wife, Helen; Mr. Alex Jefferson and his wife, Kathryn; Mr. Joseph Meeker and his fiancée, Miss Rica Adams. Of course, you are acquainted with Mrs. Belinda Gray from the train, and this is her husband, Mr. Carl Gray." Danielle presented herself politely and took the time to hug Belinda, whom she was pleasantly surprised to see again.

"Rosa, she is just as lovely as you described her to be. We are so pleased to meet you." Whether spoken in truth or just politeness, it did not matter. Helen Jackson had no idea the positive impact her words had on Danielle.

About that time, everyone was asked to be seated for dinner. Both girls were very self-conscious at the beginning of the meal, but it became a relaxing evening due to all the joking and teasing among friends. Neither Danielle nor Madison had laughed so much in their lives. Feeling sincerely welcomed, the girls' uneasiness soon subsided.

After dinner, some of the guests continued their conversation as they drank coffee at the table, while others mingled about the room.

"Danielle, please come join us." Helen offered the empty seat next to her.

"Belinda just mentioned you're a seamstress, and Rosa told us you designed the dress you're wearing. You seem quite talented."

"I do love to sew. I had hoped to try my hand as a dressmaker when I arrived in Bristol, but work was scarce in the city. Thankfully, Rosa was kind enough to offer me the head of housekeeping position. I'm immensely happy there."

Impressed with Danielle's work, Rica could not keep from sharing her opinion. "Well, if what you're wearing is an example of your work, then I would say you are an excellent dressmaker. It's beautifully designed and meticulously sewn."

The other ladies all agreed and shared their own compliments toward the well-made dress.

Danielle was flattered and humbled by the comments. Their opinions made her feel a little more self-assured. Immediately, her mind flickered back to the many times Esther and Delbert had used the word *worthless* in reference to her.

"If you're interested in working as a seamstress, I can offer you a parttime position. You see, I design and sew for a boutique in the West. My daughter, Bethany, substituted at a mission orphanage there for several months. The circumstances required her to work, and eventually she was blessed with a job making dresses. Soon after, the owner asked me to join them. The proceeds are used to support the orphanage. As it is, designer gown orders have increased, and I need help keeping up. Would you consider working with me? I'll pay you well." Helen had been looking for a dependable seamstress with whom she would feel comfortable working—and she was confident Danielle was that person.

"I would first need to discuss it with Rosa."

Having sensed on the train how much Danielle wanted to be a seamstress, Belinda could not keep quiet. "Danielle, Rosa is the one who suggested it."

Rosa offered a supportive smile.

"Then *yes*. I *am* interested in the position. I have plenty of spare time in the evenings. How do I begin?" Danielle could barely control her enthusiasm.

All the ladies were pleased to hear of the arrangement. A time and date for training were set for Danielle to meet with Helen at the Jacksons' home. Since Danielle had no transportation, Rosa volunteered to take her.

That night Danielle and Madison returned home, having had the most fulfilling evening in both of their lives. Neither girl had ever been included in such an impressive gathering. It was an occasion they would not soon forget. Danielle's small world was beginning to expand.

⚜

On the day of the scheduled meeting, Rosa had shown up in Hattie's drive exactly at noon as promised. They were leaving town early since Rosa wanted to show Danielle some of the local sites along the way. The attractive chauffer had also packed a lunch for them to share at an overlook not far from town. Rosa was looking forward to their trip as much as Danielle was.

When they did arrive at the Jacksons' home—one of the finest in the area—Rosa noted that Danielle was not impressed—suggesting Danielle might be familiar with a wealthier lifestyle.

Upon being welcomed in, the two visitors walked into the parlor to find Rica Adams and Helen deep in conversation. Helen eagerly greeted them with warm sisterly hugs.

"Rica, this is a surprise. I wasn't expecting to see you today. Although from the looks of things, I think I know why you're here." Rosa picked up the pad of paper lying on the table in front of the couch. There were several drawings of wedding dresses sketched on it.

"Your suspicions are correct. I've come to convince Helen she is the only person I trust to make my wedding dress. After seeing the exquisite bridal gown she designed for her Bethany, why would I not beg Helen to take it on?"

"Rica, I'm certain there are many ladies who could—" Helen started to protest.

"Not to mention she has become like a second mother to me, and I am trying to model my life after hers. Is it any wonder why Bethany turned out to be the wonderful person she is, with a mother such as this?" Rica lovingly took Helen's hand and laid it between hers.

Tears filled Helen's eyes, but not just for the beautiful compliments Rica had paid her. It was in recalling the troublesome and disagreeable person Rica once was, compared to the lovely Christian woman she had become.

"Rica, you are so sweet to say such things—"

"Here. Here. We will not accept a denial, Helen." Always in a hurry to get to the next task, Rosa took things in hand. "What Rica proclaims is truth—every word of it. Now Miss Rica, let me see that stunning ring once again. Not that anyone was surprised by your engagement to Joe, but we had assumed it would be longer. We were all elated to hear of your plans to marry soon."

"Danielle, the church is hosting an engagement party for Rica and Joe. It will be held here since our home is centrally located for everyone. These affairs do tend to start early and run late. You must come and bring Hattie and Madison,"

Rica joined in, "Oh, yes, Danielle. I would love for you to come. Please say you will. It would be such a blessing to have you there."

Danielle was further encouraged by their enthusiastic pleas for her to attend the party. "That is so kind of you both, and I appreciate it—but I don't attend your church."

"You don't have to attend Faith Chapel. Besides, you just received a personal invitation." Helen was not about to let Danielle off the hook.

"But there is no way for me to get here. I don't own a horse, much less a carriage."

"Why don't you drive Hattie's buggy? Mercy is an extremely gentle horse, and she practically guides herself," Rica suggested, eliminating any excuses.

"I know nothing of horses. I'm afraid I never had the privilege of riding in my youth." Danielle's face turned red from the embarrassment.

"Then I will send someone over to show you how to hitch up Mercy and give you a driving lesson or two. Hattie will be with you in case you need assistance on the way to the party. Besides, the horse has Hattie's usual routes memorized." Helen knew the solution had been found.

"Johnathon can take Hattie home when she gets tired. My husband doesn't like to linger at these affairs. It'll allow the two of us and Madison to stay for as long as we choose."

"Perfect. Danielle, you have no reason to miss the party!" With Rica's declaration, the matter was dropped.

For the first time in her life, Danielle felt as if she was being accepted as an adult.

Rica and Rosa visited while Helen explained to Danielle the sewing techniques she used. Since Danielle caught on quickly, it did not take long. The two enjoyed each other's company just as Helen had expected. "Danielle, I have heard the story of how you ended up in Willow Weep. So where are you from, and who are your parents?"

Danielle knew the day would come when she would not be able to tiptoe around her past life, but until that day, she was going to withhold as many details as possible. "I don't remember my father, but his name was Daniel Harrison."

Helen gasped. "Excuse me, did you say your father's name was Daniel Harrison?"

"Yes."

"By any chance do you have relatives who live in this area?"

"No. Or at least not to my knowledge. I know little to nothing of my father or his past or his side of the family. He died soon after I was born."

"Oh, I see." Helen decided to act as if she was changing the subject and could see Danielle was relieved. "Yours is such a pretty name. Is your middle name just as lovely?"

"I like to think so. My full name is Danielle Valerie Harrison."

A few minutes later, Danielle went to the shay to retrieve the samples of her beading, embroidering, and piping for Helen to assess. On her way back to the house, she was surprised to see Hunter Jackson walking toward her, leading Rosa's sorrel, Skyler.

"So, Miss Harrison, what brings you to the Jacksons' home this afternoon? Or will I get in trouble for asking?" Hunter intentionally teased her to see if they were still on friendly terms.

"Well, Mr. Jackson, not that it's any of your business, but I'm here for instruction from Mrs. Jackson. She has asked me to sew for her." Danielle smiled to let him know she, too, was teasing. "Although, if I remember correctly, we agreed to be on a first name basis."

"We did, but when we last met, you left in such a hurry that I was afraid maybe we were back to our old ways." Hunter acted as though he was joking, but inside he was unsure.

"Nothing of the sort." Danielle quickly moved on to another subject, not wanting to speak of him and Sally Meeker. "It didn't occur to me that you might be related to Mr. and Mrs. Jackson. Am I correct in believing you are a relative?"

"You are. I'm Mel's nephew. He's hired me to supervise his property and employees. How did you come to know my aunt and uncle?"

"Earlier this week, Rosa asked me and Madison to dine with some of her close friends from church. The Jacksons were among the group. They're a wonderful couple. It was a blessing to have met them, as well as the others." Danielle looked admiringly at Hunter's strong, handsome face and wondered why she always felt the need to speak so formally to him.

"I'm glad to hear you approve of Mel and Helen. I highly admire them. I respect how they live their lives. The way my uncle represents himself in business and to others is a rare find. They're an excellent example of a Christian couple."

Danielle took note of the sincerity in Hunter's voice and recalled what Rosa had said of him.

"As supervisor, why are you the one caring for Skyler and not the stableman?"

"Keith was busy, so I told him I'd take care of the horse." Although the explanation was correct, he had omitted a few details. Having noticed Rosa and Danielle coming up the lane, Hunter had volunteered to look after Skyler—hoping for an opportunity to speak with Danielle.

The rest of their conversation was pleasant, but just when it seemed they were beginning to enjoy each other, Danielle seemed to become uneasy.

"Danielle, is something wrong? Are you afraid Sally Meeker is here?"

"I guess, I am. She doesn't like finding us together, and I don't want to distress her. She seems offended by our friendship."

Somehow Sally Meeker had managed to interfere in their meeting whether the girl was there or not.

"Let's not bring Sally into the conversation. I assure you Miss Meeker is not on the premises."

It bothered Hunter that Danielle had referred to him as a friend, and this was not the way he had wanted the conversation to go.

"I must get back to the house. Helen needs to look over these samples. It was nice seeing you again." She gave a slight drop of her head in acknowledgment and walked away.

What Hunter and Danielle did not know was that the three ladies inside the house had wandered to the window one at a time to watch the couple's *chance* meeting.

Rica was the first to make a comment. "Not that I'm surprised, but I think my future sister-in-law, Sally, will need to look elsewhere to capture a husband."

"And during my past visits here, I've never noticed Hunter taking a personal interest in the care of my horse." Rosa thoroughly enjoyed pointing out the fact.

Helen added, "I was beginning to wonder if there was a girl alive who could gain the interest of my husband's nephew."

Then noticing that the conversation between Hunter and Danielle had ended abruptly, they all stated in unison, "That didn't go well."

They couldn't keep from giggling as they hurried to where Lonnie had set the table for tea. Fortunately, the group of ladies had sufficient time to collect themselves before Danielle's return.

19

ALONE AT LAST

Danielle had a delightful time visiting with the ladies at the Jacksons' home and felt welcomed into the close-knit group. To add to it, Danielle's dreams of becoming a seamstress would be complete once Helen Jackson had the fabric and sewing supplies delivered to the cottage. It was unfortunate that her encounter with Hunter had tainted the day. It was nothing he had done. It was caused by her own foolishness in finding another way to be difficult. She and Hunter were trying to build a friendship, and it was her warped sense of etiquette that created the problem.

In retrospect, she knew she had done nothing wrong. Sally Meeker and Hunter Jackson were not married or engaged. If they were a serious couple who had issues with one or the other social-izing with certain people, then it was their responsibility to work out the problem between themselves. Danielle's resolve was to be friendly, cordial, and respectful to Hunter and Sally. She would be herself when encountering either of them. So with the situation settled in her mind, the guilt lifted.

It was then that Danielle remembered the letter from Jean which had been stuffed in her sewing basket with the rest of the mail. Her dear friend's letters were always full of good news from their church and Grandville.

My dear Danielle,

I must first tell you everything is fine with Everett and me. The vegetable garden is planted and growing. My flowers are doing quite nicely, and the roses are plentiful. You will be happy to know the willow is healthy and the leaves are fuller than ever. Delbert made no attempt to cut the tree down. As a matter of fact, Delbert is one of the reasons I am writing this letter.

I have some information which came from a staff member within your family's household, and I believe it to be true. Normally I would not repeat such gossip, but I feel it is something you should be aware of. Please forgive me if I have made the wrong decision.

From what I understand, shortly after you left, Harold expelled Delbert from their home and sent Margaret to a mission in the Appalachians. Supposedly they were given a chance to change their ways but did not comply. When last heard of, Delbert was living with your grandparents.

I was also told your mother was given a similar ultimatum and did not comply, so she too has recently been told to leave. Harold sought a legal separation and sent Esther to a newly renovated home near downtown. Sherry is under the complete, legal guardianship of your stepfather and she is flourishing in his care. . .

Danielle could not believe what she had just read. The thought of Harold Simpson standing up to Esther and their children was beyond comprehension. Her stepfather had always cowered to her mother's every demand. Danielle had overheard her mother planning vicious schemes to take advantage of Harold time after time. It was good to hear that he had finally tired of her mother's behavior and had taken control of his life. Unfortunately, now that Esther's wealthy lifestyle was severely altered and her social standing was in jeopardy, Danielle knew *someone* was going to pay.

⁂

Helen tapped lightly on the study door. She did not like to interrupt Mel when he was concentrating on his paperwork. If he was deep in thought, the slightest knock would go unnoticed.

"Come in, my beautiful wife," Mel responded with his most patient and caring voice. His smile always reflected the love he felt for his Helen whenever he looked at her.

Helen entered and walked over to his desk. She waited for him to acknowledge her presence. When he looked up, the expected smile consumed her heart as a reminder of how blessed she was to have a husband such as Mel.

"What is it, darling? I can tell you have something serious on your mind." Melvin Jackson could read his wife like a book.

"I'm sorry to bother you this late, but I believe I have made a life-changing discovery for the Harrison girl and possibly her family."

"And how so?" Mel could tell his wife was shaken by the news and gave her his full attention.

"I was attempting to acquaint myself with Danielle—which is difficult since she seems to evade most questions concerning her personal life. Anyway, I asked who her parents were. The first thing out of her mouth was that her father's name was Daniel."

"Daniel? That *is* interesting—although it's a common name."

"But when I asked if she had relatives around this area, she told me she knew nothing of her father or his family. However, she did volunteer her full name. Are you ready for this?" Helen could not help but keep her husband in suspense.

"I'm intrigued." Mel, knowing his wife's story telling techniques, played along.

"Her full name is Danielle *Valerie* Harrison." She waited for his response.

"The *child?*" Mel was stunned.

"I'm assuming so, but I didn't know what to do or ask afterward. So, I dropped the subject. I thought I should speak to you first. You usually know the best way to approach such issues."

"I have no idea how to approach it. I don't even know if we should interfere. . . but of course we will." Mel's brow furrowed, knowing he was about to meddle in Joshua Harrison's family affairs.

✶

Danielle could not wait to get out of her uniform and into a comfortable dress for walking. It was such a perfect afternoon that she did not want to spend a minute of it inside.

She chose a lightweight dress of white eyelet and let her hair fall down her back. Just as she was about to tie it with a ribbon, there was a knock on the door. Danielle opened it to find Hunter Jackson.

Neither spoke. They just stood looking at one another. Danielle was trying to hide her pleasure in finding him there, and Hunter was looking at Danielle's long, blonde hair, thinking it looked even prettier than he had imagined.

Realizing neither had spoken, Hunter intruded on their thoughts. "Are you ready?"

"For what?"

"I was told you were expecting a driving lesson today. Did you forget?"

"Oh—yes. It slipped my mind. I don't know how I could've forgotten. I've been looking forward to it. How did you get roped into teaching me?"

"Aunt Helen sent a message to the stable asking for someone to give you driving lessons, and I drew the short straw."

Danielle laughed, "Just my luck! Well then. . . let's go." She joined Hunter, completely forgetting to tie back her hair. Hunter noticed but decided not to mention it.

Once they crossed the cottage bridge, Hunter grabbed Danielle's hand and led her to the barn. She pretended not to notice.

Hunter first gave a complete demonstration on how to hitch the horse to the buggy. Then he removed all the tack so Danielle could hitch up the horse alone. Danielle did it correctly while following his instructions. When she was done, he carefully helped her into the buggy and handed her the reins to begin her first lesson.

Danielle was a natural, so their ride was more about talking and laughing than training. It was the first time Hunter and Danielle had been together without something out of the ordinary happening to cause confusion between them. Occasionally, Hunter would make suggestions or explain ways to make driving a horse easier. At other times, he would put his hands over hers to demonstrate how to make stopping and starting smoother. The ride lasted much longer than necessary, and neither cared since they were not ready for the session to end.

When they returned to the cottage, Hunter had Danielle detach the buggy, remove the driving harness, and put the tack away properly. He then explained the correct way to brush Mercy, pick her hooves, and bed her down comfortably. They were talking and laughing, finally having the chance to enjoy each other's company—that was. . . until a hand slipped under Hunter's arm, catching him and Danielle off guard.

"I waited for you at the willow until nearly dark. I see you've found something more interesting to do this evening. Do you suppose you can tear yourself away and drive me home?" Sally Meeker made it sound as if she was hurt that Hunter had failed to keep their date.

Hunter was shocked at the girl's audacity and was just about to set Miss Meeker straight when Danielle touched him on the shoulder.

"Thank you for the driving lesson. I feel much more confident. Please tell Mrs. Jackson I am indebted to her. Good evening to you both." With that, Danielle exited the barn, leaving Hunter alone with Sally.

20

BURN IT TO THE GROUND

Esther had taken most of the day to mull over her current circumstances *and*—for the first time in her life—felt scared. It was obvious the news of their separation was already known within Grandville society. Having attended a ladies' luncheon earlier in the day, she had been subjected to the coolness of her peers. Not to mention, Mrs. Dirksen, who was known for her directness, had made derogatory remarks about women who could not maintain a marriage because of their roaming eyes.

Previously, Esther had planned to subtly work the trauma of their separation into the luncheon conversation—painting Harold as an insensitive and inattentive tyrant and therefore drawing sympathy from the ladies. She now realized such tactics would not work in her favor.

Harold's Christian parents and grandparents had been wealthy, well-respected, and dearly loved throughout the Grandville area. Harold, too, was revered as a good, honest businessman. No one would believe him to be a villain. In addition, Esther was now certain her reputation as a homewrecker had leaked into her social circles. It appeared she was sentenced to succumb to living a middle-class life on the allowance Harold offered her. Yet Esther reasoned that the ladies she so wanted to impress would ignore her improprieties if she could somehow attain wealth again. Money could cover a multitude of sins.

Refusing to live the existence of a pauper and a "nobody", Esther vowed to find a way to get every cent of Harold Simpson's money.

After failing to impress the young lady he was interested in courting, Delbert had returned to drinking and gambling. To his grandparents' relief, Delbert immediately had moved in with his mother after Esther sent word that she, too, had been evicted by Harold.

So having fabricated a devious scheme to re-attain her wealth and status, Esther was particularly pleased to see her son return home late that night, obviously inebriated. Wasting no time in conveying to Delbert her despair over her predicament, she quickly reminded him that her loss of social status would mean he would be blackballed as well. Of course, Esther knew Delbert—like she—relished his position among the elite. As she had anticipated, her words captured his attention right away.

"And whose fault is it that you and I have been reduced to poverty? What type of man casts his son and his wife out onto the street to fend for themselves among the undesirables? An uncaring, ruthless, weak, sniveling man such as your father, that's who! He is nothing but a money-grubbing coward. And we have stood by and allowed him to rob us of our rights to his fortune. He is taking advantage of us."

Esther watched out of the corner of her eye to see if her words were rallying her son.

"You are correct, Mother. What kind of man indeed!" Delbert threw back his head and downed the alcohol he had just poured into his glass.

Seeing her son was ripe to blame Harold, she continued, "Who do you suppose will get our money when he dies? It's not to go to you, Margaret, or me. Oh, no! At present, much of it will go to Sherry—a little girl. But, if the truth be known, I can assure you, the rest of our inheritance will go to Danielle—the person who has caused nothing but misery in our lives.

"I watched him around her. Mark my word. Harold favors her. I could see it in his eyes. She has weaseled her way into his affection. That girl knew exactly what she was doing. Danielle will be granted the rest of *our* money."

By this time Esther was leaning down and looking Delbert directly in the eyes. "Our money!"

Delbert met her gaze, while slowly nodding his head in agreement. Then he poured another drink. But Esther grabbed the glass and bottle—not wanting him to get staggering drunk. She still had more manipulating thoughts to plant into his head.

Delbert started to grab the bottle from her but perceived it was not the time to cross his mother.

Esther proceeded, "If I were a man, I would see to it that your father dies a pauper—just as he has condemned us to do. I would take a torch to his beloved shipping business this very night! I would burn it to the ground. A *man* would burn it to the ground! Danielle Harrison would not receive a cent of our money—not one cent."

Then Esther poured Delbert a small glass of the liquor and

repeated her thoughts to him, ranting over and over about their penniless future. She skillfully outlined in her son's head the information on how to destroy Harold's business—wanting him to believe the ideas were his own. His groggy mind soaked up every detail. By the time Esther left the room, her son was primed to carry out the deed. A short time later, Delbert left home driving the buggy which had been conveniently equipped to carry out the scheme of torching his father's business.

Although Esther had felt extremely satisfied as her son stalked out the door that night, it had not occurred to her that Delbert would go straight to another bar. Finding his friends inside, he joined them and ordered a drink. Before staggering from the bar, Delbert Simpson—with a tongue loosened by liquor—had admitted his financial status, had revealed being barred from his own home, and had bragged of his plans to set fire to his father's company. Not only had his cronies witnessed his admissions. . . but so had a stranger sitting alone at the table next to them.

✦

It was Harold Simpson's night to work late on ledgers at the shipping company. He was still dumbfounded, after having just spoken to his attorney. The audit Harold had requested revealed that his accountant had altered Harold's financial records. Having feared prosecution, the man had confessed that Esther and her father had used the accountant's previous, undisclosed embezzlement accusation to blackmail him. The three had managed to swindle Harold out of over one-third of his life savings. If Danielle's flight had not stimulated him to seek investigative actions against Esther, she and her father might have ruined him completely. As it was, thanks to some recent investments, he hoped he would be able to restore much of his losses. Harold chastised himself for not keeping tabs on the man he had thought to be his trusted friend.

There was no chance of recovering the stolen money from Esther or her father since it already had all been squandered on overseas trips and lavish parties. He knew they had set out to use him from the beginning. Yet Harold almost felt sorry for his wife and in-laws. They truly believed themselves to be part of the upper class simply because they had a few nickels to rub together in Grandville.

As Harold began sorting through the day's mail, he found two letters from Elm Branch. The first letter was from Margaret, stating how she despised him for sending her to live among the people she referred to as *the wretched Appalachians.*

The second letter was from the mission minister informing Harold that Margaret had run away. The local people had banded together to search for her with no success. But as it turned out, the next morning she had been located by a young, visiting pastor who had found her shivering in the deep woods with a twisted ankle. Grateful to have been rescued, Margaret had changed her attitude toward the mission and the people of the mountains. She was working to gain their trust and had turned her life over to the Lord. The senior pastor, feeling there was a strong attraction between Margaret and the young man, was prepared to grant the two permission to court if Harold had no objection.

For Harold Simpson, the news that Margaret might be saved from a life of selfishness and might someday become a loving and caring individual was encouraging. He bowed his head and thanked God for the miracle He was performing in Margaret's life.

It was then that Harold heard an unsettling noise that caused him to check its source. Finding nothing out of the ordinary, he returned to the mail. However, as he reached to open another letter, he sensed an eerie presence behind him. Before he had time to react, everything went black.

21

A GRUESOME DISCOVERY

Since the man who had overheard Delbert Simpson's threat to burn down the shipping business had gone directly to the police, the fire department had been summoned quickly. Therefore, only two buildings had been destroyed in the fire. One of the buildings belonged to a neighboring business, but the contents were of little value. The other building did belong to Harold's company but had been abandoned and was scheduled to be demolished. Unfortunately, the part of the building where Harold's office was located had been badly damaged.

The authorities had found presoaked oil rags placed around each of the remaining buildings. It appeared Delbert might have succeeded in destroying the entire complex if he had not fallen drunk with the lighted torch still in his hand. A policeman had cuffed and taken Delbert to jail by the time the investigating officer was ready to inspect the building where Harold's office was located.

"Sir, over here! It looks like a body!" The rookie officer who spoke had never made such a gruesome discovery.

The investigator pulled the charred boards off the unfortunate victim. "Call the coroner. We'll be needin' him."

Esther watched the glow of the fire from a distance and smirked as her husband's business went up in flames. Everything had played out just as she had wanted. The heartless woman was confident in believing that no one would ever know she had been on the premises and that no one would ever know it was she who had murdered Harold Simpson. However, that was not all Esther Simpson had planned for that night.

Benjamin Dice had spent a late night at his office and was on his way home when he noticed the sky ablaze. There was no doubt in the attorney's mind that it was the shipping company.

Having preconceived notions before arriving at the scene, Benjamin Dice was not surprised to learn that Delbert had been arrested for the crime. However, Dice was not prepared to hear that his loyal friend had lost his life in the fire. He refused to accept the news and, without permission, went into the building where Harold's body had been found.

The investigator started to reprimand him for entering the crime scene but relented when he was told Dice was Harold Simpson's lawyer.

Benjamin started to reach down to examine his friend when the investigator shouted, "Let me remind you we're still collecting evidence. So don't tamper with the scene. But can you identify the body?"

"I. . . will be most happy to identify Harold Simpson. Why are you making the assumption he's dead?" Attorney Dice could see no evidence of severe burns or anything else to support the officer's conclusion of death.

The policeman ignored Dice's question and continued to treat the investigation as an accidental death having resulted from the fire.

After a thorough examination by the coroner, Benjamin Dice was found to be correct. "I have found breath within the man and a faint heartbeat. We must get him to the hospital at once."

The coroner had made another crucial discovery. "The man does suffer from a few bad burns and a bit of smoke inhalation, but his condition is not due to either one—or by fallen debris. Mr. Simpson has suffered a severe blow to the head caused by a blunt instrument."

"Sir, he'll soon recover. Correct?" Benjamin sounded desperate for the doctor's assurance.

The coroner turned honest eyes toward the attorney, "I have no idea. . . but I fear there is little hope."

After Harold had been taken to the hospital, Dice stayed to see if he could be of any assistance to the officer who was now investigating an attempted murder. Ben also was preparing to move the company's files to a secure place where he could easily access them. Unbeknownst to Esther, Benjamin Dice had been named executor of Harold's affairs in all circumstances.

While the officer completed the investigation, Ben scanned the office to make certain nothing of importance had been left behind.

That was when he discovered the broken portion of a peacock feather. The colors had blended with the rug, making the feather nearly impossible to see. He and half of Grandville knew Mrs. Simpson usually wore a lavishly adorned hat with three peacock feathers. He suspected one of those feathers was now missing its eye. Ben felt the eye was a major clue since Esther had often boasted that she only visited Harold's business once and would never set foot in the barbaric place again. The evidence was brought to the attention of the officer.

As ruthless as Delbert was, the attorney could not believe the boy capable of murder—but Esther. . .

22

COLLECTING WOMEN

As he dismounted Petra, Hunter gave a cheerful wave to Hattie, who was watering her flowers. He had wondered if Danielle would remember their scheduled lesson and was glad to see her waiting on the bench in front of the cottage. Although he was charmed by her bright, blue-violet eyes and inviting smile, it was her unassuming manner that made her even more appealing to him. Noticing she had removed the pins from her hair, he hoped she had done it for him. As Danielle stood to greet Hunter, he felt mesmerized in her presence.

"You look quite lovely tonight, Miss Harrison."

"Thank you, Mr. Jackson. I see you have had a hard day at work."

Hunter, realizing she was referring to his soiled jeans and well-worn boots, began to apologize. "Well, yes, my work day and our meeting didn't coincide well. As you can tell, I had to make a decision— " Then he noticed her mischievous smile.

"To be honest, I wasn't certain you'd remember the lesson. You did run off before we could agree on the time." Even though Hunter found Danielle's constant disappearances frustrating, he didn't think it wise to ruffle her feathers just now.

"I didn't want to keep you and Sally from— Never mind. Do you want me to start with hitching up the buggy?"

"Why are you always concerned about Sal— Oh well, anyway. . . yes, start with the buggy."

"You kids have a good time. Teach her well, Hunter. My life may depend on it," Hattie called out as she gave another wave and went inside.

Danielle, having managed to avoid another conversation about Sally Meeker, hurried into the barn and began gathering the tack for Mercy, while Hunter pulled the buggy forward.

"Here, you guide the shay to get a feel for maneuvering it into place like this."

As Danielle reached to take the shafts, her fingers brushed Hunter's hand, causing them both to jerk away as if they had been stung. Feeling awkward for their reactions, they timidly looked up into each other's eyes. Danielle, embarrassed for allowing her feelings to show, pretended as if nothing had happened and went back to work.

Hunter stood motionless for a moment—his eyes fixed on Danielle. *If she has feelings for me, why does she keep pushing me away?*

Danielle tried to convince herself nothing had happened between them. He belonged to Sally Meeker. She would have to find a way to keep her distance from Hunter Jackson.

By the time Mercy was hitched up, they were back to feeling at ease with one another. Danielle coaxed the obedient horse from the barnyard and down the street as if she had grown up doing so. The thrill of controlling a horse filled her with excitement.

Hunter was seeing another glimpse of her true personality. This was the Danielle he wanted to know. She was fun loving and full of life—everything he had believed her to be. He longed to see

Danielle free of the burden she was carrying and free of whatever was keeping her from revealing her true feelings for him.

Having the excuse of showing Danielle more ways to handle the horse, Hunter again—quite intentionally—put his hands over hers and was satisfied to notice that she did not resist or pull away.

"Slap the reins like this—with confidence. It won't hurt her. The horse needs to feel you're in charge. You're doing great."

Danielle smiled, pleased to know he was happy with her progress.

"Like this?" She gave the reins a robust snap and off Mercy went into a gallop.

Laughing at the sudden lunge, they both turned to share a playful glance. Hunter then explained how to gently slow the horse. Before long, the two were involved in conversation—Hunter sharing antidotes from his childhood and Danielle admitting to her humiliating waitressing experiences.

"I'm sorry you had such a rough start at the inn. But according to Rosa, you've more than made up for it."

"It *is* embarrassing not to be able to work closely with people. I don't know why it affects me so."

"Evidently there's no lapse in your concentration when you're sewing. My Aunt Helen is extremely impressed with your work."

"Thank you for telling me. I hope she is."

The conversation continued to flow, as Hunter took the liberty of putting his arm onto the back of the brown leather seat. Although neither would have spoken the words, it was obvious they both wanted to spend more time together.

"Well, I think you're ready to take to the road. You're a natural. Although, you might need a few more lessons before taking on a team of horses. And remember, Hattie's a great driver when she's feeling up to the task. You'll both be in good hands."

Pleased to have earned his approval, Danielle, without thinking, gave Hunter a quick kiss on the cheek. Being caught off guard, Hunter stepped back, causing Danielle to lose her balance. In response, Hunter put his arm around her waist. Again they were face to face. There in the quietness of the evening, they both could feel the longing between them. Hunter then made one of the hardest decisions of his life—*not* to kiss Danielle Harrison.

❧

"My name's Robert Wilky. Feel free to call me *Rob*. Most of my friends do." Rob was the handsome assistant Rosa had hired to replace Chef Fran, who would soon be retiring.

"Well then, you may call me *Danielle*. I certainly don't mind forsaking a few formalities. So why did you choose the Willow Inn to begin your career? That is, if you don't mind my asking." She was impressed with the comfortable way in which the lanky, brown-eyed chef presented himself.

He smiled and ran his hand back through one side of his blonde hair, forcing a few strands into place. "I have Rosa to thank for my position. I grew up near Remington, and we attended the same church. I made money on the side by cooking for church functions, weddings, and the like. Anyway, she noticed I had a flare and a passion for cooking, so she offered to finance my culinary training in New York City. In return, I agreed to work at the inn for a few years. She's a generous and caring lady."

"She certainly is. She took me under her wing too. So you attend Faith Chapel? I've recently become acquainted with a few families from there—the Jacksons, the Grays, Miss Adams and her fiancée. Of course, Rosa and her husband, Johnathon, and my landlord, Hattie."

"Except for Miss Adams, I've known the others for as long as I can remember."

"Rob, will you be attending the engagement party the church is hosting for Miss Adams and Mr. Meeker?"

"As it turns out, I will be catering the party for the Willow Inn. Chef Fran isn't interested in catering any longer, and since the church is familiar with what I can do in the kitchen—"

"And having the congregation in your back pocket—" Danielle teased.

"Well, that too. . . and the fact that Rosa is donating the food." He smiled back, recognizing her cleverness.

"I suppose you know Hunter Jackson? He's Mr. Jackson's nephew."

"I've never met him personally, but I know who he is. He arrived at the Jacksons' about the time I was leaving for New York. I understand he's doing a great job as manager of Mel's property—real dependable. Am I detecting a bit of interest on your part for the young Mr. Jackson?"

Danielle blushed at his comment. "Mr. Wilky, you're terrible to draw such a conclusion just because I mentioned his name." She hoped her reply had deflected his assumption.

Robert Wilky chuckled at her response.

"Well, Danielle, I suppose I should go inside. The lunch crowd will be here in a couple hours. Glad we had a chance to officially meet. Maybe I'll see you at the party—if not before."

Rob nodded to indicate he was leaving, and Danielle gave a slight bow of her head in return.

On their ride to the engagement party, Danielle and Hattie laughed and chatted continuously. The outing reminded Hattie how much she missed being out and about, and supervising a new driver made her feel useful and lifted her spirits. Although there were a few times Danielle needed a little direction, she did quite well considering her lack of experience. Having each other's company made the ride to the Jacksons' home seem much shorter than it was.

As the guests were arriving at Rica and Joe's engagement party, Hunter anxiously waited outside the carriage barn for Hattie and Danielle to appear. Since the two were running much later than expected, he began to chastise himself for possibly misjudging Danielle's driving abilities. Fearing they had been in an accident, he was on his way to the barn to saddle Petra when he noticed the small shay coming down the driveway.

As Danielle's hopeful suitor and as the driving instructor with a vested interest in the safety of the two ladies, Hunter went directly out to meet them. Having nearly reached the halted carriage, he noticed Robert Wilky was already there. Hunter's eyes narrowed and he picked up his pace.

By the time he reached the carriage, Wilky had Hattie by his side and was on his way to assist Danielle. Hunter, ignoring Wilky, then took a lengthy step forward and offered her his hand. "Here, let me help you. I was just about to ride out and look for you two. How did it go, ladies?"

"Oh, it was a wonderful drive and such a grand time. Danielle is a good, confident driver. Hunter, you should be proud of yourself." Hattie, being refreshed by their adventure, felt the need to brag on them both.

"We started later than planned. It never crossed my mind you might be concerned. I'm sorry." Danielle smiled at Hunter, still remembering the time they had shared during the driving lesson.

"Was this your first time driving? You should've mentioned it. I could've made arrangements to bring you." Robert Wilky was not certain what his own feelings were for Danielle Harrison, but noting Hunter's demeanor, he took pleasure in allowing Hunter Jackson to believe he might have competition.

"Oh, allow me to introduce you. Hunter, this is Robert Wilky. Rosa has hired him as the future replacement for Chef Fran. Rob mentioned the two of you hadn't officially met."

Danielle was unaware of the questioning look on Hunter's face as the two men shook hands. Hunter was uncomfortable hearing Danielle refer to Mr. Wilky as *Rob* and did not appreciate having been a topic of their conversation.

Just as their handshake ended, Rob's smile turned sour as he noticed the covey of young ladies who had trailed after Hunter. Then his attention went to Sally Meeker, who was rubbing Jackson's shoulder to gain his attention.

Although Rob had eagerly looked forward to meeting Mel's nephew, his favorable impression of Hunter Jackson changed to one of a man with questionable character. He thought highly of Danielle and did not want to see her hurt. Rob did not care for men who took pride in collecting women. Not to mention, he had been somewhat interested in Sally Meeker before he had left for New York.

Not noticing Sally Meeker's arm entwined with his own, Hunter watched Danielle's smile disappear as she accepted the arm of

Robert Wilky. He stood dejected as Rob escorted Hattie and Danielle across the yard.

"Hunter darling, when did you give her another lesson? Was it last night? No wonder I couldn't find you." Embarrassed that Sally's possessive questions had been loud enough for Danielle and Rob to hear, he pulled his arm from Sally's grasp and walked away.

Once Danielle had helped Hattie get settled among a group of her friends, the next thing on her agenda was to find Madison Neely. Madison had been invited to attend the party, but instead had chosen to work the early shift as a server since the wages were twice her normal salary. As it turned out, Madison found Danielle and begged to be excused from their time together. Ronald Coats, a well-to-do boy from Willow Weep, had asked to accompany Madison after she had finished serving.

"I just can't believe a boy from such a nice family would want to spend time with me." Madison's voice began to waver. "I'm from the poor side of town, and I'm not even attractive."

Danielle gave her a hug, glad to see another glimmer of happiness in Madison's burdensome life. "Madison, you are a beautiful girl, inside and out. You must not judge yourself so harshly."

"But I'm nothing special. Why would a boy like Ronald Coats—"

"Madison, God has placed us all in different lifestyles and granted us different attributes.

"You're caring, intelligent, responsible, and possess common sense, and Ron Coats is wise enough to recognize those qualities in you. Now, let go of your misgivings and enjoy the evening with him." Madison gave her a hug and hurried back to work. Danielle hoped her words had boosted her friend's confidence.

"Well said, Miss Harrison. I hope she will take your words to heart. We often seem to judge others too quickly and too harshly." Hunter's masculine voice surprised her.

"And is there a hidden message for me in your statement?"

"Actually, I was trying to be profound as well. But now that you've mentioned it. . . things aren't always what they appear to be." Not wanting to risk causing any friction between him and Danielle, Hunter chose not to continue.

Danielle giggled. "Are you referring to having a string of girls following you wherever you go?"

"Is that what they were doing? I need to pay more attention. I hadn't noticed." He gave a sheepish grin.

She giggled again. "Some girls would be jealous. I think you should be more aware."

Hunter wasn't sure how to interpret her remarks. "Danielle, I know those girls from church. They just stopped by the barn to talk. They're funny when they're together. I'll introduce you later. You'd like them."

"Personally, I think they're *all* taken with you."

"Well, what can I do?" Hunter gave a sneaky, dismissive wink to make Danielle laugh.

"You *should* be careful." This time her eyes seemed serious.

Again Hunter was puzzled but let the implication slide. "Have you been through the receiving line? I was on my way there. Care to join me? It's about time for it to end."

Danielle hesitated, wanting to say *yes* but thinking it was inappropriate—especially with Sally only a few feet away and within hearing distance.

Hunter tilted his head toward the line to entice her to join him. His eyes were too inviting, and Danielle could not refuse. Not waiting for her reply, he gently placed his hand beneath her elbow and led her over to congratulate Rica and Joe on their engagement.

Sally Meeker immediately made her way to the line and slipped her hand under Hunter's arm.

Rica, recognizing Sally's interfering move, seized the opportunity to address her future sister-in-law's insolent behavior. "Hunter and Danielle, it's so good to see you two together. I hope you are having a nice time."

"Sally, why are you in line?" Joe questioned. "You *are* my sister."

"I'm here to keep Hunter company."

"It seems Hunter already has company," Joe commented, further emphasizing the fact that he was correcting his sister.

Sally, humiliated by his comments, said nothing, but gave her brother a hateful stare as she pulled her hand from Hunter's arm and walked away.

23

WHO ARE YOU

As soon as Hunter and Danielle had congratulated Joe and Rica, Hunter was called away to assist a friend. Being left adrift, Danielle wandered aimlessly through the crowd pondering what the exchange between Joe and Sally Meeker had meant.

"*Miss Harrison*, I'd like to have a word with you!"

The voice sounded so angry that she could not believe it came from such a feminine girl as Sally Meeker.

"Of course, Miss Meeker. What is it?"

"It's this. . . I want you to stay away from Hunter Jackson. It's clear to see you have your cap set for him, and it's causing problems between us. He's forgetting what we mean to one another. I'm tired of finding you with him every time I turn around. Stay away from him or I promise. . . you will be sorry." Sally offered Danielle a glare equal to the one she had just given her brother. Then she picked up her skirt, gave it a shake to show her frustration, and stormed off.

Danielle's conscience was pricked by Sally's verbal attack, and she was ashamed of herself. Some of the things Sally Meeker had accused her of doing were true.

"I'm so glad I finally caught up with you." Rica looped her arm

157

around Danielle's in a sisterly gesture as they strolled across the lawn. "I'm so blessed. I will soon be married to the most wonderful man in the world. He is gentle and understanding and was in love with me even long before I deserved his affection. My life is turning into a dream come true. I never believed I'd see the day when so many friends and family would wish me well for *any* reason."

"Why would you say such a thing? You're dearly loved." Danielle was astonished to hear such a self-demeaning comment come from Rica.

"You have no idea what I was like before I gave my life to Christ. It hasn't been long ago that I was a mean, selfish, wicked person."

"Rica, I don't believe a word of it."

"Oh, it's true. When the Lord saved me, He took away all the maliciousness within me. And to be honest, I had plenty of it.

"My parents are wonderful people, but they were older when I was born. They spoiled me beyond reason and allowed me to rule over them and everyone around me. Joe's oldest sister, Eloise, who still doesn't trust me, once called me *possessed.*"

"I still find it impossible to believe. You're kind and caring."

"Honestly, Helen's daughter, Bethany, could tell you some horror stories about me. But you'll have to learn of my past ruthlessness from someone else. I can't bear thinking of my life before I was saved.

"By the way, Eloise is the one wearing the green and pink dress over by the rose garden. She's a nice looking girl but very studious—absolutely no interest in romance whatsoever."

"I beg to differ with you. It so happens I've been watching an exchange between her and the thin gentleman with the reddish hair—who also looks studious." Danielle was excited to share her discovery with someone.

Rica watched as Eloise and the young man nonchalantly stole glances of one another. "Mr. Mirks? He attends Faith Chapel too. It never would've occurred to me."

"It might be possible to win Eloise's favor if you could find a way to bring the two together."

"I'll definitely try. They'd make a perfect match. Thank you, Danielle. Maybe I can put some of my old finagling skills to good use for a change." Rica was gushingly excited at the thought.

"Anyway, the reason I was in such a hurry to speak with you is because it appeared Sally was reprimanding you for some reason. May I ask why?"

"Between us. . . Miss Meeker requested I stay away from Hunter." The words had leaped from her mouth before considering that Rica was marrying into the Meeker family. But the relationship between Hunter and Sally was so confusing to her that she needed to confide in someone.

"Oh, yes. Sally does have big plans for the young Mr. Jackson." Rica glanced in the direction of the barn and then back at Danielle. "Yet, if you notice, he doesn't seem to care."

Danielle looked toward the barn where Hunter stood surrounded by another group of admirers.

"If I were you, I would *not* keep my distance from Hunter Jackson unless *I* so chose. Well, I believe I'd better catch Mr. Mirks before I miss my chance at matchmaking." Rica gave Danielle a warm hug before leaving. "Seriously, dear, follow your heart."

As Rica walked away, Danielle was not certain she understood her new friend's advice. *Follow my heart? Is Sally and Hunter's relationship one sided?*

"Nephew!" Mel summoned.

Hunter, glad to have a reason to excuse himself from the ladies surrounding him, went to join his uncle.

"I see you have quite a collection of girls to keep you entertained. What will Miss Meeker think?"

"They're just friends from church. . . but why would I care what Sally thinks?"

"It's a natural assumption since Miss Meeker is usually on your arm. . . and from what I've been told, you do drive her home on a fairly regular basis."

"I assure you I have no interest in Sally Meeker. I only accompany her home because she's so insistent. As a gentleman, I feel obligated when a lady needs an escort—but that girl seems to appear out of nowhere expecting my assistance. I'm sure she'll be a great match for some guy, but she's too pushy and highfalutin for me."

"So, you're telling me you're frustrated with Miss Meeker?"

"I am."

"Have you told the girl how you feel? You don't want to mislead the young lady. That's not very gentlemanlike either. You're also giving people the impression there's an understanding between you."

Hunter took time to mull over his uncle's words. "I guess I've never looked at it from that angle."

"According to Helen and a few of her friends, they seem to think you're interested in the Harrison girl."

"I am. . . and I think the feeling is mutual. . . but for some reason, she pulls away." Hunter's face displayed his uneasiness in having this conversation with his uncle.

"Do you suppose your actions toward Miss Meeker might've given Miss Harrison the wrong impression?"

"Okay. . . now I see where you're going with this." Hunter finally understood how blind he had been.

"Look Hunter, I've only brought up the situation because another young man close to me struggled with this same issue. As a Christian, sometimes a gentleman must take the initiative and be direct with certain young ladies. It's not easy to tell someone you aren't interested in them. But it *is* the right thing to do—especially when it comes to protecting people's reputations. . . and the relationship with the one you love." Mel hoped his words were not too direct.

"Thanks, Mel. I guess there's more to being a gentleman than just being accommodating. Looks like I have a few situations to deal with."

"You're most welcome, son," Mel slapped Hunter on the back as they shook hands and parted.

After taking care of a couple unexpected problems to keep the party in motion, Hunter finally found Danielle standing near the gazebo. "Danielle, I'm sorry. I didn't mean to walk off and leave you alone like I did. One thing led to another—"

"Led to another group of lady friends?" She pressed her lips together and widened her eyes to emphasize her point.

"Like I told you before, they're friends and nothing more. They're only being sociable."

"Somehow, I doubt it—at least not most of them."

"Well, I can't speak for them, but there are no attractions on my behalf. Although. . . maybe I should be more discerning in the way I present myself. I suppose people can get the wrong impressions if we're not careful."

It was then that those in attendance were asked to be seated for the evening meal.

"May I persuade you to join me for dinner?" Hunter was determined to rectify his past mistakes and be more direct in his approach to Danielle. He didn't want her to misinterpret his intentions any longer and intended to explain his relationship with Sally Meeker as soon as possible.

Danielle's first thought was to follow her heart and accept his invitation. But she suddenly froze, intimidated by the sight of Sally Meeker's threatening eyes across the lawn.

Having noticed the long pause, Hunter followed Danielle's gaze which led to Sally. He, in turn, gave Sally a disapproving look.

"If it's Miss Meeker who's causing you to hesitate in accepting my invitation, I can assure you there's no need for concern."

"Then yes, Hunter. . . by all means."

Hunter escorted her to the table where his Aunt Helen and Uncle Mel were seated along with the Smiths and Hattie. Even though their friends were all elated to see Hunter and Danielle together, they attempted to hide their exuberance.

Despite Sally's scolding and the shyness in making an appearance with Hunter for the first time, Danielle still managed to notice every detail of the party's decor. The tables and chairs were draped in white linen, and lemon lily wreath centerpieces encircled large, white candles. The guests of honor were seated on the gazebo, which was draped with white satin and accented with wreaths of lilies. The decorations were simple but delicately elegant. Danielle had never allowed herself to dream of sharing just a beautiful celebration with a man who loved her.

Those in charge of the festivities were in good spirits, friendly, and accommodating. The meal—prepared by Chef Wilky—was pleasing to the eye and delicious. A string quartet played softly in the background, allowing those present to converse unhindered, while being served by ladies in white uniforms with yellow aprons.

Everything seemed perfect—except Danielle secretly wished Hunter had chosen a more secluded table where they could have been alone.

When the guests began to mingle again, Hunter—also anxious to be alone with Danielle—tried to seize the opportunity to take her on a tour of the Jackson property. But to Hunter's dismay, just as they were about to leave the table, Helen and Mel approached them.

"We're sorry, but may we borrow Danielle long enough to introduce her to a few friends?" Helen hoped her nervousness did not show.

"Of course, I don't mind waiting." Hunter was not being exactly honest.

"Hunter, please join us." Helen gave him a pleading look to let him know he might be needed.

"Certainly."

Danielle allowed Hunter to take her hand as they followed Helen and Mel to a gathering of three standing by the veranda. She thought the man with the clerical collar holding his wife's hand appeared to be the pastor and his wife from Faith Chapel. Next to them was a nice-looking, older gentleman with a tan face and white hair. He appeared to be in his mid-sixties, tall, and still in good physical shape.

"We're sorry to interrupt your visit, but Helen and I would like to introduce this young lady."

The older man stared at Danielle as if she were a ghost. "Who *are* you, child?"

"Joshua, this is Miss Danielle Harrison." Mel had not expected an immediate reaction from Joshua.

"Danielle Harrison? Who are your parents? Where are you from? What's your father's name?" The older man seemed beside himself.

Taken aback by his abruptness, Danielle responded, "I. . . I. . . I have been told my father's name is Daniel Harrison. That. . . that is all I know of my father."

Joshua Harrison let out a loud gasp. "Your mother. . . who is she?"

"I. . . I'm sorry, sir, I'm not comfortable sharing such information."

Danielle knew her response was overly frank, but she wanted to protect her identity. The Simpson name might be easily connected to the well-known Grandville shipping company.

"I suppose not. Well, I can enlighten you on anything you might want to know about your father. You're the spitting imagine of my Valerie—your late grandmother."

Joshua Harrison's hand was trembling as he pulled a handkerchief from his pocket to wipe his forehead.

"I know beyond any doubt, that *you* are my granddaughter. Your middle name is Valerie? True? "

"Y. . . yes sir. My middle name is Valerie. I don't understand."

Seeing that Danielle appeared faint, Hunter put his arm around her and looked for a place for her to be seated. Mel grabbed a couple chairs from nearby.

"My Dani! I was afraid I'd never lay eyes on you again." Joshua took a seat on the chair facing his granddaughter.

"Joshua and Danielle, we are sorry for bringing the two of you together in this manner. We thought it might be easier this way, but we were wrong. It's been too much of a strain for both of you."

Joshua waved his hands and shook his head. "No. . . no, Mel. There isn't a right or wrong way to approach such an issue. I'm just grateful you've brought my granddaughter to me. I'm beyond words. Thank you." Joshua was beginning to calm down and think clearly again.

Danielle, baffled by what she had just been told, looked up at Hunter in confusion, then back to Joshua Harrison.

"Is it true? You're my grandfather? My grandmother's name was Valerie?"

"Yes, my dear Dani, every word of it's true. I would've known you anywhere." Joshua stood to his feet and reached out to her.

Danielle stood just in time for Joshua to hug her and then smother the top of her head with kisses. Feeling his arms tighten, she relinquished her fears and lovingly embraced her grandfather.

"My girl. . . my long-lost, baby girl."

It was a beautiful scene to watch unfold. Mel, Helen, and Hunter felt blessed to be part of the reunion. For Hunter, it was his first glimpse into Danielle's guarded past.

Joshua Harrison's granddaughter seemed more composed than she felt. Danielle was almost afraid to hope that she might have just met a family member who would love her.

She and her grandfather stayed together among their friends until the party's conclusion. Hunter, knowing the discovery was a lot for the two to absorb, kept a close watch over them.

As it so happened, Hunter was well acquainted with Joshua Harrison and had even asked the man to grant him the first chance to bid on the Harrison farm if the older man ever decided to sell. The two men held each other in high regard, and learning that Joshua was Danielle's grandfather made Hunter respect the man even more.

When the party ended, Danielle promised her grandfather she would visit him early the next day. Rosa, having heard about their reunion, had insisted she take the day off.

⁂

Hunter accompanied Danielle to the buggy immediately after the horse was hitched up and Petra was tied to the back. He had every intention of driving Danielle home—especially now that her mind was focused on meeting her grandfather for the first time.

Just as he was assisting Danielle into the buggy, he noticed Sally Meeker stalking her way toward him. "Hunter, what are you doing? You know I expected you to take me home tonight. Why are you with *her*?"

"Not that I need to explain anything to you, Sally, but I've asked to escort Danielle home. And why should you assume I'd drive you home?" After having just witnessed Danielle's life changing event earlier, he was not in the mood to humor Sally Meeker.

"You always do. You know by now I count on it." Sally had raised her voice to sound more authoritative.

"Well, you shouldn't. I'm afraid I've been much too lenient in our acquaintance. You must no longer rely on me to accompany you when you find yourself unescorted. Since your parents drove you here, maybe you should return home with them. Excuse me, Sally. I have a long drive ahead."

"There's no reason for you to trouble yourself, Mr. Jackson," the handsome chef interrupted as he approached Hunter and Sally. "I'm on my way back to Willow Weep, and I can drive Danielle since we're both going in the same direction. One of the staff can take my rig."

"See. *He'll* take her." Sally was pleased to have an argument to present to Hunter, but it made her sound even more desperate.

Rob, having once been impressed by Miss Meeker, was insulted by her insolent reference toward him and now saw her as self-centered and arrogant.

Hunter, disgusted by Sally's presumptuous behavior and the chef's impudent attitude, climbed into the buggy. He had Danielle to consider. "Then I have the perfect solution. Since Danielle has accepted my invitation, maybe *you* would like to escort Miss Meeker to Willow Weep. . . since you're *both* going in the same direction. Good evening, Mr. Wilky. Miss Meeker."

Giving the reins a whip, he and Danielle drove away, leaving Wilky and Sally standing alone in the dark.

"Well! As if Hunter Jackson gets to decide who will take me home. I don't just jump in a buggy with *any* man—like that Harrison girl."

Then, with hands on her hips, she commanded in her most disrespectful voice, "So, go get your buggy!"

Sally's impudent tone did not suit Rob Wilky. "Miss Meeker. Did I overhear Mr. Jackson say that you arrived at the party with your parents?"

"Yes, I did. Why?"

"Well, then. . . it's fortunate you have a ride home. You see, I just don't let *any* girl hop into my buggy." He tipped his hat and walked away.

24

CALL ME GRANDPA

After a few minutes alone on the road, Hunter looked over to see how Danielle was coping after the reunion with her grandfather. He hoped his presence brought some comfort to her flustered heart. This was not the time to explain his association with Sally Meeker or to be admiring Danielle's silhouette in the moonlight. He would have to be satisfied with just sitting beside this lovely girl. Hunter prayed that someday he would be able to win her heart completely.

"Is there anything I can do?"

"I'm fine. I just have all these feelings coursing through me. I'm elated and shocked. . . joyous. . . sad. I feel blessed, but I feel cheated. I have someone in my life who might love me just because I exist. . . and I'm afraid to hope it's true. I've never been happier. . . and that makes me resent the one who kept me from a loving family. I feel as if I'm wandering through a maze."

The conflict within Danielle was evident in her voice. It saddened Hunter to know that her past was overshadowing the happiness of being reunited with a devoted and loving grandfather.

Hunter put his arm around Danielle and pulled her close. . . and she let him.

Hunter had asked to switch his day off, so he could drive Danielle to the Harrison farm the following morning. Since she was unfamiliar with the area, he did not want her to get lost and was glad to have another reason to be alone with her.

After crossing the bridge to the cottage, he found Danielle in her favorite place on the bench. "You're looking lovely as always, and it appears you're ready to leave."

Danielle, lost in her thoughts, was startled by Hunter's voice. "Yes, I couldn't sleep from the excitement. I was forcing myself to sit here waiting for time to pass. I don't want to arrive too early since— And why are you here, Mr. Jackson?"

"I couldn't sleep for worrying that you might get lost on your way to your grandfather's. The farm is a bit tricky to find when you don't know the area. Besides, it's secluded, and I keep remembering the day you met up with the Brewster boys. I decided to take the day off to accompany you. That is, if you would allow me?"

"How kind! Thank you, Hunter. I— " Danielle paused, touched by his thoughtfulness and hoping her teary eyes were not detectable. "To tell the truth, I was leery of making the trip alone. I thought about asking Hattie to ride along, but she didn't seem herself when I checked on her this morning. I guess the engagement party was too taxing. I'm beginning to worry. She doesn't seem able to do much of anything."

"Everyone has noticed Hattie's decline. We're all concerned.

"If we leave now, I think we'll arrive at a decent hour. Besides, I have another challenge for you." Hunter's smile revealed he was pleased with himself. "I brought something a little bigger, and I want you to take the reins. Come on. Let's see what you think."

When they arrived at the back lot, Danielle found he had chosen a two-seated buckboard drawn by two horses. She suspected he had chosen the rig to distract her from overthinking the visit with her grandfather.

Danielle's eyes opened wide as she watched Hunter climb into the seat and offer her a hand up. "I have to admit the horses and buckboard do look daunting."

"Don't worry. I won't mind helping you when it's needed."

Danielle had an easy way with the team, and Hunter only assisted when necessary. She wasn't going to entertain any thoughts of Sally Meeker today. Still she wondered why she felt guilty for being alone with Hunter.

The two entertained themselves by a friendly competition of sighting wildlife until they had begun passing buildings and fields that belonged to the Harrison farm. "To think, *my* father walked and worked in these very fields." Danielle spoke the words as if Daniel Harrison had been royalty.

As the lofty, white Harrison farmhouse came into view, Hunter took the reins to hurry the horses along. He watched as nervous excitement rose within Danielle. A sleek haired, brown dog romped toward them through the manicured yard, barking and wagging its tail.

Joshua Harrison had risen from his rocker on the wraparound porch as soon as he heard the team and buckboard coming down the lane. Hunter pulled the horses to a stop, jumped from his seat, and lifted Danielle from the buckboard so she could meet her grandfather halfway. Joshua's arms were ready to enfold her, and Danielle was willing to oblige.

"My little Dani! You know I love you. God is so good! I hope you don't mind if I use your pet name. We've always referred to you as *Dani*."

"Not at all. My close friends, Everett and Jean, call me *Dani*. They were the only people I ever knew who were like family to me." Danielle stopped herself from saying any more while Hunter was present. She wanted to reserve such information for when she and her grandfather were alone.

Although he did want to know everything about Danielle Harrison, Hunter perceived that what he had just overheard was meant to be private and understood he should excuse himself when the Harrisons were ready to speak in depth.

"Hunter boy, thank you for seeing to Dani's safety. Won't you both please step inside? Lacresha has insisted on fixing a meal to blend breakfast and lunch. Believe me, whatever it is, there will be plenty of it, and it will be the best you've ever had.

"Lacresha, bring that husband of yours and come on in here and greet our Dani. I know you're listening." Joshua laughed at his own wittiness in knowing what he had said was true.

"Well, you certainly nailed that one down, Josh. She had her ear to the door, and you'd a thought she'd been shot when you called her out."

"Oh, hush, you two. Of course, I was listening. I've been waiting to see this little one as long as the two of you have. Where is our girl? I want to lay my eyes on her, so I'll know this isn't a dream."

Lacresha took Danielle's face in her hands and looked deep into her eyes. "You are your father's daughter. That's for sure." Then she put both arms around Danielle and squeezed her close, as her husband did the same.

"Danielle, this is Jeremiah and Lacresha Williams, my two best friends—my family—and the ones who keep this farm going in the right direction. Jerry took the position as overseer here at the farm a few years before you were born, and Lacresha took charge of the house. They felt the pain of losing you and your father just as deeply as we did."

Jerry and Lacresha were the most handsome couple Danielle believed she had ever seen. Their dark skin only added to their attractiveness. Although Jerry's hair was graying, they both looked much younger than their years. Their constant smiles caused Danielle to feel at ease, and she loved them at once.

"Come on, everyone! The meal is set out, so it's time to eat." Joshua was correct. The buffet was brimming with food of every kind—fresh bread and buttermilk biscuits, ham and fried chicken, butter and cheese, jellies and salads, and an array of fruits and vegetables. The menu was ingenious and seemed unending. The men eventually joined the ladies at the table with their plates stacked high.

Danielle sat quietly, overwhelmed with the wonder of the new world she had stumbled upon. Hopefully, she and her grandfather could put together the missing pieces of their relationship.

After the meal, Lacresha began clearing the table and Jerry headed back to the barn, while Joshua led his granddaughter and Hunter to the parlor where family pictures were on display. He took the time to explain how each person was related and a brief history of their lives. It had never dawned on Danielle that there might be an entire family in existence on her father's side—and many of them still living.

"Here. . . this is your Grandmother Valerie on our wedding day." Danielle was stunned to see there was more than a striking resemblance between her and her grandmother. In fact, it appeared to be her own likeness set in the sterling silver frame. Suddenly the void in her heart was filled. It could not be denied that she was truly part of this family.

"This is another one of Valerie—not long before she passed. Your grandmother was a kind and humble Christian woman with a servant's heart. As a matter of fact, there wasn't much of anything good in people that couldn't be found in your late grandmother. Her hair might've grayed over time, but the years didn't deprive her of beauty. However, the unexpected loss of you—and later Daniel—did rob Valerie of that extra spark within her. It never returned."

Danielle took her grandfather's calloused hand. "I'm truly sorry. I wish I'd known her. How long has it been?"

"Your grandmother passed two years ago last month."

Seeing the sorrow the memories brought to her grandfather made Danielle wish she had not asked.

"I can see what you're thinking, but these are the matters we need to discuss if we want to have a close relationship. I want that bond between us, and I hope you do also. I sense you've had a difficult life, and I want to help you heal."

Joshua was being as sincere and vulnerable as a man could be, and Hunter could see both those qualities were something a man must strive to attain.

"And *this* is a picture of your father around the time he and your mother were married." Joshua looked at the picture briefly and handed it to Dani.

Danielle accepted the picture as reverently as it had been handed to her. She looked at her grandfather in awe. "This is my father?"

"Yes, Dani, that's your daddy." Joshua fought to keep his emotions under control.

"I never dreamed I would ever see his face." Danielle lightly ran her fingers across her father's picture as if all the love she had held in her heart for Daniel Harrison had finally transferred to him. Unlike her grandfather, Danielle gave in to her emotions.

Joshua reached out to embrace his granddaughter. Finally he was able to be the loving grandfather he had always wanted to be. Hunter sensed it was time to excuse himself.

The mood in the room changed not long after Hunter left. Grandfather and granddaughter took seats opposite one another—Danielle in the wingback and Joshua in the rocker. It was the first time the two had been alone together.

Danielle was the first to speak, "Grandfather, you have given me a special name. Is there another name you had in mind for me to call you? I've noticed your brow wrinkles when I say *grandfather*. Since everything is new between us—"

"*Grandpa*. I always imagined you would call me *Grandpa*. I'm not a poor man by any stretch, but I'm a farmer. We're more relaxed out here. We're county folk. *Grandpa Harrison* or *Grandpa Josh* or both will be fine. You may save the name *Grandfather* for polite company. Valerie would've liked you to call her *Grandma*."

Danielle could tell he was pleased she had asked. "Then *Grandpa* it is."

There was a long silence. Then Grandpa Harrison reluctantly spoke up, "I believe we should address the most difficult subject before us. That would be how your mother and father's relationship affected your life. I'm a direct man, and I'll be candid with you. Understand it's not my intention to insult you in any way. However, when it comes to your mother, I must tell you I don't have a high regard for her. . . to say the least."

Danielle nodded. "I understand."

"Well then, I'll proceed. Your mother and father met at a summer party. At the time, she was staying with a wealthy aunt and uncle in Bristol. The couple, by the way, have since lost their money—foolishly wasted, from what I hear. But that's been the way of the Gilded Age."

Outside, Hunter had not realized the chair he had chosen on the porch was by an opened window. He could clearly hear the conversation between Joshua and Danielle. As much as he wanted to understand her past, he could not allow himself to eavesdrop and decided it was best to join Jerry in the barn.

"Your father, being young and having little knowledge of women, was overly taken by Esther's beauty and beguiling ways. They were married within weeks—unbeknownst to me or your grandma. It was plain for everyone involved to see your mother was using Daniel and had no love for him.

"Less than three months into the marriage, she was already seeking a divorce—but stopped the proceedings after finding she was expecting. Your father, still infatuated with the woman, did everything possible to make Esther happy. However, it seemed that belittling him was her only pleasure in their bond.

"Soon after your birth, her threats and her character assassination of Daniel escalated. Then one evening, your father arrived home to find Esther had packed her belongings in your grandma's bags, taken you, and left."

Joshua explained how Daniel had discovered the marriage traps Esther had set for him and later for Harold Simpson. He explained how Harold had smuggled her to visit her father and how the two new friends had planned a secret, legal case for Daniel to gain custody.

Danielle was astounded by the story. She never would have guessed Harold and her father had once been close and had plotted to rescue her from Esther.

"What a wonderful God we serve! If He hadn't led me to Willow Weep and then to you, I might have never known my dad loved me." She looked into her grandfather's eyes. "Thank you, Grandpa."

"You should know that your dad and Harold would have won the court case. They had more than enough evidence. Unfortunately, your daddy was taken by pneumonia not long before they were to submit their findings for trial.

"Your grandma and I tried to find a way to get custody of you but were told we had no legal rights. Somehow Esther got wind of our plans, so we received the same threats as Daniel had. For your sake, we obeyed." Joshua Harrison scooted forward in his rocker. "I'm sorry, dear one. We could do nothing."

Danielle reached up to touch her grandpa's cheek. "I do understand. It's never wise to cross Esther."

"Thank you for saying that. It's a relief to know you understand.

"Now, my dear Dani, I'd like it if you shared the details of your past with me. Not knowing has been torture for us. I want to know everything."

Danielle gave her grandpa a faint apprehensive smile.

25

THE ACCOMPLICE AND THE MASTERMIND

The night of the shipping company fire, Esther had been extremely busy:

Now that Harold was out of the way, the next thing on Esther's list was to find a way to break into the Simpson home and take possession of her daughter. She knew she needed to act fast to prevent Benjamin Dice from finding a way to keep Sherry from her. If in possession of her youngest daughter, she assumed she would be in control of Sherry's portion of the Simpson fortune. Her staff's buggy needed to be returned before the caretaker awoke, so Esther gave the horse several lashes to keep him moving through the empty streets to accomplish her mission.

On the way to her former home, Esther reviewed the possibilities for entering the house without being detected. Knowing there was a watchman on site, she assumed the man would be concentrating on the backyard and the main entrances. The staff members at the Simpson home were not dedicated employees, so she knew they were never concerned with what went on within the household after they retired.

That night, Esther took care to park the horse and buggy in

a grove of trees beyond the house. Then she sneaked through the shrubbery to the tiny door which opened onto the first landing on the cellar stairs. Her hunch had been correct. The door was left unlocked. After having slipped inside, Esther hurried to the study where Harold stored his mother's jewelry. Having discovered and memorized the safe's combination years before, she wasted no time in helping herself to the jewels that would have been part of her daughter's inheritance. Then she made her way to Sherry's bedroom with the ease of an alley cat.

Upon entering the room, she found Sherry snuggled with her doll, Molly, and sleeping peacefully. Esther lit a candle, grabbed a bag from the closet, and shoved the child's clothing inside. Then she walked over to Sherry and placed her hand over her daughter's mouth, frightening the little girl awake. "Hush, Sherry!" she whispered loudly. "It's Mother. Get your clothes on. You're going to your grandparents. Your father's *dead*, so you're to live with me now."

Sherry cried out, "No. No. Not my Daddy!" Having been told in such a cruel way that her father had died was devastating. Instead of comforting her daughter, Esther took the little one by the shoulders and gave her a good shaking. "You hush, now! I don't want anyone to hear us. Get these clothes on."

The child was so alarmed by her mother's harsh treatment that she quieted out of fear. Then Esther removed Sherry from the sanctuary of her home, not caring that her little girl was traumatized.

When Esther reached her parents' house, she parked at the back and broke a door window to gain entrance. Sherry was left alone, trembling in the dark foyer while Esther went to rally her father.

"What are you doing here at this hour? I might have shot you if I'd heard the window breaking. What on earth is going on that couldn't wait until a decent hour?"

As he and his daughter entered the parlor, Elmer Snodd was so disgusted that he yanked the ties on his robe so tightly it pained him.

"There's been a fire at the shipping company. Harold died in the fire, and I'm fearful that Delbert was responsible." Esther tried to act as though she was concerned for her son.

Elmer shut the door to the parlor so his wife would not hear but was still unaware that Sherry had been left in the foyer and was overhearing the horrible details of her father's death. The little girl was mortified beyond words and fell to the floor in aguish, too shaken to even cry aloud.

"Harold was burned in the fire? Surely not! When did the authorities contact you about the death?"

Esther suddenly realized she had divulged too much information. "They haven't informed me. I saw the fire from my window and feared Delbert had followed through with his drunken threats to set fire to the company. It's Harold's night to work late, and Delbert has been furious with his father for leaving us destitute." Esther paused as she nervously fiddled with the collar on her cape.

"And there is something else you must know. I knew Dice would look for a way to keep Sherry from me, so I went directly to fetch her before he had the chance."

Snodd paced back and forth. "I thought you were barred from the house, and Harold has a watchman on the property? How did you get her?"

"I used the tiny cellar door on the side of the house, and I simply walked in and took my child without being noticed." Esther foolishly presented the facts of her devious plan, thinking herself to be quite clever.

"You took the child without telling anyone? Where on earth is she?"

"I left her in your back foyer. I want you and mother to keep her until I can make proper arrangements. As her guardian and mother, I will soon be moving back into the Simpson home." Esther strutted the room as she imparted her expectations.

"Now, I wouldn't be so hasty in drawing such a conclusion if I were you. What was in the legal agreement between you and Harold concerning the child? I need to see the documents to ascertain who has legal custody. You told me Harold had disinherited you. But then he signed papers making you the child's legal guardian if something happened to him? That doesn't make sense." Her father was not convinced of her confident scheme.

"I. . . I don't exactly know what I signed. The lawyer was explaining the papers to me. He did tell me to read them, but I didn't. I wasn't concerned about it at the time. I just wanted to leave. Once I understood they were aware of my. . . *our* indiscretions, the last thing I wanted was to end up in court. Father! Dice's findings would have exposed us publicly and ruined us. I couldn't risk it."

Esther began wringing her hands and pacing with her father.

"Are you crazy? Do you know what taking the child might mean? No, you take the child with you. I can't be part of this. You get me those legal papers too."

"I can't take her to my home. The house staff is completely dedicated to Harold and Dice. They can't know that we have the child. You must keep her here. There's no alternative." Finally having realized she could be jailed for kidnapping her own daughter, Esther panicked.

"Now, explain this nonsense about Delbert!"

"No, I don't have time. I need to get home before I'm missed." Esther ran from the room to avoid further questioning from her father. Then she disappeared into the night, leaving Sherry on the foyer floor and Esther's father uninformed of the details of Delbert's entanglement in the fire and the death of Harold Simpson.

Elmer Snodd, so infuriated by Esther's exploits, returned to bed—forgetting that his young and frightened granddaughter was alone in the dark foyer.

✦

When Edna Snodd descended the stairs the next morning, she discovered Sherry in a heap on the floor.

"My goodness, Sherry! What are you doing here? Get up and come with me to the sitting room." Edna grabbed her by the hand and pulled the child to her feet.

Sherry, being in anguish, disoriented, and frightened, made no attempt to answer her grandmother.

"Well, child, speak up." Her grandmother waited. "Answer me! Honestly, I have no time for this. Come sit down. I'll speak to your grandfather to find out what on earth is going on with you."

Again, Sherry was left with her heart torn—lonely and afraid, with no one to recognize her trauma or to share her grief. Worst of all, there was no one to trust. She sat frozen—her eyes fixed as if disconnected from the reality that surrounded her.

Other than when her grandmother had dropped off a few stale

finger-sandwiches and weak tea, Sherry was left in the parlor to fend for herself.

✦

When brought before the judge, Delbert was shocked at the many charges made against him, but none struck him as deeply as the one for attempted murder.

"The attempted murder charge will be changed to a first-degree murder charge if your father passes as expected. *Son*—and I use the term lightly—you will be held without bail!"

"Judge, I didn't do it! I would never try to kill my own father! You have to listen! It wasn't me!" Delbert turned to his mother who had shown up in court in her most conservative dress, hat, and hairstyle. "Mother, tell them! I was drunk!" Delbert, seeing his mother was not coming to his defense, suddenly understood.

"It was you! You *used* me! Tell them! I could be hanged!"

"Order in the court!" The judge yelled as he hammered the gavel. "Keep this up, and I will add contempt to the charges. Get him out of here!"

Benjamin Dice closely watched the exchange between mother and son. Esther pretended to be both humble and hurt. She played the loving mother who understood her son's accusation as cries of desperation and grasping for straws. Her performance was believed by most in the room, but Benjamin Dice knew Esther Simpson was a woman devoid of feelings. He watched as Delbert's dumbstruck expression reflected the sudden realization that his mother's deceitful manipulation had transformed him into a malicious brute who would do her bidding. Esther saw it too—but did not care.

Delbert's devious mother exited the court room a free woman, and Delbert had been unsuccessful in his attempt to expose her as the mastermind of the company fire and attempted murder. Fortunately for Esther, her son was known as a dishonest troublemaker within the community, so his accusations in court were viewed as the rantings of the liar he was.

Her flawless plan to make Harold's murder look like an accident had not gone smoothly. It would have *if* Harold had not somehow survived the blow to the head and *if* the man's body had been so severely burned that the wound had gone undetected.

Following Esther from the court house, Elmer Snodd confronted his daughter. "Do you think I haven't figured this all out? If you were going to kill the man, you should've done a thorough job of it, and if you knew Delbert was coming to torch the place, why didn't you make certain Harold's body burned. The boy was drunk. He never would've known the difference.

"Listen, I'm not the only attorney who'll likely conclude that *you* were the mastermind and Delbert was only the accomplice in these crimes. You'll both be executed if Harold dies! And now, you've brought Sherry to my house and have placed me and your mother in the middle of this mess!

"And as for the custody papers you had delivered, I've looked them over, and you have absolutely no legal right to Sherry. You could be arrested for kidnapping. Come to the house and get her immediately!"

⚜

Esther did not follow her father's demands but went straight to her home. The housekeeper met her at the door. "Mrs. Simpson, I need to inform you that two police officers were here with papers to search the house. I had no choice but to let them. They did seize two or three items from what I could tell. I noticed one of them tagging your favorite hat. I'm afraid that's all I know of the matter. May I be so bold as to ask how Mr. Simpson is doing?"

"You're cozy enough with him. Find out for yourself." Being in such a hurry, Esther tripped on the steps trying to get to her room.

She had no intention of fetching Sherry from her parents' home. Esther pulled her bags from the closet and began to pack her most valuable gowns. She was leaving for New York City where no one would find her.

Within the hour she had lowered the two huge travel bags from her window, taken the unused servants' stairway to collect them, and carried the overstuffed bags to the train station nearby. Esther decided to take the first train out of town and find her way to the city by an alternative route. Once settled in New York, Esther planned to sell the Simpson jewelry and live quite comfortably.

26

TERRIFIED

Benjamin Dice raced from the court room as soon as he received the message. *How could this have happened? What type an incompetent staff does Harold have within his household? He has taken steps to secure every other matter in his life, so why didn't he make certain his staff was trustworthy and loyal? I'll dismiss them all if necessary.*

The coachman drove the distance to the Simpson home in record time. Benjamin Dice leaped from the carriage before it came to a complete stop and impatiently pounded on the front door.

The head housekeeper, Elsa, showed him in, trying not to make eye contact.

"Gather the entire staff immediately! The police are on the way, and I want to get to the bottom of this. I can't believe you were all so inattentive."

Elsa scrambled to gather the others, knowing her job was at stake since the child was assigned to her care. Fortunately, it took only a few minutes for the help to assemble in the foyer.

"How did it happen that the Mr. Simpson's entire staff had not noticed Sherry was missing until this late in the afternoon." He paused and waited, but no one seemed willing to answer.

Finally, one of the girls from the kitchen spoke up. "When she didn't come down for breakfast, I took a tray to her room. I thought she was asleep, so I left the meal on the tea table. When she didn't come down for the noon meal, I knocked on the door and told her the tray was outside the door if she was hungry. I assumed she'd been told about her father and was too upset to eat. I'm extremely sorry I didn't wait for her to reply."

"Understandable on your part, I suppose. Who oversees her care?" he demanded.

The head housekeeper spoke up, "We all share the chore, but I assume the main responsibility is mine." Knowing, as head housekeeper, the child's welfare was definitely in her job description caused her shoulders to develop an involuntary twitch.

Then trying to pass the blame, she continued, "I don't believe it was my responsibility to tell the child her father was near death. I assumed someone such as yourself or her mother would be along to speak with her. We are accustomed to Miss Sherry staying in her room for hours at a time and running the grounds unsupervised at will. We *do* have other duties to perform."

"I don't recall asking you to inform the child of her father's misfortune. . . but I am informing you that not knowing the child's whereabouts at any given time is neglecting your duty. We will address this matter later."

There was a sudden knock on the door, and three officers were ushered in. At that point, the police began their inquiry into what might have happened to Sherry Simpson. Each staff member was given a full and lengthy interview.

But Benjamin Dice did not need an investigation to know Esther Simpson was responsible for the kidnapping and reprimanded himself for not being sharp enough to come for the little darling immediately after the fire.

✦

Attorney Snodd slammed his fist on the dining room table. "No, Edna. I'm not going to find Esther. Esther has likely packed her bags and left town. They know the child is missing by now. That will throw suspicion on us. But rest assured, I'm not going to get caught with her. I'll be back in an hour. Get the child ready for traveling and choose a bonnet that hides her face. She won't be spending the night."

✦

"Come in, man! I don't want anyone to see us together." Snodd was not pleased with the man he had hired as a chaperone, but he was in no position to be choosey.

"Edna! Come here. We have work to do."

"Who is this? He's perfectly filthy." Edna covered her nose with the back of her hand in disgust.

"Never mind who he is. The less we know of him, the better. Draw him a bath so he can bathe and try to give him a haircut. Then find one of my old suits and give it a good pressing. He must look like a gentleman when we're done." The attorney was determined to take care of the situation in short order.

When Mrs. Snodd completed her husband's demands, the bum looked somewhat the part of a gentleman. Then she and El-mer coached the man in etiquette in an attempt to keep him from drawing attention. Once he was given the address and the necessary instructions, Sherry was summoned.

"Now remember, bud. . . watch your manners when eating and don't talk to anyone unless it's absolutely necessary. Do *not* bring undo attention to yourself.

"I've already telegraphed your contact. Follow the instructions exactly and you'll receive payment upon your arrival with the child. Once you've made the delivery, I never want to hear of you being in Grandville again. Do you get my meaning?"

The man lifted his head slightly to indicate he understood, then grabbed Sherry by the arm and started for the door.

"Don't grab her like that, you imbecile! You must treat her like your daughter—a little lady. Show him, Edna." She then demonstrated how to accompany the child and had the man practice.

A short time afterward, the Snodds handed their terrified granddaughter over to a complete stranger of seedy character—who then was expected to deliver the child to another person of questionable character.

❧

When it was time for them to board the train, the man was itching to take control of the child. Seizing the opportunity to boss someone around, he bent down and looked at her with his beady eyes. "Now ya listen here, girlie. Ya do as I says, when I says, and only if I says. . . and if ya don't, I'll surely give ya a beatin' ya won't forget. Ya hear, girl. I'm only doin' this for the money, so I don't cares what happens ta ya and neither does yer grandpappy." He grabbed her arm tightly and pulled her toward the awaiting coach.

Sherry took the seat beside him, still fearing for her safety.

She wanted her daddy, but her daddy was dead. Danielle was the only other person who cared for her, and she was gone too. *Jesus, please help me.*

✦

It was a hot night on the train, and even the open window did not seem to offer relief. The man who was her keeper removed a bottle from an inner pocket of his jacket and took another drink. He finally dropped off to sleep, allowing Sherry a moment to relax.

Early the next morning, ignoring all tutoring given by the Snodds, the vagrant took his ward by the arm and led her from the train and into a restaurant for breakfast. Sherry just pointed to something on the menu when the waitress took the order. The lady returned with bacon, eggs, toast, and hot cakes for the stranger and a bowl of oatmeal for the child. Sherry tried to give the impression of taking several bites so the man would not get upset. Her little hand trembled each time she raised the spoon to her mouth.

After the meal, they re-boarded a train, but Sherry was too shaken to tell if it was the same one. The man gave her a controlling sneer and pushed her down into the seat. The time seemed to creep minute by minute.

During the rest of the ride, the bum frequently removed a bottle from inside his suit pocket and took a drink. Once again Sherry was relieved when he fell into a deep sleep, allowing her to doze without him constantly eyeing her.

When they reached their stop, the stranger again took Sherry by the arm, intentionally squeezing it to cause pain as he steered her from the car and onto the platform. Then he stooped down to where they were eye level. "Now ya do ever thing I's tells ya to.

Ya understands me?" He waited for her to reply. "Answer me, ya stubborn, li'l goat." This time his voice was even more threatening.

When Sherry didn't reply, he pulled the child to the side of a building and picked up a stick from the ground. "I'll teach ya not ta answer me." He then struck her on the back. It was not until the third strike that a strong hand reached out and grabbed the bum's wrist, bringing the intended strike to a halt in midair.

"I'll not stand by and watch you beat a little girl." The husky guy gave the bum a shove, causing him to land on the ground with a hard thud. He then cried out in fear while trying to crawl backward to escape what he expected to follow. The huge man grabbed his arm in a vice-like grip and pulled him to his feet.

About that time a horse and wagon passed between Sherry and the men. Even while still feeling the effects of the beating, she used the interruption to escape from her captor and whatever fate her grandfather had in mind. Unfortunately, instead of running toward the people gathered to watch the altercation, she crossed the tracks and ran up into the woods.

"She a mean'n. Dats wa I whooped 'er." It then registered that he had given himself away.

"You're no gentleman! Why are you dressed to look like one? I'm taking you to the police."

When the rescuer leaned down to pick up his hat, the bum kicked the guy in the knee, causing him to loosen his grip. He then wrenched his arm free, burst through the crowd, and headed toward downtown.

Afraid the vicious stranger was close behind, Sherry forced herself to keep moving. Being wise enough to weave through the thicket slowed her down but allowed her to run a longer distance before becoming winded and giving in to the pain in her side. After resting, she walked aimlessly for several more hours, but by then, Sherry knew it had been a mistake to run into the forest. Yet she had come too far to turn back and no longer knew which direction the town was. Lost and confused about what to do next, she could no longer keep herself from crying. The child sat down between two boulders to hide and drifted into a deep sleep.

The noise that woke Sherry seemed deafening. She scuffled to sit up and peek over the rock. There, only a few feet away, a bear stood on its hind legs, exposing its teeth while making slow sweeping movements with its head. The frightened child then noticed the cubs not far away. The face of Harold Simpson flashed through her mind. She knew that no matter what happened, he was waiting for her in Heaven.

Sherry bravely prepared herself to be mulled.

The snarling bear charged directly toward her. As she braced herself, another black bear stormed forward, lunging and sinking its teeth into the mother bear's shoulder. She retaliated by digging her jagged teeth into the other bear's neck. Their intimidating roars echoed throughout the woods. As they wrestled, their bodies slammed against the rocks which sheltered Sherry. Then their aggressive battling began to move them farther away as they attacked one another again and again.

Thinking quickly, Sherry crawled from the rocks and edged from tree to tree away from the area. Once out of range, the terror-stricken girl began to run, continuing to push her way into the dense forest.

Her escape was long and arduous. Sweat on her neck and face

from the heat brought menacing gnats and swarms of mosquitoes, raising numerous, itchy welts. After two days with little food, even the berries looked tempting, but knowing they might be poisonous, Sherry trudged on—hungry and distraught.

Late in the day, Sherry heard an eerie sound that convinced her someone was following close by. Fearing the abusive derelict had finally located her, she ran wildly on, giving no thought to her surroundings. The shadows in the forest made it impossible to distinguish that the rise she had ascended was a ridge running along a creek bed. The little girl found herself tumbling down a steep, rocky hill, suffering painful cuts and scrapes, and eventually plunging into the swiftly moving waters. Choking on gulps of creek water, she coughed violently as the current pulled her along and under.

✦

It was completely dark when Sherry regained consciousness and felt the sand and gravel beneath her. She could feel the roughness of the log that held her in place against the flow of the creek. Sherry could not swim and knew that only the hand of God had kept her from drowning.

By then, the multiple scrapes and bruises had become extremely painful for the little girl. To make things worse, it was a cold night. Sherry was wet, chilled, and shivering with no hope of relief. There was a sharp pain in her chest and left arm. The slightest movement of either brought tears to her eyes. Unfortunately, she had no choice but to find a way to get to her feet. The challenge proved to be agonizing. She wanted to find a place of refuge there, but was fearful of snakes near the creek bank and preferred to face the other dangers that might be lurking in the woods at night.

Jesus, I'm scared.

Trusting Him, the little girl walked away from the creek and back into the forest.

As Sherry staggered on, the unquieted grief within her heart was even more painful than what she was enduring within her body. Adding to what she had already faced, she was beginning to feel ill and was developing a wheezing cough. Until the recent traumatic events in her family, Sherry had never known any form of hardship. Now, hardship had crept in and was totally enveloping her life.

Feeling herself becoming weaker with each step, Sherry thought it would be impossible to get back up if she fell. It was then that a hint of light flashed in the distance. The sun was rising. She had been unconscious on the creek bank much longer than she had imagined.

The dawning sun soon exposed a dirt road, bringing her hope. In anticipation of finding help, Sherry tried to run, expending energy that could not be spared. Stepping from the woods, the exhausted, little girl began to feel faint and collapsed by the roadside.

⚜

"I told ya not ta touch that white girl. Nothin' ta do with us. Stay on the road, and I mean what I say!" the dark-skinned father nervously warned his son.

"But Papa, she's lookin' bad. Can't leave 'er," the oldest boy pleaded.

"Ya touch that girl and no tellin' what trouble it might cause us. Cover 'er face with somethin' so she don't get too burnt. Look at thum clothes. She's a rich one. Someone'll be along fer 'er. I'd help 'er, but I gotta protect muh own family first. Too dangerous.

We hafta leave 'er."

The family of five walked on—each burdened by the decision.

Rand, for his own safety, had followed the family on his way home from town. Although he had heard the father's advice, he did not heed it himself. Once the group was out of sight, he scooped Sherry into his arms and headed into the woods.

The tall, muscular, young man banged on the door—his dark forehead dripping with sweat, "Miss Zelda, it's Rand. Please hurry, ma'am!" He could hear the woman moving around inside the tiny cabin. It seemed an eternity before she reached the door.

"What is it?"

Rand pushed past the nurse and carried Sherry to the cot-like table used for examinations. "Miss Zelda, I know ya got your trainin' ta work with us folks, but ya have ta look at this white girl. She's bad off."

Zelda followed as she tried to analyze the patient's condition. "She sure is. Fetch me some water. How did you come by her?"

Rand grabbed the bucket to head for the well but stopped long enough to answer. "I was followin' a family back from town, and they passed 'er up. The dad wouldn't take the chance of bein' seen with 'er. Anyway, she was layin' unconscious beside the road. I just couldn't leave 'er. I was afraid she'd die in the heat."

"I can't blame them, Rand—even though I'm ashamed to say it."

Rand went for the water while Zelda undressed the child and discovered the bruises on her back along with multiple cuts and scrapes. She covered Sherry with sheets so Rand could come in. "Take a look at this. She's been beaten." Doc Zelda pulled back the cover just enough to expose the marks. "The rest of her injuries could be from falls. Any idea at all where she came from?"

"One of the towns, I reckon. They're all 'bout the same distance from where I found 'er."

"Well, I need to get some liquids down her. I don't like the sound of that cough either. And she's chilling, even in this heat. This isn't any average child. Look at that dress. She comes from money." Even so, Doc Zelda was genuinely concerned for the little, white girl who had mysteriously appeared in their woods.

"I'm sorry, Doc. I hate ta leave ya hangin' with this one, but I have ta ask ya not ta tell who brought 'er here. I might be blamed for what happened ta 'er. I'm sorry I involved ya." Rand felt like a coward but knew it could cost him his life by just being involved in the situation.

"Sure, Rand. I'll keep it to myself. And I'll take good care of her. The little thing's been through a lot for some reason. Although I'll have to give this situation some serious thought myself before I chance reporting her to the authorities." Zelda smiled at the kindhearted boy. "Now you take on out of here and make sure no one sees you."

✦

Zelda was wearing a grave expression after completing the examination. She had treated several lacerations and wrapped the child's chest to protect her ribs. All were injuries which would heal in time. However, she was especially worried about the raspy cough, which apparently was caused by fluids that had aspirated into the child's lungs.

Zelda Fields was an excellent, young nurse who had received

her current training under the watchful eye of Dr. Kent Fields, her adoptive father. She had grown up in a white community with many advantages and was the sole heir of her parents' estate. Since being told her birth parents had died of a fever, she had dreamed of working among her people as a physician. In honor of both sets of parents, Zelda was determined to earn a medical degree and was actively seeking a college that would accept ladies of color.

But her immediate concern was her patient on the cot who was fighting a high fever. She only hoped the child had not fallen into the waters at the Burr Creek crossing where most of the cattle in the area watered. The water there would be contaminated, and it would not do for bacterial pneumonia to set in.

27

THE GIFT

Hunter pulled into Hattie's drive with the hopeful excuse of familiarizing his favorite student with a different breed of horse and type of buggy. It was an impromptu visit, but he was able to catch Danielle just as she was leaving the yard to take a walk by Willow Creek. He slipped over and took her by the hand. "And where do you think you're going. You have a driving lesson tonight."

Flustered by his sudden appearance, Danielle began to apologize. "I'm so sorry. It completely slipped my mind. I just— Wait a minute. This is my night to sew. You know that. We have no such plans." She cocked her head suspiciously. "So, what brings you here? Be truthful." She arched her eyebrows and waited.

"Can't a guy surprise his girl. . . *a* girl. . . with a riding lesson on a great day like this?" Hunter, not necessarily regretting the slip of the tongue, continued his case. "With everything that has unfolded in your life lately, I thought you might need to relax and clear your head."

Danielle heard the slip, and while it may not have been what he meant to say, she hoped it was what he had wanted to say. "That's very thoughtful. Thank you for caring enough to take the time."

"I do care, Danielle. . . a lot. . . and I have at least one reason to believe you might care for me." Hunter raised his hand to show that their fingers were intertwined.

Danielle gave a hesitant smile but did not deny his claim. Not certain how to reply, she turned toward the bridge.

"Listen, there's something I'd like to explain to you about Sally Meeker."

Danielle's heart dropped at hearing Hunter bring up the girl's name, and she began to prepare herself for what he might say.

"It's been brought to my attention that I've been giving the wrong impression when it comes to Sally and myself. I want you to know that I'm not—nor have I ever been—the least bit interested in her. I only felt obligated, as a gentleman, to escort her home when she asked. It didn't occur to me the gesture might be viewed as some type of relationship between us."

"So, you're saying the two of you *aren't* a couple?" Danielle had not meant to interrupt him—especially since it made her look overly enthusiastic.

"Like I said. There's absolutely nothing going on between us. There never has been and there never will be. I'm sorry if my actions were misleading. Just didn't think the situation through. To be honest, I found the whole ordeal with Sally irritating—not that I'm insinuating she isn't a fine girl. Actually, I hardly know anything about her." The confession made him feel awkward and naïve.

"I can understand how you felt obligated as a gentleman. . . but you don't owe me an explanation. We've never discussed the possibility of there being anything between us."

"That's the *point,* Danielle. I do want there to be something between us. I have since the first day we met. I can't believe you haven't noticed." Hunter gave her a crooked smile which had a little bit of teasing mixed in. "So now. . . I'm asking *you* to be truthful."

Danielle smiled—apprehensive and embarrassed to answer. "I must admit there were certain actions on your behalf, here and there, that indicated you might be interested in me, but then Sally would show up. I was left to draw my own conclusions. Then. . . when she confronted me at the engagement party— "

"What do you mean? Did it concern me?"

"She basically told me to stay away from you because I was causing trouble in your relationship. . . and if I didn't, I would be sorry."

"Danielle, I never would've guessed Sally was so manipulative."

"I wasn't certain what to believe."

Hunter stopped and took both of her hands in his. "Danielle, I want you to understand that you are the only girl I've ever truly cared about or have wanted to be with. Will you please consent to my seeing you on a regular basis? I want to know that you're *my girl*."

Danielle, completely stunned by his words of commitment, was left nearly breathless. "Hunter. . . of course, I will."

He breathed a sigh of relief and gave her a wink.

"Then I need to speak with your grandfather."

Danielle lovingly took his arm as the two made their way to the buggy. She looked at Hunter trustingly, free to allow her eyes to meet his without a hint of guilt. And while doing so, she realized she had fallen in love with Hunter Jackson.

On her next visit to the farm, Danielle brought Mercy to a halt in front of her family home. Again, Joshua was waiting on the porch, eager to give her a welcoming hug. She did not need to wonder if her grandfather's love was unconditional. It was evident in his eyes and in the way he pampered her. Danielle hoped he felt that same love in return.

Joshua Harrison was handsome and agile for his age. It was plain to see a hard day's work would not faze him. One only had to meet Joshua to know he was extremely wise, honest, and caring. Danielle believed her own father would have been equal in character. The thought made her proud to be a Harrison, but it saddened her to think the last years of her father's life were spent in misery and turmoil.

"My dear Dani, I can hardly believe you're finally here for me to spoil until my heart's content. I have a lot of making up to do in that department, so I shall lavish you with love and gifts to the best of my ability for as long as I'm able. Which means. . . before we tour the farm, I want to introduce you to your first gift."

"Grandpa, meeting you is all the spoiling I've ever needed."

Joshua put his hand to her cheek for a moment, as if to make certain he was not dreaming. Then going to the back of the carriage, he collected the bags Danielle had brought for her visit. "Now if we hurry, we can take a gander at that present. . . and the property. . . and not be late for the special dinner Lacresha has planned."

As he sat the bags on the porch, Joshua suddenly recognized the black one with the ring of red roses woven into it and the other one with wildflowers as being those Esther had stolen from his own darling wife. He took only a few seconds to recall the incident and thank God that Valerie's beloved bags had returned. Then he rushed his granddaughter off to the barn.

Joshua grabbed the door handle and slid it wide open, causing time to momentarily stand still for Danielle. She had not expected to see Hunter standing there with his sleeves rolled up exposing the muscles in his upper arms.

"Well, my sweet Dani, what do you think of her?" Joshua's voice jolted Danielle back into the moment. "She was bred from a prizewinning stallion, and I want you to have her."

Hunter proudly led the animal forward for her inspection. Danielle's eyes finally moved from Hunter to the horse. She took in a deep breath at the majesty of the mare. It was an Arabian with a sorrel coat that shined like a new penny. Her long mane and finely chiseled head made a dramatic impression.

Grandpa Harrison put his arm around his granddaughter's shoulders. "I chose this mare because you're a novice. She's good natured and calm, about five in years and fifteen hands, if I remember correctly. I thought the two of you would be the right match. She has the fine lines that a lot of the ladies like in a horse and moves likc a ship on calm waters. The gal is trained and ready to ride."

"Oh, Grandpa! She's amazing! I'm not accustomed to receiving gifts— and never extravagant ones. Are you certain? She must be worth a fortune."

"Of course I'm certain or we wouldn't be here. I want you to have the best of everything. Now go over and take a good look."

Danielle walked toward the horse, noting each lovely curve. She reached out to gently stroke the mare's neck while speaking softly to her. The horse gently nuzzled her nose into Danielle's shoulder as she slipped her arms around the mare's neck.

"Thank you, Grandpa. I never allowed myself to dream of owning my own horse." Danielle left the mare's side long enough to squeeze her grandpa tightly and kiss his cheek.

"Well, it's worth every cent to know she means so much to you, but you'll want to come up with a more fitting name. This fine animal deserves a more original name than *Sugar*.

"Lessons will begin tomorrow, my dear. I might need to mention that I'd like you to train on a cross saddle to start. I don't care what silly opinions people have on the subject of lady riders. I feel riding astride is safer. If you like, you can take on the sidesaddle once you've had a decent amount of experience. Of course, it's your decision."

After spending some time with Sugar, Joshua and Hunter took Danielle on an extensive tour of the Harrison farm. The trio surveyed the barns and stable before taking a wagon ride to view the crops and the orchard near the pond. The final stop was an emotional visit to the family cemetery where Danielle was shown her father's and grandmother's graves. It was a peaceful setting where she knew she would be spending time.

Once dinner was over, Lacresha and Jerry decided to stay for a while to visit with Danielle. As it turned out, they all enjoyed themselves so much that it was quite late before everyone decided to retire.

However, after the others had departed, Hunter lingered. "Speak up, boy. Obviously you have something on your mind. What is it?"

"Well, since you put it that way, I guess I'll get to it. I haven't mentioned this to you, but since your granddaughter has moved to Willow Weep, I have become very fond of her. You know my character—"

"I would have to be quite senile not to notice there is an attraction between the two of you. Why else would you drive Dani home the night of the party, escort the girl here for her first visit, and show up just before she arrived this afternoon?"

Hunter chuckled at his friend's observation. "Well, then, I would like to have your permission to court Danielle."

"Of course, son, you have my permission. . . but I do ask you to consider how deep your affection is for Dani. I'm being blunt, but you must understand where I'm coming from. She has had a lonely and hurtful upbringing, and I don't want to see her further devastated by someone's careless infatuation. Be honest with your feelings, but please don't speak to her of love and the like unless you're absolutely certain. Pray before you speak. I'm not talking about breathing a prayer. I'm saying pray it through until you know God's will. Feelings do grow stronger over time, but they can also fade. I'm asking you to be careful with her heart and not mislead her."

Hunter gave a nod. "I can understand that you don't want us to rush into anything. I assure you I'll be careful."

But in his heart, Hunter felt he was more than ready to profess his love to Danielle.

28

STAY WITH ME

"Come over here, darlin'. I want you to see your new saddle. I picked it out because it's on the smaller side and doesn't weigh as much. But we have all types of saddles around here. You're welcome to use any of them. Valerie loved the English saddles and only tolerated the sidesaddle when need be."

"Thank you, Grandpa. It's beautiful! You didn't need to buy me a special saddle. I'm sure any of the others would've been adequate." Danielle ran her hand over the fine leather which had been painstakingly tooled with roses and other adornment, indicating it had been costly.

Joshua walked over and placed his hand on another saddle. "You might like this western one to start your training with. It's the type of saddle you'll see me using on *and* off the farm. I have no interest in the English ones. Hunter has volunteered to teach you the English riding styles. . . if you're interested. The young man is well versed in English and western—quite accomplished compared to most."

"I don't actually know the difference. I've only heard my brother and sister talk of riding. All three of my siblings have horses."

Danielle mentioned it nonchalantly, even though the thought hurt her deeply.

"I don't believe there's a great difference, but I think it's advisable for you to get at least a little training in both styles—then the sidesaddle. Well, at least we're approaching the twentieth century. The day is coming when ladies will completely abandon the method. However, Lacresha has agreed to take on the challenge. She's an impressive rider, especially when it comes to the sidesaddle. It's still an unfortunate necessity in public."

Joshua stopped speaking long enough to imprint this memory in his mind. He was finally spending time with his granddaughter after so many years of praying for the privilege. Knowing he was living a miracle, he offered a prayer of thanksgiving in his heart.

"Well, if you're ready for your first lesson, let's get—"

"Trinity!" Danielle smiled at her grandfather. "Actually, I'd like to give her two names. . . if it's acceptable to you. . . Trinity's Rapture."

"Trinity's Rapture. In reference to Christ's return? Nice! The name suits her. It'll look good on her papers.

"Well then, I believe we need to fetch Trinity's tack. Time to get her saddled up."

It was not long until Joshua and Dani were riding across the meadow together—as they always should have been.

⚜

Hunter had asked permission to drive Danielle back to Willow Weep, so she and Grandpa sat on the porch steps waiting for her escort to arrive. It was a pleasant summer evening, and they both were happy to have a few extra moments in each other's company.

Even though Joshua was not certain he should approach the subject, he had prepared a speech and could not bring himself to put it off. In his opinion, enough time already had been wasted. "It may be a might early to discuss such a lofty subject, and I do realize you have just settled in and feel comfortable in Willow Weep. . . but. . . I want to ask you to consider coming to live here on the farm. After all, this is your rightful home, and we've been separated far too long."

Danielle did not speak. The question had taken her by surprise. There were so many things to consider before making such a move. Rosa and Hattie first came to mind. Yet the thought of having a proper home where she was wanted and loved was tempting.

"Grandpa, thank you so very much for the invitation. It's the most desirous offer I've ever had. It's not that I don't want to come live with you. It's just that I feel an obligation to Rosa and Hattie because of their generosity toward me when I first arrived in Willow Weep. I owe them so much."

Joshua hesitated to make certain that his reply did not sound demanding. "I understand completely. They certainly have been your devoted mentors. But I also know that Rosa and Hattie are compassionate and understanding ladies who wouldn't want to stand in the way of your happiness.

"Maybe we can come up with a compromise. Why don't you move here and keep your job until you feel comfortable in leaving? I can provide you with transportation. I know it isn't ideal. . . but if it would give you peace of mind—"

"But what about Hattie? She isn't doing well and has come to depend on me."

"I do understand you have details to work out, so I'm only asking you to give the move some serious thought. Pray on it. God didn't bring you this far and not have a complete plan for your life.

He has the answer."

"Grandpa, as far as I'm concerned, I'd move to the farm tomorrow. It's just a matter of coming up with something satisfactory for everyone. Like you said, I need to give the move serious thought and spend time in prayer. He'll make a way."

"Well then, Dani dear, let's not wait to begin our praying." Joshua took his granddaughter's hand, and they shared the first of many prayers which would guide their family through the years to come.

⁕

Hunter gave Mercy a little encouragement with the reins. "I asked Joshua for permission to court you."

"You did? What was his answer?" Danielle squeezed his hand, excited that Hunter had taken the initiative to speak with her grandfather.

"Of course he gave me permission. . . along with a stiff lecture not to break your heart."

"And no warning that I might break yours?" They shared a playful look.

Then Hunter became serious. "I would never intentionally break your heart, Danielle."

She only smiled demurely, but those words had caused her heart to open up to his love even more.

By then the carriage was out of view of the Harrison farmhouse. Hunter lovingly put his arm around Danielle's waist and pulled her close. "I guess having your grandfather's consent officially makes you my girl."

Danielle leaned her head on his shoulder, happy to know they belonged to one another. Hunter bit his lip to control his satisfied smile as she cuddled up to him.

Not long after, Hunter took a side road and eventually pulled over as they entered a canopy of trees. Danielle was a little suspicious as he helped her from the carriage. "You're being mysterious. So. . . why are we here?"

Hunter winked at Danielle and brushed her cheek with a kiss. He then took her hand and led her toward a well-worn path.

"It's slippery here, so watch your step."

"What's that roaring sound? I've never heard it before."

"Just a minute longer. It's worth the wait."

The noise gradually became louder as the path took them through a series of rock formations and ended in front of a cascading waterfall. The sun streaming through the mist created a rainbow on the billowing water below. Danielle was in awe of the scene before her.

"It's magnificent. I've never seen a waterfall. May we stay awhile?"

Hunter extended his hand toward a large willow. A picnic basket sat on a quilt beneath the tree.

"Hunter, you never fail to amaze me. When we first met, you seemed so—"

"So *what*? Don't leave me hanging."

"We'd better let it go."

"No. I'd like to know your first impression of me."

"Remember, I warned you. Well, one of my first impressions was that you were much too blunt and bossy."

"Okay, I can handle that. But you sidestepped the real question. I want to know what your exact first impression was. You're hiding something." Hunter placed his hand against the rock wall beside Danielle to indicate he was waiting.

"All right then. . . I thought you were extremely handsome."

"Handsome?" Considering their explosive encounter and how frightened she was, Hunter had not expected her first impression to be so complimentary. He recalled how demanding he had been after finding her in such a dangerous position with the Brewster boys.

"It may not have been my first thought when I happened across you and the Brewster boys, but once they had moved on, I thought you to be the loveliest girl I'd ever seen. You are, you know."

"Truly?"

Hunter recognized the question as being sincere. "Truly."

Her eyes twinkled as he gently ran a finger across her lips and felt their softness.

This time, he could not resist. Hunter tenderly lifted Danielle's chin and lovingly kissed her for the first time.

29

A DISTURBING LETTER

Later in the week, Danielle was relieved to find a letter in the mailbox from Jean. It had been far too long since she had heard from her dear friend. As always, the letter started out with news of the gardens and Everett's latest projects. Danielle could almost see the flowers in bloom and taste the sweet, sun-warmed tomatoes picked fresh from the vine. She could envision Everett in the workshop perfecting a piece of furniture and could nearly smell the scent of newly turned wood. As always, Jean's writing made Danielle feel as if she was standing right beside her friend witnessing it all in person.

Then the letter continued with the news from home:

> I have been withholding some disturbing news longer than I should have. I was hoping I would receive further information which might be a comfort to you. Unfortunately, I haven't.
>
> According to the newspaper, Harold Simpson has been badly injured during a fire at the shipping company. There were only two buildings which completely succumbed to the fire, one owned by the shipping company and the other owned by a neighboring business. Neither structure was

considered a great loss, but the fire did spread to the building which housed Mr. Simpson's office. God must have been looking after your stepfather because the authorities were informed of a potential fire early on. As a result, the office building was spared with only partial damage. Had the building not been saved, he might not have survived.

Evidently, Mr. Simpson had been working late at the office and, prior to or sometime during the fire, it has been established he was hit from behind, sustaining a life-threatening head injury. He also suffered from smoke inhalation which added to his fragile condition. At this time his fate cannot be determined.

No, Heavenly Father, not Harold! Danielle, shaken by the news, had to stop reading until she could contain her emotions.

I'm sorry to report that your brother Delbert was found lying outside the burning building and in his possession were a lighted torch and other items used in starting fires. During the arraignment, he did plead not guilty but was charged with arson and attempted murder. He's to be held in jail until the trial is concluded.

The staff at the Simpson home hasn't been out and about as usual, so I haven't been able to gather any further details.

I know your first instinct will be to return to Grandville, but I don't think it would be wise on your part. Harold Simpson will receive the best of care. I'm not certain what has happened to Sherry. It's my concern that your mother is

*enraged over her current circumstance, and you'd
be an easy target for her revenge. Please, I pray,
stay where you are, and I'll try to inform you
of any further news.*

*The best way to help is with fervent prayer for
all concerned. Your mother and brother need
to come to the Lord. Only Jesus can soothe a
troubled soul and spirit. Keep in mind that
our Heavenly Father can handle the situation
without your presence.*

Danielle's first concern was for Harold, whom she now loved for having been her father's devoted friend when he had needed him most. She refused to accept that Harold might be leaving this world but clung to the belief that she would someday see him face-to-face to thank him.

Then her thoughts went to Sherry. Danielle knew how cold the staff and Esther could be. The little darling would be left to face these horrible circumstances on her own.

Finally, her mind was swept away to Delbert, whose self-centered meanness had been molded by Esther for her own advantage. Danielle had no doubt that her mother was behind the attempted murder of Harold Simpson. Even though Delbert could be evil, she knew Esther *was* evil. Many of Delbert's attacks on Danielle had been conjured up by the woman herself.

No longer able to bear the depressing news alone, Danielle sought comfort in prayer.

Heavenly Father, I come to You in the name of Jesus.

I pray for your protection over Harold, Sherry, and Delbert who need your intervention. Please, touch Harold so he'll recover quickly and grant him the long and happy life he deserves.

I pray for my little Sherry who must feel scared and abandoned. Grant her comfort and love until she's reunited with her father.

As for Delbert, please don't allow him to be punished for crimes he didn't commit. Touch Delbert's hardened heart so his eyes will be opened to accept Jesus as his Savior.

And please, Dear Father, make it clear to me if I need to return to Grandville.

Amen.

This was not the only prayer that went up to Heaven from Danielle for the Simpson family—for she did seek the Lord often and fervently.

⟡

Ever since warm weather had set in, the Willow Inn had been booked to capacity and every minute of Danielle's workday was consumed with countless demands. Not to mention, spending time at the farm meant working late into the night to complete the dresses Helen needed.

Danielle was concerned that Madison had not even been told that she and Hunter were courting. When the two girls finally did arrange to meet on the back steps of the inn to talk and enjoy a cool breeze, it was not a time for sharing good news.

"Madison, what's wrong? You haven't seemed yourself lately."

"It's my sister. I do love her, but whatever I do at home seems to be wrong in her estimation. Tally is one who likes to do everything herself and then gets mad at me for not helping. No matter what needs doing, it must be done her way.

"I'm sure Tally wants me to move out. She's all but said it in words, and I'm beginning to believe it would be best for everyone.

The house is too small, and I never have any privacy."

"I'm certain your sister doesn't mean to make you feel that way. Caring for a home and your siblings must be monotonous. Tally is most likely just taking her frustrations out on you. She may feel trapped at home."

Danielle could tell her words had exasperated Madison and made her feel worse than she already did. Madison had needed someone to listen and empathize while she sorted through her feelings about her sister's behavior. She wasn't ready to reason.

"I don't think so. Tally has always said she would never marry. As far as I can tell she plans to live at home and look after father. Oh well, there's no use talking about it. I have no other options. Maybe I'd better get back inside. I have work to complete and a second shift to look forward to." Then the frustrated girl hastily disappeared through the kitchen door.

Madison had needed a friend, not a lecture. Unfortunately, the subject would have to be addressed again to set things right between them, and Danielle had no idea when that would be.

A couple evenings later, having caught up on the sewing for the mission, Danielle was on her way to the bench with a book when she found Hunter outside holding a bouquet of flowers. Danielle grabbed the flowers and gave him an excited hug.

"Thank you for the roses. They're beautiful. They're the first flowers I've ever received." She placed a kiss on his cheek.

"You're welcome, and it's an honor to know I'm the first to give you flowers. Now please tell me you're through sewing for the evening. I have plans for us."

"As a matter of fact, I'm all caught up. So, what do you have in mind?" She raised her eyebrows quizzically, certain Hunter was again going to keep the secret until the exact time for it to be revealed.

"I think you'll love this one. So, close your eyes and come with me." He took her hand and led her across the bridge. Once they crested the hill of Hattie's back driveway, he spun Danielle around three times just for the fun of it. "Okay. Open your eyes."

Danielle gasped. Tied behind Petra was Trinity, all decked out and ready to ride. "Grandpa allowed you to bring her all this way?"

"Well, there were a few promises made on my part, but I did get him to agree. I also have permission for Trinity to stay here until you head back to the farm. I had to promise to escort you on your next visit." Hunter made the statement as if it would be a burden.

She placed her hands on her hips and gave him a stern look as a reply. Then shook her head and gave an adoring smile.

"'Umm, I forgot the sidesaddle," Hunter admitted. "Not sure what to do about that. Didn't even cross my mind when I saddled her up."

Danielle pressed her lips together while studying the oversight, then shrugged. "I don't know how to ride a sidesaddle anyway."

Hunter laughed, "I'd better check to see if Hattie has one. If she doesn't, then we have a legitimate excuse in case someone notices."

Before he left to talk to Hattie, Danielle tugged on his shirt and gave him another kiss on the cheek to thank him for bringing Trinity. In return, he gave her a tiny kiss on the tip of her nose. "I won't be gone long."

As it ended up, Hattie did not have a sidesaddle, but the problem did not discourage Danielle. She changed into an older skirt she had purchased to remake. To give the illusion she was riding aside, the skirt was draped over both sides of Trinity and bunched where her leg should be. The two rode to the edge of town without notice.

After a lengthy ride, they found a shade tree along Willow Creek where they could enjoy each other's company.

"This community is such a lovely place to live. It's difficult for me to imagine leaving the area. I've only been here a short time, but I've grown fond of the town."

"I understand why you're so taken with Willow Weep, but I'm looking forward to you moving to your real home. Your grandfather needs you, and I'd like you close by so I can see you more often. Besides, you have a horse to think of. Hattie's paddock is small. Trinity needs a place to run. She's young."

"You know I want to move to the farm to be with grandpa and be closer to you. I just don't see a solution at present."

"Danielle, I guess now would be a good time to tell you. When I was picking up a crate at the station, I met up with Hattie's son, Hugh, who was changing trains. He mentioned that he and his wife were concerned that Hattie is becoming too feeble to live alone. If she has another spell like the last one, they'll have to close the house and insist she move in with them on a permanent basis. They're already making accommodations for when the time comes."

"That's horrible. Hattie thrives on her independence. It would devastate her, I'm sure."

"I'm sorry I had to be the one to tell you, but I believe you should prepare yourself. Besides, she has made a few comments lately that make me think she is mentally readying herself. Not too long ago, she asked if I'd come by to check on the house if something happened. This evening she asked if I knew of anyone trustworthy to do yardwork. You must keep in mind that God may be preparing her for the changes to come in her life. We all have to make adjustments from time to time."

Knowing Danielle needed comforting, Hunter pulled her a little closer.

His words reminded Danielle of the path God had secretly constructed to reunite her with her grandfather. She looked up into his eyes, "Yes, I've had to make several adjustments in my life recently. Our Father's always working behind the scenes to provide our needs—even before we ask." She snuggled into Hunter's arms.

"Hopefully, going to live with your grandfather won't be the last time you move."

"Isn't it a bit early in our relationship to speak of such things?"

Danielle, you know there have been a few girls in my past—only one that I had any feelings for—but I've never felt for anyone the way I feel for you." Hunter had not meant to be so bold, but the words had come so easily. He did have deep feelings for Danielle and would have spoken all that was in his heart—if Joshua Harrison's words of warning had not come to mind.

Just then, a dilapidated wagon came rattling along to break their daydreams of a future together. After the wagon passed, the two took a romantic walk along the creek before returning to Willow Weep.

The sun was setting by the time Trinity was comfortably situated in Hattie's barn. But, as they were leaving for the cottage to say good night, their eyes were drawn to Hattie's garden.

"I can't leave it in this state. Let me walk you to your door. I need to come back and pull as many weeds as I can before dark."

"No, I want to help. Obviously, she hasn't weeded in days. I hadn't noticed. I feel so neglectful."

Danielle began working on the patch in front of her. Hunter chose a spot nearby.

"Hattie is known for her immaculate garden with its superior vegetables. Finding it so overgrown concerns me. She must not be doing well at all." Hunter stood up and looked around. "We won't put much of a dent in it tonight but let's do what we can."

"I can get up early in the morning and work until I leave for the inn—although it's going to take more than a couple weedings. I'll need to start checking on Hattie more often. Something is terribly wrong."

"I have to pick up a load of lumber tomorrow or the day after. If I have any free time, I'll see if I can get some more done."

"What if Hattie is hurt to find we've been weeding? She'll know we've noticed she's slipping."

"It can't be helped either way, Danielle. Someone was bound to figure it out, and it's better sooner than later."

30

THE JAILHOUSE DOOR

It was early afternoon when Miss Simpson's train arrived in Grand-ville. In her previous way of life, Margaret would have been eager to return home to brag of shopping trips, high-class balls, or lavish vacations. But this arrival was different. Margaret did not step onto the platform with foolish nonsense to share but hurried through the crowd with urgent matters to address. Since the streets were crowded, Margaret did not bother to hire a cab. Having become accustomed to walking in the mountains, she believed better time could be made on foot. She only hoped that she was not too late.

When she left town, Margaret had spewed her contempt on Harold for sending her to the Appalachians. Now, that same young lady loved her father dearly and was concerned for his welfare. She prayed for the opportunity to hug him tightly and thank him for rescuing her from herself.

There was also Delbert to see. Even though she and her brother had been close while growing up, their closeness had been wrong-fully used to manipulate circumstances and intimidate others to their own advantage. Margaret could not recall ever having shared a conversation of substance with Del or feeling the supportive love siblings normally have for one another. She regretted that they had wasted their years together on self-serving ambitions—and now she had come to rectify their relationship. Delbert would most likely mock her in the end, but her brother was going to hear her out—whether he wanted to or not.

As far as their little sister was concerned, Margaret could not wait to see the dear one she had neglected. Never had she played a game with Sherry, read a book to her, or even hugged the child. The most attention she had ever directed toward Sherry was to demand the child be silenced or removed.

Even worse was the way she acted toward Danielle. Margaret recalled the hateful condescension and taunting she and Delbert staged against their older sister to the satisfaction of their mother. She thanked God that Danielle had been wise enough to escape their torment.

Even though Margaret was ashamed of her past behavior, God was now directing her life, and she believed He would help her make amends to those she had misused.

"Hello, I'm Margaret Simpson, and I was directed to meet with Attorney Dice before going to the hospital. Is he in? I'm desperate to see my father." Her heart was racing for fear of using valuable time that could be better spent with Harold.

"Yes, my dear. He's expecting you. Follow me." The secretary picked up the file from her desk and showed Margaret into the office.

"Margaret! Come in and have a seat. I must say I'm surprised it has taken you so long to arrive. I haven't talked to Delbert, but

I'm certain he's anxious to see you. I assume you will be going directly to the jail."

"I apologize that my arrival has taken so long. Your letter was much delayed and making arrangements for a train trip isn't as easy in the backwoods as in the city. Then there was the money to consider. Of course, I plan to see Delbert as soon as possible, but I *must* see my father. So, I don't mean to be rude, but if you would please tell me why you requested that I meet with you first, it would be most appreciated. I'd like to be on my way."

Attorney Dice was immediately suspicious of Margaret's seemingly desperate need to see her father. "Well, I have to admit to being skeptical when it comes to your motives—especially after the demeaning references you made toward him before you left—not to mention your treatment of him in the past. You do realize your father is in a very fragile condition and still unresponsive. He could not withstand any drama."

Margaret was hurt by the lawyer's bluntness but understood he had every reason to be cautious.

"The old Margaret would have been outraged, would have insulted you, and would have vowed to get even. But as the new Margaret, I will take a different approach to the derogatory remarks." Margaret stood to her feet and held out her hand. "Hello, Mr. Dice. Let me introduce myself. . . I am Margaret Simpson, a born-again Christian, as well as the daughter of Harold Simpson, whom I love and respect." Margaret could not prevent smiling at the befuddled look on the lawyer's face.

Benjamin Dice did shake her hand—although, he was not convinced of the sincerity of the introduction. Staying true to his legal instincts, he took some time to absorb what he had just heard.

"Are you honestly telling me that you have accepted Christ as your Savior and have turned your life over to Him?"

"I am and I have," Margaret answered without hesitating.

"I'm certain you understand why I am reluctant to take your profession of faith seriously. Can you quote John 3:16 for me?" he challenged.

"*For God so love the world, that he gave his only begotten Son, that whosoever believeth in him should not perish, but have everlasting life,*" Margaret stated without even blinking.

"Romans 10:9," Dice fired back.

"*That if thou shalt confess with thy mouth the Lord Jesus Christ, and shalt believe in thy heart that God hath raised him from the dead, thou shalt be saved.*" Margaret gave a little nod to let him know it was his turn.

Dice raised his eyebrows, indicating he was impressed but not yet convinced. However, his next question was asked with a little softer tone. "So, you have put your unprincipled past behind you?"

"I have," Margaret answered sweetly.

"This isn't a phase?" he scrutinized one final time.

"It's not a phase."

At that, Benjamin Dice enfolded Margaret in his arms and gave her a fatherly hug—not just because she was Harold Simpson's daughter, but because she was a sister in Christ.

When they were seated, Benjamin still did not hold back on his directness. "My heart is so full of joy on your behalf that I can barely contain my emotions. I never believed that sending you to a mountain mission would be the way to touch your heart for the Lord. To be honest, I was afraid you might have been too spoiled and self-centered to be reached—mainly because of the hold Es—" He stopped himself from uttering the words.

"The hold Esther had on me? Yes, I've come to see my mother and grandparents for the unfortunate people they are. I guess I always knew how horrible we all were, but selfishness and greed are sins that continue to tighten their grip. I thank Jesus for giving my father the insight to find a way to set me free. Once God did open my eyes to sin, he propped them wide open. Hopefully, someday the rest of my family will be reached with the gospel."

Blessed to hear Margaret's confession, Benjamin reached over and patted her hand.

"I'm sorry to have misjudged your motives. But now I should prepare you for seeing Harold. To begin with, your visit will be limited to a few minutes. He's only allowed one or two visitors twice a day. So far it hasn't been a problem—since I've been the only visitor."

"I hadn't thought of that. I've pictured myself sitting by his side for hours."

"Your father is still bandaged from the burns, so be prepared for what you'll see. They should be removing some of them soon. From what I understand, the burns should heal with little scaring. He did suffer from smoke inhalation, but it has cleared up. It's the head injury that's the major problem. There's swelling due to a fractured skull. It's still too early to know if he'll survive the trauma. Just don't expect your father to look like himself."

"Head injury? The telegram stated he had life threating injuries but— Tell me what happened. . . please!"

❧

Margaret paused after placing her hand on the handle of the jail-house door. She was devastated after seeing the condition of her father. If it wasn't for the Holy Spirit's prompting, she would not have been able to face Delbert. At the same time, she was certain that Delbert was not the only one involved in the attempt on Harold's life.

Upon entering, she was taken to a small room and left waiting for almost an hour. When the door finally opened, a haggard man was placed in a chair across the table from her. It took a moment to recognize him as Delbert. Her brother had dropped some weight and appeared despondent.

"Since he hasn't had any visitors so far, I'll allow you thirty minutes. . . but no more," the guard informed her.

Margaret's first thought was to tear into Delbert with both fists and tell him what a horrible person he was, but after looking into his eyes, she could see he was a broken man—not at all the arrogant bully he had always been. He did not seem to be mistreated or scared but did seem devastated. Margaret's heart filled with sympathy for her brother.

"Del?"

He slowly raised his head to look at her. "Maggie?"

"Yes. It's good to see you. But, are you all right? You don't seem to be yourself."

He placed a shaky hand on hers. "No, Mag, I'm not all right. I've been accused of trying to murder father. I suppose you know that by now."

"Yes, Benjamin informed me of the details earlier today. Do you feel up to talking about it? Or would you just like to visit?"

Delbert gave a huff and shook his head in frustration. "I guess Dice is chomping at the bit to get me behind bars or see me hang if father doesn't pull through. I can't say as I blame him.

"How is father? I haven't been told anything." Delbert looked down at the floor in shame.

"There is some change from what I understand. The burns are healing, and his lungs are clear. The head injury is the main concern. It's still too early to tell." Margaret tried to ease Delbert's mind the best she could.

"I hope he makes it and not just to save my own skin. It may be difficult to believe, but I do care. Thanks for letting me know. I don't have a lawyer. Since I'm being painted as an arsonist and accused of attempted murder—and have no money—no one is jumping at the chance to take the case." Delbert pounded the table with his fist.

"I'm sorry. I'll see what I can do to find a good lawyer while I'm in town. I should be here often—at least for a while. You see, I've been accepted in a nursing school not far from here. There's a desperate need for a traveling nurse in the mountains, and I believe God has called me to fill the position.

"Attorney Dice advised me not to postpone my schooling while we wait for father to recover. . . and for your case to unfold. I'll be back to visit you both on weekends whenever possible."

Margaret was surprised to see the grateful smile on Del's face and was even shocked that he had not criticized her when she had gone on to mention her intimacy with God and His call on her life.

"I also have a young pastor as a suitor, and he is in love with the mountain people as I am. It's too early to tell where our relationship might lead, but so far, he's willing to wait while I'm in training. He hopes to set up another mission somewhere in the mountain region while I'm away." Margaret noticed that Delbert had become somber, indicating that good news and general conversation wasn't what he needed.

"Del, what possessed you to start the fire?"

The question rallied Delbert. It was the first chance to tell his side of the story. "I'm not convinced that I did start the fire. I had set out to, but I have no recollection whatsoever of starting it. Of course, I was staggering drunk by then."

"What put such an idea into your head in the first place?" Margaret could picture Delbert taking revenge against their father, but she didn't believe him capable of murder.

"I came home after stopping by a bar for a few drinks. When I went inside, Mother was in a rage over how badly father was treating us and had determined that Sherry and Danielle would get our entire inheritance. She was telling me father deserved to live penniless—just like he left us. She kept repeating the same arguments, over and over, saying if she were a man, she'd burn the company to the ground. I was drawn in. I had a couple more drinks while I was at the house, and before I knew it, I was in a buggy on my way to burn down the shipping company."

"So, it was Mother who planted the thoughts in your head." Margaret recalled similar methods their mother had used over the years to coax Del and her into doing her bidding.

"I lost my nerve on the way there, so I stopped by the bar for a little more encouragement. The next thing I remember was waking up in jail. The prosecutor accused me of packing the buggy with what was needed to start the fire, but it's not true. That buggy had to have been packed by someone else. I didn't do it. That I know for certain."

"Are there any witnesses that can support your story?"

"There were a couple of my buddies at the bar. They confirmed that I was bragging about burning the place. And I most likely was. I don't remember." Delbert leaned his head back, feeling he had little hope for the future.

Margaret suddenly noticed that it was the first time she had heard Delbert talk like a man—not like the hellion he had been raised to be. He sounded like someone who desperately wanted to change. He might even be open to the gospel.

"What about Father's head injury? Do you deny the accusation?" Margaret needed to hear his answer.

"I had to be staggering drunk if I was found on the ground at the scene. In that state, there's no way I could've made my way to Father's office or managed to be quiet enough to sneak up on him." He looked into Margaret's eyes. "I'm telling you I didn't attack Father."

"Then do you have any idea who did try to murder him?" she asked, already knowing the answer.

"Well, our mother did show up at the arraignment. No one—not even my own grandfather—had bothered to tell me about Father's injuries. Before I knew it, I was being accused of trying to kill him. I even pleaded with Mother to defend me during the hearing. But she acted innocent. . . and said nothing. My own mother and grandfather allowed me to take the blame and watched as they hauled me back to jail. I suppose you've heard that she and our grandparents left town not long after?" His tone reflected his resentment. "So, who do *you* think tried to kill Father?"

Margaret left her chair to pace the floor. "I assumed it was Mother. I got the impression Benjamin Dice feels the same way. I also have the feeling he wants to help you, but his hands may be tied because he's Father's attorney."

"Dice help me? That will never happen. He knows what kind of person I am. He has decent people to represent."

Del's statement gave Margaret hope.

"I'm afraid I have some more unsettling news. It's about little Sherry. She's missing and they have no leads as to what happened to her. Benjamin has his opinions on the matter, but he wasn't at liberty to share them—although, I doubt either of us would be surprised as to what his theory might be."

Delbert raised his head, "Our poor little sister. Who knows what they've done with her? No doubt Mother reasoned she would gain control of the Simpson fortune if she had custody of Sherry. At least we know all of Esther's angles. With the Snodds, it's always about big money and being somebody. What suckers we've been! Groveling. . . willing to do anything for Mother's attention and approval. You know. . . I really believed she loved us. I even believed she loved Sherry. But Esther Simpson loves no one but herself.

"And I keep thinking of all the years I laughed at Father for letting Esther walk all over him. But, to be honest, she's done the same to us. Anyway, once Father did stand up to her, we bucked him all the way." Delbert took a deep breath and released it.

"I wonder why we refused to see the good in him. I was equally abusive to Father when he sent me away. I hated him and everyone at the mission and ended up running away. That is when it hit me—there was no one in the world who had any reason to care for me or would miss me if I never returned. I was ashamed of my sinful ways. Then one of the verses the pastor had required me to memorize came to life in my mind. 1 John 1:9 *If we confess our sins, he is faithful and just to forgive us our sins, and to cleanse us from all unrighteousness.*

"I finally understood that, even though I was an unlovable person, God loved me anyway. That's when I accepted Jesus as my Savior. His transformation in my life was immediate. He will do the same for you, Del."

"No, Maggie. There are things I've done that I can't even speak of. They can never be made right. I'm unforgivable."

"Del, you must listen. If there's one thing you love on this earth, it's animals. I've seen you go to great lengths to save strays. Remember the dog that was covered in tar. The poor thing couldn't help himself and would've died in that state. Other people threw rocks at him to run him off, but not you. Even though he was an undesirable mess, you took him in and worked for days to remove all that tar. When you were through, he had been transformed into the beautiful animal he was meant to be. You gave him another life.

"Delbert, can you try to see God in that light? We get ourselves in all sorts of tangled messes, and there's nothing we can do on this earth to save ourselves. Yet, our Heavenly Father takes us just the way we are and begins working in our lives. It's the reason Jesus died on the cross. Only His perfect shed blood can cleanse us of our sins."

The door abruptly opened and in walked the prison guard. "I'm sorry, miss. Time's up."

"May I, at least, have time to say goodbye?"

"Make it short." Then the guard stepped back outside.

"Del, here are some verses and writings on how and why we must give our lives to the Lord."

"Sis—"

"I won't take *no* for an answer. You will read this. . . because you love me, as I love you. God will forgive everything, Del. Promise you'll spend time in prayer."

"I don't know how to pray."

"Prayer is talking to God."

"Margaret, this isn't going to work."

"Del, please. I can't stand the thought of us not being together in Heaven."

Margaret grabbed her brother and hugged him with all her strength, and Del reciprocated in loving desperation. It was the first time the twins had shown affection for one another, but it would not be the last.

31

WHO ARE THESE PEOPLE

"Rand, what are you doing here? I thought we agreed you shouldn't come around. You know what the consequences might be if it's discovered you have any connections with this girl." Zelda Fields reluctantly opened the door and allowed him to enter.

"Believe me, Doc. Wasn't my idea. Granny sent me for some medicine. She's gotta cut on the bottom of 'er foot that's not healin'. She reckoned ya'd know what's needed." Rand stood near the door with his hands tucked in his pockets, eyeing Sherry from a distance and wondering if it was safe to get any closer.

"Seriously? How does that sassy, old lady expect me to know what's needed without examining that foot. It's only a short distance. Maybe I can run over when I'm certain my little patient is resting well. Do you know anything about the cut?"

"Only that it's deep and oozing pus. Cut it on an ax last week. That's all I was let know."

"Well, it's too late for stitches. I wish she'd sent someone when it happened. No telling what's going on with the cut this late." Zelda walked over to the cabinet and began packing the appropriate instruments and medications for the trip to Granny's.

"How's the little 'n doin'? I can't help but be worried about 'er."

Zelda motioned him over to Sherry's cot so he could see for himself. "She's well on her way to recovery but still has a difficult time ahead. It's going to take awhile for her to bounce back. Poor dear doesn't seem to have the will."

About then Sherry went into a harsh coughing spell and winced with pain until the cough subsided.

"Girl looks awful pale. Course it's hard ta tell with white folk. They're all different colors. Seems tuv been sick a terrible long time ta me." Rand put his hand on Sherry's forehead.

The gentleness of the touch caused the child to respond. When her eyes fluttered open, Sherry's groggy mind managed to make out two bodies standing in front of her. The sight gave her a terrible fright, jogging her memory of running from a man. *Who are these people? I've been caught!* For that brief moment, all hope of being free of her captors was gone, and she relented to despair before falling back into a deep sleep.

"Sweetheart, can you hear me?" Zelda smacked Sherry's cheek lightly, hoping she would rally again. "Well, at least it's a good sign she's on the mend. Although it's bad timing since I need to see Granny. No telling when the child might wake up again or for how long."

"S'pose I can stay with her—if you're desperate." Rand's facial expressions reflected he did not care to be left alone with the sick girl.

"I hate to ask you to, but from your description, Granny needs to be seen right away. I don't seem to have any other choice." Zelda finished throwing the last of the needed supplies into the bag. "I'll try my best to hurry. Promise me you won't go outside, and for goodness sakes, don't answer the door for any reason."

"No, Miss Fields, I don't plan on doing either of 'em."

"If the child wakes up, introduce yourself and try to explain what she's doing here. She could be lost, but I still think she's a runaway. If so, she isn't going to trust you. I'm sorry you were brought into this situation, Rand."

Zelda then walked out the door, aggravated that she had to fear for a good man's safety while he was doing her a favor.

Not long after Zelda left, Rand grabbed a skillet and scrambled a couple eggs to ward off his hunger pangs. Yesterday had been a long workday, and he had fallen asleep on the porch swing without an evening meal.

It was about the time Rand sat down to eat that Sherry's eyes opened once more. The scared little girl surveyed the room, trying to make sense of where she was. The walls were made of logs, and she recognized a stone fireplace with two chairs and a fancy tea stand between them. She could see a man sitting at a kitchen table with his back turned to her. There was a tiny cook stove and a cabinet with dishes, pans, and food supplies.

Sherry raised her head and saw a small window with pretty, lace curtains and a door near the corner which she thought led to a bedroom. Beside her cot was a white cabinet with what looked like medicine bottles and medical equipment. Sherry had never been in such a small home, but if she hadn't been so frightened, she would have welcomed the clean, cozy feel of the little dwelling.

Dropping her head back on the pillow, she tried to remember how she had come to be in the cabin, but it was of no use. The last thing Sherry could remember was trying to reach the road ahead. She feared the hateful bum had caught her and delivered her to the people her grandfather had hired to hide her.

"Hi there. Ya must be startin' ta feel better. Ya sure did give us a fright when ya first got here. Ya been real sick. Still aren't fairin' too well, but I guess ya can tell that yerself." Rand had walked over to check on Sherry and was glad to have found her awake, but Sherry pulled back.

"Now ya don't need ta be scared of me. I mean ya no harm. The lady who's lookin' after ya, Miss Zelda, will be back shortly. She had an errand ta run. I was the only one handy who could watch after ya."

Sherry was not ready to trust anyone, but the young man had a way about him that drew her in. "My name's Rand. May I ask ya yours?"

Instantly, the inkling of trust she had considered putting in him was whisked away with that simple question. Sherry turned her head away from Rand and squeezed her eyes shut. If he did not know her name, she was not about to tell him.

"No, no, no, no. Li'l girl, I didn't mean ta upset ya. We've just been wonderin' who ya are and how ya came ta be alongside the road. Ya can't blame us for wonderin'. We aim ta help ya."

Even though his words made sense, Sherry was wise enough to reason that she could be tracked by her name. She refused to open her eyes and stayed quiet until she fell back to sleep.

❧

When Zelda returned, Rand told her what had happened and apologized for distressing Sherry.

"You did fine, Rand. There's evidently something strange going on with that child. It's most likely going to take time to reach her.

"That silk dress and the undergarments were ruined by the muddy creek water, so I had to burn them. I'll have to make her something fit to wear. She'll just need to make do with a plain dress until we figure out her situation."

"Somethin' bad's goin' on with that child. Wasn't just fear I saw in that girl's eyes. There was a kinda sadness. A loneliness. Like 'er heart was broke."

"Having money and nice things doesn't necessarily mean happiness. The wealthy can be just as miserable as the poor."

"Money might not make ya happy, Miss Zelda, but I sure would like givin' it a try."

Zelda laughed, "I was raised with every advantage, and I must admit it was nice. I do miss it, but I wouldn't trade my former life for my work here with you good mountain people for anything. This is where I belong, and it's where I want to be."

"That's sure good news, Miss Zelda. We need ya bad. But ya' haven't mentioned Granny's foot."

"It's a bad cut, but it should heal just fine. That's if she'll follow my advice."

Rand stood to his feet and went to look out the front window. "Reckon I'd better head on outa here. The rain's stopped and there's plenty work ta be done. I'll take out through the woods in back. Usually not much goin' on out that way."

"Thank you for watching her. And take care not to mention you were here or that you know anything about the child. We can't afford a slip of the tongue."

Rand gave a curt nod, then walked out the door and headed for the woods.

⚜

It was early evening when Sherry woke again, still feeling as weak and tired as she had previously. When Zelda noticed her movement, she didn't speak but heated up some thickened chicken soup.

"I understand that you don't know where you are or how you came to be here, but let's not worry about that. Right now, you need to eat and start regaining your strength." Zelda lifted the spoon to Sherry's mouth and waited.

Sherry did not want to eat for the woman, but the food smelled good and she was extremely hungry. Zelda had placed a few pieces of bread in the broth to soak, hoping to make the soup more enticing. "Eat slowly. I don't want to make your tummy queasy along with everything else." The child did as she was instructed and was even disappointed when told she had eaten enough for the first time.

Afterward, Zelda removed the stethoscope from a drawer and listened to Sherry's lungs. "They sound much better. I've every hope that you will be on your feet soon. You need to rest and allow that meal to do its part in making you feel better."

Sherry was barely tucked in when another coughing attack began. The nurse rubbed her back and encouraged her to relax. When the incident was over, Zelda cooled Sherry's forehead with a damp cloth and helped her find a comfortable position. Her reassuring manner reminded the weary child of her longing for a mother's tender care.

Sherry was confused by the kindness shown to her by the two adults and prayed they truly were good people who had found her along the road—and not those involved in her grandfather's plan to get rid of her.

32

AN UNWANTED KISS

Danielle tapped lightly on the office door, not wanting to disturb her boss but knowing it was necessary. As it was, she had put it off too long. Grandfather would be expecting a decision soon, and she wanted, at least, to be able to tell him she had spoken to Rosa about the move.

"Come in." Rosa looked up and sighed. "I was wondering when you were going to get around to mentioning you would be moving to the farm."

Danielle's eyes widened. "How did you know? I haven't told anyone."

"It just makes sense. The two of you were separated for all those years, and it's time you were together. I would do the same thing."

"If you don't mind, I'd like to keep my job for a while. I'm not quite ready to give up all my newfound independence." Danielle then looked up at Rosa sheepishly.

"You can stay for as long as you like, and there won't be any hard feelings when you decide it's time to leave. I'm happy for you. My only request is that you help train a suitable replacement.

"Besides, Joshua needs you. Since you've come into his life, he is a changed man. He's been lost without Valerie. Even though I'll be losing my most cherished employee, I think it's for the best."

"I appreciate your understanding, Rosa. However, I probably won't make the move right away. Since Hattie's not doing well, I haven't had the heart to speak to her."

"Any other time I would disagree with you, but we all see the difference in her. Sadly she sees it too."

"I owe Hattie and you so much. I love you both for taking a chance on me when there was absolutely no reason for you to do so.

"Well, it's time for my shift to begin. My *boss* expects me to start work on time."

Just before leaving the room, Danielle gave Rosa a hug and whispered a thank you in her ear. A short time after the door closed, Rosa wiped a stray tear from her cheek, saddened to hear she soon would be losing her new friend from her staff.

Things were still icy with Madison. It was disheartening to Danielle that her impromptu comments about Tally had hurt and annoyed her friend. It was evidently one of those situations that needed time to heal. During the process, Danielle would try to find a way to make it up to Madison—although the whole ordeal did make the workplace uncomfortable and the days lonely.

During lunch break, Danielle chose a picnic table under the maple tree near the back porch and was immediately joined by Rob. "I hear you and Jackson have decided to make it an official courtship. Are you certain this guy is all he's cracked up to be? It's none of my business, but I hope you keep an eye peeled when it comes to a guy who can have his pick of women."

"Are you trying to tell me something?" Danielle smiled at him, but after seeing his face, she realized he was serious.

"I just don't want you to get hurt. I'm suspicious of his innocent act when it comes to Sally Meeker."

"You mean to insinuate that Hunter can't be trusted?"

"I'm saying it's highly possible."

"Excuse me, Rob, but I need to speak to Alyssa." Danielle was furious. *How dare he cast aspersions on Hunter in such an opinionated way! He was certainly right—what goes on between Hunter and me is absolutely none of his business.*

Danielle spoke with Alyssa briefly and then took a short cut toward the willow to calm down.

⁘

Sally managed to block Hunter between the big rock and the post office step while he was sorting through some mail.

"Sally, what are you doing here? If you remember, I asked you to keep your distance. I don't want to be seen with you. Some people have misunderstood our acquaintance. You know that Miss Harrison and I are officially courting. Now if you will please step aside, I can get on my way." He took a step forward, hoping she would relent and free him.

"Hunter, you didn't suppose I took you seriously. If you think I'm the type of girl who gives up so easily, you're mistaken." Sally tucked her chin down and looked up at him with enticing eyes.

"Listen—"

Sally suddenly, but purposefully, leaned in and kissed him near his lips. She then quickly stepped over, took his arm, and looked up with adoring eyes.

Danielle, who had just come into viewing distance of Hunter and Sally from the other side of the street, arrived just in time to see the kiss and the girl take hold of Hunter's arm. Instantly wounded and mortified, she ran back to the inn.

Sally, who had already seen Danielle coming from a distance, had intentionally created the scene hoping to cause trouble between the two. Hunter, unaware that Danielle had witnessed the display, pushed Sally away.

"You listen to me and listen well. If you don't immediately stop pestering me in this humiliating way, I promise you I will go speak to your father, and I will bring my uncle with me when I do. Do I make myself clear?"

Sally did not answer but perched her lips as she lifted her shoulders from side to side and walked away extremely satisfied.

⚜

Danielle sought seclusion on the side of the inn by the tall hedge. Refusing to give into tears, she tried to decipher what she had witnessed. Just as she had calmed down enough to catch her breath, Rob appeared out of nowhere and sat down on the step beside her.

"I've been looking for you. I want to apologize for what I said earlier. I guess I'm still sore over Hunter's abrasive behavior toward me the night of Rica and Joe's party. No one likes to feel like a loser. I'm afraid I've become overly fond of you. Can you forgive me?"

Danielle fought back tears as she looked into his eyes. "I can. . . and I'm sorry too. I don't think Hunter and I were thinking much of anyone else's feelings that night. You see, I'd just been introduced to my grandfather for the first time. It was totally unexpected. Hunter was trying to get me away from the crowd so I could sort through everything that had happened. He was being protective."

"I hadn't heard. Here I was feeling sorry for myself. Maybe I've been a little hard on the guy. I must admit I was hoping to steal you away from him. Then seeing all those girls following him and letting it go unchecked, I thought—"

It was at that moment they heard Sally Meeker's voice on the other side of the hedge. Walking down the sidewalk beside the inn, she had caught sight of Rob and Danielle sitting on the steps. It was the perfect time to finish off the relationship between Hunter and his little sweetheart. Since the two could not see Sally, she pretended to be talking to a close friend as she passed.

"Didn't I tell you Hunter would come crawling back to me as always. He's just not ready to settle down, and I understand that. Miss Harrison is the kind of silly girl he always goes after. He toyed with her like he did the others, but now that he finally has her corralled and believing they're going to ride off into the sunset together, he's bored. Let's say she's due to be dropped sooner than later. He apologized only minutes ago and asked me to take him back. I did. . . but this time it was with a warning that I have other offers pending and that he needs to straighten up or he might lose me altogether. Although, I must admit, I do enjoy watching him squirm."

After passing the target area, Sally made up general conversation until she was out of hearing range. Pleased with her ingenious plan, Miss Meeker congratulated herself for a job well done.

Rob watched as the color drained from Danielle's face, but when he tried to put his arm around her for comfort, she pulled away. He grabbed his cup, flung the coffee into the shrubs, and went inside—angry at Danielle for trusting Hunter and furious with Hunter for deceiving her.

Hunter finally found Danielle walking down a sparsely populated backstreet. "Did you forget I was supposed to pick you up at the inn after your shift. I was beginning to think you'd been raptured."

Danielle turned and gave him a harsh look that let him know he was in trouble, but for the life of him, he did not know why. "You didn't like the joke?"

"Why are you here? Haven't you had enough fun at my expense? You *are* one of those men who enjoy collecting women. You have no heart at all. You should be ashamed of yourself. So go to your *Miss Meeker*. The two of you deserve each other." Danielle started toward the creek.

Hunter sat in the buggy, appalled and unable to grasp why Danielle was so furious and why she would hurl such horrible accusations toward him. He was hurt and unable to take the searing words lightly. Once he gathered his thoughts, he jumped from the buggy and followed after Danielle. When he caught up with her, he took hold of her hand so she would have to stop and face him. "I have no idea what's going on, but I don't appreciate the demeaning insults. I, at least, deserve to know why you chose to verbally attack me for no reason."

"Then let me refresh your memory. I just so happened to be near the post office today while you and Sally were cozied up together just like old times. I saw her kiss you and take hold of your arm. It appears the two of you have rekindled your relationship after intentionally misleading me."

"So that's it. How long were you there?"

"Long enough to see what I needed to."

"If you had stayed a second or two longer, you would have seen me push her away and would have overheard me threaten to speak to her father if she didn't stop her unbearable pestering."

"I must admit you are quick with answers. But let me give you a few more facts. I was privy to a conversation which exposed you as the person you are. I almost feel sorry for Sally. I can't understand why she would want a man like you when she has other prospects. If you'll excuse me, I have sewing to do."

"Wait! I have no idea what you're referring to. I have never intentionally dishonored any woman. My worst crime is for putting up with Sally's antics, and for that I'm sorry. I don't know what you have heard about me, but I can only say that any gossip that would make you turn on me so violently is nothing but lies. What's difficult for me to take is that you were willing to believe hearsay."

Looking into his eyes reminded Danielle of how she had wounded him the day he had been fly fishing in the creek. She had hurt him that day. Now she had hurt him again.

"Why didn't you come to me before jumping to conclusions? The only thing I've ever wanted from you. . . is to *trust* me. You've always been willing to believe the worst of me. Why? This is getting old. I don't know. I just don't know anymore."

After Hunter had his say, he got into the buggy and drove away—leaving Danielle standing alone.

33

A FRACTURE THAT COULD NOT BE REPAIRED

As Danielle rode Trinity alone for the first time, she felt the consequences of her lingering insecurities. It was the first time since the breakup that there was little to occupy her thoughts, and she could not prevent herself from dwelling on the ugly scene. The ride through the countryside was a welcome distraction.

Since business had picked up at the inn, Danielle had not been able to visit her grandpa. Today she was on her way to the farm to spend a long weekend which Joshua had secretly arranged with Rosa.

It was late afternoon when she rounded the curve near the Harrison homestead. As the house came into view, Danielle could see the yard was filled with people, and camping tents were set up along the pasture fence line. She had no idea what it all meant, but having to deal with guests was the last thing she needed.

"Here she comes!" Joshua Harrison called out as he clanged the dinner bell for all present to gather around to greet Danielle. "Shake-a-leg, everyone!"

By the time she was ready to dismount Trinity, a large group had congregated around Danielle. "Grandpa, you have me at a disadvantage. Who are these good people?"

"They're your relatives, my dear one. They've come from far and near in order to meet you." A round of applause rang out, along with calls welcoming her back to the family.

"Lacresha, Jerry, and I started planning this affair right after your first visit. It was a challenge trying to set a date, but we all finally settled on this weekend. And here we are! The first family reunion in years! I hope this meets with your approval."

"It most certainly does." Danielle conjured up an appreciative smile and a loving hug for her Grandpa, while vowing to herself to be kind and cheerful no matter how she felt.

"And where's Hunter? I was expecting him. He didn't mention that you'd arrive unescorted." Joshua stated disapprovingly.

"He had other obligations, and as you see, I did nicely on my own." Danielle felt guilty for practically lying to her grandfather, but under the circumstance, it could not be helped.

Fortunately, her answer appeased Joshua, and he began the task of introducing her to the family members, giving a short biography of each one. Danielle did love meeting her newly-found relatives and was touched that they cared enough to sacrifice their time to become acquainted with her.

Regrettably, with everything else going on in her life, Danielle began to feel overwhelmed—that is, until she was introduced to a most stunning second cousin whom she found extremely engaging. "And this is Gayle Harrison, your dad's former partner in mischievousness. And, I still believe she was behind most of their plots—although she denied it every time."

"Uncle Joshua, you'd have this lovely child believing such poppycock? I was a sweet child and *sometimes* things just happened to happen. However, I do recall a little impishness on Danny's part. Your father was the true troublemaker. I just tagged along." Then the charming lady smiled a smile that helped refresh Danielle's cluttered heart.

She had no idea why, but Danielle wanted to grab hold of this lively cousin and share every joy and sorrow she had ever known. When the woman opened her arms, Danielle nearly leaped into them—while Gayle's reaction exhibited the same intense emotions. Neither understood, but at the same time. . . each knew.

Grandfather was called away, so the two ladies joined arms and took a stroll toward the flower garden. Gayle was the first to open up. "So, you're my darling cousin, but I've never had the opportunity to lay eyes on you before this day. My dear Danny—I loved him so—even though we were ornery beyond reason."

"Really?"

"Oh, yes. You see, I spent much of my youth here on the farm, since my mother passed away when I was two and father had to travel for business. Daniel and I played in hay lofts, splashed in creeks, hunted for night crawlers, rode horses at full speed, and even sat the woods on fire. We were active—to say the least."

"Well, you would never know it today. You are so refined and beautiful."

"How kind of you to say so! And I return the compliment. I can't believe I'm standing here speaking to you. You've only existed in my dreams thus far."

Gayle lifted Danielle's chin. "I wish I could have watched you grow up. There wasn't even one picture to visualize what you might have looked like."

"I'm afraid you might have been disappointed. My life was very mundane—and at the same time very stressful. I don't remember ever being a child. I had responsibilities."

"I heard your mother's husband was very well-off."

"He was, but—" Danielle had not planned to share her life's story with this already beloved cousin but felt compelled to do so. The only other person who knew her story was her grandfather. Not even Jean and Everett were aware of everything.

"I felt such a connection with you when we were introduced. It was almost like meeting the mother I would have chosen for myself. Your children must adore you."

"And I felt as if I'd met my perfect daughter. As far as my children go. . . I'm the maiden cousin. I was engaged when I was twenty and was planning our wedding when my fiancé was killed in a hunting accident. I was devastated and mourned his loss for several years. After experiencing such sorrow, I no longer was interested in marriage. Instead, I sought a college that would accept me, and then poured myself into establishing a most lucrative business."

"Very impressive."

"Thank you. Danielle, I just know we are going to be great together." The two embraced once again, knowing their relationship was meant to be closer than cousins.

Soon afterward, Lacresha and Jerry—along with Joshua's brother Ray and his wife Ruth—began bringing out the food to add to the celebration. Golden fried chicken and fish, mashed potatoes and gravy, fresh fruit with cheese, fried-down green beans, and freshly baked bread were all placed on the serving table. There was a choice of chocolate cake with caramel sauce or sugar cream pie for dessert. To Lacresha's pleasure, several of the relatives went back to the table for seconds and even thirds. They complained about being stuffed, yet wished they could eat more.

Afterward, the women volunteered to clean up, and Danielle used the opportunity to get to know the ladies of the family. The rest of the evening Danielle spent sitting around a campfire listening to the family reminisce. Great-uncle Lytle and Great-aunt Dorothy were the biggest cut-ups in the group. Lytle savored the attention for his storytelling, but Dorothy usually followed with the realistic side of the story—which was often funnier than his version. As it turned out, dealing with unexpected guests was exactly what Danielle had needed.

The next morning, there was an early breakfast of oatmeal, scrambled eggs, bacon, and toast.

Danielle had learned that another get-together in honor of the visiting family was to take place later in the day. Friends, neighbors, and church members who were close acquaintances to her relatives would be joining the group. The entire family was rushing around setting up borrowed tables and chairs, games, canoes rides, and anything else one might find as entertainment at a picnic. Out by the barn, Joshua and Jerry were keeping a close eye over the pig on the spit.

At exactly three o'clock, the carriages began to arrive. The first one brought Rosa and Johnathon. The next was Helen and Mel Jackson, and then Rica and Joe, who were followed by several people Danielle had not yet met.

Everyone appeared to be having a glorious time getting reacquainted. However, the evening meal was not served on time, since the meat was not ready. This was fortunate for the latecomers—of which, one was Hunter Jackson.

Upon seeing him, Danielle escaped to the kitchen to ask if she could help Lacresha and Tenzy set up the food. However, the two had all the assistance they needed and shooed her off to visit with the relatives. Not wanting to face Hunter, Danielle stalled for time by taking a sneak peek at the dishes the ladies had prepared. An overabundance of potato salad, deviled eggs, baked beans, slaw, yeast rolls, cookies, pies, and cakes were being removed from the kitchen and placed around the succulent roast pork. Long before the prayer was offered by Pastor Strong, guests began congregating around the serving table, hoping to be among the first in line for the tempting meal.

✦

Once the meal was over and the dishes were done, Danielle went to see if she could help with the games. She was quickly paired with a shy, little girl in the three-legged race. To her dismay, she and the girl were placed in line beside Hunter Jackson and a young boy. When the race began, she and the little girl worked well together and had made it nearly to the finish line when Danielle twisted her ankle, leaving her embarrassingly sprawled on the ground in front of everyone.

Out of the corner of her eye, Danielle could tell Hunter looked perturbed but felt obligated to help her. She accepted the outstretched hand when it was offered and was immediately restored to her feet. However, when she looked up to thank him, she saw it was Rob Wilky. Rob guided her over to the side and checked her foot to make certain all was well. The two then walked over to watch the sack race and later the egg roll. Although Danielle did appreciate Rob's company, it was uncomfortable with Hunter nearby—that was until she saw Sally Meeker walking the premises.

Hunter was devastated as he watched Danielle walk away with Robert Wilky. At the same time, he feared there was a fracture in his relationship with Danielle Harrison that could not be repaired.

Sally, too, had watched the contests and was ecstatic to see Danielle walk away with Rob. She knew her scheme had worked. In fact, she had been following Hunter from a distance, hoping to stage a chance meeting, but had been drawn to eavesdrop on two ladies who were passing by:

"Danielle is everything Joshua described her to be. I'm so happy he finally has his granddaughter back in his life. The separation had placed an unbearable strain on the whole family, and then to lose his son. . . and knowing she would never meet her father. . ."

The wheels began to turn in Sally's head. *Danielle Harrison? Joshua Harrison? She's Joshua's granddaughter?*

Sally wished she could remember what she had heard about Joshua's son and grandchild, but she had always been too self-absorbed to care about the details of other people's affairs. However, she did remember Joshua had a son who died and there was something about a long-lost child.

Sally then realized she had become the victim of her own wrongdoing. Joshua Harrison was like a second grandfather to her, and she adored him—as he did her. She could not bear the thought of him being disappointed in her or learning how devious she had been in causing Hunter and Danielle's parting. *Why didn't someone tell me who Danielle Harrison was?* Sally wondered how she would get out of this precarious situation without losing Joshua's approval.

34

TOO LATE

Sally Meeker had checked inside the house, all though the yard, around every game area, and even down by Willow Creek. She knew Hunter had not gone home because Petra was still in the paddock. The only place left was the horse barn, and she was on her way there.

Not only had Rica been watching Sally flit about the yard in what appeared to be a state of panic, she had also noticed that Hunter and Danielle had been keeping their distance from one another. There was no doubt Sally was up to something, so Rica went to get Joe.

✦

"Hunter."

"Sally, I made myself perfectly clear at the post office that the next time you pestered me, my uncle and I would speak with your father. You need to leave, or I will go get my uncle right now. The choice is up to you."

Hunter's countenance indicated he was determined, and Sally

knew he would not waver.

"Please, Hunter. Don't." Tears of fear burst from Sally's eyes. "I need to tell you what I've done. Please, hear me out. I'll leave immediately afterward."

"Miss Meeker, I'm asking you to leave. Anything you have to say can be discussed in front of your father."

"Hunter, listen. It's about you and—"

"Feel free to let her speak, Hunter. I'd love to hear the confession Sally wants to share so desperately. Rica and I are here as your witnesses." The veins in Joe Meeker's neck pulsed as he glared at his younger sister.

Sally knew she was in trouble but was relieved to have the opportunity to admit to her deception. "The reason you and Miss Harrison are no longer courting. . . is my fault. When I detained you at the post office, I knew Danielle was watching. That's why I kissed you and took your arm. Then on my way home, I saw Danielle sitting near the hedge at the inn, and I faked a conversation, hoping she'd believe you didn't actually care for her and had come back to me. I staged it all."

Rica raised her fingers to her lips to cover her gasp, while Joe shook his head in disgust. Hunter only stared blankly at the ground.

"Why would you do such a thing? Hunter is a fine man, but he isn't interested in you. I'd hoped you had more respect for yourself than to pursue someone after being told to back off. You should be ashamed. You owe Hunter and Miss Harrison a sincere apology with the promise not to interfere in their relationship again. If I find out differently, I'll speak to father myself."

"Sally, when I told you about my past, you knew it was to discourage you from the path you are taking. Instead, you used the information to wreak havoc in Danielle's and Hunter's lives. Don't you care that your friends are beginning to avoid you because of your behavior? You need to stop manipulating people, or you will end up alone and miserable as I did. Joe and I are trying to help you."

Sally hung her head, seemingly ashamed of her actions. "Hunter, I'm so sorry for the trouble I've caused you. I will speak to Miss Harrison this very day. But please don't tell Joshua. He's always favored me. I don't believe I could bear it if he discovered the trouble I've caused his granddaughter. I didn't know who she was."

"So that's it! If you hadn't found out she was Joshua's granddaughter, you would still be causing problems. No, my dear sister, I am taking this to father."

Sally followed Joe from the barn, pleading for him to reconsider, but Joe didn't slow his stride.

Rica took the opportunity to speak with Hunter. "I'm so sorry you have fallen victim to Sally's schemes. It shames me to see all the suffering such actions can cause. Would you like me to be there when you speak with Danielle? I'd like to help set things right."

Hunter paused while giving the offer consideration. "All I've ever wanted of Danielle was that she would trust me. It was one of the reasons we weren't together when she first arrived. So just when I thought she had faith in me, this happened. She believed Sally. . . over me. Rica, I think it's too late."

"I will not hear of it, Hunter. If there are two people who deserve to be together as much as Stewart and Bethany Jefferson, it is you and Danielle. How dare you give up so easily!

"Do you know how patient Joe had to be with me? I cared absolutely nothing for him, and I used him over and over. Instead of walking away, he prayed for me. . . and he continued to pray until I turned my life over to Jesus. Joe stood firm and believed in God's timing. He told me he always knew I was the girl for him but was waiting for a few *spiritual modifications* in me first."

Rica laughed at recalling Joe's words but returned to her prodding. "The only thing I know about Danielle's past is that she was taken away by her disloyal and deceitful mother as an infant and the father was barred from her life. Have you considered how her upbringing might have caused her to hesitate when it comes to affairs of the heart?"

Hunter did not answer.

⚶

Danielle's heart ached as she watched Hunter watering the horses in the paddock.

"Miss Harrison. . . may I have a word?"

The voice was unmistakable, and Danielle just wanted Sally to go away. "I don't believe—"

"Sally has a confession, as well as an apology, to offer you, Miss Harrison. I ask that you please hear her out," a bass voice requested.

Danielle turned to see that it was Mr. Meeker who had spoken, and standing beside him were Joe and Rica.

"I don't understand."

"You will shortly. Go ahead, Sally." Mr. Meeker raised his eyebrows at his daughter to spur her to speak.

"I'm responsible for your breakup with Hunter. I knew you were watching when I forced a kiss on him and took his arm. Later in the day, I pretended to be talking to a friend. It was all a lie.

"I'm sorry for all the trouble I've caused and hope you will forgive me. It won't happen again." Sally was too embarrassed to look Danielle in the eye. "I truly am sorry," she repeated.

"I see." It was the only response Danielle could manage.

"Sally will not be going to Europe or away to school this year as planned. It seems she has some growing up to do. Please accept my apologies as well." Mr. Meeker escorted his daughter directly to the carriage where his wife joined them before they drove away.

Sensing Danielle needed to be left alone, Rica gave her an empathetic squeeze of the hand before leaving.

All the terrible words she had spoken to Hunter while he stood before her and denied the accusations came back to her. It felt as if she had ripped her own heart out with her own hands. Danielle could see it was she—and not Sally—who had destroyed the relationship.

As she walked away, the realization of her unreasonable assertions caused her to feel nauseous. Her legs began to feel weak, but she managed to move from the view of the guests. Just then, a steadying arm reached around her waist.

"My dear, come with me to the garden."

Once seated on the garden bench, Danielle fell into Gayle's mothering arms and poured out the heartbreaking story. Gayle held her and did not speak, wanting her cousin to release all the disappointment and hurt she had been holding inside.

Joshua began to speak as he approached them. "Dani, my girl, are you all right? I knew something was amiss when Hunter didn't arrive with you this afternoon. I just haven't had a proper moment to speak with you about the matter. Mrs. Meeker informed me of the whole affair before they left. I dearly love Sally, but I did see a calculating streak developing during her teens. I'd hoped she'd grow out of it. I'm sorry about all this, my darling girl."

"Don't hold it against Sally, Grandpa. It was my jumping to conclusions and refusing to believe Hunter that caused the parting." Danielle sniffled as she wiped the tears from her eyes.

"Granddaughter, if I had the answer to this situation, I'd gladly intervene."

"Grandpa, I fear Hunter has already given me his answer."

Gayle placed a loving hand on Danielle's cheek. "Sweetheart, you must remember that Jesus is the answer."

"Uncle Josh, will you keep watch and let us know when we can sneak up the back stairway. I want to take Dani upstairs so she can freshen up. She has family and friends to entertain."

Hunter had never felt more abandoned and wronged. Why he was still at the Harrisons' party, he did not know. Yet, he had accepted the invitation and decided he did not want to insult Joshua by leaving too early. Once the horses were watered and fed, Hunter headed back toward the creek to help with canoe rides—only to find that Rob Wilky had taken over the position. Even more upsetting, Danielle was there keeping him company.

". . . so, maybe you could accompany me to the. . ."

The last thing Hunter wanted to do was listen to Wilky wooing Danielle. Fortunately, the dinner bell rang, so he joined the others in the backyard. After grabbing a cup of coffee, he went to sit down with Helen and Mel.

"We haven't seen you around the house lately. What have you been up to?" Since Mel and Helen had noticed that Hunter and Danielle were not acknowledging one other, Mel felt he should keep to general conversation for the time being.

"I. . . uh. . . I'm a little behind schedule on the barn. Thought I'd better get caught up. Been working a few extra hours."

"Hunter, aren't you going to eat? The barbeque is delicious."

"I'm not hungry just now, Aunt Helen. Maybe I'll grab something later."

"Oh... excuse me. There's Rosa. I want to speak with her," Helen intentionally left to allow Mel time alone with Hunter.

The two men sipped coffee and discussed the barn until their dialogue began to lag. By then Mel thought it was safe to bring up the subject. "We happened to see the Meekers leave early with Sally in tow. Do you have any idea why?"

"I can't be certain."

"I've also noticed that you and Miss Harrison have been too busy to speak."

"I'm sure everyone here who's aware that we've been courting has noticed."

"I have a feeling Sally Meeker has been up to something. Would you like to talk?"

Hunter rubbed the back of his neck. "It's gone beyond Sally's meddling."

"Rob Wilky?"

"I don't know what's going on between Danielle and Wilky."

"I'm offering my ear, but if you're not interested, we can drop the subject. Although I do think you need to sort things out—if not for the two of you as a couple, at least for yourself."

Hunter rubbed his chin. "I don't really want to talk about it, but someone has already given me something to mull over. I might as well get an older man's opinion."

Mel chuckled. "At least you didn't call me an *old man*."

After listening to Hunter's stance on what had taken place, Mel offered his view. "I agree Danielle did issue some serious charges. Since she won't open up about her childhood, it's possible she's dealing with some underlying trust issues from the past. If you take the disagreement at face value, then you have every reason to walk away. I guess you need to decide if the principles you're guarding are worth giving up the young lady you seem to care about. Are you prepared to go on without her? I believe I'd explore my feelings on those subjects. . . but it's only *my* opinion. Sometimes love does come with a high price tag."

"But then there's Wilky. I guess I'm wondering if she has already moved on. They seem to be on the chummy side."

"You can't blame the guy for trying. But if she cares for you, then Rob won't be an issue. There's only one way to find out."

As Hunter passed the porch, Joshua called out, "Son, I don't believe you've met my niece—my son's closest cousin while they were growing up."

"Gayle, this is Hunter Jackson."

"Nice to meet you, Hunter." Gayle extended her delicate hand.

"It's nice to meet you, ma'am." Hunter was taken by Gayle in much the same way as Danielle had been.

"This fine gentleman is a close friend and a hard worker. He's among the first to help when it's needed. This is also the young man who has been seeing my granddaughter."

Hunter's eyes opened wide. "Well. . . we are. . . so to speak."

"What's wrong with you, son? Something upset you?" Joshua asked to get to the point.

Gayle took Josh's question as a hint to leave. "Hunter, I'll be visiting Joshua for several weeks. Hopefully we can chat at another time. As it is, I have responsibilities and must rush off."

Hunter understood what was taking place. "I take it you

know, then?"

"Mrs. Meeker informed me before they left, and I've since spoken with Danielle. My granddaughter is hurt. Son, I warned you not to move too fast."

"In all due respect, Danielle made the choice not to trust me, and I was rightfully offended. I assume she knows Sally lied."

"Sally and Mr. Meeker did apologize to her. Danielle is also aware of her own offenses and has explained to me how the incidents had looked from her point of view. I must say though, I'm sorry your courtship has dissolved."

The two friends shook hands, and Joshua gave him a slap on the back as they parted.

Hunter watched Joshua walk away. What bothered him was the finality in which Josh addressed the breakup. Evidently their friends and family were already beginning to dismiss them as a couple.

Even so, despite his frustration, Hunter wasn't sure he could walk away from the girl he loved.

⁂

As dusk approached, family and friends gathered on the front lawn. Hunter watched as Wilky continued to hover over Danielle. Again he pondered whether they had become more than co-workers—or was Rob only seeing her through a rough time?

It then occurred to him. . . he had just caught a glimpse of how Danielle must have felt when Sally was following him everywhere.

The screen door slammed, as Joshua approached him carrying a guitar.

"Come on, everyone! What this party needs is a few songs. Hunter, would you mind starting us off?"

Hunter was not in the mood, but instead of being difficult, accepted the guitar and sat down on the front step. As he began picking out a catchy tune, his crisp, clear voice filled the air, and the others joined in. It was followed by an upbeat hymn.

Before he could pass the guitar along, someone requested a popular love ballad about a misunderstanding between lovers. Hunter hesitated a moment before beginning.

The requested song emphasized the soothing quality of his voice, but the lyrics made Danielle uncomfortable and she decided to walk away. Rob was obviously angered by the song and followed close behind.

Danielle's departure with Wilky tore at Hunter's heart. As soon as the song was over, he handed the guitar over to the next volunteer that Joshua had drafted. He was more than ready to pull Petra from the paddock and head for home. He could no longer watch the romance play out between Danielle and Rob Wilky.

When Hunter entered the horse barn, he saw the outline of two people in the distance. The one was a man who walked away giving the distinct impression he was upset. The other was a woman who was stroking a horse. Hunter's saddle was hanging on a rack a few feet away, and he hoped the lady was aware of his presence. He lit a lantern and then caught sight of her tear-stained face. "Danielle? Did Wilky do something to upset you?"

"No. The other way around."

Hunter paused. "Is it because of us?"

Danielle stared at him, then looked away.

Unable to resist, Hunter reached out and pulled Danielle to his chest, hugging her closer than he had ever dared. He then leaned over and kissed the top of her head.

"We can work this out."

35

GOING TO THE POLICE

"Good morning, sweetheart. I'm glad you woke early. I just finished making breakfast and decided to let you sit at the table today. Would you like that?" To the nurse's disappointment, Sherry only offered a couple nods.

Zelda had been working to earn Sherry's trust, hoping she might speak or at least make a sound. Since it was still not obvious whether the girl was mute or just refused to speak, the nurse hoped the questions might eventually catch the child off guard. "Do you need help, or would you like to try walking on your own?"

Sherry didn't answer, so Zelda helped her from the bed and went to pull the chair from the table. The child walked slowly but did not stagger. Once seated, she looked back at the cot as if pleased with her accomplishment. After bowing her head, she watched as Zelda uncovered the plate before her. Sherry's eyes lit up at seeing pancakes and syrup—instead of the usual eggs cooked yet another way.

"A neighbor brought me some flour from the store, so we are celebrating your recovery with hotcakes. Folks around here need to walk a long way to get food supplies, so we don't always have what we want at our fingertips. For most of the people in this area, money is hard to come by as well." Zelda hoped the little girl understood her meaning.

Suddenly Sherry remembered her silk dress and looked around the room for it. She wondered if the dress might have been the reason the nurse had made the statement.

Zelda sat down across the table from the girl, and the two shared breakfast in silence. Sherry devoured the pancakes as ladylike as possible and would have indicated she wanted another one if she had not been too shy.

When the meal was over, Zelda had another surprise. "I have a bath ready for you out in the shed. I can't wait to see how that beautiful, blonde hair of yours looks when it's clean and brushed out. Do you think you are up to a bath?"

Sherry gave a bit of a nod and followed the nurse to the shed.

The refreshing bath and clean, untangled hair did go a long way in making Sherry feel better.

Zelda liked the feel of combing through the long locks. "Your hair is just lovely. I'm glad washing it and taking a simple bath is no longer a problem. . . although I do have some disappointing news. I'm sorry, but I had to burn the clothing you were wearing when you came to us. The dress and your underthings were ripped and ruined in what I imagine was creek water."

Sherry acted as if she had no interest in what happened to the clothes and waited for Zelda to continue.

"I did make you a new dress and undergarments. I know they aren't nearly as nice as what you're used to, but they're functional and will have to do while you're here. Your new things are hanging over there by the door. I'll leave so you can dress."

Not waiting for Zelda's departure, Sherry made her way to the door and removed the dress from the hook. The fabric was pink cotton sprinkled with tiny, multicolored flowers. Not only was she pleased that the dress was made from a simple pattern, but it also looked cool and comfortable compared to her fancy clothing. Sherry could not wait to put it on. She looked at Zelda as if to thank her.

The nurse had not expected gratitude from this child. Judging from Sherry's former attire, she had thought the girl would find the dress beneath her.

"I'll be in the kitchen when you're through dressing."

When Sherry returned to the cabin, Zelda asked her to take a seat at the table where a slate and chalk was lying. "I need you to write your name and address so we can reunite you with your family."

Fear instantly filled Sherry's eyes, and in resistance to the request, she turned her head to the side and would not look at Zelda. Impulsively, she jumped up, knocking her chair over, and almost made it to the door before being caught by her caregiver.

"Okay, okay. It's all right. Come sit down. We'll drop it for today."

Sherry was still panicked as she was led back to the table. Although still wary, she was intelligent enough to have perceived that Zelda *was* a good person and had not been hired by her grandfather. She knew the woman would still want to know who she was and why she was so fearful. But Sherry could not let that happen.

"Since you don't want to give me your real name, you still need a name other than. . . the girl. . . or the child. So as a compromise, I'll give you a name for the time being. Would you like to help me choose one?"

Having calmed down, Sherry gave a half nod.

"Good. How about Bertha, Ethel, or Blanche?"

Sherry moved her head slightly back and forth, letting

Zelda know she did not approve. Zelda laughed. "Mabel, Elizabeth. . . Minnie?"

Sherry did not react to them.

"Ellen. . . Anna?" Sherry's eyes lit up and she gave a nod for *Anna*.

"All right, *Anna* it is. Now for a last name. Smith, Jones. . . Brown. . . Hill."

Sherry gave a nod.

"Hill? Anna Hill? I like it. Short and simple. We won't tell anyone, except Rand, that it isn't your real name. Please write the new name on the slate."

Sherry complied and handed the name to Zelda with a questioning look.

"Since you won't give me information about yourself, I'll need an answer when I'm asked where you're from. I suppose I'll have to tell people that you must live in the country and don't know your address. I dislike stretching the truth, but you've given me no choice—although, I do plan to get to the bottom of this mystery."

Sherry relaxed a little more but feared what might be next on this woman's agenda.

✦

A few days later, a lady and a little girl showed up at the cabin while Sherry was sitting on the porch. Because she did not know who they were, she left the bench and walked backward to the door to find Zelda.

"Elna, so good to see you. What brings you my way?"

"Asha and I were out huntin' fer berries or anything else we might find ta eat. Thought we'd happen by fer a visit and a drink a cool water. . . if you'd be obligin'."

"You know you're always more than welcome. . . and help yourself to all the water you can drink. The dipper is hanging by the well as always."

Elna filled the dipper and handed it to her daughter to drink while she waited for her turn.

"How'd ya come by that white girl. Surely is a strange one."

"Passed out by the road. She was extremely ill, and I'm still doctoring her."

"So, who she belong to?"

"I don't know just yet."

"Did ya ask her?"

"She appears to be mute."

"Well, that's a fine fix. What ya gonna do with that child?"

"Right now, I'm going to finish nursing her back to health."

Asha, a little charmer, kept her hands clasped behind her, as she twisted back and forth and watched Sherry. Her hair was in perfect, tight braids and her dress was clean and still looked neatly pressed.

"Ya want ta go pick some flars? I know where there's some real perty ones. They don't make ya sneeze or itch either. My mama knows all 'bout wil'flars."

Sherry was hesitant to react right away. She had spent most of her life playing alone or with Danielle. There was seldom a chance for her to be with children her age. When she was with friends, it was normally during dinner parties or weddings where she was expected to act like a lady. Most of her schooling took place at home, since Esther insisted on the best of tutors to impress her friends.

"Well, ya comin'?"

Sherry went to Zelda to wait until she was acknowledged.

"Is there something you need. . . Anna?"

Sherry pointed at Asha.

"I ask 'er ta go pick flars. Is it all right? I know which ones."

Zelda motioned Asha over to her. "Sweetheart, do you know what it means to be mute?"

"Means she kin't talk, but I don't care. I kin talk for both of us."

"That's the truth. My girl kin talk up a storm. She don't need nobody 'round ta listen either."

"I guess it wouldn't hurt for Anna to get a little exercise. But don't go far and don't stay long. It wouldn't do for her to get overly tired."

"I'll be shur she don't git too tard, Miss Zelda. Kin I show 'er the feesh at the bridge if she's up ta it?"

"That's a grand idea."

Asha took Sherry by the hand, and the two girls walked off together. Zelda noticed Sherry was wearing a bit of a smile—the first Zelda had seen on the girl's face.

"Pretty li'l thing. Looks downcast though. Hope ya know what yer a doin' keepin' 'er. Ya be careful and wise 'bout all this."

✦

It was evident the knock was from a strong hand. Zelda opened the door to find Rand, who looked as if he was tired from a long day's work. She would expect nothing less from the young man. Sherry was sleeping, so she stepped outside to join him on the porch.

"What brings you here?"

"Just stoppin' by to let ya know I passed by Granny's today. She's up and around and as feisty as ever. Almost patched up."

"It's a wonder. I don't believe that woman's ever listened to another soul in her life. It's a blessing she didn't wait longer to send for me—might have lost her foot or worse. So why are you really here?"

"I was just wonderin' how the girl's doin'. I don't reckon anyone will be makin' a connection between me and her this late. Just that she's gotta place in my heart."

Zelda had thought the girl was asleep when Rand arrived, but the knock had awakened her. Sherry had been too sleepy to open her eyes before the nurse stepped outside, but she could easily hear their conversation through the window.

"She's nearly recovered, but I'm still taking a few precautions." Zelda went on to explain what had transpired the first day Sherry had been allowed to walk unassisted.

Rand was also puzzled by the child's reaction when it came to being reunited with her family. "Don't fret. I'll keep it a secret that *Anna* isn't her real name."

He then took Zelda's hands in brotherly concern. "Doc, please, have a good plan before ya start askin' the law 'bout that child. She's runnin' for some reason—scared nuf ta make it all those miles through that thick forest and 'cross that big creek from somewhere far off. Somethun's terribly wrong from what I can see. Ya know yer also takin' a chance havin' a white girl in yer care. Think on that too before ya act."

Zelda knew Rand's warnings were justified. "Most of the law officers respected my father and counted on him to come through in emergencies. They know me well since I worked with him, and I think I have their confidence. Don't worry, I won't divulge anything unnecessarily. I care for that little girl too."

Sherry did not know why, but it was as if she was acting on instinct. She slowly opened the cabin door and peeked out to be certain it was Rand. When she saw it was, she could not keep herself from going directly to him and crawling into his lap. Sherry snuggled close to him and the tears began to flow. Wrapped in his arms was the first time she had felt comfortably safe since Esther had removed her from the sanctuary of her home.

Sherry was learning to love the people in her hiding place and thanked Jesus for her haven every day. However, she kept up her guard and never completely relaxed.

❦

Sherry stayed with Elna and Asha while Zelda went to town to purchase food and medical supplies. The trip would take the entire day, so she promised to bring back a sack of candy as a treat for the girls.

When she left Sherry, Zelda had on her mind another errand which she had not mentioned. The nurse had no choice but to stop by the Arlington Police Station. Arlington was the farthest of the three towns where she would be making inquiries about a missing child. She reminded herself to be guarded.

"Hello, Officer Likens. Remember me—Zelda Fields—Dr. Kent Fields' daughter?"

"I'd know that pretty face anywhere. Was just thinking of your dad the other day. We sure do miss him 'round here. Can't get these young doctors to respond too quick in an emergency or travel the distances like Kent would. What brings ya in?"

"We had a child show up, and I was wondering if you knew anything about it?"

"No, haven't had any reports of a missing kid. The streets are full of abandoned youngsters of every color. The orphanage is running over. If she's not a burden or giving you any trouble, she'd be better off staying put."

"I understand but thought I'd stop and check. Well, I'd love to stay and chat for a while, but I need to start for home if I want to get there before dark." Zelda then offered a proper goodbye and left. She was relieved to have fulfilled her duty of reporting the lost child and pleased the visit was barely notable. Still, there were two more towns where she would need to make similar inquiries.

standing alone. Eventually Madison did appear, and it was apparent she was upset. Danielle motioned her to step outside for privacy.

"Do you need to talk?" Danielle asked out of concern, but Madison shook her head.

Danielle understood why Madison did not want to confide in her. "I came to ask if you were serious about finding a place of your own."

She nodded and blubbered something about not having a choice.

"Madison, I'm on my way to work, so I've only a minute. I don't have time to go into detail, but Hattie is moving to her son's home and I'm moving to Grandpa's farm. I told Hugh that you might be interested in moving into the cottage. They need someone on the premises to look after the place in exchange for rent. Mercy will be at your disposal as well. If you're interested, then you must go immediately and make the arrangements."

Madison's mouth dropped open, "Danielle, you have no idea how things have escalated with my sister. If you're teasing me, please say so."

"You know I'm not teasing. Since it's your day off, maybe you can be moved in by the time I get home. Feel free to remove my clothing, and I'll pack when I return. You may have anything else in the cottage that belongs to me. I should be able to move out in a matter of minutes."

Madison took Danielle's hands in her own. "Thank you for this, dear friend."

"I'd like to take the credit, but this is Divine intervention on everyone's part. Now, hurry!"

Danielle stepped into the street and watched as Madison ran toward God's answer to her prayer. In addition, He had mended their friendship.

After work, Danielle hurried to the cottage and was relieved to find Madison had already made the move and had even added a few decorative touches of her own. Danielle packed her belongings, as the two again marveled at God's perfect timing.

"Living in this little cottage has been such a lovely dream. It will be the same for you." Danielle gave a final glance around the room, picked up her bags, and walked out the door with Madison following close behind.

"I'm sorry I've been upset with you."

"It wasn't your fault. I should have known you just needed someone to listen."

Madison hugged her friend and watched as she started to walk away.

Danielle paused long enough to give the safe, little refuge one last look. Precious memories of life there flashed through Danielle's mind. The cottage belonged to Madison now.

Joshua, Gayle, and the Williamses relaxed on the front porch, enjoying the cool breeze of the evening. "Someone's coming. If I didn't know better, I'd think that was Danielle, but she just left last evening." Joshua stood to his feet, trying to get a better look.

Jerry walked over to join him. "No, Josh. That's our girl for sure. I wonder what brings her back so soon."

Lacresha clasped her hands together. "I hope nothing's wrong. That child has been through so much. I don't think I could bear to hear she's been hurt again."

"No, dear. I believe she's smiling." Gayle comforted.

Joshua stood at the end of the walk and took hold of the halter to bring Trinity to a stop. He and Jerry removed the bags attached to the saddle and the one Danielle had been balancing in front of her.

"What is all this? Is something going on?" Joshua then helped her dismount.

Danielle turned to face him. "Yes, Grandpa, something *is* going on. I've moved out of the cottage, and I'm getting ready to move into the farmhouse before me. I hope I'm still welcome."

The look of happiness that radiated from Josh's face was exactly what Danielle needed to see.

He pulled her into his arms and was soon joined by the rest of her loved ones who wanted to take part in the embrace. The little group rejoiced as they offered up praises to the Lord.

After a lengthy visit, they all went upstairs to her father's room to help Daniel's daughter set up occupancy. Not wanting one thing that belonged to her father disturbed, Danielle only allowed her clothing to be put in drawers or hung in the closet. She would live in the room just as he had left it.

⚘

Hunter raced Petra down the road. Even though he had wasted half the evening in Willow Weep trying to locate Danielle, he was ecstatic when he learned she had moved to the Harrison farm. He did not want to interfere with their family time, but his heart was set on seeing her.

⚘

Since she had missed dinner, Danielle insisted on making her own meal and looking after Trinity. She always took pains when bedding down the mare and did everything possible to make the stall cozy. It was just as she was lifting a small scoop of grain from the barrel that a hand grasped her own to assist. Then her hair was pulled aside, and a kiss lightly brushed the back of her neck.

Danielle let go of the scoop and put her arms around Hunter's neck to give him an affectionate kiss in return.

Once she turned to finish her work, Hunter wrapped his arms around Danielle's waist, pulled her close, and rested his chin on top of her head. They stayed in that position, enjoying a few peaceful moments together. Unfortunately, one of them had to speak.

"Danielle, we need to get to the bottom of this. I don't want you always believing the worst in me. I've gathered enough here and there to know your childhood was a difficult one. Is that the cause of your distrust?"

"Hunter, I wasn't exposed to many people while I was growing up. . . and I had little reason to trust most of them. I suppose it does influence the way I feel toward others."

"Yet, you put your trust in Rosa, Joshua, and several others right off. You even trusted Rob." Hunter let go of her and walked away as he ran his fingers through his hair. "I don't understand."

Danielle dumped the grain into the trough.

"I'm sorry I didn't come to you before believing Sally. . . and you know Rob's only a friend."

"Some friend—I heard him ask you out."

"And you were there when I told him I wasn't interested."

They both paused to give thought to what had been said.

"Why do you insist on keeping your past from me, Danielle?"

"For my safety. Too much is known about me already. Grandfather and Gayle will tell you the same."

"But we're courting."

"You're right, Hunter, I should tell you, and I will someday. But right now, it's too painful. I just want to enjoy my life as it is."

"I can't help but wonder what it's going to take to earn your complete trust."

Danielle looked into his eyes but could not answer.

37

BERNADETTE PEPPERCON

Leaving the attorney's office, Bill stepped aside to allow the gentleman with the cane to enter. Filling in for Harold Simpson as company president—while doing his own work—had proven to be a challenge for the shipping foreman. Even though the double salary made it worthwhile, he was glad to hear arrangements had been made for the executive job to be taken off his hands.

Benjamin Dice, too, was relieved to get the management of the shipping company back under his control. Now he would focus on how to find Sherry.

"The child is still missing and there are no leads. I'm positive Esther is the kidnapper, but we don't have proof to support that. Not even Mr. Long has come across any hard evidence."

The secretary listened patiently as Attorney Dice vented.

"The three adults most assuredly had someone purchase their train tickets, disguised themselves, and left the station during a high traffic time of day. I can only pray that Sherry was with them."

The secretary made several suggestions as to whom they might hire to help Long track the missing family and child, but none of them met her boss's standards. Having failed at her first attempt to find a suitable detective, she handed over the morning mail and returned to her desk to do further research.

Out of utter frustration, the attorney put Sherry's case aside to shuffle through the mail. It was all expected correspondence, except the last envelope which had a general mail address. He reached for the letter opener. Inside there were legal papers signed by Elmer Snodd.

Dice quickly read through the papers and, thinking he was mistaken, read them again. *Esther's asking for a divorce!*

Benjamin was elated. He scrutinized the documents to make certain everything was in order. Fortunately, when it came to Esther, he and Harold had anticipated nearly every angle to protect the Simpson assets. *The woman will have her divorce.*

Even though he would try, there was little hope of tracking the Snodds by the documents. Elmer Snodd was, of course, too wise to send mail from the city where he was living. He had obviously bribed someone within the Lancaster postal service to mail the divorce papers and retrieve the return document.

Disgusted that he had been thwarted again by the crooked attorney, Benjamin turned his attention to getting the paperwork completed and in the mail. He did not want anything to interfere with the swift divorce action Esther's father was attempting to finagle. The sooner Harold was free of Mrs. Simpson, the better.

❧

Taping his fingers in anticipation of Margaret Simpson's arrival, Benjamin Dice rehearsed in his mind what needed to be said.

When the door opened, the pretty brunette walked in and laid the Simpson file on his desk. "I thought I'd save your secretary a few steps."

Margaret took a seat and reached for his hands. "Tell me, Benjamin. Has my father passed away? Is that why you've called for me? Please don't hold back."

"No, Maggie, you dad is still with us, but I'm afraid what I want to speak to you about might not be pleasant either. I have been informed by your father's physician that there is nothing further to be done for Harold. He will be released to home care tomorrow afternoon."

"What does this mean? Is he to live the rest of his life in a comatose state? Will he live?"

"I can't give you those answers. Only time will tell. I'm sorry to be so vague."

"Of course, you don't know. I could tell there hasn't been any change in father recently. So I must be content in what the future holds and see this in a positive light. Now that the doctors have left my father in God's hands, I believe we will soon see a miracle."

"I'm happy to see you taking the news so well. I must admit I was worried about your reaction. I will leave it up to you to inform Delbert, unless—"

"I'll tell my brother. It will be easier coming from me. He truly does care about father's condition—which brings us to what I've been waiting to tell you. Delbert has been shaken by father's injuries and by all that has transpired since the fire—so much so that he's a changed man. Thanks to our mother betraying him at the indictment, Delbert's eyes were opened to her deceit and the dreadful person he had become. As a result, he's given his heart to the Lord. It has only recently happened, but I don't think he's put down his Bible since."

Shocked by the news, Benjamin stood to his feet. "There's no doubt in your mind that he isn't using it as a ploy?"

"None whatsoever. I wept with him as he confessed his sins to our Lord and Savior. He's truly born again—a free and gentled man."

"Well then, glory to God! Harold has definitely proved me wrong with his plan to rescue you kids. It was obviously the Lord's leading. I do hope you know it was difficult for your father to strip you both of the lifestyle to which you were accustomed."

Once they finished discussing Delbert's transformation, Benjamin went on to explain the visitation adjustments that would be needed for Harold. "The move and medical changes could prove to be a problem for your father for quite some time. You need to understand that your visits will be even more limited for a while. He'll only have a nurse to look after his needs. We just can't take chances."

"It seems I have so little time with him as it is. Still, I understand the precautions."

"Thank you for your tolerance. Now, let's move on to the changes made within the Simpson household.

"Maggie, as your father's executor, I've replaced his original staff with the people we had hired to watch over Esther. By the way, the house he had provided for her is in the process of being sold. As far as the new staff members, they are extremely dedicated to your father and his wishes."

"To be honest, I don't know that I could recognize any of our former staff, and I barely remember hearing mother was set up in another home. Rest assured, none of those changes matter to me.

"Benjamin, when Sherry is found—and if our father should pass on—what's to become of our little sister?"

"If such a thing should ever happen, she is to live with me

and my wife. We would count it an honor since we haven't been blessed with children."

"I'm certain she would be most happy there. You would both make wonderful parents."

"Thank you. I appreciate your confidence in us. Now, about the divorce. . ."

Margaret left Benjamin Dice's office that day with the assumption that Esther had finally divorced Harold for a more lucrative offer. Glad her mother's action would put an end to her father's misery, she prayed he would live to have a long and happy life.

"I told you *one teaspoon*, you featherbrain. You are a poor excuse for a maid. I believe I'll have to look elsewhere for help." Esther made the statement, not only because she enjoyed belittling people, but because her funds were almost depleted. She would need an excuse to dismiss the servant if money ran out before the wedding.

Esther—now using her middle name, *Bernadette,* to help conceal her identity—laughed as she visualized Benjamin Dice's face when he discovered the divorce papers. She knew Dice would have done whatever was needed to see that the papers were sealed and delivered in record time. But she was confident that—instead of divorce papers—they would be receiving a letter informing them of Harold's demise.

Mrs. Simpson had played her cards right. Selling her mother-in-law's jewelry had given her enough time and money to infiltrate the right circles and quickly land a wealthy husband. The wedding plans to become Mrs. Ulysses Peppercon were in place, and if need be, her father—as always—had the right contacts to finalize the divorce before that date. She would soon achieve the rank she sought and the riches to do whatever she wished. The groom was a bachelor nearly thirty years her senior and was no longer sharp witted. Fortunately, he had been ripe to be taken in by an alluring face and attractive figure. All she had to do was wait him out—and in her estimation, that would not be long.

Esther Bernadette then sauntered over to the cream-colored wedding dress hanging on the closet door. Taking it to the full-length mirror, she held it in front of her for another look. She began swirling around the room, smirking at how everything was falling into place.

However, the day of the wedding did not turn out to be the triumphant affair she had expected. Esther had been blindsided at receiving the divorce papers—instead of being told that her ex-husband was dead. She feared Harold had caught a glimpse of her the night of the fire. Should he still be in his right mind—with his testimony and a little circumstantial evidence—she could be indicted for attempted murder. The thought overshadowed any type of victory she felt.

Although Esther had longed for a magnificent wedding that made the headlines of the society page—to protect her identity—she had to settle for a small, but elaborate ceremony.

After enduring a boring honeymoon with her elderly husband, Esther felt rewarded when, soon after, Ulysses fell ill and appeared near death. Esther, being overly excited by the news, sent for his physician. "Well, tell me, doctor. Is there any hope for my darling husband? We have only just married."

"I'm sorry to disappoint you, Mrs. Peppercon, but you have presumed too much. Your husband is not slipping away. He has a virus. Most likely it will last a week or so. I do think I should mention that Ulysses has the constitution of a man in his forties. It wouldn't surprise me if he lived to be a hundred. I will let myself out."

Esther picked up a vase and threw it at the door as soon as the man was out of hearing range. The physician had seen through her motives for summoning him. Although she could not risk taking her anger out on her current husband, the thought that she might have to live decades with the disgusting, old codger sent her into a rage.

It's Danielle who is to blame for the life I have been forced to endure. It's she who is always at the core of my problems, hindering me from achieving the life I deserve. If Danielle had never been born, everything would have gone as I had planned.

38

AFRAID OF WHAT MIGHT LURK BEYOND

With Sherry following her everywhere she went, Zelda felt as if she had a puppy. Even when she stepped over to the kitchen, the child was directly behind her. The little girl had started panicking after being left at Elna's overnight while the nurse had delivered a baby. Zelda assumed Sherry had felt abandoned, and whatever had happened in the sad child's past was causing her to be desperately needy.

It wasn't long after breakfast that the familiar tap was heard. "Come on in. You will anyway," Zelda yelled.

Sherry hurried to the door and pulled Rand toward the kitchen chair. "Wait just a minute, sweetie. Got some business ta tend to. Doc, can we step outside?"

Zelda turned to reassure Sherry that they would be on the porch and that she could stand by the door while they talked. Sherry shook her head violently and grabbed Doc around the waist. They finally agreed the door would stay cracked so the child could see them.

"Miss Zelda, I've been thinkin' ya better keep Anna close ta the cabin and not let on much that she's here. If ya told anyone else ya might want to speak to 'em about it. I hope ya don't mind but I already spoke ta Elna and asked her ta hush 'bout it. She said they haven't seen nobody ta tell and promised not ta breathe a word. Ya don't know who might be lookin' for Anna or why. Your lives could be in danger, and there are folks who would sell ya out for a few coins."

"I don't remember mentioning Anna to anyone other than Elna and the officer, and he wasn't interested. He didn't even ask for a description. I don't know if anyone else has seen her or not. I was considering putting her in school if she ends up staying. You're right though. Maybe we'd better continue sending her to the bedroom when patients show up."

"Remember ta be careful if anyone does come lookin' for her." Rand followed her to the door.

"I will be. By the way, I haven't told Anna you're staying with her while I go into town. I guess we'd better go explain. I have a lot of ground to cover before it gets dark. I hope she isn't any trouble while I'm gone."

"Not a problem. Ya know how Anna likes ta play them games. We'll be fine."

When the nurse left for Remington, Sherry was curled up on Rand's lap. Zelda assumed the girl would be asleep within minutes. She was still somewhat weak after the illness, and any undue stress seemed to exhaust her.

❧❦❧

Zelda typically bought her supplies in Bristol, but today, even though the prices would be higher, she felt obligated to go to Remington. Because the trip was a little longer, she had borrowed a mule to load with medicine and other provisions.

Since Zelda was already tired when she stepped into the Remington Police Headquarters, she was glad to be greeted by the matter-of-fact officer. "We've taken in a white child up our way. We haven't been able to find anything out about the little one. Would you happen to know if there's a report on a missing child?"

The officer didn't speak but rummaged through a book and a few files. "Nothing here— Any of you officers heard anything about a missin' kid?" Without looking up from his desk, he continued working.

"Evidently not. Never know about them whites up your way. The maw may be dead. Could have a worthless drunk for a dad. Probably belongs to a moonshiner who don't care much about 'em. Too many homeless kids on the loose to keep track of. Can't help ya. Have a good day, ma'am."

Zelda replaced the straw hat she had worn to keep the sun off and left the station without uttering another word. The man had written Sherry off as white trash, just as if those children did not matter. The thought pained her heart.

Because of the storm and the detours the flooding had caused, it was late when Zelda returned to the cabin. Rand had made stew, and it was warmed and waiting for her. Sherry ran over to give her a hug and then went back to the table to read.

"I was about ta send a searchin' party out for ya. That sure was a bad storm that passed through. Gettin' too much rain for the crops. I'm worrin' 'bout it. How'd ya fair?"

"First of all, how did *you* fair?" The nurse walked over next to Rand while he was dishing up the stew. "She's reading?"

"I found that *Swiss Family Robinson* among your books while she was dozin'. When she woke up, I started ta read it ta her, and before I knew it, Anna took the book from my hand and went to sit at the table. Been sittin' there readin' ever since. Makin' good time at it too."

"At least we know she's educated—which means she can write well, but won't. What is she hiding?" Zelda whispered back, still wondering if the girl could talk.

The young man shook his head. "I don't know, Doc, but I wouldn't force it."

"Rand, I've been thinking. The child needs to socialize. We can't keep her completely secluded. Anna needs to be around people. It might help her open up. Otherwise, we may never draw her out of the desperate state she seems to be in."

"Again I don't know. It sure seems ta be takin' a chance for the both of ya. With those nice clothes she had on, someone's bound to be lookin' for 'er."

The two continued to talk quietly. "The sheriff brought up the scenario that she could be from a motherless family, and the father might be a worthless drunk who doesn't care about the kids. See, we don't have to lie. . . exactly. We'll just talk around it. You know a lot of the mountain people are superstitious, and with her being a mute, maybe we *can* pass her off as a poor child that I've taken in. . . and I *have* taken her in."

"I don't like lyin', Doc. Besides, it won't work anyway. That Sykes' family came across Anna first. They most likely will remember her and that dress."

"The Sykes probably only looked at her for a few seconds."

"All right, I'll go along with it, but I'm not likin' it. I'll stop by Elna's to tell her what you're thinkin'. I'd talk to the Sykes', but I don't know if ya can trust 'em. Okay, how we goin' 'bout this?"

Sherry may have been looking at the book and turning the pages, but she was fully aware of what the two were discussing, As much as she longed for the companionship of Asha and other children, Sherry wished Rand had persuaded Zelda to keep her location a secret. The child was not ready to test the waters by being exposed to people who might not be trustworthy. She was content in this little, hidden world and was afraid of what might lurk beyond it.

Certain the greedy bum would be back, Sherry prayed for Jesus to protect her. She felt as if she could bare anything if there was hope her daddy was looking for her. . . but she knew he was not.

39

THE WEDDING

Danielle laid the letter aside. Jean had written to say Sherry was still missing and there were no leads. According to local hearsay, the child was believed to have been taken by her mother when she had left town. Even as horrible as that thought was, at least her little sister should be safe—but then again, who knew when it came to Esther.

It was also disappointing to hear Harold had been released to home care. From what Jean told her, there was nothing else to be done for him. Danielle wished she knew what that meant, but she still refused to believe that God would not restore him. The best and only thing she could do was to continue believing and praying for her Grandville family.

Trying to keep her mind positive, Danielle walked back to the treadle machine where she had left the dress mid-stitch. She finished sewing the trim before giving it a final examination. Danielle was pleased since it was the most elaborate gown she had ever attempted to design.

The front of the bodice had a sweetheart neckline with sky-blue silk sewn within the princess seams and came to a point at the waist.

Loops and brocade covered buttons aligned the front. The rest of the bodice and the slender skirt were made from matching brocade with an iris pattern woven in golden thread. Danielle had chosen the fabric to highlight her Grandmother Valerie's blue sapphire pendant and earrings that she would be wearing.

The elbow length sleeves were puffed at the shoulder, and instead of a bow, she had chosen a small Daisy Tampico bustle. The rest of the details she had painstakingly added made the dress even more eye-catching.

After trying the dress on and then seeing that it was pressed well, she hung it in the closet—completed and ready for the up-coming affair. At that point she heard the familiar tap on her door.

"Danielle dear, Lacresha and I have come to see the dress. We won't take *no* for an answer."

She could hear the two ladies outside the door giggling over their bold demand. Opening the door to let them in, she placed her hands on her hips, pretending to be disgusted. "But it's supposed to be a surprise."

"It will be. . . to everyone else. Where is it? We girls have waited far too long." Gayle pointed her to the closet.

"All right, I hope it's to your liking. If not, pretend it is." Danielle removed the dress from the closet for the two ladies to inspect.

"My goodness, girl. It's beautiful." Lacresha held the dress up while she and Gayle inspected every detail. "To think our little Dani has such talent. I bet it fits perfectly."

"Dani, you are an outstanding seamstress. It's simply exqui-site. The fabric is the exact color to complement Valerie's jewelry. Wonderfully done, my dear."

"Thank you both. It means so much to have your approval. I've never worn a sweetheart neckline before. I do hope it's acceptable."

"The neckline doesn't seem to be cut too low. I love it."

"I agree with Lacresha. You've managed to keep the neckline modest. So, don't start nitpicking at this lovely gown. Lacresha, we'll look like wallflowers beside her tomorrow."

"You both are being too kind. I hope Hunter likes it. After all, he's the one I want to impress."

"He definitely will. Although, I doubt he gives one feather for what you'll be wearing." At the thought of Danielle and Hunter together, Lacresha pulled her hands to her chest. "That boy is head over heals in love with you."

Danielle lowered her head and then peeked up in shyness. "I hope so."

"I'm telling you, Uncle Joshua, our girl is an extraordinary seamstress. Lacresha and I can't wait until you see the gown. No wonder Helen snatched her up."

"Well, it's high time I see at least one of the dresses I've been hearing about. However, there is no doubt in my mind that Dani is gifted."

"I'd venture to say this dress is among her best work." Lacresha was too excited not to add her opinion.

Their enthusiastic conversation was postponed by a knock at the door. Since Joshua was standing, he answered it. "Come in, Hunter, and have a seat. Gayle and Lacresha have just been raving about the frock Dani's made."

"Joshua, I've seen Danielle's work. I'm certain their opinions are correct. . . and if your granddaughter is wearing the dress— "

Hunter stood captivated as he watched Danielle descending

the stairs. "You look— "

Joshua, overwhelmed, removed his handkerchief to wipe his eyes. "The dress is beautiful and is only surpassed by your own beauty, my dear Dani. I see you have on Valerie's jewelry. That sapphire set with the diamonds was her favorite. It does my heart good to see you wearing them."

Stepping forward, Hunter reached for her hand as she took the last two steps. He felt as awkward as a schoolboy going to his first dance.

Danielle, seeing her young man in formal attire, did not think it was possible for him to look more perfect. "And you look. . . strikingly handsome."

Suppressing their sighs, Gayle and Lacresha stood by, watching silently.

Since it was getting late, the family had no time to linger and hurried out the door to their awaiting carriages.

Helping Danielle into her seat, Hunter completed his first thoughts. "You are stunning. I'm concerned you might divert attention from the bride."

"I was just thinking you might do the same to the groom. Thank you for the compliment. However, I doubt it would be possible to compare to Rica's beauty."

"Then you should look in the mirror more often."

Danielle responded with a charming smile. Hunter was glad to see her deep dimples had finally returned. It was the first time he had seen them since the stress of their disagreement seemed to have stolen them away.

Hunter gave Petra a little lash with the reins to hurry him along.

"You have no idea how I've been looking forward to this day. I've never attended a wedding—much less an extravagant one."

"Well, be prepared. The Adamses are much older than our parents, extremely wealthy, and have only one daughter to spoil. The sky will be the limit."

Danielle hugged Hunter's arm. "I certainly hope so."

When they arrived at the church, a line had formed for the valet parking, so Hunter was concerned that, if Danielle's family did not arrive soon, a backup might make them late for the ceremony. To help alleviate the parking problem, he assisted Danielle to a bench near the entrance to wait and parked the carriage himself. Several other gentlemen followed suit.

Danielle was in awe from the moment they walked into the sanctuary. She had never seen a room look so heavenly. Snow-white tulle lavishly adorned the walls, while glowing white candles were arranged to enhance the ambiance. White roses of varying arrays were placed throughout the room to add romance to the scene. To maintain the illusion, music played softly in the background. Danielle was enraptured, and Hunter loved watching her reaction.

As she gazed in awe, he carefully guided her to a pew in front of Helen and Mel. Danielle tried to nonchalantly look about the room but actually wanted to stand and turn in a circle to capture it all. She was eventually brought back to reality when Joshua, Gayle, and the Williamses joined them.

Danielle turned and whispered to Gayle and Lacresha. "I can't believe this is our quaint, little Faith Chapel. If this is the sanctuary, I can't wait to see her gown. I was so mesmerized that Hunter practically had to pull me to my seat." Gayle and Lacresha smiled in agreement.

Just then, the string quartet played the intro for the processional, and everyone grew quiet.

Joe Meeker and his five groomsmen took their places at the front of the church. Immediately after, four lovely bridesmaids in white, silk gowns and stylish hats trimmed in miniature white roses gradually made their way down the aisle. Danielle noted that two of the bridesmaids were Joe's sisters, Sally and Eloise.

It seemed to delight everyone in attendance to see that all those participating in the grand procession were dressed in white to blend with the décor.

"Leave it to Rica to choose white for the entire wedding." Hunter would have expected nothing less from her. He knew she was about to prove to those present that choosing all white for the wedding would not draw attention away from the bride.

Regardless, Danielle was most interested in catching a glimpse of the matron-of-honor. Leaning back, she watched as the lovely, wisp of a girl made her way toward the front of the church. She was just as feminine and charming as Rica had described her to be. Bethany Jefferson blew a kiss from her fingertips to the tall, handsome man seated by Helen. Stewart Jefferson smiled back at his wife affectionately.

The guests quickly forgot the fashion choice when the bride entered the room on her father's arm. Rica, looking graceful and dazzling, wore a white silk gown. Her lovely face was emphasized by the high collar of the Queen Anne neckline, while the lace sleeves brought attention to her olive skin. The skirt was sewn in a slender godet style, with inserts of gathered lace that sprayed elegantly to the floor with the back vee flowing into a magnificent train. The bridal veil was floor length tulle with a headband of lace-covered silk.

Instead of a bouquet, Rica carried two long stemmed roses,

one white and one red, in remembrance of Christ's atonement for her sins—Isaiah 1:18. . . *though your sins be as scarlet, they will be as white as snow. . .*

It was as if there was only one dress in the world for Rica, and she had found it. The gown was intentionally meant to be shockingly understated compared to current fashion. There were no pearls, no rhinestones, no bustle, nor even the slightest puff of a sleeve. But on Rica, it was *simply* beautiful.

Without a doubt, the seamstress to be credited for the fabulous wedding gown was none other than Helen Jackson, who was uncomfortable with all the attention she received because of it.

The ceremony was equally romantic as the setting. While taking their vows, Rica blinked away tears, as Joe fought the lump in his throat, causing him to stammer through his words of commitment. It was an emotional time for all present.

✦

Once the ceremony came to an end, Hunter carefully guided Danielle through the reception line. He did his best not to be curt to the other members of the wedding party, but he was anxious for her to meet Bethany.

"Hunter, I'm so happy to see you." The two exchanged a quick hug.

"Bethany, I want to introduce you to Danielle Harrison, Joshua's granddaughter. Danielle, this is my cousin, Bethany Jefferson."

"So nice to finally meet you, Miss Harrison. My mother and Rica have nothing but the highest praise for you. I also happen to know Hunter concurs."

"Thank you. I've heard nothing but the highest praises for you, as well. . . and please call me *Danielle*."

"Thank you, and I would love for you to call me *Bethany*. I hope to speak with you both again at the reception."

It was time for them to move along, so Hunter edged Danielle over to Rica who gave them both a joyous embrace and added that she was looking forward to attending their wedding soon. They both blushed—but at the same time, the thought pleased them.

40

THE RECEPTION

As they had hoped, Rica and Joe's reception was held on the Jacksons' lawn. With the gazebo, the verandas, the lake, and the extensive grounds, it was a must. Of course, due to Helen's fondness for the bride-to-be and since Rica was Bethany's best friend, little persuasion was needed to secure the location.

To no one's surprise, the tables, centerpieces, candles, and other decorations were in pure white. The meal, prepared by a French chef, was superb and was served while the guests dined to the soothing sounds of a six-piece orchestra. Friends and family enjoyed each other's company while eagerly awaiting the afternoon festivities—the cutting of the five-tiered wedding cake and the exciting departure of the bride and groom riding into their future in a white, gold trimmed carriage.

After the meal, Hunter went to check on the guests' horses while Danielle was drawn to the big willow by the lake.

"Am I mistaken, or do you have a fascination with weeping willows as I do?"

Danielle turned to find Bethany following close behind. "You are not mistaken. At my stepfather's home I had my own willow, or at least I thought of the tree in that way. I spent much of my private time there in the summer. It was my refuge."

"It was the same for me under this dear tree. I miss it terribly... but I happily exchanged it for the comfort of a driveway lined with weeping willows and a new way of life. I'll never forget the day Stewart took me to our home after we were married. Every willow was swaying in the wind."

"I understand. When I left my willow, God brought me to Willow Weep to friends and family that I love and who love me. I've never been so happy."

"I suspect it isn't just friends and family who love you. I've seen the look in Hunter's eyes, and I hear it in his voice when he speaks your name. He's definitely a man in love."

"I hope that's his true feelings—although, Hunter and I seem to have our difficulties. I wish it wasn't that way."

"I'm certain most couples need to do a little sorting. Stewart and I went through a very difficult time, and we're grateful for it. We've even had a tiff or two since we wed—and I happen to know mother and father do on a rare occasion. One time mother vowed to leave my father over turnips. We still laugh about it." Bethany raised her eyebrows as if divulging a family secret.

"Now, *that* is comforting to hear. Maybe there's hope for Hunter and me." Danielle recognized Bethany's sense of humor as being similar to her own and felt they would someday be close friends.

"Mother told me you designed your dress. Well done. Do you enjoy sewing to support the mission?"

"Very much. It has fulfilled my desire to be a seamstress. Do you miss your work there?"

"For a while I did... but I was blessed to have been there during the rough times when the mission was struggling. I'm certain it's a totally different place now that it's running smoothly. God has worked miracles."

Danielle followed Bethany as she stepped through the willow's branches to take a seat on the big rock. "I believe this tree rivals my own willow. It might even rival the one in Willow Weep."

"You are making your comparison to the wrong person. I'm totally prejudiced toward this one.

"So, to get back to our previous conversation, are you in love with my favorite cousin? Please, don't tell any of my other cousins I said that, but Hunter and I have always been close. He's more like a brother. So, am I correct about your feelings for him?"

"I guess I will at least admit that I'm falling in love with him. I hadn't meant to. It just happened. I wish I'd known earlier that he was available. It certainly would've made things easier between us."

Bethany gave a playful smile. "I've heard the story."

"So. . . you and Hunter confide in each other?"

"I think my cousin needed to talk. He regrets the Sally situation."

Just then, they heard voices and could see Hunter and Stewart walking in their direction.

Bethany grasped Danielle's wrist as they left the willow. "Danielle, I want you to know that you can trust Hunter. He is and always will be a man that can be taken at his word—maybe outspoken at times, but always honest and truthful."

"Thank you. I do believe he is." As Hunter came close, her heart seemed to flutter. Danielle Harrison *was* hopelessly in love with Hunter Jackson, and there was nothing she could do about it.

Stewart reached his hand out for Bethany while Hunter casually put his arm around Danielle's waist. The gesture, along with the conversation with Bethany, had strengthened her confidence in him.

"We've come to ask if the two of you would like to join us in a boat ride. . . but we wouldn't want to interrupt your visit." Stewart waited for a reply.

"I think I can speak for the both of us. We definitely would love to go with you, but as you can see, it would be quite a feat to get these dresses safely inside a boat. So, we must respectfully and lovingly decline. But thank you for asking." Bethany stood on her tiptoes and gave Stewart a kiss.

Hunter wasted no time in removing his jacket, and laying it neatly folded on the rock. "Well, old man, it looks like it's the two of us. How about a row down to the dam and back?"

Stewart also removed his jacket. "Sounds fine, but being an old man, I think *you* should do the rowing."

"Without a doubt. I wouldn't want you to strain anything." Hunter rolled up his sleeves in preparation and started for the lake.

Danielle watched the two walk toward the dock. Hunter was a strong, confident man who could handle himself in most any situation—a man who had proven that he meant to be her protector. And she loved him for that.

In no time the two young men were gliding across the water. Staying close to the bank, Hunter took advantage of the cooling breeze offered by the shade. Even though it was late in the summer, Rica and Joe had managed to have their wedding on one of the most pleasant days of the season.

Hunter finally rowed as close to the dam as he dared before stopping to rest. Stewart used the opportunity to question him. "Am I mistaken, or have you found the young lady you want to spend your life with?"

"Well, there's nothing like getting to the point. . . but I do believe Danielle *is* that girl. I don't mind saying I'd be devastated if she didn't feel the same. Why do you ask?"

"Oh, I got wind of a little disturbance between the two of you, and I was just wondering if—"

"Helen? She's like a mother hen. I'm not complaining. She only wants the best for us. I do have a problem with Danielle not trusting me the way I think she should, but I did give her reason to feel that way. It's taking time to get past it."

"Bethany and I went through something similar just before our wedding. She felt I'd given her a reason not to trust me, and it seemed rightfully so. She wouldn't even listen to me. I won't go into the details, but I do know how you feel. We thought it was over between us, but God used the situation to correct a few issues in our lives. If you believe Miss Harrison is the girl you've been waiting for, then have faith in what you have in each other. The Lord will have your back."

"That's a good piece of advice. Thank you. I'll try my best to do just that." He grabbed the ores and—after giving Stewart a good splashing with one—began the return trip.

⚜

Danielle and Bethany were waiting on the dock by the time Hunter and Stewart returned. It was time to join the rest of the guests at the gazebo for the cake cutting.

Rica wore a radiant smile as Joe's hand covered hers while cutting the slice to share as husband and wife. They laughed out of the sheer pleasure of fulfilling the tradition and having their friends and family gathered around them.

A short time after everyone had been served, Rica made a point of finding Bethany to say their goodbyes. Then the bride and groom hurried to the carriage to escape the heavy showering of rice. As the two waved goodbye, everyone cheered and wished them a blessed life together.

Hunter pulled Danielle close to him and wondered how far in the future their special day would be. Seeing the way she looked up at him, he knew Danielle was wondering the same thing.

⚜

That evening, Hunter, Danielle, Joshua, and the rest of the Harrison household were asked to join the Jacksons while they dined on the food kindly left by the chef.

"I've always been a fan of home cooking, but I must say, I could get accustomed to a French meal now and again." Mel folded his napkin and laid it beside his plate. "Tell me, Bethany, we don't want to bore our guests, but what news have you from the mission? Helen only speaks of the business end of things."

"Then you will be interested to know that Sandra and Elmer have adopted a little boy by the name of Mark and are in the process of adopting a little girl. They have also moved into a larger home to accommodate everyone."

"Well, I have some news from Lena that's not just business." Helen gave Mel a smug smile. "I only had a moment before the wedding to read the letter I received from her yesterday, but. . . she and Burt have adopted an infant."

Bethany clapped her hands. "How wonderful!"

"They're overjoyed at being parents. And, the best part, my dear Bethany. . . the little girl has been named Bethany Helen. To have a little one as a namesake is such an honor." Helen retrieved her handkerchief and dabbed her eyes.

Bethany fell silent at the thought of Lena and Burt caring

enough to name their first child after her and her mother. "That is the highest compliment I believe I've ever been paid."

Stewart cleared his throat in response to his wife's statement. "Oh, really?"

"Uhh. . . *other than* my dear husband choosing me for his companion in life." She rubbed his arm lovingly.

Stewart smiled in satisfaction. "And I have news of my old college buddy, Matt, and his family. They have decided to trade their country home and his original job for a house on a California beach. Matt is opening an architectural business nearby."

After hearing all of the good news, Mel added, "We must admit that each story is a true miracle of God."

"Which reminds me. . . what are our hopes for grandchildren?" Helen had just broken her resolution not to approach the subject.

Stewart laughed. "Why did I know that was going to be brought into the conversation? Bethany and I have every hope of children in our future, but until then, we are cherishing our time together."

Afterward, Bethany recapped the history of the mission and its effect on the people and town of Pike City. The news of so much happiness in the lives of other couples drew Hunter and Danielle closer, causing them to continue to dream of a lifetime together.

41

DECISIONS TO BE MADE

Gayle sat up straight in the kitchen chair as she nervously stirred her coffee. "Now that dinner is over, I'd like to speak to everyone. Lacresha and Jerry, would you please stay? It shouldn't take long.

"I suppose you've all been wondering why I've come for such a long stay when I have a business to run. The answer lies within this envelope." Gayle paused and stared at it as if contemplating something.

Lacresha sat motionless, fearing what might be inside the letter. Over the years, she and Gayle had become as close as sisters, so anything concerning Gayle affected her too.

"Here, girl. Don't keep us in suspense. We're fearing the worst."

Danielle and Hunter nodded in agreement.

"No, Uncle. It isn't bad news. As a matter of fact, I hope you'll all view it as the best of news. You see, not long before I arrived, I received an offer for my company that no one in their right mind should refuse. It seems my glassware has become stiff competition for a major company, so it is more feasible for them to buy me out than to compete. For me, however, the business has never been about the money. It was the way I filled my life. While most women were caring for their families, I was seeing to details that would make the business grow and become more profitable.

"My first instinct was to decline the offer, but when I realized everything important to me could be bought and signed away in a moment, I had to face how empty my life had become. I suddenly longed for my family. . . and since I wanted to meet Daniel's dear daughter, I decided to come home while considering if I was ready to put my life's work behind me."

"Gayle, I never dreamed you were contemplating such a difficult decision. You've seemed not to have a care in the world." Josh felt bad for not being more perceptive.

"Actually, you all have made the choice extremely easy. This extended visit has made it very clear to me that I need my family. Uncle Josh, would you mind if I moved in with you. . . at least until I decide what I want to do with the rest of my life?"

"Mind? I'd be over-the-moon with joy. You're welcome to live here until the end of your days if you so choose. Lacresha and Jerry, can you believe what we're hearing? When will you make the move, my dear?"

Danielle and Lacresha grabbed each other's hands while waiting for her answer.

"Well, I was fairly certain of my decision before I left. So, I did inform my staff that I would most likely not be returning. I also have a company ready to move my household belongings as soon as they receive word. Therefore, if you all agree to my staying, I'm prepared to sign the contract at this time." Gayle turned her head and issued a pert, little smile with an optimistic nod.

The entire family, including Hunter, ecstatically encouraged her to sign the papers. Gayle removed the contract from the envelope and, with a few strokes of a pen, retired from the world of big business.

"I'm now an unemployed, free woman. I never imagined I'd be so relieved after selling my company, but you've all made it *impossible* for me to return."

"So, cousin, will you ever work again?"

"Danielle, I have no idea. . . but if I do, it will be something simple. . . such as a millinery shop."

"Say, let me get my carriage ready in the morning," Joshua broke into the conversation. "We'll ride into town to make certain that contract is properly mailed. I haven't had a meal at the inn for quite some time, so I'll treat everyone to lunch."

Before Dani's arrival, Joshua, Lacresha, and Jerry had set-tled into a mundane life, but having Gayle permanently joining the household lifted their spirits even higher than they had ever imagined.

By the time the movers had finished placing Gayle's furniture in the attic, there did not seem to be a square inch to be had anywhere in the room.

"I hope you didn't leave anything in a drawer, because you won't be able to get to it until the furniture is removed." Lacresha stood in the door of the attic while admiring all the lovely pieces from a distance. "You certainly have good taste in furniture."

"Anyone can have good taste if they have the money and are willing to pay the price. When I purchased these items—other than my business—I had nothing else in my life. Now, I could care less about any of it. They're just pieces of wood. It's interesting how our perspective can change."

Danielle and Lacresha were astounded by her statement. Neither had realized the depth of Gayle's disappointment in the way she had spent her life.

"Gayle, you must not view your life in that way. You entered a business world dominated by men, and you were successful. You've accomplished a great deal, and you're an example to women who don't feel they fit into the family way of life. Just because you see it in a different light now, doesn't mean the time you spent there was a waste. Think of the jobs you provided. Remember, it was enough for you then." Lacresha had not meant her words to be a reprimand.

"But it wasn't done because I didn't want a family. I did it because I was running away from life. I just couldn't see it then. I've finally allowed the Lord to set my eyes on what is important. I want to love and be there for those I love."

Danielle and Lacresha could see that Gayle was not being cynical. She was being grateful that she was free from her own captivity.

❧

Once the movers pulled from the driveway, Hunter and Joshua excused themselves to explore a piece of property Joshua had recently purchased. An elderly neighbor had decided to give up farming to move closer to his family and had offered the property to Josh for a good price—*if* he would make the purchase within the week it was offered.

Since things were still a bit strained between the two men—due to Hunter and Danielle's misunderstanding—Hunter decided to take advantage of the time to set things straight. Fortunately, their excursion did prove to be a time of healing, and Joshua's faith in Hunter was restored.

It blessed Danielle's heart to see all her loved ones finally relaxed and interacting—free from the constraints that had weighed heavily upon their hearts. Much had happened within the short time she had been with them, and now it was beginning to feel as if they had always shared their lives together. Everything seemed settled, and she could not imagine being happier or more content.

Later that evening Hunter and Danielle held hands as they scouted a few of the trails that weaved their way through the Harrisons' woodland. The couple's closeness had been well restored, and they were once again concentrating on what their future might hold.

When they reached a little meadow covered with wildflowers, the two took time to gather a bouquet. Danielle breathed in their fragrance and then held them out for Hunter to enjoy. Instead, he placed his hand around hers and lowered them.

"The flowers are beautiful, but I can't think of anything in life that I'd rather look upon than you. Granted, we've had our difficult times. . . but on my part, it was because I wanted so much to know you were mine."

She tipped her head slightly and looked reassuringly into his eyes to let him know he had no reason to worry.

"Danielle, out of respect for your grandfather, I've never told you this before now. He wanted me to be certain before I spoke. . . but I've *always* been certain."

He reached out and lifted her chin so she could not mistake what he was about to say. "Danielle, I'm in love with you. I don't think it's earthly possible for anyone to love more than I love you. . . and I hope someday you can return that love."

Danielle took his hand and slid it down her cheek to kiss his palm. "But I do. I began falling for you the moment we met. Hunter, I *am* in love with you."

"Are you certain?"

Danielle gave him a look to convince him she was most serious. "I am."

"Then we are truly in love?"

"It seems we most definitely are."

Hunter did not give her the tender kiss she expected he would. Instead, he took her by the hand and led her deeper into the woods, close to the road that ran parallel with the Harrison farm. There they found another clearing where a picturesque stone house stood near the creek. The home was situated in a sunlit spot, surrounded by an abundance of shade trees that connected the yard to the forest. Danielle had never been to the area and was impressed with what was before her. "This is such a lovely home. I wonder who lives here."

Hunter smiled down at her with a mysterious but lovingly hopeful smile. "*You* will. . . if you so choose."

"I don't understand."

I just signed a contract with your grandfather to purchase this property. I know the house needs work—which I'm more than willing to do in order to restore it to its former glory. "But—"

Hunter then got down on one knee. "Danielle, it's with your grandfather's permission that I ask— Will you please accept my proposal of marriage and live with me in this home? I promise I will do everything within my power to make you happy." He then opened a small, velvet box to reveal a glistening engagement ring as further enticement.

Danielle—completely shaken by Hunter's unexpected proposal—broke into tears, unable to give an answer.

Hunter stood and quickly enfolded her, patiently waiting for her reply.

"Yes. . . I will marry you. . . and I'll be most happy to live in this home."

To his own surprise, he was overcome with quieted emotion as he took her delicate hand and placed the ring on her finger. And that is when he *truly* gave Danielle the most tender and loving kiss the two had ever shared.

42

NO STONE UNTURNED

Hunter had not taken Danielle into their future home immediately after his proposal. It was late in the day, and he wanted to show her the house in the brightest of sunlight. Not to mention, they wanted to share the news of their engagement with the Harrison and Jackson families.

✦

"I must admit I was disheartened at the thought of you leaving home one day soon. . . so I jumped at the chance to keep you close by. After all, your new house will be only a stone's throw away."

"Grandpa, it's definitely more than a stone's throw away."

"Not when I'm done. See that patch I started clearing this morning. When it's completed, it will only take a few minutes to be on your doorstep."

"But it took Hunter and me much longer than a few minutes to reach the house."

"He doesn't know the lay of the land as I do. That house sets back a lane and at a sharp angle on the property. It's just right through those trees." Joshua was proud of his witty plan.

"Oh, Grandpa, that will be wonderful. It will be almost as if I'm still living upstairs. We can see each other anytime we choose."

It was then that Hunter pulled into the drive with a wagon full of supplies, ready to take Danielle to see the inside of their home. She ran to greet him and urged him onto the porch so her grandpa could share the news.

"Right through that patch of trees? I never gave it a thought. Can the house be seen from here?"

"It can—if you'll let me clear the trees up to the yard."

"By all means. Clear as much as you like. The house does seem a bit too secluded. So, why don't we take a walk from here to get an idea of the distance? Anyone interested in coming along?"

"You bet we are." Lacresha stood to her feet and descended the porch steps. "Surely you didn't think it was possible to go without us."

"No, I don't suppose I did. Maybe you can talk that husband of yours into helping me and Josh unload this wagon at the house this afternoon."

"Hold off, everyone. It appears the Jacksons have come to join us." Jerry stood and waited to assist Helen from the approaching buggy.

"We figured Hunter should be arriving with that wagon load about now, so we've come to get a look at that fine house we've been hearing about. I'd like to check the roof and basement walls. Then there's the outbuildings." Mel wore work clothes so he could do his part.

"I was concerned we might be intruding, but it looks like everyone is going." Helen was wearing a casual dress for rummaging through the house.

"We're pleased you've come. Everyone's input is welcome.

Whether or not we take your advice is a different matter." Hunter grinned and then took Danielle's hand, ready for Joshua to lead them through the woods.

When the party arrived at the property, rays of sun streamed down to showcase the house at its best. "Oh my, that house does make a statement. We didn't know the family, so we've never been here. I wasn't expecting it to look so stately. Hunter, what a nice home for your new bride! It's perfectly lovely. Mel, I'm so proud of our nephew."

"I would have expected nothing less from the boy—although I assume Joshua had a hand in this."

Seeing that Danielle was getting anxious to look inside, Hunter walked over and picked her up in his arms. "Might as well practice. Would someone get the door?"

Everyone laughed, but Joshua spoke up, "Why don't the two of you take some time to look inside first. We'll be content having a gander at the yard and buildings. Looks like that garden needs some tending." Josh then reached over and opened the door.

"Thank you, Josh. We'd appreciate a few minutes."

Hunter walked in and placed his bride-to-be in the middle of the foyer, directly in front of the cherry staircase leading to an open landing. "And this is your future home." He then gave Danielle an affectionate kiss on her forehead as he put his arm around her. "I hope you approve."

"Very much—especially if the foyer is any indication. I wasn't expecting it to be so luxurious inside, and it's been so well-kept."

"Come see the rest of the house. I think you'll be exceptionally pleased. I know I was. The kitchen needs some work, but it shouldn't take long. That's about all I've noticed so far."

Hunter and Danielle held hands as they walked for room to

room—both excited that they would soon be spending their lives together in this wonderful home. They agreed that the large kitchen needed new floor covering, cabinetry, and an updated stove. There was a formal dining room, two sitting rooms, and a library located on the first floor. Upstairs there were six bedrooms—three of a nice size and two smaller ones, one which could be used as a sewing room and the other as a nursery. Their master bedroom had its own balcony with an exceptional view of the backyard, flower garden, and Willow Creek.

When their private tour concluded, the couple went out to join the others who were patiently waiting for their turn. The men gave the inside of the house a thorough inspection and only found a few windows in need of repair. They then went to the basement before going outside to check the roof. The ladies took inventory of decorating needs and measured windows and spaces.

That evening everyone congregated in the Harrisons' dining room where the ladies put together a delicious meal from leftovers. They all had such an enjoyable time that the Jacksons stayed late into the night and had to force themselves to go home.

Again, each member within the Harrison household was astounded that so much love and happiness was continuing to be breathed back into their once stagnant lives.

Rosa stood as Danielle entered the office. "It's so good to have a moment with you. The inn has been so busy I haven't even had time to properly congratulate you on your engagement. I literally broke into tears when Hunter stopped by to tell me the news."

"I'm sorry I wasn't with him, but we were afraid the word

might get out before we could tell you together."

"I appreciate your thoughtfulness. I would have been hurt. Now, let me congratulate you with a hug."

Rosa removed a couple accounting books from a chair so Danielle could have a seat.

"Things are slowing down here at the inn. People aren't so anxious to endure the end of summer heat. However, we are still booked solid for the weeks of the fall foliage and for the holidays."

"Now, why do I sense you have something else to speak to me about besides the engagement?"

After hearing her boss's references to the inn's upcoming bookings, Danielle felt her request was ill-timed but was ready to trudge ahead. "I've come to speak to you about cutting—"

"I know what you are going to say, but you don't have to feel you're letting me down. I've already spoken to Madison. She's willing to pick up your hours. And when the time comes for you to leave, I believe she will be an excellent replacement. Madison has made great strides under your guidance."

"Thank you for being so kind to me. From the time of my arrival—"

"All right, none of this sentimental talk. I want to hear the details of the engagement, the plans for the house, the date. . . "

Danielle was more than eager to oblige her.

✦

Jean had written to say Delbert's trial had been delayed and to send a few newspaper articles which all stated that there was little hope of her brother being acquitted. Fortunately, according to the articles, he did seem to have a decent and dedicated attorney. Jean had also spoken to Harold's new housekeeper, who thought the trial had been delayed because the prosecuting attorney believed Mr. Simpson's condition to be most grave.

Danielle had no intention of giving into the severity of the situations. There was nothing that Jean had supplied or had written that would convince the girl that God would not intervene in Delbert's and Harold's lives. She then took time to pray over both matters and included a prayer for the Lord to protect Sherry while she was in her mother's care.

As long as Benjamin Dice was involved in her Grandville family's lives, Danielle knew that not one stone would be left unturned when it came to Harold Simpson's affairs. The attorney was a good Christian man with the highest of ethics. He would not abandon Harold, Delbert, or Sherry.

43

THE PURSUER

"What I'm trying to explain, Margaret, is that the prosecuting attorney is thorough in all he takes on, and the defense attorney is equally astute. They're good Christian men and are well-qualified to gather the evidence necessary in determining what took place the night of your father's attack.

"I don't consider myself qualified to take on an attempted murder case. My expertise lies within the business and personal realm. I'm not a criminal lawyer."

"Ben, you have to step in and do something. It's looking bad for Delbert, and I'm afraid he's going to end up in prison for crimes he didn't commit."

"I'm fully aware of that fact, Margaret, but I've done all I can do for Delbert. The case is in God's hands now."

Frustrated with her father's friend, Margaret clamped her mouth shut. She refused to allow herself to revert to the obnoxious remarks she would have used in the past. As tears welled up in her eyes, she collected her things and left Benjamin Dice's office without uttering another word. The girl knew what he had said was true, but she was not ready to accept it.

When Margaret Simpson arrived at the jail, she found her brother trusting the Lord for justice, but seemingly had resigned to going to prison or being hanged if it was required. Feeling ignored in her efforts to rescue Delbert from his fate, she insisted that he get on his knees and join her in prayer for his deliverance. The courtroom battle might be out of her hands, but the Heavenly battle was not.

Sherry had become accustomed to the brown faces around her and had grown to love the people and their ways. Even though it was a simple life of poverty, she much preferred it, compared to living with her mother or grandparents. The little girl wanted to let her guard down and fully embrace her time in the foothills, but she could not.

Being convinced the bum would find her someday, Sherry never ventured far from Zelda or Rand. Every unexpected twitch of a twig, faint rustle in the weeds, or unidentified movement in the distance left her feeling uneasy.

Sherry's fears were justified, since Oscar Cain—the vagrant Elmer Snodd had hired to deliver Sherry—had never left the city where she had escaped. To support himself and his liquor habit, he had continued as the thief and pickpocket he had always been.

Even though Cain was a stupid man, he was smart enough to recognize that Elmer Snodd was hiding the child away for an unscrupulous reason. Since he had been deprived of the money he had been promised for the delivery, he came up with another way to capitalize on the deal. In order to do so, he began to search for Sherry. Once he found her, the girl could be used to blackmail her grandfather. Should Snodd refuse to meet the monetary demands, then he would report what he knew. The man was positive Elmer Snodd would not want that to happen.

To locate the girl, Cain began questioning the townspeople. Because of his unwelcome questions and his unseemly appearance in the now dirty and ragged suit, he was reported to the local police. Considered a menace by the authorities, he was no longer allowed to loiter on the city streets.

Under the circumstances, the tramp was forced to take up residency in the forest near the train station. There he wandered the wooded foothills until he needed to return to town for whisky and food—or to scan the area for Sherry.

Unfortunately, that day, Cain awoke with a hangover and missed the arrival of the morning train. He had hoped to pick a few pockets at the station, but instead went down to the creek to take a dip and wait for his headache to subside.

That is where he noticed a group of people passing in the distance and was sure he had caught sight of a white face among the darker ones. Still feeling disoriented, he decided not to follow them and soon forgot about the ordeal.

However, Sherry *had* seen the man who was bathing in the creek and was nearly certain it was her vicious abuser. She knew he was here to capture her.

✦

The next day on Oscar Cain's way back from the station to his camping site, a girl ran in front of him and jogged his memory. He then recalled having seen a white person among a group of dark skinned people walking through the woods. Cain concluded that

Sherry was most likely living among the settlers in the foothills. If so, he would find her. He began scouring the area and spying on every home and settlement he found.

Zelda's peaceful, little cabin was hidden from the road by clumps of trees and bushes. That morning when Sherry had stepped out the door to draw a bucket of water, she looked up and caught a clear glimpse of Oscar Cain staggering down the road.

The girl crouched down beside the pump in a state of panic, and that is where Zelda found her a short time later. The nurse questioned her, but Sherry only clung to Zelda and refused to write down what had caused her distress.

Although she wanted to tell Zelda and Rand about the man who was her pursuer, she did not dare. Sherry knew revealing the story would mean being returned to her mother or grandparents. Both scenarios petrified her.

Oscar Cain continued his day-to-day search. In fact, he had never been so dedicated to a task in his pathetic life—even astonishing himself. It was greed that caused the man to be so persistent, for he was expecting to be wealthy by the time he was through with Elmer Snodd. Thankfully, the bum had not discovered Sherry or the cabin—but that only postponed the inevitable.

44

ANOTHER WOMAN

"So, who is this *Joshua Harrison*?" Furious with Hunter, her middle son, Agnes Jackson wadded the letter up and pitched it on the floor.

"He's a farmer who lives near Mel and Helen. A good man. Successful enough. Well respected." Lucas Jackson picked up the letter his wife had thrown on the floor, straightened it, and laid it on the desk. "The girl's his granddaughter."

"Hunter is engaged to a common farm girl? He knows our expectations when it comes to marriage. We should've known he'd do something like this for spite."

"Calm down, Agnes. I'm sure she's a fine young lady. Hunter, like Mel, wants a different way of life than we do. He's doing well for himself. Actually, I'm beginning to admire his independent thinking."

"Lucas, since Hunter left college, you've made no qualms about your disappointment in his behavior. You promised me you'd see to it that he'd settle down and fall into step with the rest of our family. You even made a point of preaching to the boys that an advantageous marriage is just good business sense. I said nothing when you allowed him to temporarily go his own way. Now Hunter wants to marry an unrefined, country bumpkin, and you admire him for it?"

Lucas rubbed the back of his neck as he leaned on the over-stuffed chair. "I know. I'm just tired of fighting Hunter on his every whim. As I said, the boy is like Mel. He isn't impressed with our lifestyle. No one could change Mel's mind, and I doubt we'll be able to change Hunter's."

Agnes walked over and stood in front of her husband, "So you're telling me you're not going to keep your promise to get him in line?"

Lucas took a few paces and stopped as he considered the question, then turned to face his wife. "Yes, I am. I don't think we can change him."

"Well, Lucas, if you think *I'm* going to allow him to go through with this wedding, you are highly mistaken."

⚜

Even though most of their spare time was used to work on their future home, Hunter made certain he and his fiancée found time for romantic interludes. He told Danielle they should enjoy their courtship because he planned for it to be short-lived. Danielle did not argue with him.

With the entire family assisting, the renovations were going far better than expected. Joshua had continued to work overtime on the shortcut between the two homes and would soon have it completed. Along with everything else, Gayle had a surprise for the newly engaged couple and finally called another family meeting.

"Again, this should only take a few minutes. . . but I want you all to know that I've decided to make the farm my permanent home.

I've become so accustomed to having family around that I don't think I could return to living alone."

Needless to say, everyone began to express their happiness over the news, and she had to interrupt them to share the rest. "But wait. . . there's more. I know Hunter is doing well financially, but I've also heard these two discussing the meager pieces of furniture they plan to begin housekeeping with. . . and it simply won't do. That's why, Hunter and Danielle, I would like for you to accept my furniture as a wedding gift. I know my things won't fill the entire house, but it'll be a good start."

Hunter and Danielle looked at each other in disbelief.

"Gayle. . . thank you. . . but Danielle and I can't allow you to do such a thing. It's far too generous."

"My dear cousin, I do thank you, but I must agree with Hunter. It's not that we wouldn't love to have the furnishings, but we can't possibly—"

"Unless you don't care for the furniture, then I insist you take it off our hands. Otherwise, it will be left in the attic to gather dust. Please, I want to do this for the two of you."

"The only way we could possibly accept it is if you'd allow us to purchase it."

"I won't hear of it. Besides, the style is perfect for your home."

The discussion did continue back and forth, but in the end, Gayle won.

⚜

Rosa hurried to catch up with Danielle. "I'm so glad you're still here. I desperately need your help. While I ran to the post office, the new server took a reservation for a large party this evening, and I just found it on the book. The girl didn't even write down the name. All the staff who are willing to work overtime have gone home. I did catch Madison in time, but I need one more waitress at the very least. If you'll stay, I'd promise to have a boy deliver a message to Joshua, so he'll know you're working late."

"I would love to help you, but I just can't. I still panic at the thought of being a waitress." Danielle was ashamed of her reaction, but she couldn't put herself in that position again.

Rosa placed a hand on her forehead, trying to think what to do. "I would send for one of the other servers, but there isn't time. The party is due within minutes. What if I do the serving, and you just deliver the platters and drinks to the buffet along the wall. I can serve them from there and instruct you at the same time."

Seeing how distraught Rosa had become, Danielle agreed to chance humiliating herself once more.

It seemed only seconds until the guests arrived, and Danielle was relieved. . . at first. . . to see that the host and hostess were none other than Mel and Helen Jackson. They were followed by a very distinguished couple and an extremely pretty and proper, young woman. Behind them were Mr. and Mrs. Meeker and Sally, Joe and Rica, who had recently returned from their honeymoon, Pastor and Mrs. Strong, and Mrs. Belinda Gray.

Once everyone was comfortably seated, Mel requested that Danielle come to the table where he took the reluctant initiative to introduce her to Hunter's parents, Mr. and Mrs. Lucas Jackson, and their guest, Miss Marka Bricker.

Danielle was totally shocked. She already knew she looked a mess—especially after working a full shift in the extreme heat. This was not the way she had expected to meet her future in-laws or her fiancé's past love interest. Hunter had planned for them to visit his parents' home for the introductions. He, also, had explained that the visit, most likely, would not be a pleasant one.

The situation totally flustered Danielle. Fortunately, she thought to take a few deep breaths to calm herself.

Danielle managed a polite greeting—which was coolly received. Not to mention, her nervous reaction did not go unnoticed by Agnes Jackson or Miss Bricker, who both smiled back at her quite judgingly.

Rosa stepped forward to intervene. "I must apologize. Your reservation did not have the name of your party. Had I known it was the Jackson family, I wouldn't have asked Danielle to serve tonight, so she could've joined you."

"Very interesting. Hunter did not mention you were a working girl, as well." Agnes ignored Rosa and lowered her head, while keeping her eyes on Danielle, to make it clear she did not approve.

Danielle's face reflected how belittled she felt.

Mel was furious but did not react. He was afraid he would not be able to control his tongue if he spoke. However, he leered at his brother disapprovingly.

Helen was still putout that Lucas, Agnes, and the Bricker girl had shown up on their doorstep unannounced, but she, too, managed to keep quiet. Rica, on the other hand, was livid and did not. "Danielle is one of my most cherished friends. I simply scramble to get a moment alone with her. Your son has done well in choosing his future bride."

"I assume if one lives so near the country, as you do, becoming acquainted with a farm girl or two is unavoidable." Agnes Jackson then offered a brief smile.

Rica, was preparing to retaliate, when Rosa cut in. "I guess I should mention the specials while we pass out the menus."

Fortunately, the tactic worked, and everyone's interest was

swayed to look at their dinner choices. However, the empty chair beside Miss Bricker caught Rosa's attention. "We seem to be missing a guest."

Agnes Jackson raised her head pompously, as her eyes scanned the room and finally connected with Danielle's. "Hunter will be joining us. I expect he will want to spend every possible moment with Marka once he sees she's here."

The private dining room became silent.

Danielle left the room hurt—uncertain she would be able to function at all.

Rosa followed, as she tried to place a comforting hand on the girl's shoulder. "My dear, if I'd had any inkling it was to be the Jacksons, I never would've asked you to serve."

Danielle held up her hand to let Rosa know it was all she could do to keep from falling apart. At the same time, the situation made her determined not to give in to the rudeness of Hunter's mother.

As it turned out, Danielle was able to work quietly in the background by following Rosa's all-inclusive instructions. However, it was when Danielle came from the kitchen with the last platters that she saw Hunter, her protector, enter the room.

"My darling son, you're late. I can't imagine what kept you. We've already placed your order." Agnes then lifted her head, turned her cheek, and waited for his welcoming kiss.

He did not oblige.

Hunter's eyes were set on the attractive Miss Bricker. As a matter of fact, he only looked away from the girl momentarily and only offered a brief nod toward the others present. Unfortunately, included in that distracted glance was his fiancée. He had totally ignored her in front of so many she loved.

Shocked by what they had witnessed, the entire group began to eat in near silence. Only the tingling of crystal and silver could be heard. At that moment, almost everyone present had a change of heart toward Hunter Jackson.

As it so happened, Rob Wilky had momentarily stepped out of the kitchen to consult with Rosa and witnessed what had taken place concerning the favored Mr. Jackson.

By the time the meal was over, the situation had become so uncomfortable that the guests began inventing reasons to be on their way. The pastor and his wife were the first to excuse themselves.

After their departure, Agnes Jackson spoke up. "Hunter dear, since you and Miss Bricker once had an attachment, I think it only proper for you to drive her home and renew your friendship. It's been quite some time."

Hunter stared at his mother a little longer than need be before answering. Totally unaware of his family's and friends' newly formed opinions of him, he rose to assist Marka Bricker from her chair. "Yes, mother. I'm looking forward to speaking to her alone."

With his intended standing only a few feet away, Hunter left the room with the young woman on his arm—not even giving Danielle a second glance.

The rest of the party, except for Mr. and Mrs. Lucas Jackson, watched in utter disgust. Those who loved Danielle could almost feel the stab of pain in her heart.

As those remaining prepared to leave, Rob entered through the swinging doors, wrapped his arm around Danielle, and took her through the kitchen to spare her the torture of facing the others. "Don't worry, sweetheart. I'll see you home." He then kissed her lightly on the forehead.

Rosa, admiring Rob's kindness, was relieved he had thought so quickly and gave him a nod to excuse him for the evening.

However, Sally Meeker had watched as Rob easily stepped in to comfort the hurting girl. . . and it was not admiration, she was feeling toward him.

45

THE SPY

Joe and Rica followed closely behind Rob and Danielle as they set out for the Harrison home. Rica would not be able to rest until she was certain her dear friend was properly comforted. Since Rob felt it was his place to console Danielle, he was disappointed they had tagged along. Once they arrived, he found himself obliged to wait on the front porch with Joe. Unhappy about the situation, he soon excused himself and went home.

On top of everything that had happened at the inn, Gayle had met the girls in the parlor with the news that Joshua had fallen ill. "Don't panic. The doctor has given him a full examination. He does fear Uncle Josh might've had a light heart attack. We're to monitor him closely and make certain he gets plenty of rest. For the first few days your grandfather should only be disturbed for medical reasons. So Lacresha will care for him during the day, and I will take the night shift. Don't worry, Danielle. He'll be back on his feet in no time."

"How could this happen? He was laughing when I left this morning. It's because he's been working too hard on clearing the lane, isn't it?"

"Danielle, Uncle Josh has worked hard all his life. His condition can't be blamed on just one incident. He's a strong man." Gayle tried to reason with Danielle, but the girl could bear no more and excused herself to go lie down.

Once she was out of hearing range, Rica found Gayle. "I think you need to know that hearing of Joshua's condition is not the only matter Danielle's dealing with tonight. It appears Hunter has betrayed her. At the inn, Hunter totally ignored her and left with a girl from his past on his arm. I don't even know what to make of it myself." Rica unfolded the rest of the story, leaving Gayle appalled at Hunter and his conduct.

When Rica and Gayle eventually joined Danielle, they found her sitting at her dressing table, now dry-eyed, and staring into the mirror. "Hunter didn't even acknowledge me. From the moment he entered the room, all of his attention was focused on his former love."

"Surely there's another reason for his conduct." Gayle poured water into the basin and wet a cloth to place on Danielle's swollen eyes.

"The reactions of our friends at the inn indicated they saw the same thing. Anyway, what other explanation can there be?"

Rica sat down on the bed beside Danielle and rubbed her shoulders to help calm her. "It's true. We were all disillusioned and confused by Hunter's actions. Even so, I suggest you give it some time and wait to hear from him. You do recall how much he wanted your trust?"

Gayle and Rica said little else, not wanting to give Danielle false hope in Hunter's love *nor* discourage her faith in him. They only left her side when she finally agreed to lie down.

Danielle felt guilty for deceiving Rica and Gayle into thinking she had fallen asleep. But, she just wanted to be alone, forget what had happened at the inn, and concentrate on praying for her grandpa.

Periodically, Oscar Cain would abandon his stakeouts and walk the back roads to see if he could locate Sherry. Most of those he met along the way would not stop to speak to him since he was a stranger and obviously a derelict.

However, on one such occasion, Oscar came across a junk dealer who was a good-hearted soul who could not bring himself to be unkind to anyone. Cain held up his hand to get the dealer to stop. "Aw hates ta hold ya up, but I'm in these hills a lookin' for a stray young'un. A white girl, 'bout tall as that bush yonder, skinny, with yeller hair. Ya seen any kid like that?"

The junk man rubbed his chin as if it helped him reflect. "Not usual ta see a white'un in these parts. There's a moonshiner, by the name of Riggle, with a bunch of kids. They live east a here 'bout three miles or four. I'd say they got at least a dozen or so. May of took in a few. Don't figure though, cuz the daddy's not much fer providin'. Poor as church mice. All of 'em kinds got different colored hair. Why ya lookin' fer this girl?"

"I wuz a doin' a favor and the rascally thing got way from me. Ran in the woods, she did, and I can't find the li'l dickens. I'm afeared fer 'er." Cain was proud of himself for coming up with a nearly truthful answer.

"I see. Some of thum critters can be onery. Never had none ma'self. Anyway, most of the whites er east a here. But all of 'em folks has a bunch of young'un too. Sorry, that's 'bout all I know ta hep ya. Best be on ma way." The man gave Oscar a friendly wave and signaled the mule onward.

Cain had only taken a few steps when the dealer stopped the mule and yelled back at him. "I don't know how long ya been lookin', but I did see that nurse in these parts with a li'l, white girl the last time I wuz up this way."

"And where 'bouts this nurse live?" Cain was careful not to act overly eager.

"I can't hep ya there. Stands to reason it would be in these parts though. Have a dandy!"

The bum paid no attention as the man pulled away. Oscar was already trying to decide whether he should go east or try to locate the nurse.

He finally decided to check out the Riggle family, and their place was easily found since he could see smoke coming from the chimney. Oscar Cain spied on the family for almost two days trying to catch sight of all the children who lived there. He did not care about their sad faces, worn clothing, unwashed bodies, or thin frames. The bum was only interested in the color of their hair. Once he surmised there was not a blonde among them, he moved farther east.

Being lazy, the hike up the mountain took him longer than most men, but to his credit, he did find the general location of the white settlement. Oscar almost immediately happened upon a church gathering and was able to get a fair view of the children there. The Snodds' granddaughter was not among them. Nonetheless, the size of the congregation indicated there were several white families in the area, so Oscar continued to snoop around.

During his stay on the east side, Cain saw several girls with light colored hair and about the right size and age, but he did not see Sherry. Frustrated for making the wrong choice, he headed back west to find the nurse.

As it happened, a rainstorm moved in unexpectedly, leaving Oscar stranded without shelter. After being drenched, he stripped down to his trousers and wrapped the shirt and jacket in a tight bundle to protect the two bottles of whisky stashed within them. The storm soon passed, but the rain set in as if it were a plague.

Just before sunset, he finally noticed a small cavern within the rocks. While trying to get to it, he had to cross a gushing stream which had been newly formed by the downpour, and the shivering tramp was swept to the bottom of the hill. Cain received several cuts and bruises from the slide and even more while slipping and falling in the mud as he climbed back up to the hollow in the hillside. There was nothing to eat, but he was not concerned since the alcohol had survived the ordeal just fine.

The rain continued to hound him into the next day but disappeared once he reached the general area of where the nurse was supposed to live. Cain was fully aware he had been a fool to look elsewhere. There was now no doubt in his mind, that when he found the nurse's dwelling, he would find Sherry.

However, Oscar Cain's tiring journey had not been a total waste of time, since, along the way, he had devised the perfect plan to locate the woman. All he had to do was wait at the crossroad for someone to pass by.

Since it turned into a nice day, the cocky tramp did not need to wait long before hearing a group of people coming his way. He quickly broke open one of his wounds and used his shirt to soak up the blood. Then he wrapped the shirt tightly around his arm. "I needs help! Ha'da bad fall. Broke ma arm and the bone's ran clean through the skin." Oscar acted as if he was about to pass out.

One of the men reached out to keep Cain from falling. "Anyone here knows how to set a bad arm." No one in the group responded.

"Best see Zelda Fields. She'll know what ta do."

The bum had to force himself not to smile. "Would ya be sa kind as ta shows me the way er give me d'rctions. I'm 'fraid I's 'bout ta give out."

As quickly as that, Oscar Cain had the information he needed. So, after taking time to do some lucrative thieving in town, he made the long trek back up the mountain to monitor the home of Nurse Zelda.

⚜

"I'm telling you, Rand, Anna has gone back to being my shadow since the day I found her crouched by the well. I have to force her to go outside, and that's when I'm with her. Whatever she saw or heard that day has frightened her beyond reason. I'm at my wits' end."

"It's plain as daylight Anna saw whoever she's been afraid of since gittin' here. Barney just told me he'd heard somebody askin' 'bout a white girl. What we need ta figure out is if they're meanin' to harm 'er."

The nurse admired Rand for his intelligence and wisdom. She believed he someday would be very successful once he had the chance to get away from the hills. Rand spent his spare time looking for ways to make life better for himself and those around him. He was an honest and caring man who loved the Lord dearly.

"It's highly possible that Anna saw someone. . . or maybe it was just an animal that had frightened her when she was lost."

Rand rolled his eyes. "Ya don't believe that any more than I do."

"Then why don't they just come to the door and ask about Anna."

"Maybe she just seen them, and they haven't found her yet. If not, they will soon, and they're probably not to be trusted. I think it's best I take up sleepin' on the porch. Can't be around much durin' the day, but I'll be here as soon as my workday ends."

Sherry overheard their conversation through the window and realized her friends were close to unraveling the story. She found a piece of paper and wondered if it was time to write down how she came to be lost in the forest.

The thought of falling into the hands of the brute who was pursuing her petrified the child. However, she feared being returned to her mother or grandparents just as much. Even as an eight-year-old, Sherry understood that, for some reason, they had sacrificed her safety for their own advantage. Her family had proven their love for her was not sincere.

Still the child could not help believing that her pursuer might overlook her and give up the search. If so, she could stay on this hillside haven with Zelda and Rand. Sherry decided not to reveal her secret.

Sadly, the little girl's idealistic hopes put her at risk. Oscar Cain was camped only a short distance away from Zelda's cabin. It was only a matter of time.

46

ALONE WITH MARKA

They were out of town before Hunter could speak to Marka Bricker calmly. She was seated much closer to him than necessary and was wearing a more pleased smile than she had the right to be.

"I can't say that I'm happy to see you, Marka." Hunter's statement was dry, and his expression was most serious.

"You certainly have a poor way of showing it. You rushed to my side the moment you recognized me and haven't taken your eyes off me since." Marka leaned back in her seat, satisfied with her reply.

Hunter wasted no time in getting to the point. "Only because I was furious, and I wanted to put an end to this charade before it went any further. I understand completely why you and my parents are here. They don't approve of Danielle, and you still hope to keep me dangling."

Marka gave a little huff. "Surely, Hunter, you're jesting."

"If you'll recall, there was another time you pretended that you wanted to rekindle our relationship. That was when I was still a bit infatuated with you. Like most people, I didn't care to be told that the person I was interested in doesn't want to see me anymore. But by that time, I was older and had caught on to your game. So,

I guess I should've made my feelings clear at the time. It was only my ego and not my heart that you wounded when you went your separate way. I have never been—nor will I ever be—in love with you, Marka."

"Oh, what a convenient tale you've fabricated. I'm glad to hear you have consoled yourself with those thoughts."

"Stop it, Marka. You know what I'm saying is true. So, when did you and my parents become traveling partners?"

"Your mother asked me to join them with a party of friends at the coast. I was free and decided I'd like to go. Your Uncle Mel's home is only a stop on the way."

"I'm surprised you're so willing to be used in mother's scheme."

"My, you are free in your opinions. Evidently your imagination has been working overtime on my behalf. We've barely spoken this evening. I've made no overtures, nor did I plan to do so. Not to mention, your mother and I have had no discussions about you."

"Of course, not. . . it would've only been implied. Look, Marka, we grew up as childhood friends, so I'm going to be honest with you. You were always a nice girl—at least until you were allowed suitors. I must say, you did the right thing by ending our relationship after learning I wasn't interested in the lifestyle you and our parents enjoy."

Marka smoothed her hair and gave another agitated huff.

"But when I started seeing other girls, your behavior toward me suddenly indicated you still cared—but, of course, you didn't. Like I said, I was wise enough to see what you were up to. You didn't want me, but you didn't want anyone else to have me either. It was only a ploy to keep me interested in you. For some selfish reason, you want the men in your past to continue pining for you.

Marka, you're a grown women and you're still engaged in the same childishness."

She opened her mouth to protest, but Hunter's words caused her to realize how obviously self-absorbed she had been.

"I'm taking you to Mel's house, and I never want to deal with this again. I'm in love with Danielle, and she doesn't deserve to be hurt by you—or my parents."

"Well, Hunter, if you have no feelings for me and truly care for her, why did you treat the girl so inexcusably at the restaurant?"

"What are you talking about? Danielle wasn't among the guests."

"No, she wasn't." Your betrothed was one of the servers. You didn't even bother to acknowledge her."

"You must be mistaken. She doesn't work at nights and she's not a server."

"I'm not mistaken. When your parents and I first arrived, your uncle introduced her to us. She is a smaller girl with blonde hair."

"No. . . no, I didn't see her. You have to be mistaken."

"Hunter, you looked right at her. Rather coldly, I'm afraid."

"If you're being truthful. . . then I've wounded her deeply. I was livid when I walked in and saw you. I don't even remember dinner. All I wanted to do was get you back to Mel and Helen's before any problems were created."

"Hunter, I'm sorry, but, before you arrived, the girl had endured some brutal insinuations from your mother. And she did seem devastated when you totally ignored her."

"Danielle is truly the love of my life, Marka. Since we met, all I've wanted to do was keep her from harm. There's no way that I'll be able to rectify this mess tonight. By the time I take you back to Mel and Helen's, it will be far too late. And I have commitments tomorrow that can't be put off. How could I have overlooked her?"

"Hunter, I'm sorry for my part in this. Much of what you're saying is true. I do like it when men are pining for me. Will you forgive me?" Marka wiped her eyes with her handkerchief.

"I do forgive you, but I'd appreciate it if you would keep your distance. We have nothing further to discuss."

Arriving in the foyer, Hunter stopped briefly to wish Marka Bricker well on her journey.

Upon entering the parlor, he could feel the tenseness in the room and assumed the two Jackson brothers and their wives were not on the best of terms. After acknowledging him, Mel and Helen left the room so Hunter could be alone with his parents who sat close together at one end of the sofa.

Hunter's stiffened jaw indicated that their son was more upset than they had ever seen him. Alarmed by it, Agnes Jackson was unable to wait until he spoke. "Don't blame your father. It was all my doing. I'm the one that vowed to stop the marriage."

"As much as I would like to allow your mother to take the blame, I stood by and did nothing while she followed through with that absurd plan." Lucas, as always, tried to appear the gentleman.

Agnes flinched when she saw the flash of anger in her son's eyes. "I don't think there's anything left to say that Mel hasn't already said or that we haven't concluded ourselves. You're a grown man, and I had no business interfering in your life. I just want the best for you. I apologize, Hunter."

"Danielle *is* the best for me, Mother."

Agnes, being nervous, tried to smooth things over. "Mel and

Helen have explained who she is. The girl and her situation aren't as bad as I had thought."

"Mother, I love you. In so many ways, you are a wonderful person, but you have done and said enough. Not only did this humiliation take place in front of our friends, but Danielle also believes I intentionally ignored her. I was so angry that I didn't even notice her presence. There's no doubt you were successful in creating a division between us."

At hearing her son's last assertion, Agnes Jackson lowered her head.

"I assume you both will be leaving in the morning, so in all due respect, I'm saying goodbye and wish you well in your travels. I'll be spending the night at the inn."

Hunter left the parlor.

Mel and Helen rose early to see their guests off but offered no regret for their departure. As they drove away, Mel shook his head. "I suppose I should feel bad for being so outspoken with Lucas and Agnes, but I can't bring myself to be. I've watched them turn their noses up at people over the years, and I refuse to allow them to do so to our friends. That poor girl was crushed by the time dinner was over. The way Hunter treated Danielle was disgraceful. I never would've believed he was capable of being so callous. I've a good mind to fire the boy. And why isn't he downstairs and ready to go? We have an important meeting to attend."

"Mel, when the Bricker girl asked to speak to Hunter this morning, Agnes told her that he had spent the night at the inn. I'm beginning to think maybe things weren't as we supposed."

It was then that Hunter entered the foyer with no greeting, wanting to set the record straight. "Before we leave, I'd like to explain a few things to the both of you. When I arrived at the inn last night, Rosa was still up and gave me a piece of her mind concerning my actions toward Danielle and Miss Bricker. I assume all of my friends and family who witnessed the display have the same opinion of me."

"You assume right." Mel folded his arms.

"Mel. . . Helen, you know I love Danielle. Please understand that I was terribly upset when I received your note saying my parents were in town. It was clear they were here to make things difficult. I was irate when I saw Marka." Hunter continued with the explanation.

It took some persuasion, but soon Mel and Helen had settled down enough to think the situation through rationally and volunteered to explain to the rest of the dinner guests what was behind all their misconceptions. Hunter was somewhat relieved to know he would soon be vindicated with the other witnesses. Yet, it was Danielle's forgiveness that he coveted above all.

47

I MUST FIND HER

The following morning there was no noticeable improvement in Joshua. The stress of her grandfather's condition mingled with the devastating rejection by Hunter had taken its toll on Danielle.

Trying not to remember what had happened at the inn was useless. Even when managing to dismiss a hurtful thought, another one followed. Denied any escape from her thoughts, she had spent a long, sleepless night.

"Danielle, I'm so sorry. These letters came last week, and somehow a book was laid on top of them. I meant to give them to you yesterday. I do hope any news they might have will cheer you up."

Gayle laid the letters on the wicker porch table beside Danielle. "Would you like some company, dear? I have all day to catch up on my rest."

"Thank you, but it's probably best that I'm alone. There's a lot to sort out. My main concern is for Grandpa. His recovery is more important to me than what I'm feeling."

"Remember, Danielle, the doctor told us it might be a few days before we see much improvement. We're only to call Doc if there's a notable decline, so try not to worry. Your grandfather is a resilient man. Now, I'll leave you to your thoughts, but remember I'm here if you need me." Then, respecting her cousin's wishes, Gayle went inside.

Danielle was considering which letter to open first when she noticed a chaise coming up the driveway. The young driver confidently brought the horse to a stop in front of the house. Danielle rose and was surprised to see it was Sally Meeker. "Miss Meeker, I wasn't expecting you."

"Please. . . call me Sally. I know we haven't been on the best of terms in the past, but I would like that to change."

Danielle took Sally's hand and squeezed it tenderly. "Of course, I would like that too."

"Then I hope you don't mind my intrusion, but I saw how distressed you were after dinner last night, and I think I might be able to shed some light on the matter. But if you don't mind me saying, you look even more upset today. Am I correct?"

"It's just that when I arrived home last night, I learned that Grandpa had fallen ill. The doctor believes it was a light heart attack and that he'll come through just fine—although it'll be a while before he's back on his feet."

"Oh my! This comes as quite a shock. Joshua has always been so strong. I don't remember him ever being sick. Please, give him my love and tell him the Meekers will be praying for a swift recovery.

"Is there anything we can do to assist? Bring supplies? Sit with him? Meals?"

"Thank you, Sally. But so far, Gayle and Lacresha are managing his care. Jerry and I can get anything else we might need. Unfortunately, I won't be able to give him your message just yet. The doctor wants him to have complete rest, so I'm not allowed to see him for a few days."

"Would it help if I tell our friends? They'll want to know."

"Of course, that would be wonderful." Danielle offered her a grateful smile.

"Then consider it done." Sally smiled back, pleased to know she had found a small way to ease some of the family's burden.

"Would you like to have a seat?" Sally took the wicker chair, and Danielle sat back down on the sofa.

For a short time, there was an awkward silence, but Sally knew it was best if she spoke first. "I don't think there's any other way to go about this than just to say what's on my mind. Last night at dinner, everyone was appalled at the treatment you received from Hunter and his parents. I can't speak for the others involved, but I feel I might have some insight when it comes to Hunter. Remember, he had reason to give me more than one unpleasant facial expression."

Danielle giggled in agreement, seeing that Sally was trying to make their conversation lighthearted.

"Our friends were watching Hunter—but not *studying* him as I was. Danielle, the looks Hunter was giving that Miss Bricker weren't out of admiration or love. They were caused by frustration. Even though little was said between them, Hunter spent the entire meal trying to keep the girl from making a spectacle.

"He also glared at his mother for requesting he take Marka home—and for bringing attention to the fact the two had been more than friends."

Danielle turned away from Sally, as if she didn't want to hear any more. "I saw none of that."

"Please listen, Danielle. Since no one bothered to include me in their conversations during dinner, I had the advantage of watching the entire episode. From my perspective, you were distressed and weren't thinking clearly by then. Besides, you only glanced at him occasionally."

Not convinced, Danielle again removed her eyes from Sally.

Noting her reaction, Sally delved deeper into her observations. "When Hunter arrived, he was already angry and became more so when he saw Miss Bricker. As he greeted everyone at the table, I believe he saw a group of friends but wasn't seeing anyone individually. He seemed so stricken by what, most likely, was a plot by his parents that he couldn't see beyond it."

"How can you not see the one you are supposed to be in love with?" Danielle blinked away tears.

"Why would he even consider that you were there? You never work evenings—and especially not as a server. Remember, you *were* in the background the entire meal."

"Then why was he so anxious to be alone with Miss Bricker?"

"I can only tell you that neither his face nor his countenance indicated he was happy to be leaving with that girl. Danielle, don't be so foolish as to judge Hunter without speaking with him. There's more to this story than what you and those in our party have imagined." Sally hoped her passionate plea was having an effect on Danielle's heart.

"I don't know that I can be so easily convinced."

"Is it any more far-fetched than what you're willing to believe about the man you love?"

Shocked by her bold statement, Danielle caught her breath.

"I *am* being forward, but you must consider what I'm saying. Hunter is a good man who would never intentionally hurt you. He loves you dearly. If I can see it. . . surely you can."

Just then a young man on a bicycle came rushing up behind Sally's chaise and skipped up the steps. "I have a wire for a Miss

Danielle Harrison."

"I am she." Danielle took the telegram and gave the boy a tip from the change she had in her pocket.

Sally watched as Danielle's face took on a look of panic. "What is it?"

"I can't say just now. I'm sorry, but I must cut our visit short. Do you suppose you could do me a favor by telling Rosa that I won't be coming to work this week? I have urgent business to attend to."

Sally had no choice but to say goodbye. She prayed Danielle would heed her warning and that the telegram would not cause her new friend more sorrow.

As soon as Sally left, Danielle reread the telegram:

STILL WAITING FOR YOUR REPLY ON ELMER SNODD'S
SISTER'S NAME AND ADDRESS IN BRISTOL. A POSSIBLE
LEAD IN LOCATING SHERRY.
BENJAMIN DICE, ESQ.

She then remembered the two letters and realized they might hold the necessary information she needed to understand the message.

The first letter she grabbed was from Jean. It was short and to the point.

My Dear Danielle,

I hope I've made a decision that's in your best interest. It was difficult to know what the right thing to do was, but I trusted the decision to the Lord.

Your stepfather's attorney, Benjamin Dice, has just left. He was seeking information on your whereabouts, hoping that you might know the address of your Grandfather Snodd's sister. He didn't give me any details, other than he believes Sherry might be living with your great-aunt in Bristol.

Since I felt it was the right thing to do, I did give him your address and a brief explanation of your life as it is now. I would have never done such a thing if I hadn't become acquainted with the new staff at the Simpson home. They all hold the attorney in high regard.

I'm also including yesterday's news article on Delbert's trial. I'm sorry, but it doesn't look promising for him. . .

Danielle then ripped open Benjamin Dice's letter. She skipped the formalities and scanned down to the necessary information.

I do apologize for invading your need to keep your location private. However, since this involves finding your sister, Sherry, I felt it necessary to seek you out.

Your friend, Mrs. Jean Johnson, was good enough to share your location, current way of life, and what you are aware of in reference to your family in Grandville.

I believe it is best to fill you in on what may have happened to Sherry. This is strictly off the record, and I hope you will guard this information.

Shortly after finding an announcement of your mother's recent marriage in a New York newspaper, an associate of mine was sent there to gather information. While there, he was able to befriend a staff member at the Peppercon residence. Being suspicious of your mother's motives for the marriage to their elderly boss, the longtime employee was most cooperative. From that contact, we learned of a conversation between your mother and grandfather. The informant told my man that they had overheard Esther and your grandfather state that Sherry had been sent to Mr. Snodd's sister in Bristol.

What I need from you is the name and address of your great-aunt. The information could be invaluable in locating our dear Sherry. If we weren't in the middle of Delbert's trial, I would be in Bristol myself, trying to locate the woman.

I think it's important for you to know that the Snodds and your mother have a reason for hiding your sister. Your mother does not currently, nor shall she ever, have legal guardianship of Sherry. That honor would belong to me and my wife. Therefore, your mother and your grandfather know that she, and possibly both, could be brought up on charges of kidnapping.

Hopefully, Sherry will soon be safe in our care once we find your great-aunt.

This is all the information I feel comfortable sharing at present. Please telegraph me with your reply as soon as possible.

I must add that I was astounded to learn where you happened to make your home. I can only assume it was the

Lord that miraculously delivered you safely into the hands of your father's relatives.

Thank you for your assistance and may God bless you in your new life.

Sincerely,

Benjamin Dice

Danielle looked up in time to see Jerry coming from the stables and yelled to ask him to get the shay ready. She then ran upstairs and packed a bag before finding Lacresha. "By any chance is Grandfather doing better?"

"Why yes, he's beginning to rally. I was just about to come tell you. He'll be up and around soon." Seeing the look on Danielle's face, Lacresha's smile waned.

"I can't tell you what a relief that is to hear. It makes what I have to do so much easier."

"What are you talking about? Is something wrong?"

"You must keep this quiet, but I have received information indicating that Sherry was sent to my great-aunt's home in Bristol. Do you happen to know if Grandpa has the woman's name and address? My stepfather's attorney is asking."

"I'm almost positive he doesn't. He did hear the family's home was foreclosed on, but that was shortly after your father passed. No. There was no reason for Joshua to have any contact with them. I do remember the woman's name was *Myrtle. Myrtle Milk, Musk. . .* the last name was four letters and started with an "M"."

"At least that's a lead, Lacresha. I know you won't agree, but it's imperative that I go to Bristol to try to find Sherry. She must be terribly frightened. I just can't believe my mother and grandparents were so uncaring as to send her among strangers. . . especially after what happened to Harold."

"I can't let you go on a search like that alone. Let Jerry go with you."

"No. He's needed here to help with Grandpa. I'll be fine. I've become familiar with Bristol. Besides, it's better that I meet mother's family alone."

They both heard Jerry bringing the shay around, and Danielle started toward the front door.

"Wait! Why is it better to go meet them alone? I don't like this. Let me get Gayle to go with you. Jerry and I can manage Joshua ourselves."

"Thank you, Lacresha, but I can do this myself. Please, tell Grandpa I love him. Don't worry. He'll understand why I have to do this." She then ran from the house, jumped in shay, and was off to Bristol.

48

ESCORT HER OFF THE PROPERTY

Sally Meeker parked in the back lot of the inn and hurried to the office to inform Rosa of Joshua's heart attack. Alarmed by the news, Rosa's first reaction was to insist they pray. She then made a list of restaurant dishes to be delivered so Lacresha and Gayle would not need to cook. To assist her, Sally volunteered to contact the Women's Aid Society so they could provide the rest of the meals.

Before Sally left, the two ladies briefly discussed Hunter's behavior the previous night. Sally was relieved to hear that her summation of the incident was correct and that she had not led Danielle astray.

On her way out, Sally did find Rob Wilky taking a break outside, "Rob, I'm glad I ran into you. May I have a minute of your time?"

"Why?" Instead of rising out of courtesy, Rob threw up a hand to indicate she could have a seat.

"I want to ask you to leave Danielle alone. She and Hunter are in love, and it was obvious that you planned to use what happened last night to try to win her."

"*This* coming from *you*—after chasing Jackson and intentionally causing trouble between them. Sorry, I'll look elsewhere for advice."

"That's true. I did pursue Hunter shamefully and did a lot to interfere in their relationship. Thank goodness Joe stepped in to prevent me from making an even bigger fool of myself. I'd like to spare you such embarrassment and the disapproval of the people close to them—*if* you'll listen to me."

"Surely you're not comparing my caring for Danielle to your intentions to trap Hunter."

"Just because you've been subtle doesn't mean there's a difference between the two. Besides, I can't fathom Danielle leading you on. I'm sure you've been told she has no romantic interest in you. Yet, last night you intentionally took advantage of the situation. Can you deny it?"

Rob did not answer.

"I've just confirmed that Miss Bricker was brought here to cause problems between Hunter and Danielle, and he recognized that right away. Hunter has absolutely no interest in the Bricker girl and put an abrupt end to the plan."

Her frankness forced the young chef to question why he had become so fascinated with Danielle Harrison and had developed such disdain for Sally. It only took a short time to trace it back to the night of Rica and Joe's engagement party. Hunter had embarrassed him by disregarding his offer to drive Danielle home, and Sally had been condescending toward him. From that moment on, winning Danielle from Hunter had become a challenge.

Having a clear picture of what his motives were, Rob Wilky realized he *had* been devious and felt ashamed for trying to maneuver his way into Danielle's affections. There were definitely a few things he needed to discuss with Miss Sally Meeker.

Esther—having just heard that Delbert was about to be found guilty of the fire and attempted murder—let down her guard. Now she thought the only thing holding her back from living life completely in the open was Sherry—and the authorities would have to find the child before they could accuse her of anything. However, Esther knew that was not about to happen, since she was finalizing preparations to have her aunt send Sherry to an overseas boarding school.

In the meantime, she had a long, overdue score to settle. Mrs. Ulysses Peppercon was looking forward to ruining her eldest daughter's life the way the girl's birth had ruined hers. Esther would now set her focus on locating Danielle.

Even though Danielle was able to make it safely to Bristol, it was a challenge to drive a horse on the busy city streets. However, her concern for Sherry far outweighed any fears she had. Her first stop would be at the telegraph office to contact Benjamin Dice. Then she would need to devise a plan to find her great-aunt's residence.

The library did have a street directory, but it was of little use without an address. Hoping to jog her memory, Danielle sat down to make a list of four-letter family names and words that started with the letter *M*. It seemed she had heard her Grandfather Snodd mention the name on occasion, but she could not recall it.

After spending several hours at the city library looking for clues, Danielle laid her head on the table. She knew she could not give up, but the task was beginning to seem impossible. God had never failed her—so she sought His wisdom.

The next thing she knew, a librarian was shaking her awake and asking her to please vacate the premises. Danielle apologized profusely and soon found herself outside in the fading daylight without a place to spend the night. Fortunately, she happened upon a store which had few customers and a very friendly and obliging clerk. The lady gave her the name of a cozy hotel on a backstreet and a place to board the horse. Still exhausted, Danielle checked into her room, put on her gown, and slipped into bed without a hint of dinner. She would worry about food in the morning.

At daybreak, Danielle stayed in her bed going over and over the list of possible names, but to no avail. It was only after morning prayer that she thought to say *Myrtle* with each name on the list. Finally, about a third of the way through, *Myrtle Mart* jumped out at her. Instantly, Danielle remembered Esther taking her to her grandparent's home to collect some legal papers from the aunt. It was one of the few times Danielle had been in the Snodd home. The name *Myrtle Mart* had been written on the envelope in bold letters.

Knowing her aunt's name was the crucial clue she needed to find Sherry.

Danielle was still struggling with the next piece of the puzzle. Information pertaining to where someone lived was much more difficult to attain in the city. In Willow Weep, people could direct you anywhere if you asked—but not in Bristol. And since she knew her aunt had little money, it was doubtful a telephone directory would be of use.

Staring out the restaurant window, Danielle noticed a milk wagon turning down a side street. She raised the cup of tea the waitress had just set in front of her and watched as the driver maneuvered the many carriages parked along the avenue. That was when the thought suddenly came to her. She took a few sips of tea while finishing her toast and summoning for the bill. Now she had a plan.

With God's blessing, Danielle thought it might be possible to find Sherry by the day's end.

"Stop! Oh please, sir! Stop!"

The older gentleman turned and gave Danielle a friendly smile. "What can I do for you, young lady? I certainly didn't think I missed any of my customers. Pride myself on being accurate."

She had to take a moment to catch her breath. "Not a customer. . . just desperately needing information." Danielle had to wait again while breathing deeply. "I'm looking for someone with the last name of *Mart*. The lady of the house is *Myrtle*. Does the name sound familiar?"

"*Myrtle Mart*?" The kind man gave it some thought. "No, doesn't ring a bell, but I'll check my book. I did pick up a few customers last week." He checked the new names but there was no match.

The only choice left was to share a doctored up version as to why she was trying to locate her great-aunt. After doing so, she was invited to the creamery to speak with the other milkmen employed there. Being aware that a worker could be fired for giving out a customer's personal information, Danielle did her best not to draw the attention of their employer.

Since the men did not come and go at the same time, it took most of the day, but she was blessed. God had directed her to the right place. Myrtle Mart *was* a patron on one of the routes.

To her disappointment, it was too late for a young lady to be seen on the streets alone, so the reunion with Sherry would need to be postponed until the next morning. She dreaded another night alone—fretting about Grandpa Harrison's health and contemplating Sally Meeker's disturbing words. Taking all of her hurts and worries to the Lord, she finally drifted off to sleep.

The following morning Danielle rushed to the shay that had been left for her in front of the hotel. Most people had already arrived at work, so the streets were not crowded, and the milk man's directions were easy to follow. As she entered the housing district where Myrtle Mart lived, Danielle began rehearsing what might be proper to say to an aunt she had never met. Being wise enough not to expect much of a reception, Danielle reminded herself that getting Sherry to the safety of the Harrison home was all that was required from the visit.

It was a very old section of town. The homes had been grand at one time, but most were now rundown and many seemed beyond repair. Even at that, Myrtle Mart, being true to the family delusion of social standing, lived in the house that had once been the grandest of them all.

A butler in a faded uniform answered the door as if he had been trained to give guests the illusion they were about to be received by nobility. He then directed Danielle to a parlor.

Finally, after waiting for an unreasonable amount of time, a stern-faced woman entered the room wearing a stained and out-dated, green silk gown. On top of a head of thinning hair was a lopsided hairpiece in much need of restyling. The woman stopped midway across the room to give a haughty, intimidating stare. Out of respect, Danielle stood.

"Your last name is *Harrison*?"

"Danielle Harrison."

"The product of Esther's disgraceful marriage to a dirt farm-er, I assume."

"You are mistaken, dear. I am the product of a good and honest, young man who was tricked into marrying a Snodd. However, I bear that disgrace as best I can."

The aunt's eyes widened at Danielle's response, but the woman was unable to come up with the words to retaliate. "State your business."

"My business is simple. I'm here to collect my sister, Sherry."

"The child that Elmer was supposed to have sent to be left in my charge?"

"Grandfather? Yes. . . of course." Hearing for certain that her Grandfather Snodd was involved in Sherry's kidnapping had thrown Danielle off for a moment. She managed to regain her hardnosed persona.

"His check for the child's care arrived, but the child did not. He was informed by telegram but never replied. I can't help you."

The thought of where Sherry might be frightened Danielle. But wanting to maintain composure in front of the staunch aunt, she looked directly into the stone-faced woman's eyes. "I'm not certain I believe you."

"Butler!" It was not a page befitting a lady—but a full-fledged bellow of one losing control.

The butler appeared—wild eyed and trembling.

"Give this woman a complete tour of the house and grounds. She's just accused me of lying about harboring a child. Afterward, escort her off of my property."

"Aunty Myrtle, how courteous of you!"

Danielle turned to the butler. "Shall we proceed?"

✦

After seeing the state of the home, Danielle was almost embarrassed for the woman. Each room possessed discolored, sagging wallpaper and chipped paint which must have been beautiful in bygone years. It was also apparent that little cleaning had been done in most places. Danielle was surprised the hateful woman would allow even the lowly product of a farmer to view the home in such horrendous condition and wondered if the pretentious aunt had ever lifted a finger in the way of housekeeping.

Sadly, Danielle had seen nothing within the house or on the property to give the impression a child had recently been on the premises. Even though there had been ample time for Sherry to have been removed from the home, Danielle doubted that was the case. She was fairly certain that Sherry had never arrived. With little hope that Elmer Snodd had taken Sherry to live in New York, Danielle decided to go to the police.

An officer held the door for Danielle to enter the precinct. Several policemen milled around the noisy room, while others sat at their desks taking information from the people in front of them.

Seeing the counter, she approached the officer standing behind it to ask for assistance. "I'd like to know if there has been a little girl reported missing."

"You're gonna have to be more specific than that. When? What'd she look like?"

"I can't say for certain about the dates. She's eight, small for her age, and has long, straight, blonde hair. It's beautiful. . . her hair, I mean. She's beautiful too."

"She have a name?"

"*Sherry. . . Sherry Simpson.* She's very intelligent for her age—a wonderful personality. You'd remember my little sister if you'd seen her." Danielle smiled in recollection.

"Well, I don't remember her, so I must've not seen her. Let me check the records." After combing through several books and files, he returned with a frown. "No reports. Nothing recorded."

"But you must have. You have to have!" Danielle was beginning to panic." She then gave a modified version of Sherry's story.

Out of sympathy the man gave a whistle to get the other officers' attention and repeated Sherry's information to them. No one responded. "Sorry, honey. Without some type of a report our hands are tied. Leave your name and address. If we learn anything, we'll be sure to contact you. Next."

Disheartened, Danielle drove to the train station and questioned the ticket agent who shook his head at her for even supposing he could recall the girl.

Remembering that the cabbies would be arriving and leaving the station throughout the day, she spent the rest of the time interviewing them and the other employees at the station. When it became too late for her to be out alone, Danielle had to force herself to return to the hotel—however, not before sending Benjamin Dice a telegram to inform him of her findings. She had to face the fact that locating Sherry was beyond her capabilities. It would need to be handed over to professionals. There was nothing left to do but return home in the morning.

After having a light dinner, Danielle went to her room where again she was alone with her thoughts.

49

SEARCHING FOR DANIELLE

Farmers throughout the country were discontented. They still complained of unfair treatment due to tariffs, inflated shipping costs, monopolies, overpriced equipment, high interest rates, low crop prices, and the list of protests continued. People were losing their farms because they could not pay back mortgages.

Mel and Hunter were meeting with other farmers in the district to sort out which problems applied to their area and then find solutions for them. However, things had not gone well.

Because there were so many complaints, a single day's forum turned into an extended stay with the meetings running late into the evening. While Hunter was extremely concerned about the problems and corruption facing the farming industry, he was much more concerned about his relationship with Danielle.

By the time he and Mel arrived home, it had been over three complete days since the disastrous dinner at the inn. Once again, it was too late to call at the Harrison home.

Since the misunderstanding, the only communication between Hunter and Danielle was the wire he had sent to her from Cumberland just before the meeting. There was so much that needed to be said about that night. The message ended up consisting of only two words.

⚜

Hunter knocked on the Harrison's backdoor at seven the next morning. Instead of a cool reception, he received an unexpected embrace from Gayle. "I'm so glad to see you. Come in. We're so worried about Danielle."

Lacresha got up to pour him a cup of coffee while Jerry shook his hand and offered him a seat.

Confused by their kindness, Hunter began a rambling explanation. "I wanted to speak with Danielle the night of the dinner, but I had things to see to first—which made it impossible. Then we were held over at the meeting in Cumberland. Is Joshua here? I'd like to see him before trying to speak with Danielle. I assume you all know what I'm referring to."

Gayle looked puzzled by his response. "Of course, we know what happened at the inn. Didn't Helen tell you she came by to explain how your actions had been misconstrued?"

Hunter's shoulders dropped in relief. "No, I wasn't aware. Mel and I arrived home late last night, and I didn't stay for breakfast this morning. So, Josh and Danielle know and understand?"

"I'm afraid not."

Gayle first told Hunter the details of Joshua's heart attack, explaining that he was getting stronger and should recover without issues. Hunter was relieved to hear his friend was improving so quickly. He knew Joshua was not ready to give up any of life's pleasures.

"So. . . Danielle is unwilling to forgive me? May I speak with her alone when she comes down?"

"Danielle wasn't here for Helen's explanation. She left for Bristol that day to find her little sister. She received word that Sherry might be living there with an aunt."

"In Bristol? I don't like the idea of Danielle wandering the city streets alone—especially for this length of time. What part of town does the aunt reside in, and what kind of people are they?"

Lacresha stood to pour Jerry more coffee. "Those people lost their home years ago, so they're probably renters. We don't exactly know anything about their character, other than they're her mother's relatives." Lacresha suddenly dropped the subject, remembering that he did not know much about Danielle's family.

"Hunter, there was nothing I could do. She was determined to go by herself and was out the door before I could stop her. Thank goodness, we've convinced Joshua that he's not ready for visitors, so he hasn't insisted on seeing her."

"No one is blaming you, Lacresha. But I'm going to Bristol to find her. Once I have, I'll try to locate her sister. But I'll need some leads?"

By then Lacresha was fairly certain the aunt's last name was *Mart*. She then retrieved the letters and telegram Danielle had received before she left and gave them to Hunter to read.

Knowing Danielle had resolved to tell Hunter about her relatives in Grandville and realizing how serious the situation might be for the little girl, Gayle took it upon herself to inform him of the history of the Snodds and Simpsons. Since Joshua was doing well, Jerry insisted on taking the day off and riding along just in case he was needed. Hunter had to stop by the Jacksons' to pack a few things, so Jerry agreed to meet him on the north road to Bristol.

The two men decided to start their search at the police station.

"*Danielle Harrison*? Yes, the girl looking for her little sister. She was upset after finding the aunt here in Bristol didn't have the child. I've since sent an officer out to check on the Marts, and he came up with the same conclusion as Miss Harrison. Before you ask. . . there's no missing child reports on record."

"I'm her fiancé. Do you have any idea where Miss Harrison went from here? I've been out of town, and Danielle only told one person before leaving. She's been gone longer than expected. We're all concerned."

"I think she mentioned going to the railroad station. Let's see, I believe I have her. . . yes, here's a couple of addresses—a rural route and the Primrose Hotel here in town." He wrote down the directions to the hotel and handed them to Hunter.

Hunter and Jerry thanked the man for the information and started walking toward the door.

"Wait. . . I was about to contact Miss Harrison. I happened to recall the nurse from up around Rock Creek asking if we had any reports on a missing child. It's been a while back though. Anyway, she didn't try to file a report."

"So, the child was a girl?"

"She didn't say. There's so many orphans living on the streets now days, we just don't have the manpower to keep tabs on them all. Sad days.

"Well, that's all I have for you. Nonetheless, I'm sending a man to follow up on Miss Harrison and to make certain the two of you are on the up and up. I hope it all ends well. Have a good day."

"Bart!"

When Hunter, Jerry, and Officer Bart arrived at the hotel, they learned that Danielle had checked out to return home. The hotel clerk seemed very personable and caring, so Hunter was not surprised that she knew a little of Danielle's dilemma.

When the lady mentioned Danielle had arrived late after checking at the train station the previous night, Hunter pictured the love of his life frantically searching for her little sister. It was then that he recalled having witnessed a scene during the summer. He was leaving the station with a shipment that had come by rail and had unintentionally driven his wagon in front of a crowd watching two men fighting. He distinctly recalled seeing a little girl running across the tracks and up into the hills. At the time, he had even marveled at how much she looked like Danielle.

Putting together what he had learned about the nurse at Rock Creek and his remembrance of the little girl at the tracks, Hunter shared his theory with Jerry and the officer. "Jerry, would you please make certain Danielle arrives home safely? She must have taken the road south of town or our paths would've crossed while we were on the way into Bristol."

At that point, Jerry left to guarantee Danielle's safety, Officer Bart returned to the station to report what he had learned, and Hunter prepared to head for Rock Creek.

50

UNNECESSARY BITTERNESS

Hunter went to the station to find the place where he had seen the little girl crossing the tracks. At the time it happened, he had not questioned why such a well-dressed child would be running into the woods. Now presuming it had something to do with the two men fighting, he decided to investigate further.

It did take valuable time to find and question workers at the station, but he eventually found a person in maintenance who remembered a fracas over a man striking a child. The time frame the worker gave matched Hunter's. Surmising that the child was fleeing from at least one of the men was all the information he needed to begin searching the Rock Creek area. Hunter was certain that once he found the nurse, she could direct him to Sherry.

Oscar Cain had been spending his time watching the movement around the nurse's cabin. He assumed all the activity during the day was created by patients coming and going for treatments or medical remedies. That was definitely an obstacle, but what disturbed Cain most was the young man who had begun sleeping on the porch. That arrangement had put an unwelcomed twist on his hope to grab Sherry at night. The nurse only left the premises once during the bum's watch, and it was in the evening—which put the girl in the boy's strong, capable hands. If the nurse and girl stepped outside during the day, the child stayed glued to the woman's side. He had only seen Sherry fetch water once, but the well was only a few steps from the porch and the door was left open. The girl was in clear view of the nurse.

He could easily overpower the petite lady, but the problem was finding a time when no one was around to prevent him from doing so. Still, Cain was running out of time and knew he must snatch her at the next opportunity. More than one person had spotted him lurking around, and he could tell they were suspicious.

On the other side of things, Sherry spent much of her time sneaking peeks out the window. She constantly worried that the bum might be waiting to abduct her, but at the same time, wanted to believe he had left the foothills. If he had, her dream to remain in her mountain home might come true. That is why she still could not let Zelda know the secrets harbored within her heart. Sherry breathed another prayer for God to make the man go away.

✿

Everett answered the door with his usual kind smile. "Hello there, ma'am. May I help you?"

"I'm Mrs. Peppercon, and I'm here to see Jean." The uppity woman did not offer a hand.

"Well, if that's the case, please have a seat in the parlor here, and I'll go fetch her. She's clearing out the garden, so it may be a few minutes. Make yourself at home, Mrs. Peppercorn."

"That's. . . *Mrs. Peppercon.*" Esther sniffed at the thought. "*Peppercorn*, the very idea!"

Everett snickered at his little joke, as he hurried off to find his wife.

Esther had no intention of leaving the house without knowing where Danielle had gone. Having resolved that it was time for her to come to terms with that so-called daughter of hers, she began rummaging through the Johnsons' desk.

"Jean, when did you start taking in such highfalutin clientele? That one I left in the parlor is dressed to the hilt. Could barely spare a word."

"What are you talking about? I don't have anyone scheduled today, and I'd never describe any of the ladies I do alterations for as highfalutin. Let me get to the pump to clean up, and I'll see who you've let in."

Everett, being curious himself, followed Jean back to the house.

Before leaving town, Mrs. Peppercon instructed the hired driver to take the street that ran in front of the Simpson home. There was no reason to drive by the place, but she just wanted to do so out of sheer curiosity. Even though Esther no longer needed Harold Simpson's fortune, she still wanted it. The self-centered woman dreamed of taking his money and flaunting it before all of Grandville.

Jerry did finally catch up with Danielle about two miles from the house, but little was said between them once he had told her Hunter had gone to look for Sherry. He decided to let the ladies of the house explain the rest.

When the two travelers arrived home, Gayle and Lacresha welcomed Danielle at the door and rushed her to the kitchen for a decent meal. They were sorry to hear she had not found Sherry, but their hopes were restored when Jerry told them Hunter had stayed behind to continue the search. Danielle's face indicated she felt betrayed that they were so accepting of Hunter.

Jerry decided it was time to find some chores to do outside and leave the women to help Danielle sort through her feelings.

Lacresha set a glass of lemonade on the table as she lovingly placed a hand on the back of Danielle's head. "We know what you're thinking, but I assure you that we have reason for speaking of Hunter in such a good light. As a matter of fact, here's a telegram from him. It came the day you left for Bristol."

Unwilling to read it, Danielle laid it aside.

Gayle and Lacresha could tell it was time to explain the situation encompassing Hunter that night at the inn.

After hearing the account Hunter had given them, Danielle still seemed unmoved by the explanation. Becoming miffed, Gayle folded her arms. "Surely, Danielle, you've been in a position when you were so focused on a matter that you weren't aware of your surroundings."

"Yes, I have. It's just that he seemed so overly mesmerized by Miss Bricker."

Lacresha was baffled by Danielle's ambivalent feelings toward Hunter. "Danielle, we've told you what was on Hunter's mind when it came to that girl. He followed through and gave her the tongue lashing she deserved. My goodness, girl, Hunter went searching as soon as he heard you were alone in Bristol. He's trying to find your little sister this very minute."

Gayle, also frustrated with Danielle's attitude, chose to continue the lecture. "Young lady, you've been given a logical explanation for what occurred at the inn. It's time for you to decide whether you're *ever* going to believe in the person you so desperately wanted to marry only a few days ago. Hunter is a good man. He doesn't deserve his feelings being constantly abused by you."

"Abused?"

It was like a slap in the face. Gayle had never been so direct. Danielle might have reacted defensively, except the statement was wise and correct. There were so many times she had been rude to Hunter and had walked away. Even when they had enjoyed wonderful outings together, she often had ended them by leaving him hurt and confused. Not sharing her past indicated a lack of faith in him. Danielle had to agree that she *had* abused his feelings.

Seeing the sadness in Gayle's eyes for having to speak so directly, Danielle reached for her cousin's hand. "Thank you, for your honesty. I've been wasting precious time on unnecessary bitterness. If I'm truthful, he has never given me reason not to trust him. There have been so many times that he's proven his love and devotion for me." She reached over and took Lacresha's hand as well.

Danielle, then opened and read Hunter's telegram. Shame filled her heart as she lovingly passed her fingers across those very telling words—*Trust me.*

❧

Once the midday meal was over, Lacresha and Gayle told Danielle they had a surprise. Gayle swept her hand toward the doorway where her grandfather stood looking much stronger and healthier than she had imagined.

"There's my Dani. I was beginning to wonder if I'd ever see you again."

Danielle ran to put her arms around his neck. "I'm sorry I couldn't visit, but we both know it was for the best. Evidently the doctor's strict precautions have paid off."

"Just so you know, the doctor has given me a clean bill of health—but only if I promised to take it easy for a while. He even prescribed a daily walk to restore my strength. I also have the doctor's permission to attend the annual fish fry."

"That's wonderful news, Joshua. I heard last week that Rosa is planning to host the meal outside in the back garden. It's a lot more work for the staff but much appreciated by the rest of us. The evenings are so comfortable this time of year." Lacresha then cleared a place for him at the table.

"Uncle Josh, this will be a first for me and Danielle. Hearing you were all spending a late-summer's evening together with family and friends always made me homesick."

"I work at the inn. Why haven't I heard of this?"

Lacresha took Danielle's plate. "Rosa's been hosting the evening for so many years that I guess everyone took it for granted you knew. It's a wonderful time. You'll enjoy it—especially since none of us will have to cook."

While everyone else laughed, Danielle wondered if she could enjoy the evening if Hunter had not returned with Sherry.

51

PREPARE TO MEET YOUR MAKER

Hunter slapped his heels against Petra's side to peak the hill. He had taken the road—not much more than a widened path—to what was considered the Rock Creek area.

After scouting around, he discovered that the families did not live on or near the main road. The homes Hunter did manage to find were on makeshift trails that twisted and turned through the woods. The seclusion, which was so important to the residents, meant Hunter would have to comb the forest to find anyone who lived there. The few people he *did* weed out were not receptive or informative. Even the white man he had come across sleeping near the creek had turned a deaf ear.

After having found only three dwellings by late evening, he had no choice but to make camp for the night. Fortunately, Hunter was blessed with a comfortable temperature for sleeping and a hefty stack of pine needles for bedding.

In the morning he took a dip in the creek and made a meal out of bread and sliced cheese. Once Petra was fed and watered, the two set out to find anyone who might assist in locating the nurse.

He decided it was best to return to the road and look for the hidden paths. The process made the search seem tiresome, but it was more effective than wandering aimlessly through unknown territory. Hunter did find a few more homes by noon, but as before, the people were evasive or just shook their heads and went about their business. It was obvious strangers were not welcome in the foothills.

"Hello, there!" Hunter called out as he and Petra approached a tiny shack. The door was wide open, but he decided not to take liberties. "May I have permission to dismount. I'm trying to locate someone in the area."

An older man, wearing overalls and no shirt, appeared in the door but did not give him permission to approach. "Whatcha want up here?"

"I'm looking for the nurse who practices in this area. I was hoping you might direct me to her place."

The man shut the door.

Having a distinct feeling he was being watched, Rand walked the property before leaving for work. Even though he found nothing unusual, there was still an eerie feeling about the place. He took time to warn Zelda to be extra cautious.

The nurse had told Rand she would do so but was contemplating whether to continue agreeing with his methods of protection. Sherry's clinginess was getting worse, and Zelda worried that Rand's safety measures were adding to the child's anxiety.

Throwing the door open, Zelda stepped out on the porch to breathe in the fresh air. She longed to be free from the fear of an intruder. Sherry was asleep, so she sat down on the bench to pretend it was a normal, carefree day. But when she did, a shiver ran up her spine. Then there was a thud, as if someone had dropped from a tree. She noticed the birds stopped singing momentarily, and there was a rustle in the tall grass. It was *not* a normal carefree day. Zelda would abide by Rand's wishes for a while longer.

Since the patient load had increased recently, it was necessary to do the laundry every morning to keep the medical cabinet stocked with clean linens. Folks knew not to show up at the break of day or after dinner time, unless it was an emergency. The set hours gave Zelda a few minutes for herself and time to make routine house calls. On this day, however, the eerie feeling lingered, so the nurse postponed the washing. Instead, she and Sherry got an early start on schoolwork.

Oscar Cain had landed on both feet when the branch had given way causing him to plunge to the ground. He had not been injured but the thump seemed to have alerted the nurse. He figured it must have kept her from doing the wash that morning, which had made it impossible to snatch the girl as planned.

Since there had been little foot traffic at the nurse's cabin, the bum positioned himself closer to the pump. So far no one had been to the well, but he reckoned they would be needing water soon. Therefore, he had no choice but to make the grab at that time—even if it meant entering the cabin to get the child. If he waited much longer, the strong, young man would be showing up.

Cain had enough money to send the telegram to blackmail the Snodds, and he was itching to get on with it. It would not do to miss his chance, so Oscar crouched down, ready to pounce when the time came.

Rosa Smith had never had a year when she did not enjoy preparing for the annual fish fry. Her friends and family looked forward to spending time visiting with one another over a simple meal. It was a time for playing a few board games, taking a group stroll along the creek, or relaxing in the garden.

Organizing the event had never been a problem before this year, but it seemed the hotel guests were going out of their way to try her patience. Rosa could not remember having clients who disturbed other patrons by carousing the hallways at all hours. To make things even more challenging, the woman who had just checked in was the most demanding and arrogant guest she had encountered in all her days of innkeeping.

The entire staff was out of sorts because of all the chaos. Even worse, Rosa was having trouble finding enough workers for the fish fry. If she had not told Madison and Rob to offer the workers double pay, the entire dinner might have fallen on Rosa and Johnathon's shoulders.

The only news to brighten her day was hearing that Joshua would be able to attend the gathering. She also hoped Hunter would be back in time. Rosa still felt somewhat responsible for the misunderstanding between him and Danielle, and she would not rest until things were settled between the two.

"Excuse me, Mrs. Smith!" Madison's face was flushed with anger. "The lady in twenty-seven is demanding to speak to you. Evidently, something else doesn't suit her. I may be speaking out of turn, but I think you have just cause to ask her and that other unruly group of partiers to leave. Their behavior is disgraceful, and they're giving the other guests the wrong impression about the inn."

Rosa never had known Madison to be anything other than compliant. The girl took pride in her work but always seemed to lack the confidence to stand up for herself or rely on her own judgment. It was a concern for Rosa since Madison was expected to take over as head-of-housekeeping when Danielle married. The proprietor was relieved to see that the girl had a little spunk. Although, if the unwelcome guests' behavior had provoked Madison to state her opinion so boldly, then the situation must be worse than she had imagined. Rosa needed to see to the matter at once.

Rand had once read of a book character who had the feeling of impending doom. That was exactly what he had felt the entire day, and he could not shake it. There was no doubt that Sherry had seen something that frightened her earlier in the week, and he felt it was his duty to protect her. Rand had never skipped out on an ounce of work in his life, and on this occasion, he had promised his boss that the landscaping work would be completed by the end of the day. He did not want to risk losing the job, but something within compelled him to return to the cabin early. He hoped he was correct in believing it was God.

Rand did not walk away from his work that day. . . he ran.

Hunter dismounted Petra to give them both a much-needed rest. As it was, every person he had encountered turned a cold shoulder as soon as he mentioned the nurse. He had been praying for guidance, but so far, he had not been enlightened. Leaving the area without Sherry was not an option, so he fell to his knees and once again asked for direction.

When he had concluded, he rose to his feet and wiped the sweat from his brow and the back of the neck. Hearing the trickle of water, Hunter took Petra's reins to lead him into the woods to find the source.

"That was a mighty fine prayer. I'm God-fearin' myself." A man with a kind face walked from among the trees.

Hunter had not even heard the snap of a twig.

"Sir, I didn't know anyone was around. I hope I haven't disturbed you."

"Naw, just breakin' camp. . . but I did enjoy eavesdroppin' on yer talk with the Lord." The older man held out his hand and Hunter shook it heartily.

"Name's Easy."

"Nice to meet you, Easy. . . Hunter Jackson. I believe your name suits you."

"Came by the name 'cause I've a way a comin' up on people without 'em hearin'. Don't intend ta do it. Just happens. I'm the junk man 'round these parts. Just finished my route up this way. Getting' ready ta head down ta flatter land."

"Looks like a good location. I camped on the other side. It was convenient for locating the families on that side of the road. You see, I'm looking for the local nurse in hopes she has information about a little white girl."

"You're the second stranger I've come 'cross within the week lookin' for that girl."

"You don't say." Hunter's heart began to pound.

"Didn't think much of it at the time, but later I got an uneasy feelin' 'bout that first fella. Wish I hadn't mentioned nothing' ta him. Just wasn't the type of man I wanna be responsible fer sendin' the nurse's way." Easy's face reflected regret.

"Where does the nurse live?"

"Got no idea. Just know she takes care of the people 'round here. But that first fella told me he'd been doin' a favor watchin' a girl, and the child got away from 'im. But he was nothin' but a tramp. Actin' all jittery. Can see now that he wuz up ta no good."

Hunter had not thought how urgent finding the girl might be. "What did this man look like?"

"He's white, average height, real thin, shaggy beard and hair, but he's wearin' a fancy suit. It's all dirty and startin' to wear. Couldn't understand that."

"So, you think he was stalking the child?"

"Sure do. Man like that don't have friends. 'Specially none with kids." Easy's description of the tramp fit the man Hunter had seen camped near the creek.

"I think I've seen the man. If he's stalking her, then he must be camped near the nurse's home." Hunter mounted Petra. The horse, sensing the urgency, began to prance.

"Thank you. I believe you're my answer to prayer. You've been a great help. May I ask you to intervene for the girl's safety? God bless you."

It definitely stood to reason that the stalker would be camped a short distance from his victim. So Hunter headed for the area where he had come across the white man in the woods. If his theory was correct, he should be able to pinpoint the nurse's cabin.

As the day went on, Zelda Field's had dismissed the haunting feeling from earlier in the day. It was time to wash dishes, so she sent Sherry out to fetch a bucket of water. Sherry had shaken her head in fright, but the nurse had placed one hand on her hip and pointed to the door. She told the little girl to leave the door open. The child reluctantly obeyed and slowly left the house with the bucket.

Unfortunately, Sherry's reluctance and slow movement caused her to play into Oscar Cain's hands. He watched as the door slowly opened, giving him time to identify the child coming outside with a bucket. He ran toward the pump and swooped Sherry into his arms.

It took Zelda a few seconds to process what she had just witnessed. Once she came to her senses, she grabbed a skillet and ran after him. He was older and could not run fast, so she was able to get in one good swing that landed on his back. He reared backward in pain and lost control of the child.

Zelda grabbed Cain's arm and wrestled him to the ground. Sherry sprang from his other arm, but instead of running into the house and locking the door, she ran into the stable. Feeling trapped and not knowing what to do, she climbed into an empty feed sack left in front of the grain.

Oscar landed in the brambles and had to fight his way out, while Zelda had fallen onto a flowerpot, which broke and cut a gash in her leg. She cringed in pain and could not get to her feet in time to stop the man.

Cain regained his footing and headed toward the stable after Sherry. He was in the building in seconds but could not see the girl as he entered. Frustrated and turning vengeful, he began to swear. It was then he saw the movement within the grain sack. With malice in his heart, the man picked up a pitchfork. "I gotcha now, ya little brat. I's teach ya ta run from me agin. Prepare ta meet yer maker." Infuriated beyond reason, he raised the instrument above his head and plunged it forward, just as Rand slid in front of Sherry. The badly aimed pitchfork landed in the side of Rand's thigh. The young man cried out in agony.

Unable to recover, Rand watched as the bum jerked it from his leg and raised the pitchfork high above his head to bring it down with deadly force. Rand, not caring for his own life, moved to cover Sherry with his body.

The evil man thrust the fork downward, just as he was grabbed from behind and flung to the floor. Hunter twisted the weapon from Cain's hand and dealt a blow with the handle which rendered the filthy man unconscious. Grabbing a rope hanging from a nail, Hunter quickly secured Oscar Cain.

"Where's the little girl?" Hunter demanded.

"Behind me! She's unharmed." Rand leaned forward so their rescuer could reach her.

Hunter opened the sack to reveal what looked like a miniature version of Danielle. He picked the girl up and hugged her to his chest. Then he looked at Rand. "I saw what you were willing to do to save the child. You're a brave man. I sincerely thank you."

"Before thankin' me, who are ya, and what have ya got ta do with Anna?"

"Anna?"

At that moment Zelda entered the building and took Sherry from Hunter's arms. "My Anna, I'm so sorry I doubted you. Please, forgive me."

As it happened, Officer Bart had been given permission to join the search for Sherry. He, too, met up with Easy, who had pointed the policeman in the direction Hunter had gone. The officer soon found Petra tied to a tree beside the road in front of Zelda's property.

Shortly after Cain was captured, Officer Bart took him into custody and escorted him to jail in Bristol. The tramp would be facing trial on several counts—in addition to the ones not yet known to local authorities.

Immediately afterward, Zelda attended to their wounds which were painful but not serious.

Later that evening the three adults and Sherry eagerly shared a meal of beef stew and fresh, buttered bread. The child seemed to accept Hunter once he had explained he was engaged to Danielle.

However, Sherry did not break her silence, nor would she respond in writing, even though she knew the perpetrator was no longer a threat. She remained the same standoffish little girl that she had become since the loss of her father and the betrayal of her mother and grandparents.

Sherry was numb. While the anticipation of being reunited with her beloved Danielle made her heart sing, the thought of leaving Zelda and Rand was breaking it. The child was torn between two worlds and knew she no longer had control over her own destiny.

Zelda tucked Sherry into bed and rubbed her back until she fell asleep.

Afterward, Hunter explained who Sherry was and what little he knew about the child's life. Zelda insisted Sherry was in a delicate state of mind, so they all agreed to be discreet in her presence.

"I'd have to be blind not to see how you've come to love Sherry. However, I must take the girl to her sister in Willow Weep. From there we'll contact her guardian. I'm sorry to be the one to take Sherry from you both."

"We do believe yer story, Mr. Jackson, but if ya think we're goin' ta let ya leave this mountain alone with Sherry, yer mistaken. Zelda and I'll be goin' with ya to Willow Weep to make sure she's happy and well cared for."

"I understand. Then I welcome the company. I'm certain your presence will be a comfort to her."

"I do ask that ya hold off on that early start. I've a commitment ta fulfill in the mornin'. I assure ya that it won't take long." Rand could not in good conscience leave without completing the job he had left undone. He prayed the unfinished work had gone undetected by his boss.

"Certainly. We'll leave when you're both ready."

And that is exactly what they did.

52

DANIELLE IS A LIAR

"I'm sorry, ma'am, but we do not furnish our guests with personal maid or butler services. If you thought you would have need of such luxuries, then you should have had those in your service accompany you. My employees have their own duties to perform."

"I absolutely *do* demand your maids see to my needs at once!"

"Ma'am, if you are not satisfied with our service, you're perfectly welcome to find a room elsewhere—although, if you're considering Bristol, we're already accommodating the city's overflow because of conventions. So, let me make myself clear. . . should you mistreat any of my staff again, I will call the police and have you escorted off the premises. Do you understand?" Even though ashamed of herself, Rosa had taken pleasure in threatening the irrational woman.

Refusing to give Rosa the satisfaction of an answer, the irate guest turned her head to the side and stuck her nose in the air.

Totally frustrated, Rosa hurried back to the lawn. Dealing with unruly guests had not been on her agenda when choosing the date for the fish fry. Because of continuously being called away to deal with their shenanigans, she had not even had time to set up the tables, and the event was only a few hours away.

Danielle and Joshua took a seat on the front porch to enjoy the warmth of the early afternoon. The cooler fall days were rapidly approaching, and they were not looking forward to giving up their summer seating.

"Grandpa, it's good to see you looking so well."

"I was extremely weak at first, but I'm over the hump. There are still several good years left in me, and I praise God for them."

Danielle took his hand. "I have no doubt I'll have many years under your watchful eye and guidance."

"Where's that fiancé of yours been hiding? I hope you haven't had another falling out."

Danielle winced. Wanting to avoid telling him about the misunderstanding, she changed the subject. "Since you asked, Hunter has gone to Bristol to bring home my baby sister." Not feeling it wise to share the entire disturbing story, Danielle made the news sound as uneventful as possible. Unfortunately, she wasn't as confident as she sounded and whispered another prayer that Hunter would safely return with Sherry.

Joshua was elated that Harold's biological daughter might soon be safely tucked away within the Harrison home. Wanting to do everything possible to make Sherry's stay comfortable, he suggested they add an extra bed in Danielle's room so the little girl could be close to her sister. As it was, Jerry was one step ahead of him. The bed was already in place, and he had also chosen a suitable horse for her to ride. Equally excited over having a child around the house, Lacresha and Gayle had made Sherry a rag doll and were in the process of baking a cake to celebrate her arrival.

Even though they had to rush to get their overly exuberant

preparations completed, the Harrison household did manage to leave for the fish fry on time.

⌖

"Make certain Joshua Harrison's fish is cooked to perfection. Even though he may have had a heart attack, he isn't going to take kindly to it being broiled instead of fried. Rosa then hurried to meet Johnathon outside. Since the back lot and garden were being used for the picnic, they both wanted to greet their friends and instruct them to park across the street from the inn.

First to arrive were the Jacksons and all the Meekers. Following close behind were Pastor and Mrs. Strong, along with Belinda Gray and her husband. They were all excited when the entire Harrison household showed up with Joshua looking the picture of health. Straight away their teasing, joking, and lively conversations began in the front lot, and no one seemed to be in a hurry to move to the garden.

⌖

Hunter, Zelda, and Rand had taken turns letting Sherry ride with them. Her caregivers cherished the time they had left with her—especially, since the little one's departure had come so unexpectedly. They had not been prepared to give her up so soon.

Still reluctant to leave her mountain family, Sherry began to tremble each time she was handed over to Hunter. As her confidence began to build, the little girl did relax somewhat, but Hunter could tell that the child's spirit had been badly damaged by the trauma in her life. Trying to calm her, he began sharing stories of Danielle's life in her new home.

Their route took them through Willow Weep, and as they approached the Willow Inn, Hunter recalled it was the night of the annual fish fry. He could already see Mel and Helen in the front lot. Stopping in the distance, he explained to the three that they were about to meet his and Danielle's close friends and relatives.

Hunter began to feel uncomfortable since he did not know how he would be received because of the misconceptions concerning him and Marka Bricker. But as the four rode closer to those gathered in the parking lot, Hunter was relieved to be greeted by his friends' smiling faces.

He dismounted Petra and lifted Sherry to the ground. Frightened by being exposed to so many strangers, the child recoiled and her little body stiffened. As she turned to Rand and Zelda for reassurance, they both leaped from their mounts to console her.

By that time the travelers had gained the attention of the entire group. The sudden silence caused Danielle to look up and see Hunter standing with two strangers huddled over Sherry. Overjoyed to see her sister, she ran to take the child into her arms. But as Danielle stooped down and held out her hands, Sherry backed away. "Sweetheart, don't you recognize me? Look closely. It's Danielle."

Still not sure that the reunion wasn't just a ploy to return her to Esther, it took several moments before Sherry had the courage to look up. When she did, she reached out with both hands and swept Danielle's hair back to reveal her entire face. She then looked into Danielle's eyes to be certain it was her beloved sister. Whimpering as she gasped for breath, Sherry desperately clutched Danielle. Realizing her baby sister needed her comforting arms, Danielle squeezed the little one tightly. Fearing what Sherry might have experienced to create such anguish and distrust pained her heart.

Everyone who understood what was taking place watched in relief while some wiped tears from their eyes.

As Danielle gently rubbed the child's back and whispered soothing words of reassurance, Sherry began to relax and released her sister. Placing her hands on her little sister's shoulder, Danielle lovingly introduced her to Joshua, Gayle, Lacresha, and Jerry, who had come to meet the child. Sherry reacted politely but did not respond verbally. That was when Danielle realized there was something terribly wrong with her little sister who had always been animated and seemed never to meet a stranger.

Danielle looked to Zelda and Rand, assuming the two might know the reason for Sherry's mysterious behavior. Their saddened expressions indicated they were as confused as she was about her silence.

Not having seen Hunter since meeting his parents, Danielle timidly looked into his eyes, as he introduced the nurse and the young man who had been Sherry's protectors.

Hunter used the opportunity to place an affectionate arm around Danielle. As soon as it happened, the incident with Marka Bricker melted from Danielle's heart and mind.

By this time, the Jacksons, the newly married Meekers, and Rosa had walked over to join them. It was just then that a loud, obnoxious voice blared through the crowd. "Well! Isn't this a touching scene—the former Danielle Harrison and her assumed fiancé, Hunter Jackson, cuddling in front of all their admirers!"

Everyone turned to see who had made such a derogatory intrusion.

Sherry reacted in stark terror and pressed her face into Gayle's clothing. Recognizing who the wicked woman must be, Gayle picked Sherry up and placed a hand gently on the back of the child's head to encourage her to hide her eyes. Rand stepped over and moved them both closer to the security of the others.

"Don't go too far away with that child. I'm her mother, and she'll be leaving with me." Esther Bernadette Peppercon, feeling cocky and smug, took several steps toward the group to let them know she had something on her mind.

"Your little party has proven to be most convenient. I must thank the inn's proprietor for letting it slip that you were congregating here this evening. I couldn't have arranged it better myself."

Joshua stepped forward. "Esther Snodd, you're not welcome—"

The hateful intruder turned to face him. "You don't want to interrupt me just now, Joshua Harrison. I'm about to enlighten you on Danielle's phony character."

Mel put his hand on Josh's shoulder to encourage him to stay calm. The rest of those present began to murmur, wondering what the woman meant. Mel and Joe drew their wives near them, as Rica reached for Rosa's hand.

"Miss Harrison is a married woman who abandoned her husband and infant child. My eldest daughter has always been irresponsible and fickle. Her young husband was also drawn in by her innocent performance. She will deny being a wife and mother, but I have evidence to prove her a liar. Here is a picture taken shortly after the child's birth."

The frame displayed the likeness of a nice looking and well-dressed, young man holding a beautiful baby girl.

Everyone stood in hushed amazement.

Danielle looked up at Hunter. His face was flushed. She wondered if he was being taken in by her mother's lies.

Shaken by Esther's ruinous comments, Danielle did not know how to explain that the accusations were untrue. . . but then the words Hunter had used to try to convince her of *his* innocence came to mind. She looked pleadingly into his questioning eyes. "*Trust me,*" she whispered.

53

IN HIS GRAVE

"That will be enough! You will no longer torment Danielle." The mountainous man towered over Esther as he wagged his finger in her face. "You've done all the damage you'll do to her or anyone else."

Esther's face turned white. "Delbert! I thought you'd be in prison."

Delbert Simpson scowled at his mother as if to speak but instead turned to those gathered. "Ladies and gentlemen, do not listen to this woman. She is conniving and dangerous. Danielle is the kind, loving, and unmarried girl you all know."

Delbert gave Esther a piercing look as he moved toward her. "As for you, Mother. . . my imprisonment, though difficult, turned out to be most advantageous. You became careless because of it and ended up flaunting your marriage. That small wedding announcement pinpointed your location, making it easy for Investigator Long to track your every move."

Delbert eyed the pathetic woman before him. "What you overlooked the night of the fire was the two young lovers secretly meeting in the shipping yard. They witnessed you coming from father's office and watched as you lit the fires around the buildings.

The two also saw you place the torch in my hand to frame me. Since their parents had forbidden the couple to see one another, they were afraid to report what they knew. However, neither could live with the secret and finally came forward."

Esther placed her hand on her chest as her eyes bulged in fear.

"Officer! This is the woman. Please, take her into custody." Benjamin Dice wore a solemn expression as he gave the order, relieved that the Snodd family would soon be brought to justice.

At that moment Margaret Simpson came from the shadows and went straight to Danielle to assure her that all was well. Just as she put a supportive arm around her older sister, a shrill scream filled the air.

"Daddy! My daddy!" Sherry wiggled from Gayle's arms and ran into the waiting arms of Harold Simpson. Feeling the security of his embrace, she began kissing his cheeks over and over.

"Daddy! You're alive! When Mother took me away, she said you were *dead*! I heard her say you burned in a fire. Grandfather Snodd gave me to that mean, dirty man."

Harold drew her closer and whispered into her ear. Whatever he said brought a peaceful smile to his youngest daughter's face.

Realizing Sherry could speak, Zelda grabbed Rand's shoulder in amazement. Then the two, beaming with relief, wrapped their arms around each other.

On the other hand, the abject horror on Esther's face was priceless. There was no doubt the woman knew she was on her way to prison. "Harold Simpson! Why didn't you die? You should be in your grave or at least out of your wits."

"No, Esther, my dear, I'm very much alive—even after having seen you viciously bring a hammer down on my head. I've had my right mind about me for quite some time. It appears you have very bad aim. . . so I *will* be able to testify at your trial.”

“You’ll never put me behind bars. I can afford the best of lawyers. You won’t stand a chance.” Esther could not prevent the quiver in her voice that hindered her bluff.

Officer Likens again was about to cuff the attempted murderess when another man stepped from among the accusers.

“Esther Snodd. . . I’m afraid you’re wrong about that! I’m Ulysses Peppercon’s attorney, Tony Black, and I’m here to serve you with annulment papers.”

“What are you talking about?” the hostile woman spewed.

“Evidently, before the marriage, you failed to disclose several legal offenses, among other indiscretions—including the fact that you have four children. . . and your actual age.”

He cleared his throat. “The day of the wedding, Mr. Peppercon’s nephew arrived too late to stop the ceremony but later convinced his uncle you had conned him into the marriage. Ulysses ordered a thorough background search on you—*and* your parents. It seems your legal battles are just beginning.”

Esther grunted in disbelief. “I won’t agree to anything unless he pays me what I feel is my share of his money.”

“You’ll not get one thin dime!” Peppercon’s attorney handed her the papers, yanked the nephew’s picture from her hand, and walked away.

Benjamin Dice moved in front of Esther. “Don’t be too upset, Esther. You won’t need the money where you’re going. Although I’ll never understand why you were so brazen as to walk into Jean and Everett Johnson’s home and steal Danielle’s letters. Surely you knew you’d be followed.” He held her gaze, hoping she would answer and further incriminate herself.

Esther did not.

Attorney Dice again instructed Officer Likens to handcuff the prisoner and take her away.

As Esther was led away, the crowd broke their silence and began discussing what they had just witnessed. Hunter turned to Danielle. "I want you to know I wasn't doubting you. I was trying to comprehend how a mother could so callously attack her daughter's char—"

Danielle placed an index finger over his lips. "Do you love me?"

"You know I do."

"Then no more explanation or apologies today. You are a wonderful man. . . and I truly do love you."

"Enough to marry me as quickly as we can plan a ceremony?" Hunter whispered.

She looked deep into his eyes to make certain he was serious. "Yes."

"Honestly?"

"Honestly."

"You won't mind having an informal wedding."

"Not at all."

Hunter wrapped his arms around Danielle—reassured that he would never have to let her go.

Since there was much to discuss, the Harrison family and their unexpected guests felt it necessary to excuse themselves from the evening's festivities. All concerned understood completely.

The Lord had once again exchanged ashes for beauty. And no one was more aware of that than Danielle.

Helen, Mel, Rica, and Joe also left the party early to spend time at the Harrisons. Gayle was the first to greet them when they arrived. "I'm so glad you came. I only wish Rosa and Johnathon could be here while we unravel all that has taken place."

Rica giggled. "I have a feeling they won't be far behind. I overheard Rosa asking the staff if they could manage the cleanup on their own."

Zelda and Rand were made to feel welcome and fit well into the family. They were grateful to have witnessed Sherry break her silence and to learn the reasons behind her fears. They had not known how much she cherished being with them or that she had wanted to stay. Sherry spent much of the evening sitting on their laps and recalling their time together. Knowing that their little love had a bright future ahead made the thought of letting go much easier.

Later in the evening, Harold and Attorney Dice offered Rand a job caring for their lawns and gardens since he seemed to be obsessed with horticulture. Harold even insisted he stay at the Simpson home while he pursued his dream of becoming a professional landscape architect.

"As for you, Miss Fields, please know that Harold and I promise to find a medical school that will accept you—not just as a woman, but as a woman of your race. We assure you that our fellow colleagues will unite to support us in this effort. You deserve the opportunity to attain a medical degree." Benjamin and Harold offered the young lady a handshake to back their word.

At that time, Danielle, Delbert, and Margaret expressed their embarrassment in the way their mother had chosen to live her life. Then Harold, Delbert, and Margaret also apologized to Danielle and the Harrisons for the way she had been treated while growing up. But the most cherished revelation for Danielle was when Delbert and Margaret told of their confessions of faith in Christ. The Simpsons had wiped the slate clean. They could begin their lives and relationships anew.

Moments later, while lemonade and sandwiches were being served, the tingling of a glass captured the attention of friends and family. "Before we leave, Danielle and I would like to request that all of you honor us with your presence at our wedding which will take place two weeks from today."

A celebratory cheer rang through the air and many well wishes and congratulations were offered to the beloved couple.

"All right, you two, what are your plans for this wedding, and how may we be of assistance?" Rica could not contain her enthusiasm.

Hunter looked at Danielle and laughed. "We have no plans. The decision was spur-of-the-moment, but we feel it's the right time."

"Gayle and I have seen a perfectly lovely, white dress in your possession." Lacresha mentioned.

"Yes, we noticed it when we were dusting your closet."

"Dusting?" Danielle, along with everyone else, laughed at their nosiness.

"Helen, may I ask for you to finish my dress? I won't have time to complete it on my own."

Helen's eyes brightened with excitement. "I'd love to do that."

"It sounds as if we need to call a meeting for tomorrow afternoon." As usual, Rica was in a hurry to get everything moving forward.

"Thank you so much. And, Margaret, I'm so happy you'll be here to discuss the plans."

Joshua rubbed his chin. "I haven't had a chance to give this wedding much thought, but, Harold, I think the Simpsons, and anyone else who would care to, should stay with us until after the wedding. It will give everyone time to get better acquainted."

After giving the offer consideration, Harold could see the advantages in accepting Joshua's invitation. Delbert and Margaret also agreed to stay. Benjamin was needed in court but promised to return for the wedding. Zelda and Rand could not stay because of their responsibilities but assured everyone that they, too, would attend the ceremony.

Having had such an eventful day, those who lived close by said goodnight, while Gayle and Lacresha encouraged Joshua to retire.

Sherry, being too excited to sleep, asked her father to take a walk to catch lightning bugs and insisted Gayle come along with them. The others decided to sit on the front porch to unwind, while Hunter and Danielle walked to the barn in an obvious pretense of checking on the horses.

Once they arrived, the two young lovers held one another close and dreamed of their wedding day—not so very far away.

54

THE BEGINNING

While her hair was drying, Danielle swept back the curtain and watched as the sun peeked above the hills to expose a glistening meadow. She had barely slept a wink. . . but what bride could? This was the day she was to become *Mrs. Hunter Jackson.*

Their relationship had been rocky from the very beginning, but each of their struggles had helped nurture the deepest love and respect between them.

A light twinkled from the barn, letting Danielle know Delbert was up and tending the horses. It was her brother's intent to make amends for all the ways he had wronged others. He also hoped to gain Harold's respect by returning to the docks as a hired worker and gradually learning the family business from the ground up.

Over the past two weeks, Delbert and Hunter had been nearly inseparable. Del had asked Hunter to teach him how to work, and Hunter had accommodated. Surprisingly, her brother had met each challenge and found that putting in a day of hard work agreed with him.

Delbert was changing into a responsible Christian man with a soft heart. And for the first time in their lives, he was seeking

Danielle out to spend time with her.

Margaret and Danielle discovered they had much in common and desperately wanted to make up for the time they had lost while growing up. The two were sorry that their time together was coming to an end but promised to meet at the Simpson home near the holidays.

Harold had blessed his stepdaughter and Joshua with stories of his and Daniel's exploits while putting together the custody case against Esther. Danielle wished her father could see the attachment that had formed between his faithful friend, Harold, and his beloved cousin, Gayle.

Just then there was a tap on her shoulder. "Couldn't you sleep, Danielle?"

"Sherry, what are you doing up so early?"

"I'm excited. I've never been a flower girl before."

"You'll look so beautiful in your new dress. Helen chose it from the ones made for the mission's boutique. I pledged to sew another one to replace it."

Sherry wrapped her arms around Danielle's neck. "I'm glad you're my sister. I hope I grow up to be just like you."

"Thank you, sweetheart. That's quite a compliment. But now, go take your bath before the other guests wake up." She gave Sherry a pat on the bottom to hurry her along.

Once she finished packing her final belongings, Danielle looked around her father's room and thanked God for the grandpa and family who had taken her in and loved her unconditionally.

It seemed only minutes before Danielle was in Willow Weep sweeping back the curtain from Hattie's bedroom window. She and Hunter had chosen the cottage lawn to exchange their vows. The miracle of being led to the cottage in Willow Weep was one of the most valued times of her life. It was while living in the tiny home that God had blessed her with friends, united her with family, and brought Hunter into her life.

Many of the guests had assembled early. Danielle was happy to see that Bethany and Stewart had arrived on the morning train as expected. Of course, the Harrisons, Simpsons, and Jacksons were already milling among the other guests. Rosa and Johnathon, along with Belinda Gray and Carl, had claimed their seats and were engaged in a lively conversation with Zelda and Rand. The entire Meeker family was just arriving, and it looked as though Sally had brought a gentleman guest. They both noticed Danielle in the window at the same time and waved. Finally realizing it was Rob Wilky, Danielle waved back enthusiastically.

Madison and her fiancé, Ron, were in attendance. She had opted not to be a bride's maid in order to serve at the reception. The two were to be married in the spring, and the salary as a server would be used in planning their own wedding.

Benjamin Dice and his wife could be seen in the background. Standing next to them were Jean and Everett Johnson. Danielle was elated to finally have an opportunity to introduce them to all the loved ones she had not known existed.

By then, it was time for the bridesmaids to arrive. But just before leaving the window, she looked up to see a cloudless, blue sky, with a full, bright sun. It was a beautiful day for their wedding.

Hunter fought with his tie, trying to achieve the fashionable look expected, while memories of their courtship faded in and out. The day he had rescued Danielle from the Brewster boys—their many disagreements—the excuses he had used for giving her driving lessons—all had become cherished memories. Having overcome many obstacles in their relationship, he knew each challenge had been well worth the battle. Today, Danielle would be meeting him at the altar.

While reminiscing, Hunter walked over to the window to view the cottage, not expecting to see so many guests mingling throughout the miniature yard. It looked as if the whole of Willow Weep had gathered. Hunter was pleased to see his family had arrived, along with Marka Bricker, who had written Danielle to apologize for her interference in their relationship.

There was a tap on the door, and the groomsmen appeared to offer their support and collect their boutonnieres. The visit was brief, and Hunter was soon leading Jerry, Delbert, and his two brothers through the trees to enter the procession near the cottage.

Down the hall, Agnes Jackson, Helen, and the bridesmaids had entered Danielle's room to assist the bride with her dress. Hugs, giggles, and tears were abundant as they all took part in the moment.

Once the final loop was placed over the last satin button of the wedding gown, Hunter's mother escorted Danielle to the mirror. Having not seen the dress completed, Danielle stood in captivated silence. The fitted bodice, long sheer sleeves, and A-line skirt were made from the whitest satin and covered with a delicate lace resembling baby's breath. Rhinestones were lightly sprinkled on the gown and the four-foot train to add a little sparkle. The waist-length veil, attached to a rhinestone tiara, glistened modestly.

"An angel could not look lovelier." Margaret dabbed her eyes, as she moved closer to admire the handiwork.

"Helen, it's beautiful. You have surpassed my dreams."

"Sweetheart, it was my pleasure to complete the gown for you."

Helen took time to give the dress a final inspection. "Well, we must hurry off. It's time to join Sherry. She's been waiting in place for almost an hour." They all laughed as Margaret, Rica, and Lacresha collected their nosegays before leaving the room.

When they were gone, Gayle presented Danielle with her bouquet and then took her hand. "You may be a cousin, but you feel more like my daughter. Since your father and I were so close, I felt much of the pain he suffered when you were lost to him. I know I'm not your mother, but may I have the honor of praying with you before you walk down the aisle?"

Danielle took Gayle's hands. "I wouldn't have it any other way."

Joshua, with reddened eyes, waited for Danielle as she descended the stairs and accepted his arm. "My Dani, you look most charming. You remind me so much of my Valerie on our wedding day. Tell me you're happy and I'll be content in giving you away."

"I'm extremely happy, Grandpa, and I believe this day is comparable to the day I met my grandfather."

"My dear granddaughter," Joshua stopped to choke back tears, "you do have a way with words. Now come, we have a wedding to attend." Joshua placed his hand over hers as they left the house.

The sweet notes of "Oh Promise Me" drifted through the air as Hunter and his groomsmen took their places in front of the cottage. At that moment the string quartet began the processional, and Sherry came into view scattering petals as precisely as possible. Hunter's mind drifted to the day at the creek when he had stormed off after ripping Danielle's flower from his hook, and he could not keep from smiling as he recalled the time he had tried saving her during a rainstorm. By the time his mind returned to the moment, Rica had taken her place beside Lacresha, and Gayle was halfway to the cottage. Margaret was prepared to follow close behind.

The music gradually increased in volume as the bridal march filtered through the forest and echoed back to Hunter. That is when he saw her—his lovely Danielle, looking like an angel.

The bride searched beyond those seated. There he stood—tan and handsome, strong and loyal, a true gentleman and her love.

Within moments, Joshua was lovingly handing his Dani over to Hunter. The bride and groom looked into each other's eyes. While cherishing every word, they lovingly exchanged their wedding vows.

It was only a matter of minutes until Pastor Strong said the words they wanted to hear— "With the authority vested in me and in the name of our Lord, Jesus Christ, I now pronounce you husband and wife. Hunter. . . you may kiss your bride."

Hunter looked down at Danielle Valerie Jackson. Her eyes were filled with the happiest of tears. The groom pulled his bride into his arms and kissed her most tenderly, leaving no doubt that Hunter Jackson was completely and hopelessly in love.

Then Pastor Strong made the announcement *everyone else* was waiting to hear— "Ladies and gentlemen, I'd like to introduce Mr. and Mrs. Hunter Jackson!"

Immediately, cheers rang out as those present stood to their feet and applauded.

After the wedding, the reception was held in Willow Park with the bride and groom's table placed by the majestic willow tree. Rob was praised as a talented chef—the extravagant cake was cut—and the best-of-the-best wishes were offered to Hunter and Danielle. After a lovely reception, the newlyweds were escorted to a carriage overly endowed with flowers and ribbons.

The couple planned to spend their wedding night at the finest hotel in Bristol. The following day they would board a train for the West to see tumble weeds, find cowboys, and visit the mission in Pike City.

As the driver snapped the reins, Hunter turned to his new bride. "Mrs. Jackson, I plan to spend the rest of my days making certain you are completely happy. God has blessed me with you, and I'm eternally grateful."

Danielle responded with a loving kiss as their carriage swept them away to experience life together.

ACKNOWLEDGEMENTS

First of all, I want to thank all those who read my first novel, *Under the Willow*, and a special thank you to those who sent me messages or spoke to me personally. You know who you are, and I will never forget your kindness in caring enough to do so. Words cannot express how much it has meant to me. I love you all.

It is with great pleasure that I thank my sister, Gayle Quinn, for donating untold hours as the *non-editor* of this book. Your patience with me through this tedious process was astounding.

I also want to thank her husband, Gary Quinn, for his encouragement and for giving up his time alone with Gayle.

Thank you to Kayla Snyder of The Brand Huntress for all of your hard work. I especially appreciate your sweet tolerance as director of this project and your meticulous artistic talent in designing *Willow Weep*. Your art degree has been a blessing to many and especially to me.

A loving thank you goes to my daughter, Yvette Snyder, for previewing *Willow Weep* and for sharing her insight.

To my husband, Jack Jones, thank you for being patient and supportive throughout the entire writing process. I love you with all my heart.

But above all, praise and glory to my Heavenly Father for His love, inspiration, and the words for this story.

ABOUT THE AUTHOR

Madge Hurley Jones lives in the countryside near Wilmington, Ohio, with Jack, her best friend and husband of fifty-four years. She considers writing to be her way of leaving a legacy to their six grandchildren: Aaron Snyder and Danielle, Samuel, Nathanael, Briella, and Elliot Mascioni. Madge's desire to write was inspired by the works of the Christian author, Grace Livingston Hill.